Remains of Life

MODERN CHINESE LITERATURE FROM TAIWAN

Remains of Life

A NOVEL

WU HE

TRANSLATED BY
MICHAEL BERRY

COLUMBIA
UNIVERSITY
PRESS
New York

Wu He

Columbia University Press wishes to express its appreciation for assistance
given by the Chiang Ching-kuo Foundation for International Scholarly Exchange
and Council for Cultural Affairs in the preparation of the translation and in the
publication of this series.

Columbia University Press wishes to express its appreciation for assistance given
by the Pushkin Fund in the publication of this book.

Columbia University Press
Publishers Since 1893
New York   Chichester, West Sussex
cup.columbia.edu
English translation copyright © 2017 Michael Berry

Library of Congress Cataloging-in-Publication Data
Names: Wuhe, 1951- author. | Berry, Michael, 1974- translator.
Title: Remains of life : a novel / Wu He ; translated by Michael Berry.
Other titles: Yu sheng. English
Description: New York : Columbia University Press, 2017. | Series: Modern Chinese
    literature from Taiwan | Includes bibliographical references. | Description based on
    print version record and CIP data provided by publisher; resource not viewed.
Identifiers: LCCN 2016053434 (print) | LCCN 2016037969 (ebook) | ISBN
    9780231544641 (electronic) | ISBN 9780231166003 (cloth : alk. paper) | ISBN
    9780231166010 (pbk.)
Subjects: LCSH: Musha Rebellion, 1930—Fiction. | Taiwan—History—1895-1945—
    Fiction. | Taiwan aborigines—Fiction. | Japan—Colonies—Taiwan—Fiction.
Classification: LCC PL2966.U82968 (print) | LCC PL2966.U82968 Y813 2017 (ebook) |
    DDC 895.13/6—dc23
LC record available at https://lccn.loc.gov/2016053434

Columbia University Press books are printed on permanent and durable
    acid-free paper.
Printed in the United States of America

Cover design: Kimberly Glyder

Contents

Introduction

On October 27, 1930, during an annual sports meet held at the Musha Elementary School on an aboriginal reservation deep in the mountains of central Taiwan, there occurred a bloody uprising unlike anything Japan had ever witnessed in its colonial history. Just as the Japanese national anthem was being played, members of six Atayal tribal villages, led by the Mhebu chief Mona Rudao, descended upon the school sports field and commenced their attack. Before noon the Atayal tribe had summarily slain 134 Japanese in a headhunting ritual that shook Japan's colonial empire to its core. The Japanese responded to what would later become known as the "Musha Incident"[1] with a militia of three thousand, heavy artillery, airplanes, and internationally banned poisonous gas. The Atayal of Musha were brought to the brink of genocide.

Nearly seventy years later, Chen Guocheng—a writer best known by his poetic pen name, Wu He, or "Dancing Crane"—traveled to Qingliu (Alang Gluban) to investigate the long forgotten Musha Incident and search for the "remains of life"—the survivors of the incident and their descendants. Qingliu is the current name of the indigenous reservation once known as Riverisle, or Chuanzhongdao. Named after the Japanese city of Kawanakajima, Riverisle is a small, idyllic community nestled between several mountains and streams in central Taiwan forty kilometers from Musha. It is also the site where the Atayal survivors of the Musha Incident were forcibly exiled after the Japanese suppressed the uprising of 1930. Living on this small reservation on and off over a span of two years during the late 1990s, Wu He, under the guise of a "researcher," began to explore the impetus behind this disturbing historical event and question the legitimacy and accuracy surrounding the event itself as well as the ways it has been rendered by historians and commemorated by politicians. In his novel *Remains of Life* (*Yu sheng*, 1999), Wu He gradually introduces a cast of characters who live in this place of exile: Girl, a former prostitute with a taste for Chopin; Drifter, Girl's little brother, who spends his days riding around the reservation on his motor scooter; Mr. Miyamoto, an older man infatuated with the spirit of the samurai; Bakan, the reservation's well-educated indigenous rights leader; Deformo, a stuttering young man who idles away his days going for long walks; Nun, who set up a makeshift Buddhist temple in a shipping container. Their stories interact with tales of the historical figures from the 1930 Musha Incident: Mona Rudao, the Mhebu tribal leader who took his own life in the aftermath of the uprising; his daughter Mahong Mona, who lived out the rest of her life in the traumatic shadows of the incident; and Obin Tado, the widow of Hanaoka Jirō, one of the central figures in the history of the Musha Incident. Along the way, Wu He offers his own ruminations and ramblings, meditations and musings that blur the line between history and fantasy, the primitive and the civilized, beauty and violence, fact and fiction.

The result is a powerful and disturbing literary voyage into perhaps the darkest chapter of Taiwan's colonial history. This one-of-a-kind work was a milestone in Chinese literature that marked the arrival of a major voice on the Sinophone literary scene. Although Wu He had begun publishing short stories in the 1970s, for much of the 1980s he lived a life of seclusion, and he did not release his writings from this period until much later. Only in the late 1990s did Wu He reemerge on the Taiwan literary world with a string of novels and short story collections that captured the attention of readers and critics. One after another, Wu He released two collections of short fiction, *Digging for Bones* (*Shigu*, 1995) and *The Sea at Seventeen* (*Shiqi sui de hai*, 1997), and a novel, *Meditative Thoughts on A Bang and Kadresengane* (*Sisuo Abang Kalusi*, 1997). But even this series of works could not prepare readers for his masterful 1999 novel *Remains of Life*. Upon its publication in Taiwan, the novel won virtually every major national literary award, including the Taipei Creative Writing Award for Literature, the *China Times* Ten Best Books of the Year Award, the *United Daily* Readers' Choice Award, *Ming Pao*'s Ten Best Books of the Year Award, and the Kingstone Award for Most Influential Book of the Year. Wu He's work has been the focus of numerous scholarly articles, book chapters, and several full-length academic monographs. In 2011 the French translation of *Remains of Life* was published by Actes Sud under the title *Les Survivants* and received great critical acclaim.

Besides its impact as a work of literature, *Remains of Life* also helped trigger a major reevaluation of the Musha Incident in contemporary Taiwan history and popular culture. At the time of its publication, there were only a handful of books in print about the Musha Incident, but within a few years dozens of new books have appeared, including oral histories, historical biographies, graphic novels, and children's books, which have collectively reintroduced the Musha Incident into mainstream Taiwanese popular culture. The extent to which this once marginalized historical trauma has moved to the center of Taiwan pop culture can best be demonstrated by the 2005 release of Taiwan black metal band Chthonic's (Shanling) full-length concept album entitled *Seediq Bale* (*Saideke Balai*), which transformed the Musha Incident into the historical backdrop for a rock opera, and the 2011 release of director Wei Te-sheng's (Wei Desheng) two-part motion picture *Warriors of the Rainbow: Seediq Bale* (*Saideke*

Balai), which became one of the most successful films in Taiwan box-office history. In 2013 another film about the Musha Incident, a documentary directed by Tang Shaing-Chu (Tang Xiangzhu) entitled *Pusu Qhuni*, actually borrowed the same Chinese title as Wu He's novel, *Yu sheng*, or the "Remains of Life."

Remains of Life may have played a crucial role in resurrecting society's collective memory of the Musha Incident, and Wu He's work also functions as an uncompromising literary statement, a novel-as-manifesto that challenges traditional historical writing, ethical assumptions, and literary conventions. *Remains of Life* stands out for several reasons. As one of the first contemporary literary works to address the scars left by the Musha Incident and its brutal suppression, the novel stimulated a renewed dialogue and cultural debate about the incident in Taiwan. After centuries of oppression, the indigenous peoples of Taiwan remain largely marginalized, and *Remains of Life* is one of the few literary works by an ethnic Chinese writer to address the plight of the island's original occupants under both the Japanese colonizers and the Nationalist regime. With extensive descriptions of the natural environment and ruminations on environmental destruction, the novel can also be seen as making an important contribution to Taiwan's burgeoning body of eco-literature. But perhaps most incredible is the way that Wu He seamlessly merges heavy themes like historical memory, state violence, and environmental devastation with equal bits of irony and humor. It is Wu He's ability to effortlessly shift gears from a mood of melancholic loss to subversive irony to deep reflection to maniacal ramblings that gives his novel such a distinct and instantly recognizable voice.

Remains of Life is not only bold in terms of its subject matter and social engagement but also noteworthy as a work of brilliant literature. Continuing the tradition of the great stream-of-consciousness novels like James Joyce's *Ulysses* and José Saramago's *The Cave,* Wu He's novel presents a major breakthrough in structure, syntax, and linguistic experimentation. Unprecedented in the Chinese literary world, *Remains of Life* contains no paragraph divisions and employs only a few dozen periods over the course of its sprawling narrative; it has been hailed as an important linguistic milestone. Innovation aside, *Remains of Life* does present real challenges for English-language readers who approach the book: the subject is a historical massacre from 1930 that is virtually unknown in the West; the setting is a indigenous reservation during the Japanese colonial era in Taiwan with a unique history and cultural background; and then there are the novel's unforgivingly experimental stream-of-consciousness style (no paragraph breaks, only a handful of periods, and unorthodox use of commas and other punctuation marks) and the narrative itself, which slips back and forth between philosophical musings (about history, the nature of civilization, and violence), observations about the people the author meets on the reservation, his investigations into the Musha Incident, and wild, magical, fantastical passages where the author's imagination takes over. The stream-of-consciousness form that dominates is not mere embellishment of an experimental literary sensibility, but a structural device meticulously designed, with each period marking a distinct shift in theme and focus. There are three themes the author explores in the novel, and each sentence break marks the transition from one theme to the next.

In the afterword, Wu He explains the three themes that *Remains of Life* sets out to investigate: 1) "the legitimacy and justification behind Mona Rudao launching the 'Musha Incident.' In addition to the 'Second Musha Incident'"; 2) "the Quest of Girl, who was my next-door neighbor during my time staying on the reservation"; and 3) "the Remains of Life that I visited and observed while on the reservation." These three items reveal the novel's circular A-B-C structure, which continues for the duration. In addition, the fractured narrative can be seen as a direct reflection and commentary on the fractured characters the narrator encounters as they live out the "remains of their lives" in the shadow of unspeakable atrocity and violence. Gradually the novel reveals the societal and political structures by which yesterday's colonial violence has been transformed into today's economic exploitation and environmental degradation.

While Wu He has described the writing process of this novel as akin to an unrestrained release of words committed to paper in a rather short time span with minimal revision, the translation process was a much slower and more arduous undertaking. Spanning more than a decade, the translation was hindered by several starts and stops, interrupted by other projects, and haunted by the myriad challenges that the original novel presented, including issues like: the romanization of indigenous names, the use of dialects, the novel's unconventional grammar, decoding original terms coined by the author, and deciphering his sometimes nonsensical ramblings. Because of the nature and number of these challenges, there was often a temptation to "simplify" things: to add conjunctions to help the narrative flow, to sneak in commas to break up long clauses, to clarify convoluted structures by making the inner meaning more legible. Ultimately, however, I decided against half-measures. This is a work of experimental fiction, and I wanted passages that were challenging or just plain weird in the original to feel just as challenging or weird in translation.[2]

Some of the other unique features of the novel include the author's employment of proper nouns for place names and character names. Throughout the book, Wu He almost never uses the word "Taiwan," instead opting for "island nation" (*dao guo*), a choice that carries direct political undertones. Likewise, he rarely refers to Chinese people or Taiwanese people (*Zhongguo ren* or *Taiwan ren*), but instead to "People from the Plains" (*pingdi ren*). "Japanese" (*Riben ren*) also rarely appears, being replaced by the "Rulers" (*tongzhi zhe*). And perhaps most confusing for some readers, the names by which some of the main characters are referred to actually shift and transform over the course of the narrative. For instance, one character is introduced as Weirdo (*Qi ren*) but later referred to as Deformo (*Ji ren*), Girl (*Guniang*) is referred to for a time as Meimei, Old Wolf (*Lao lang*) is also referred to as Daya Mona and Little Daya (*Lao Daya*), Danafu alternately appears as Nafafu and Nafu, and Mr. Miyamoto is later called Samurai. While making these names consistent and using standard terms to refer to "the Chinese," "the Japanese," "Taiwan," and other names would make the novel more legible to English readers, in almost all cases I have instead opted to preserve the author's original word choice.

This translation of *Remains of Life* marks the English-language debut of one of the most brilliant, imaginative, and challenging writers to emerge from East Asia in many years. Focusing on an actual historical incident little known in the West, Wu He's novel serves as an important addition to our understanding of both Japan's colonial project and the plight of Taiwan's aboriginal people, a group whose voice has too often been drowned under the tides of history and hegemony. At the same time, *Remains of Life* stands unique in its vision and depth, humor and humanism, beauty and strangeness.

Over the course of this extended translation process, I have incurred the debt of many colleagues, friends, and family members. I would like to thank foremost the author, Wu He, for his patience and generosity, and for entrusting me with this special book. Thanks to my family, Suk-Young Kim, Miles Berry, Naima Berry, and Beverly St. John, John and Abby Berry, and John Berry II, for their love and support. Jennifer Crewe at Columbia University Press has offered her unwavering support of this project ever since I first pitched it to her many years ago; it is a rare luxury to have an editor willing to extend the degree of patience and support that she has shown me. Special thanks to Leslie Kriesel for careful and sensitive handling of this difficult text, and to the wonderful team at CUP. Thanks also to Candy Lin, Tzu-i Chuang Mullinax, Sonny Chen, Esther Lin, John Nathan, Michael Emmerich, my former colleagues and students at the University of California, Santa Barbara, and my current colleagues and students at UCLA. Special thanks to Professor Darryl Sterk of National Taiwan University, Professor Letty Chen, and the external readers who went above and beyond the call of duty in providing detailed comments and suggestions on this manuscript. I and future readers of this book are indebted to the sensitivity, care, and professionalism they brought to the task of reviewing this difficult text. Special thanks to the National Endowment for the Arts, which supported this project with a Translation Grant. Thanks to Professor K. C. Tu, who published an early excerpt in *Taiwan Literature: English Translation Series*. Professor David Der-wei Wang has long been a champion of this novel. Not only has he published extensively on *Remains of Life,* but he also was the series editor of the original Chinese-language edition and is now series editor for this English translation. Over the years, he has been a great supporter of Chinese literature and Chinese literary studies and on a personal level, I am fortunate to call him a mentor and friend. It is with humbleness and gratitude that I dedicate this translation to Professor David Der-wei Wang, a model scholar, teacher, and friend.

M. B.

Goleta, CA

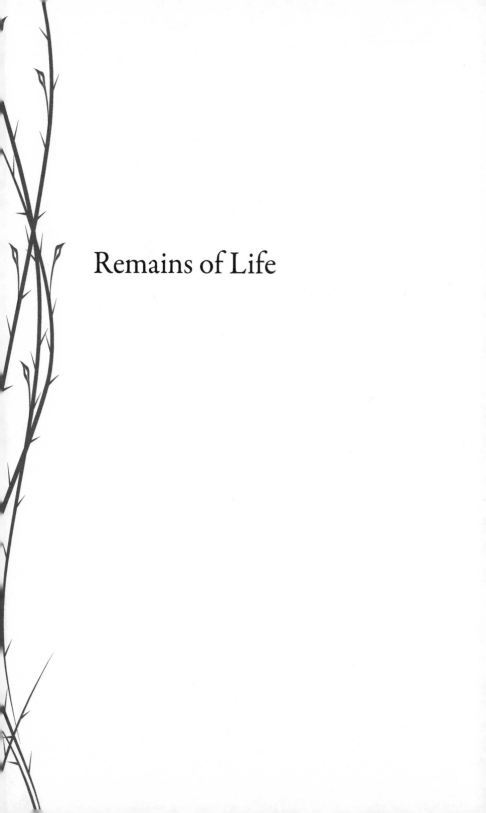

Remains of Life

Remains of Life

T
he first time I read about the Musha Incident was probably back when I was still a teenager, the White Terror[1] had passed giving rise to the simple and gray sixties, the economy of this island nation had yet to take off, there were still no McDonald's fast-food restaurants and we had yet to be bombarded by electronics, computers, and the mass media, we had more than ample time to carefully read whatever we could get our hands on, in one book I read about a brutal and bloody incident that occurred on a mountain called Musha, at the time traces of the trepidation and shock that marked my hot-blooded teenage years still clung to me, up until I read a book on the history of social and political movements among Taiwan's ethnic minorities, only then did I realize that it had happened more than a decade after everyone down in the plains had given up any form of armed resistance against their colonizers, the decision to stop resisting must have been the outcome of comprehensive deliberation wherein they were in the end left with no other choice, but didn't this information make it to the aborigines living in the mountains, I was forced into the army to carry out my term of obligatory military service when I was twenty-eight and had yet to get through all the Confucian classics required for college, for the first time I clearly felt that on our land there existed

such a thing as a "nation"—an entity in which a system of authority and power is embodied in, and transformed into, a system of violence—that invisibly controls the heart and resources of this island nation; I look back on the artistic days of my youth as nothing more than a kind of mildly insane romanticism, I was discharged from the military in 1981, at the time I came to the painful realization that I had been "castrated by the army," I decided not to immediately jump into the flames of anti-Nationalist political activities, instead I moved to Danshui, a small town on the margins of this island country, where I lived in quiet seclusion, I spent all of my time lost in historical and philosophical works, I wanted to understand the origins and meaning of concepts like the "army" and the "nation," finally after months in solitude reading about countless bloody battles, the illusions about war fostered by the history textbooks I had read as a youth had all melted away, transforming into a true "historical reality," it was perhaps then that my mind first turned to the blood spilled in our mountains, I settled down from the hot-blooded excitement of my younger days and began to contemplate the legitimacy and appropriateness of the Musha Incident. Winter '97, I was renting a place on reservation land when one evening I saw my neighbor, Girl, standing facing the misty mountains in the distance, she quietly uttered, "I am the granddaughter of Mona Rudao,"[2] every night Girl's door was left half open, the Ancestral Spirits followed the twists and turns down Valleystream until they arrived at Riverisle, throughout those difficult times, the Ancestral Spirits were with them every day, Girl always believed that if you follow Valleystream all the way upstream you will eventually find the Mystic Valley—the place where her ancestors, one after another, threw themselves off a cliff to their death, "I left everything behind to return home, now I'm taking time to recuperate and play with the shrimp and fish," Girl bent over in the knee-deep water to pick up a rock beside the stream, beneath the rock was a fish trap she'd buried there a week before, she didn't turn around but could sense me following her, carefully wading my way through the unfamiliar waters, "I have a plan," Girl uttered as she stood back up and gazed out over Valleystream toward the sea of mountains in the distance, "One day I'm going to set out in search of . . ." But is that a genuine return?, returning to the Mystic Valley where she can hold hands with the Ancestral Spirits, eating and drinking in ecstasy. In the beginning Riverisle was a place of exile, "We began by opening up the virgin land," I inquired about the tribal hunters and one of their sons told me, anyone here over seventy has lived through the hard times and should remember, it started with planting rice, the civilized rulers taught them how to sow rice paddies, from being a tribal hunting clan that stood erect they learned to squat and bend over, "They have been a tribe of rice planters ever since," as time went on some of them started planting bananas, and while harvesting the rice they didn't forget to plant some taro on the ridge beside the field, later betel palms began to sprout up everywhere, and then someone discovered that the night air in the mountains was perfect for growing plum trees and transformed the entire mountain basin behind the cemetery into a plum orchard, the mountainous slopes were filled with even larger areas of Chinese silvergrass and wild forest, but they left them pristine and untouched, only in deep autumn when the silvergrass sprouts its white buds and the forest leaves turn from green to yellow to a dull crimson do they sigh, knowing that yet another year has been spent in exile, "There haven't been any tribal hunters in ages, the only animals we catch are the squirrels and flying squirrels we trap in the fields," when his father arrived in this place of exile he was already past school age, the blood of a hunter must have still flowed in his veins, one year when he was almost thirty he went hunting in the back mountains, he returned with a wild boar or mountain goat but his fellow tribesmen did not welcome him with celebratory wine and dance, he was instead greeted by a vicious beating from the Japanese authorities,

surrounded by the silent confused gazes of his tribespeople, the rulers
used the beating as an opportunity to warn the people, "This man is
a lazy scum, instead of working with everyone out in the fields, he
sneaked off to the mountains to do evil"—there were two possible
punishments for doing evil, the first was to be forever exiled from
this place of exile, possibly chased into a cage by one of those "German
shepherd police dogs," the second was to be bound to a wild boar and
left outside in the dirt field under the blazing sun for three days, the
hunter chose the latter and in the process sacrificed his last bit of dignity—from then on all the way up to his death Dad was a farmer
who lived the rest of his days bent over in the field, he never passed on
any of the techniques or stories of the hunter, his children and grandchildren had no idea how to respect the memory of their ancestors'
lives as hunters, it was good thing then when the old rulers were replaced by a new set of rulers who legalized cigarettes and alcohol,
Dad spent the rest of his days gazing at the distant mountains and
drinking himself to death, that's right, the distant mountains, and
not the rice fields that spread out before his eyes, when I was a kid,
after dusk each day when our work in the fields was finished I would
drink with Dad, my old man would drink in silence, "It didn't seem
to matter what we said or what was going on around us," drinking
became an addiction, the bottle became the source of this addiction,
nothing in life seemed to be as important, I've heard that with de-
mocracy the people suddenly became most important, but for him
nothing was ever as important as a drink, it wasn't that he didn't understand that drinking every day will lead to what you academics call
"self-destruction," young people hit the bottle especially hard, "as a
descendent of a hunter I have lived out my life between the bottle
and the field, my time in the tribe is past, the lives of our young
people along with the brave and courageous lives of our Seediq
people have all been lived out on the road to self-destruction. . . ."
And here we are at the fin de siècle, already nearly seventy years have

passed since the incident, Mona Rudao's statue and memorial tablet stand high, overlooking the elementary school field where he carried out his massacre, on October 27 of each year Riverisle dispatches a group to bring sacrificial offerings to their former homeland to commemorate the anniversary of the incident, they also offer their favorite mixed drink of Whisbih[3] and rice wine to Mona Rudao, from the speech made by the commanding officer, they understand that even today their ancestor Mona Rudao is still heralded as the spiritual leader who led the people around Musha and Reunion Mountain, "no one ever investigated" the legitimacy of the massacre he launched because that fact had already been verified by government authorities, each year the cherry blossoms planted here so long ago by the Japanese shed their flowers and flutter to the ground for only Mona Rudao and him alone to see. . . . During the course of my investigation into the Musha Incident, I only encountered two people who had a different take on the massacre than others, both of them were Seediq tribesmen,[4] both of them outstanding aboriginal scholars who held degrees from two of the top universities in Taipei, and both of them had respect and authority in their tribe and both were approaching middle age, Bakan, a member of the Seediq Daya tribe who was living in Riverisle, believed that history had misunderstood the fundamental meaning of the Musha Incident, "The true nature of the incident lies as a traditional headhunting ritual," headhunting was an important daily ritual for the Seediq people, the motivations for headhunting may have always been quite complex, but they were never particularized, the Seediq tribe grew accustomed to this complex ritual where "you are blamed for not showing proper respect to the tribe if you don't partake in the hunt," Bakan's grand-uncle severed the head of the prefect commander with his own two hands, there was nothing really particular about that head as compared with the other decapitated heads, the civilized rulers were utterly panic-stricken by such a large-scale "primitive custom," so much so that they offered a politically inspired military assault in response to this headhunting ritual, according to the local traditions an appropriate way to bring the incident to a conclusion would have been to have the Seediq and Japanese work things out face to face and "bury the hatchet through reconciliation," perhaps some respected Han Chinese—like the Gu family from Lugang or the Lin family from Wufeng—could have come up to the mountains to serve as witnesses, but who would have imagined that the "civilized savages" would turn around and send their civilized planes, cannons, and poisonous gases to the "savage primitives" to show them the true face of civilization; customs and rituals in the end led to a horrifying and destructive cycle of revenge, the result was the historical-political entity known as the "Musha Incident," fear was always a strange thing in the Seediq people's lives, "the Ancestral Spirits will approve of Mona Rudao's headhunting ritual, but they will never understand this thing called the Musha Incident . . ." Danafu of the Seediq Toda subtribe went even a step further in denying the historical existence of "the Incident," claiming there was only a large-scale Musha "headhunting ritual," the ritual was coordinated by the clan leader of Mhebu, thus there never existed any such thing as a "Musha Incident" and the common people must learn to forget the "man who led the ritual—Mona Rudao," the Toda tribe was one of the six tribes that did not take part in the headhunting ritual, they were later recruited to form the front line of the savage search team, Danafu said that it was only in his old age that his father finally began to talk about the excitement and joy he felt as he decapitated large numbers of Mhebu people, the Mhebus had actually planned to take the heads of the seventeen people led by the chief of the Toda tribe, and so that same rush of excitement and joy existed when the 101 heads were cut off during the surprise attack on the detention center, "This is my father," Danafu points to one of the figures in the commemorative photo taken after the ritual, in the photo Danafu's father was squatting on the ground with an expressionless head propped under his arm, his father never understood what the "Second Musha Incident" was, let alone anything about its place in history, "I also think that those people writing the history books these days base everything on the explanations of government propagandists and misguided academics," the academics subscribe to the governmental line that it was a plot instigated by the Japanese rulers, and that was the only way to explain the vicious tragedy of savages killing savages, "But this is only a tragedy as defined by civilization, how could anyone ever say that we Seediqs were the ones who prompted the killing, at the time we Seediqs knew all too clearly about the rules surrounding each tribe's headhunting rituals," it had absolutely nothing to do with the plots and unrighteousness that often appear in the history books, and so, a few years later, when the Toda tribal elder came all the way to Riverisle to propose a marriage, the Riverisle elders accepted his proposal, "We are all members of the Seediq tribe, we understand one another. . . ." I found it so surprising that neither of the two intellectuals who received a civilized education viewed the surprise attack on the detention center as what civilization would refer to as a so-called "massacre," they resented the fact that civilization used their civilized tools to "massacre" the six savage tribes—almost to the point of genocide—but could not accept the idea that savages would "massacre" other savages, nor was this something that was going to be resolved by debating back and forth, nor do I believe that historians can advocate a balanced historical theory, "Primitive vocabulary doesn't even have a word for massacre," I self-mockingly thought to myself as I gazed at the fish-tailed hunting knife left behind by Danafu's father—the knife still bears traces of human hair—"Only civilization is capable of carrying out massacres," the inscription on the "Memorial to the Remains of Life," which lies on the rear side of the Riverisle reservation bears no mention of the Second Musha Incident, as a descendent of the Mhebu tribe, Bakan did not have any real opinion when it came to the way Mona Rudao was venerated by the government, neither he nor Danafu agreed with "the government's politicization of the headhunting ritual as an exemplification of the anti-Japanese spirit," during our talks Danafu seldom mentioned Mona Rudao, and it was only on one occasion that Bakan happened to vapidly mention Mona Rudao as the "hero of our tribal head-hunting ritual." I told Girl about the conversations I had with Bakan, although she never saw one, she knew what a "headhunt" entailed, however, she had absolutely no idea what a "headhunting ritual" referred to, nor did she understand the majority of Bakan's ideas, "My father never lets us talk about those things, you won't find any hunting knives hanging in our living room either," who knows when her family's fish-tailed hunting knife disappeared—she had never laid eyes on one in her entire life, I asked her about that capricious little brother of hers, she said that the only schooling her brother received was through the classes offered by the reservation church, for a while he had a job helping out around the church, he is the only young person on the entire reservation who doesn't drink or smoke, instead he spends all his time riding aimlessly around the reservation on his motor scooter, "my little brother is the most kindhearted person on the reservation," Girl's voice grew stern as she continued; unlike Bakan, who not only has *the best* education, but also is *"the best* when it comes to women and wine"; I understand what Girl is getting at, during my time on the reservation there were three "democratic elections," election campaigns in the mountains have become indistinguishable from those held down in the plains; campaign trucks decorated with colored flags drive around the streets and alleys of the reservation making a ruckus and there are a few more groups of people sitting around drinking and debating politics than usual— Bakan is one of the few tribe members who has a vested interest in the election, the majority of public servants on the reservation also fall into this category, the ball is always in their court when it comes to local elections and they are the ones who delegate power, naturally they never fail to lend their support to those among their ranks with "the greatest actual strength," in the middle are those people who "never have opinions about anything," they work in the fields during the day and sit in front of the TV drinking when they get home at night, and then there are those people like Girl who "never seem to have anything to do," at the most they get only a slight glance from men like Bakan; Girl returned to the reservation dejected and all alone, everyone in the tribe looked at her in the same way they look at those routed men who returned after ruining their bodies working in the city factories, after her marriage to a member of the northern Atayal tribe fell apart, she left her two daughters behind and, surrounded by loneliness, she left the reservation and went to Valleystream, no one seemed to care what she did, she spent her time fishing and swimming—swimming together with those fish she couldn't catch—she spoke to them, "Valleystream is the place of my dreams," she followed the riverbed, picking up rocks and pieces of dead branches along the way, "Look at these beauties, it is incredible what the handicraft of nature can do," the beauties were scattered all over her bedroom and living room, she even taught people how to distinguish them from one another, "This piece was formed by a bolt of lightning, it is like an angel of time, the rushing waters of the stream shaped this one over an extended period, it resembles an elderly man who has endured a long hard life," who knows how long it had been since the tribespeople had heard such "dream talk," most everyone thought she was insane, deep in the night I could often hear strains of beautiful music coming from nearby, during my first night on the reservation I suddenly heard Chopin's "Nocturnes" and almost thought I was back in the city at some recital hall or fancy coffee shop, the next night I heard Mozart, I pulled open my curtains to discover that all the lights were out in Girl's room, but that melody seemed to sneak out from that dark place and rise into the night, she brought a kind of mysteriousness to the reservation, leading them to confront a feeling of loss and the unknown, it was a good thing that the tribespeople had long grown accustomed to living amid the fog and mist of the mountain hillocks. It was an early autumn afternoon and rays of light were coming off the face of the courtyard reflecting a hot beam of sunlight inside through the window, I was in the living room wearing a pair of shorts and a T-shirt, reading a work by a great Japanese scholar entitled *Investigative Record of the Savages*,[5] when Girl suddenly appeared outside my door, she was also wearing a pair of shorts and a T-shirt, but her outfit was entirely black, "I know this scholar, he brought a team of researchers here to examine the Musha Incident, my grandparents were all interviewed by him, although my maternal grandfather had a bad stutter, he knew more about the incident than anybody else, they kept him the longest— my mom told me that they didn't feed him, by the time he got home he was dead tired and she had to warm up some taros for him to eat," "But didn't that scholar have to eat too?" I asked, "Didn't it enter their minds that they should feed their guest?" Girl rolled her eyes, "My mom said that Grandpa would rather starve to death than eat their sushi," Girl picked up my book and nosily flipped through its pages, "I'll bet this book about savages is no page-turner; c'mon, let's go over to the general store to sing karaoke," it is not every day that you get a chance to sing karaoke in the mountains, I was so excited that I threw my book aside, walking side by side in T-shirts and shorts we approached the bamboo forest, the trail on the way to the general store was filled with the strong aroma of blooming betel palms, the overcast chain of surrounding mountains made me feel as though I was closer to the mountains than ever before, the general store stood alone built in an arid depression, it was constructed of crude sheet iron and surrounded by a wide courtyard in front and a large bamboo forest behind, of all the reservations I had visited this one had the fanciest general store of them all, the large refrigerator

was always stacked with bottles of Whisbih and beer giving people
the happy and secure feeling that they would never go out of stock, next
door was a large karaoke hall with a full sound system and stage,
when you got hungry after all that singing the shopkeeper's wife would
cook all kinds of hot rice and noodle dishes with wild herbs so we
could sit around in a circle eating and gazing at the bamboo forest
and the mountain scenery, on the other side of the store was an arcade for the kids, the shopkeeper's scruffy black beard was a perfect
match for his wife's round white face, "I remember you from your
earlier visits, it's just your second time here and you already learned
how to hold your Whisbih, don't spend all your time wrapped up with
academics, learn a bit about real estate, there is some new land that
just went up on the market and the price is right, buy now and you
won't have to go running back and forth all the time," Girl had
already selected which songs she wanted to sing and came over to
drag me inside so I would sing with her, "Buy real estate, buy, buy,
buy . . ." I jokingly yelled as I went inside, the shopkeeper's wife
laughed harder than the lady at the vegetable market in town, Girl
had already begun singing "Return to the City of Sand," I took my
first sip of Whisbih and rice wine, the cold burn went down my
throat as I took the microphone, seven parts rice wine mixed with
three parts Whisbih was the traditional formula for the preferred
mixed drink in Riverisle, "I long to die drunk," Girl twisted her body
as she sang, "in your passionate kiss," I drank my third glass of their
standard mix as Girl finished off her fifth or sixth glass, "Are there
any tribal elders around here that I can talk to?" I didn't forget about
my research, "So, since you are always asking questions, let *me* ask *you*
one, did you know that Atayal women used to drink alcohol by the
bowl?" Girl was getting a bit tipsy, I told her, "We men also drink by
the bowl, nobody used to use little cups like they do nowadays, how
about your elders, do they drink by the bowl too?" "There is a tribal
elder who lives nearby, he's the most typical elder you're ever gonna

find, once I finish singing this 'Love You to Death' song I'll take you
over so you can ask your questions," as Girl loved him to death she
told me to, "go buy a couple big bowls to take over," love you to death
love you to death, "you don't know what it's like to drink from a big
bowl unless you try," I went into the general store next door and
bought three bowls of instant ramen; the love you to death Elder
lived right across from her cousin, we could stop by her place on the
way there to drop off the noodles, Girl's cousin lived in a two-story
building, the steel gate was left open, far off we could see a few people
sitting in the courtyard, "Just your luck, the elder you're looking for is
sitting right there waiting for you," at first I thought that Girl had
had too much to drink and was simply babbling, but among them
there was indeed an old man wearing a squirrel-gray Chinese-style
jacket and a pair of baggy pants, without any introductions they
asked me to sit down and handed me a bowl of soup, as it turns out
they had been sitting in a circle around a hotpot cooking a flying
squirrel they caught in the fields, squirrel meat is only good if you
cook it in a stew, their internal organs are good for your health, Girl
took turns flirting with several of the young men there, the old man
drank in silence with a smile on his face, beneath the table were
several good bottles of foreign and domestic spirits, everyone kept
encouraging me to try the soup first, the soup still had the taste of the
squirrel's pain as it faced its death, "that taste is most nutritious,"
someone beside me uttered before handing me a glass of brandy with
rice wine, I could tell that the old man was drinking the same thing,
they probably started drinking brandy after the economy took off as
a way to show their respect for the elders while the rice wine was to
keep with tradition, "What did you come here to research?" Girl's
cousin is the first person to ask, although she is a full-figured woman
her face still carries the distinct features of the Atayal, "There are so
few of us aborigines, what's there here worth researching? There's a
hell of a lot to research when it comes to you Han Chinese, why don't

you go home and research yourselves?" she had obviously been drinking, yet even so from her soft tone it was clear that she was not joking, "First go do some research on yourselves, you Han Chinese are the ones deserving of some real research," no one interrupted her as she spoke and I could sense that she was one of the "progressive women" on the reservation; her words not only criticized the Chinese but also shut up her fellow tribespeople, she handed me a second bowl of flying squirrel stew, "Do your research on the great Chinese race, then when you're bored you can mosey on up to the mountains to see how little savages like us carve out a life for ourselves among you great Chinese," she turned around and ordered someone to kill a chicken, saying that a cute guy from the plains had come to research her, dinner was on her, everyone at the table still sober enough to move shouted with glee saying that they should call over so-and-so and so-and-so to celebrate together—"I'm not doing any real research, I'm simply interested in understanding what life is like for the Atayal people," after getting slapped with the Atayal woman's insults, I switched to a more sincere and apologetic tone and added two lines of fruitless defense, the woman went off—probably to help with the chicken—while the old man continued encouraging me to drink more as a sympathetic smile appeared on his face; I began to reflect upon my initial motivation for coming here to "research a weak ethnic minority"—especially that well-known political incident that was aimed at them—even at my age after all these years it never once entered my mind that the Han Chinese could, or even should, be the subject of research; with such a huge population and so many talented individuals I figured that everything worthy of researching about the Chinese had already been done, reports and research materials were probably all gathered together in some massive library somewhere, in order to understand the "true nature of the Chinese people" you had to go to that library and crawl through those records to figure it out, even as I set out for this trip to the reservation I was still rather ignorant about the true nature of the Chinese people, when it comes to the "interrelationship between the aborigines and the Chinese" perhaps I needed that woman to point things out from her perspective in order for me to see a bit of our true nature, I could feel the deep resentment in her voice as she finished her last sentence, "when you're bored you can mosey on up to the mountains to see how little savages like us carve out a life for ourselves among you great Chinese," these are words of self-ridicule from someone who has been controlled and assimilated, within those words there is so much buried sadness that has accumulated after years of forced cultural assimilation, "Here is some chicken, and a bowl of chicken soup—fate has brought us together, welcome," those last words of welcome were uttered by the woman's husband, speaking with a soft voice, he was tall, skinny, and refined looking; must I keep my research a secret and avoid these Remains of Life that stand before me? The darkness of night slowly descended, the woman handed me a chicken leg, I took a sip of the brandy-rice wine mix and, facing the chicken leg at dusk, said, "I came here to see the Remains of Life left over after the Musha Incident, but first I must understand the contemporary Musha Incident," the woman translated what I said to the tribal elder, Elder nodded repeatedly as he took another drink with me, the woman told me that Elder sitting before me was regarded as the most precious member of the tribe, countless people researching tribal history and especially the Musha Incident had interviewed him, when the incident occurred he was a fourth-grade elementary school student—and he was there at the schoolyard when the massacre took place, "The Musha Incident is history, it's all in the past; as to the actual details about what happened, Elder has already told others everything he knows," the woman's husband continued, "If you want to understand the contemporary Musha Incident, then that's another matter altogether," That's right, I said, the contemporary Musha Incident is how I evaluate history through a contemporary perspective—there is no such thing as "historical history," in actuality all that ever exists is "contemporary history," the woman interrupted me to say that it was a rare occasion for Elder to be there—who knows where Girl and those young men ran off to—while the chicken soup was still hot, it wouldn't hurt to ask Elder to say a few words, "Originally you invited me over for flying squirrel stew," Elder sat up straight, "it's a good thing that we have the nutrition of the chicken soup to keep us strong, otherwise how could we speak of the intestine-cutting incident that occurred in my homeland of Musha," the woman explained that most everyone in Musha had their head cut off in the incident, although the old man survived, at the time he was in so much pain that he felt as if his intestines were cut, he ridicules himself because even today at the age of eighty-four his intestines have yet to mend, when he is asleep at night his intestines crawl out and wriggle their way up the mountain path to the old schoolyard, "I don't want to talk anymore about the details surrounding the incident or what caused it, after sixty or seventy years all the information there to find has already been collected and organized as good as it could ever be," the old man only understood his native tribal tongue and Japanese; he spoke in Japanese, his tone of voice was calm and flat, the woman's husband interpreted for the majority of the discussion while the woman spent most of the time with her cheek leaning on her hand as she gazed out at the western sky, "Someone once asked me what kind of person Mona Rudao was, he was naturally our 'people's hero,'" because of him even today the entire Musha area shines through history with the Atayal spirit of resistance, "I am a descendent of Mona, but all I can rely on are the legends passed down from the elders, it is said that when he first realized that there were only six tribes willing to join him, he sat before the burning fire in silence for a long time, the tribesmen surrounding him also sat in silence, then just as the first rays of dawn began to break through the night sky he stood up and raised his spear . . ." He risked everything on that one single venture, in his heart he understood, as did his fellow tribesmen, "Someone once asked me what he won for us, all I could say was that he won us back our 'tribal dignity,' 'the power for a people that have been oppressed and defiled to fight back,' dignity must be protected, the oppressed must resist—this is the law of history, Mona Rudao was out for justice and walked straight into this 'historical law' without ever looking back," the woman refilled Elder's cup, but Elder didn't seem to notice, "I know that some of those researchers look at me as if I'm the perfect person to come to for answers, that's me, Mr. Answers, some of them probably even suspect that I've been prepped to always say the right things, that's because I never made up any incredible moving details or explanations, it's not that I lack imagination, during the Japanese occupation I also read a couple of books that I had borrowed from the Japanese patrol officers, since the end of the war a lot of information has come out and I have always tried to keep up on all the developments, for me it was an intestine-cutting incident, weighing the whole situation, that's the only answer I can provide, I can't use my imagination to add anything or change anything, the heart of the incident remains as it ever was," Girl returned with the others, filling the courtyard with flirtatious laughter and drunken words I couldn't understand, "Sixty, seventy years later, here in this shallow mountain valley of Riverisle, I find myself often wondering: if Mona Rudao could see this far into the future—no, I shouldn't phrase it like that—if he could have stood another five, ten, maybe fifteen years, the entire situation would have radically changed, today we would still be living on the land of our ancestors, the Mhebu tribal territory on Musha would never have been transformed into the disgusting tourist spot that it is today, Mona Rudao would have led us in the fight to establish an Atayal-Seediq Primitive Hot Springs Area; I often wonder, sometimes I toss and turn in my bed at night thinking about this, but I carry no uncertainties, nor regrets." I tossed and turned all through the night, after a while my bones started to ache and I sat up in bed and rested my head against the wall, the cold mountain air came in through the kitchen from the rear mountains and snuck under my covers, just the thought of that love you to death love you to death Girl sleeping in the arms of Tchaikovsky was both amusing and infuriating, as I was leaving the woman's husband stood with me at the door waiting for Elder, a man of almost forty gazing through the darkness, a silent smile hinting of unspoken words lit up his face, I suspected that he had something he wanted to tell me about Elder, but in the end he didn't say a word, as we parted he gave me a good firm handshake—he was a humble and straightforward Atayal; Only after the first cry of the rooster did I finally decide to start organizing the wild thoughts running through my mind, I sat at the small desk beside my bed and began writing down all the things that were bothering me, 1) The first thing that got to me was when the woman raised the question of researching "Han Chinese"; 2) When Elder stood by his statement, "the facts are the facts," and refused to retract or add anything; 3) He used the phrase "resist with dignity" to approve of Mona Rudao's actions; 4) Although he thought through his answers in a extremely civilized manner, he not only seemed to have no intention of investigating the "primitive" side of Atayal culture but also expressed his hope that Mona Rudao would have waited another fifteen years for civilization; and 5) Did his answers really all match the official historical line? . . . The woman's comment about "Han Chinese research" digressed furthest from the topic at hand and I must put it aside for the time being, as for "the facts are the facts," only those who record the facts have the power to change them, in the contemporary history of the Musha Incident we read of three separate massacres: the mass killing that occurred on the morning of October 27, 1930, at the Musha Elementary School athletic field—which was led by the Mhebu chieftain Mona Rudao—the second massacre began the following day, on

October 28, and involved Japanese mobilization of several battalions of garrison troops, aerial bombing, machine guns, howitzers, poison gas, and experimental incendiary bombs, it lasted until the issuance of an imperial edict on December 30 of that same year, the third massacre occurred during the early morning hours of April 25, 1931, and involved the Toda tribe's assault on the detention center; 136 Japanese were decapitated during the first massacre, over the course of the second massacre the population of the six tribes who revolted against the Japanese was reduced from over 1,300 to less than 500 (during which official documentary footage was shot by the Japanese),[6] the third massacre resulted in the slaying of almost 200 people, over 100 of whom were decapitated, after which photographs of the heads, which are still extant, were taken, ten days later when the Remains of Life moved to Riverisle they numbered only 298; as for the later extension of the slaughter, the killing of thirty-eight other members of the Remains of Life of Musha and Riverisle, from our contemporary perspective this is truly a "tasteless" slaughter where the numbers barely add up to anything, they not only pale in comparison to the Nazi death camps of World War II but also are dwarfed by the massacres that would occur seventeen years later during Taiwan's own February 28 Incident (and this does not include the following decade of purges carried out against the Remains of Life), even so every time I delve into this page of history my heart and soul shudder—that is because the inherent nature of what a "massacre" entails is always the same, regardless of the respective process or final death toll, for a massacre involves a fundamental betrayal of life by life itself, its inhuman, cannibalistic, and empty nature has the power to give birth in humans to the ultimate suspicion—history always harshly denounces those who incite massacre, therefore, our contemporary history cannot but condemn "the Mona Rudao of the Musha Incident," yet with his civilized rhetoric Elder used the "dignity of resistance" to affirm Mona Rudao's place in history, while the intellectuals Bakan and Danafu affirmed Mona Rudao's place from the perspective of a primitive "headhunting ritual," "The civilized and the primitive" each in different ways affirmed the legitimacy of Mona Rudao's "headhunt/massacre" during the Musha Incident, it is about time that I denounce the legitimacy of the second cry of the rooster, heaven only knows just when Tchaikovsky fell asleep, after the cries of the rooster, the entire mountain reservation fell under a boundless blanket of silence; and what if Mona Rudao had been able to wait another fifteen years, "the contemporary" asks why Mona Rudao couldn't hold on a mere fifteen years, but the facts never wait for "what if," when contemporary history poses such questions is it trying to be humorous or making an outright mistake, the contemporary must always "contemporize" history, contemporary history examines history from its own pluralistic perspective, but it is helpless to raise the necessary questions, it can quietly listen but is unable to ask questions, when the rooster cackled for the third time the faint light of dawn began to illuminate the horizon—As for the legitimacy of this phenomenon, Elder's response was the same typically simple answer one can expect from history; history records the facts, but contemporary history never investigates the facts, it instead investigates the "legitimacy of historical incidents," it is obvious that while he was censuring the actions of Mona Rudao, the legitimacy of the Musha Incident was affirmed on two different levels; I opened the back door and walked down the small trail at the foot of the mountains that runs through the cemetery, most of the other people who come for early morning walks are there to enjoy the fresh morning fragrance of plum blossoms blowing down from the mountain, through the long blades of November bristlegrass one can see the reservation not far off in the distance, hidden away in the bosom of the mountain cliffs it is a place seemingly removed from both history and the contemporary, "a mountain village neglected by time," "the final resting place of the soul," the morning sun rose over the distant mountains projecting its first ray of hazy sunlight over both sides of the peak crest lines—Actually, the contemporary cannot condemn history while at the same time affirming its legitimacy. Drinking and smoking led Girl from the Valley of Dreams into a disorienting fog, she starting hanging around those places where there was a lot of alcohol, during that time she lost an incredible amount of weight, she only ate a single meal each day, usually some fish or shrimp from the nearby stream, or wild vegetables like "dragon whiskers" or "passing cat" that she found growing among the wild grass in the betel-nut field, occasionally she would add a loofah from someone's garden, there were quite a few lonely single middle-aged men on the reservation, their drunken gazes would eye up Girl's slender body, with the remnants of youth receding in their eyes, the booze would get them going, perhaps some things went through their minds but in the end they never did anything, "that's just how it is," then again, perhaps they never did have any of those intentions, they all referred to Girl as their Meimei, or "Little Sister"—dreamtalk and acting crazy were all part of Girl's sincerity, it wasn't that she was naïve, she just didn't understand the ways of the world, "I know what's going through the minds of all those guys on the reservation," as Girl spoke, it seemed as if there would never be a rest between the notes coming out of her mouth, especially as she skipped around Valleystream, she would throw a sentence rooted in reality into her dreamtalk, "How can you possibly do it without ending up having a baby, humph, it's not like I never had a baby," she insisted on going back to her hometown to live the kind of life she wanted, not having to rely on anyone, and not being controlled by anyone, perhaps there were men who secretly approached her but ended up leaving with their tails between their legs after getting an earful, or then again perhaps there were no such subtle approaches but only animal entanglements, lasting deep into the dead of night when all was quiet and soft beautiful notes would accompany the moon and stars resonating through the cold air of the mountain forest, the simple spirit of the reservation probably couldn't comprehend the gentle and beautiful sorrow resonating deep in her soul, but they embraced her. . . . One morning as I was busy comparing two chronologies of the Musha Incident, I heard Girl's voice calling out to me in a hushed call from beside the door, "Doing homework?" she was wearing a colorful Western-style dress and a European hat, Girl asked to borrow $200, twenty for cigarettes and the rest to cover bus tickets, she wanted to go down to Taichung to find temporary work, hoping to make some money to cover her living expenses, I gave her the money, "Won't you miss Valleystream?" Girl smiled, nobody cares about Valleystream, it will always be hers, she would be back soon, and Valleystream will still be waiting for her. I walked Girl to the edge of the rice fields, on the way back I decided to continue my walk, it wasn't more than a few steps before I came upon the old red brick church, I immediately realized that the local priest was someone I should pay a visit to sooner rather than later, these days there are three important local leaders on most reservations: the village head, the local representative, and the old headman, but besides these three there is often a fourth unofficial leader—the local priest—I have personally witnessed the power and authority of local priests during my time at the southern Rukai and southern Paiwan reservations,[7] during one traditional event where the tribe was called together Priest was the sole participant wearing everyday clothing, and the only one to lecture the headman, local representative, village head, and other tribe members for more than a half hour, his only lord is God, so everyone allows him to get away with not wearing traditional ceremonial robes of the ancestors, perhaps as much as half of his authority is owed to the strict social hierarchy of the Rukai and Paiwan peoples, he was dispatched from Heaven to allow the Ancestral Spirits to kiss his feet, I always felt it ridiculous how the tribespeople had allowed Priest's lord and master to handle all of their affairs concerning Heaven, Earth, and their Ancestral Spirits, I was later reminded of the great militarist Ma Ji and his theories of warfare, Priest used the art of warfare to scare away the Ancestral Spirits of Heaven and Earth, he came to this land to fight until death, he conquered the high mountains of this island nation and transformed this place into the kingdom of His children, he is the type of person that "fights for all eternity," a model to instill fear into the hearts of the indigenous people living in the mountains, at the same time, with his unwavering confidence, he also takes the Lord's classic teachings, organizations, food, and materialistic way of life and brings them into the stone and bamboo homes of the indigenous people, there must be a detailed record in Priest's file somewhere that denotes the exact time when the Ancestral Spirits of heaven and earth of the high mountains on this island nation first slipped away, I hope that the social movements of the 1990s advocating a return to traditional culture have helped the indigenous people recover their lost Ancestral Spirits, by the early twenty-first century the primitive notions of Heaven and Earth should finally be able to return home, let Heaven and Earth be the witness, the Ancestral Spirits shall call another large-scale meeting to discuss the fate of Priest and whether or not to destroy the church, but for the time being the Ancestral Spirits will probably allow Priest to temporarily preside over this "reservation subculture," the church would be turned into a school or activities center, and finally Priest would be transformed into a volunteer working for the Ancestral Spirits, he would wear traditional dress at each and every traditional ceremony helping out wherever he could, the Ancestral Spirits might give him the title of "Atayal's Eternal Volunteer" or "Rukai's Eternal Volunteer"—at the fin de siècle, it seems that everyone is transforming, priests are no exception, this is the most probable future that I see for priests, perhaps I have been standing outside Priest's courtyard for too long, Priest couldn't help but temporarily take leave of his holy hall to see if I was a lost sheep, I heard him, "Welcome! Are you settling in okay?" so, news travels fast to Priest around here, "Sorry I didn't come to see you first, but since I heard you are here to research that incident, I didn't think I needed to rush out and pay you a visit right away," Priest apologized for having overlooked his duties, he explained that he had been busy binding several new romanized editions of the Bible, once that was done the real task would be teaching God's children to read this version of the Bible romanized in their native tongue, but his confidence was not shaken, no wonder I often see the old lady living diagonally across from me spending all her free time when she finishes her work in the fields sitting under the eves with another woman reading something all the way up until dusk, Priest explained that he expected everyone to make a certain amount of progress each week, those who couldn't keep up would be fined a few dollars and forced to spend extra time studying at home, according to his plan each and every member of the congregation would have an Atayal-language version of the Bible in their hands by the time they got together to celebrate the birth of Christ at the end of the century so they could collectively welcome the coming of the Lord, "Amitummy Buddha"—my stomach couldn't help but shudder a sigh, "My Amitummy Buddha indeed,"[8] Priest asked me inside to have a tour, I noticed a lectern on the raised rostrum, the same wood was also used for the chairs and stools and it all came from the nearby mountain forests, they all displayed the cracks and fissures of the past and the termite holes of time, I figured it could very well be a historic church dating back to the Qing dynasty, but Priest laughed explaining that the entire area surrounding Riverisle had been a riverbed in ancient times, when the Japanese came there were only a few scattered settlers who had come to open up the land, the first thing one has to do before establishing a church is weigh the "economic benefit," it was only after the incident that Priest's father first heard about this place, the samurai of the Shinto shrine took pity upon God's soldiers, and what you see here is the church as it was originally built, the most fashionable red brick construction of the day, residents back then all lived in bamboo thatched huts, in sixty years it has never undergone any renovations, and that's not to preserve it as a historic site, it's just that no one ever suggested such things, Priest had a good handle on the church's books, he knew that even during the days of the economic miracle raising enough money to cover renovations would have been an impossibility so let's not even mention it during the post-economic miracle days of today, Priest attributed all of this to the rapid assimilation that took place in the postwar years, assimilation allowed people on the reservation to get a glimpse of the outside world, and provided them with more choices, the church was no longer their sole choice, that's why he must quickly succeed in teaching them to read the Bible in their native language, on the one hand to prove that the Heavenly Father also speaks their language, and secondly to fulfill the loyal-until-death tribal elder's request that holy scriptures be recited in his native tongue before and after his death, one day the church would become the center for preserving their native language, those Atayal who lost their native tongue would have to come back to the church in order to find their roots, but he didn't have anything to say about the "indigenous search-for-roots movement" of the 1990s, the church already had a secure foundation on the reservation, as long as he didn't slap any Ancestral Spirits in the face, the spirits had long forgiven the existence of this thing called a "priest," anyway, Priest looked down at the romanized Atayal Bible in his hand and sighed: movements never last, but the corrosive rot of assimilation silently goes on every second of every day. . . . I was almost completely lost in Priest's sermon, but taking advantage of the pause when he sighed, I managed to bring up my research, Priest explained that during the last decade or so before the end of the war, there were several Japanese scholars who came to conduct research on "the cause of the incident," they would often stay for extended periods of time at the luxury resort church in Riverisle, he remonstrated them with his good intentions doing

everything he could to convince the scholars that everything was
God's intention, the Heavenly Father sent the Japanese to tame the
savage nature of the Atayal people, because He had been too lax on
their savagery during the 200-year period of the Qing dynasty, the
Japanese made a small sacrifice but exchanged it for the loyalty of the
savages, examples of quite similar lessons can be found throughout
the holy books, we should not feel sadness for those who were sacrificed, for in the end savages and civilized alike all return to the embrace of the Heavenly Father for warmth, it must have been about a
decade ago that Academia Sinica sent a young girl over to research
"the impact of the incident," by then the bamboo-thatched huts
in Riverisle had all been long torn down, those with money built
modern-style two- or three-story homes, those without money stuck
with traditional Japanese-style homes, that girl naturally stayed in
one of those luxury three-story houses, he said that the greatest impact of the incident must come down to the will of God, it led the
Seediq people to move from that evil place high in the mountains to
Riverisle where they would be surrounded by mountain valleys, there
they would have plenty of land to farm, they would receive an education specially designed just for them, during the Japanese colonial
period it became a model village for the entire nation, after the war
the "Nationalist" government went even further in constructing new
roads around Riverisle, the girl interrupted him, she didn't understand, "what do you mean by roads around Riverisle," that asphalt
road that links to the outside was actually built for the agricultural
farm of a nearby public university, the girl retorted, back then wasn't
that massive mountain forest zoned as a "private farm," how come
you didn't lead the people of Riverisle in protest, that was the Seediq
people's traditional hunting ground, Priest explained that the girl
couldn't be stumped didn't have shame and never ran out of breath,
did she even know what specific year he was referring to when he said
"back then," back then was a time when decisions like this were made

in a large office building in a faraway city by someone sending down some official document, by the time the Seediq even realized that they had been "zoned" those office people's piss and shit had long dried up in the wind, no one ever talked about protesting, and Priest's business was God, he had no intention of telling the people what they should or shouldn't do, and back then no one knew what to do, "And now?" the girl asked, now it's a case of a fait accompli, a fait that is accompli so what else is there to say, just before the girl left she expressed how utterly sad and disappointed she was about the impact the incident had left, she had earned her degree in an advanced country, witnessed advanced aboriginal people and their advanced systems, she felt embarrassed and depressed by "Riverisle where all people do is drink," she left Riverisle with a feeling of shame for the "land and people," Priest ran his hands through his white hair and smiled uncomfortably, I smiled too and said: young girls are always a bit soft and tender, "tender just like chicken" but since we didn't eat her up we can forgive her, but I do feel shame for our system's lack of regulations concerning "assimilation," if Mona Rudao were alive today, he would certainly strictly regulate things like "television sets" coming into the reservation, he would also require those tribespeople who go down to the cities for employment to return for specified ceremonies in order to brush up on traditional Atayal culture, and if the "nation" did not allow autonomous rule Mona Rudao would certainly carry out his own form of self-administration anyway, he would simply "act, but not tell"—"I'm talking about our Heavenly Father, not Mona Rudao," Priest's tone sounded as powerless as a punctured balloon, no, not exhaustion but frustration, he was powerless to go any further with his little sermon, at least for now, "The Heavenly Father fills the hearts of his children, there is no room left for Mona Rudao, of course it's not that I have anything against him, I certainly know to avoid hurting the feelings of the tribespeople, those indigenous rights activists always feel obligated to talk about Mona Rudao, but when I don't mention him for an extended period of time, it becomes very difficult for him to continue on, not to mention be seen as some sort of idol, I don't object to people calling him a national hero, but I want my congregation to believe that God is ultimately their sole source of faith and support, all those in our human world that we call heroes kneel down at the feet of God, all you see are their humble backs, but you never see the face of the hero," a radiant splendor sparkled in Priest's eyes, "I do not judge whether or not Mona Rudao's actions were appropriate or just, I don't ponder such disgraceful matters, all I can tell you with any degree of certainty is that on the day of the incident the Heavenly Father was nowhere to be found in that man's heart, God never calls for senseless sacrifice that leads to nothing, it is clear that Mona Rudao's actions on that day and what followed never led to anything, you are an outsider, you're asking these questions during this obviously 'open' age, I can therefore answer these questions as I think Mona Rudao would have, but if you had showed up here twenty or thirty years ago that would have been another story, I would have said I never heard of any Mona Rudao. . . ." I also agreed that God was not in Mona Rudao's heart the day of the uprising, Priest gently put his hand on my shoulder as he walked me out of the church hall, "For many years now, the Devil has been bringing alcohol into the reservation, God must have his own holy reasons for allowing this, I cannot prevent believers from drinking, it just can't be done," the Devil doesn't drink, I silently responded to Priest's final confession, "people drink in order to withstand the burden of the holy." I took a long stroll walking along the ridges between the fields, the rays of light at two or three o'clock in the afternoon still had the power of a strong autumn sun, I ducked out of the sun to sit cross-legged under the trees in a banana orchard, surrounding me were gunnysacks filled with hands of nearly ripe bananas, gazing off into the distance I could see the road at the tail end of the mountain ridge that all the tourists took to get to the city, my conversation with Priest didn't seem to upset him, Mona Rudao's actions were obviously outside the realm of "God," even though historians and scholars of religious studies have offered all kinds of justifications for this century's massacre, some even lost their faith in God in the wake of the massacre, others used the massacre to strengthen their belief in the mysterious ways the will of God is carried out, and straddling the two there are historians and religious studies scholars who after extended discussions came to the conclusion that "no matter what may have occurred, all was carried out in keeping with the will of God, displaying His indubitable holiness," I personally utilize the word "nature" and do not accept the term "God," which I do not use in my later writings, the banana bunches that hang above me on all sides grow and ripen before my eyes, if you look around the part of Riverisle where I live it resembles an oval cradle projected down from the distant mountains, this was created by "nature," nature only carries out its inner duty but never its will, I can't be certain whether or not Mona Rudao's actions were carried out "according to the laws of nature," for although humans are born into nature, they are an animal that can betray nature, I feel the need to again return to the nature where Mona Rudao once lived, perhaps while I am there I will feel something, at the very least I will be able to ease up on "the two troubling points the contemporary has about history" that reside in my heart—the next day, I left at dawn, passing along a twisting mountain path, by the time I arrived at Lu Mountain the morning sun was still resting on the top of the plum trees, this was the former site of the Mhebu tribe, the morning sun was also resting on Mona Rudao's shoulders, I passed by the hotels and hot springs that were all indistinguishable from those at any other tourist site on this island nation, I walked deep into the mountains toward Valleystream, at first the road was paved with small grocery stalls on both sides, but then the path grew narrow until it turned into a small footpath that wrapped around the mountain cliff, along the footpath was a handrail on one side, before me was a flowing creek that emitted a thick smell of sulphur, I could sense that this was the path the Mhebu people took when they retreated deep into the mountain forests, there were absolutely no "historical markers" but there were signs everywhere marking "Hard-Boiled Egg Hot Spring this way," as if today this path exists solely for tourists to boil their "Hard-Boiled Eggs," Valleystream is around a meter wide and filled with jagged pebbles that the water rushes down over, after about a kilometer and a half the footpath ends and Valleystream opens up, as it turns out this is where the streams from three canyons converge, the canyons are so narrow that all one sees are thick brush and dense trees, hidden amid the mist, I imagined that this dense canyon forest must have been the final site of the Mhebu tribe's retreat, at the end of the footpath near Hard-Boiled Egg Hot Spring were a few makeshift structures made from sheets of cheap iron, I took a seat in one that was a teahouse and had a cup of tea, before me were the dense forests of those three canyons, my eyes remained fixed on the heart of those thick woods searching for traces of Mona Rudao patrolling all those years ago, I asked the owner of the teahouse if this was the land of the Mhebu tribe, where did those dense woods lead to, and what the future prospects were, he couldn't answer any of my questions, "There is no footpath because there are no more hunters, perhaps there are still some mountain goats and wild boars," the Mhebu tribesman laughed, "Don't you know that these days we make a living through hotels and tourism, hunting is dead," I didn't inquire about "the Incident" or Mona Rudao because I don't like to bring it up casually, "I moved back here alone, my only option was to build myself a sheet-iron house here where the three valleys meet," he had a pretty and elegant daughter who prepared and served the tea, "What my dad means is that we don't own our own land, but living here in a sheet-metal construction isn't too bad—my dad won't let me get an outside job, as long as he is alive he wants us to be together here in Mhebu," if you can imagine all the Mhebu

tribespeople who threw themselves from the cliffs and hanged themselves from the trees spread out before our eyes you would understand the meaning of those last words she uttered, I sat for a long
time gazing at that dense canyon forest and tears welled up in my
eyes, until finally the old Mhebu tribesman said, "No one goes into
the forest anymore, everyone who comes through goes no farther
than Hard-Boiled Egg Hot Spring," his daughter laughed and added,
"if you go any farther you end up in the realm of beasts and ghosts,"
I left in disappointment, I wasn't at all surprised that neither of
them mentioned "the Incident," and it wasn't that I didn't ask them
anything, even though all I did ask them was two or three disap-
pointing questions, all of the excitement of life, all of the dignity of
resistance had been buried outside of time and outside of humanity
in those dense misty woods, as far as those people who crossed paths
with the footpath were concerned it no longer had any "temporal
meaning," it has fallen into eternity, does the contemporary need to
once again enter the overgrown forest and dense fog to break the silence? If this silence remains frozen in some dense forest on this island nation, will the contemporary be unable to solve the two great
mysteries of history? Deep down I hesitated, yet my feet continued
along the footpath back, I realized that the sulphurlike smell that
emitted from Valleystream didn't just assault my nose but seemed to
drive directly into my heart, I used to ponder why "human violence"
always existed from humankind's earliest beginnings all the way up
until the present day, scholars have offered partial explanations from
the perspective of biology, psychology, sociology, politics, and so on,
but these explanations all came after the fact, I pondered the fact
that humans are a creation of this planet, they have the most advanced brains, but deep in the human heart there seems to be a burning flame just like the one raging beneath the earth's crust, it is that
primordial flame burning in the heart of man that ensures there will
never be an end to violence, the human mind has of course exerted its

fair share of brainpower exploring how to balance power and eradicate violence, all of this to limited results, we have taught people to
practice religious self-cultivation, take part in humanitarian enter-
prises, and follow the path of "nonviolence," but beneath the stream
flowing through these high mountains also flow the molten embers
of that fire, I can't help but wonder if those same molten embers also
flow through the veins of the Mhebu people who live here? that
would perhaps explain why headhunting became a part of their
everyday rites and customs, it would also explain why a small village of savages would dare resist the massive machine of a nation, and
so their resistance was not born of ignorance and stupidity, it was
driven by an anger exploding out from the depths of their hearts
even in the face of the consequences they knew all too well would
befall them, I reflected upon myself and the beast nature that indeed
lurked within this civilized person, beginning from the days of my
youth I had carried out various forms of tangible and intangible
"struggle and subversion," I took a swing and with one hit knocked
down one of the Hard-Boiled Egg signposts, I even stopped and
waited so I could hit the next person who came by to say something
to me about it, if it had been a different time and place perhaps this
would have translated into using a brick to break the windshield of a
car blocking the sidewalk, or if we switch to yet another time and
place it could be a series of missiles fired toward our island nation,
drawn to us like a moth to a flame, A friend of mine from the Bunun
tribe once brought me out behind his house to the banks of the
Laonong River so I could feel how hot the water was, he explained
that this was the best place for students to learn about nature, I almost blurted out that the long-term and repeated resistance against
the Japanese that was carried out on the mountain pass next to the
river also came from the heat of the Laonong, there have been many
"great masters" who have told people to seek peace and quietude,
there may be individual peace but can there be complete peace? Even

within peace and quietude lies a disturbing fire that burns, in the end it is the disturbance of violence that completes unmoving quietude, life is usually always wavering between peace and agitation, I'm afraid that lofty slogans like "eradicate violence" and "eternal peace" are not practical for the way humans live, people are always swaying between action and inaction, eternally swaying. . . . The reason I commit this rather emotional passage to paper is simply to use "the Incident" to make a sincere attempt at exploring the erratic nature of my own life over the past several years through this novel, I want to verify something that very well may never be verifiable—before the final "emptying of thoughts" I want to put everything I have into thinking, I found a shallow point to cross where there was a railing, I squatted down to touch the water, the fiery heat of the water was usually enough to warm people's hearts and over time can accumulate to make one's heart boil, for a moment I felt that I was a civilized person just as "primal" as the Mhebu people, back in the primitive age I would have swung my "headhunting" blade without the slightest hesitation, but in our civilized contemporary world I struggle to ponder the legitimacy of swinging that blade to commit a "massacre"? did the Remains of Life of Riverisle and those other civilized Mhebu people also once ponder this question of "legitimacy"? not far from the footpath I saw a large pile of slabstones spread out around a dilapidated two-story construction, I looked back to see "Inn of the Elder" and immediately wondered if this could be the former residence of Mona Rudao, positioned at the highest point along the entry to the canyon footpath, one could look down and observe everything down on the reservation and in the valley, perhaps because I was distracted by the "temptation of Hard-Boiled Egg" I had overlooked this place when I first arrived, I climbed through the windy pile of slabstones and found a small courtyard with bamboo and peach blossom trees, straight through the open wooden door I could see a massive stone tablet inscribed with the words "Inn of the Elder" lying on the dusty couch, on the left was a long extended bar, the large broad dance floor was completely empty, at the back of the dance floor was a black cloth backdrop crumpled up on the floor, set up on the nearby stage were amplifiers, musical instruments, and a microphone, the dust could not conceal the fact that there were many feet that once danced to the music here, traditional Atayal dance with a tinge of disco, the ancient sounds of the Seediq with a touch of heavy metal, the devoid emptiness made one sense the silhouettes of the dancing crowds, the clatter of voices, and the smell of clothes and bodies, once upon a time this was where people carried out their postmassacre carnivalesque parties, in order to stage a grand celebratory ceremony commemorating their successful headhunt, in order to provide the Remains of Life in their postcalamity years a place to display their sexuality and release themselves through dance, the smell still lingers, most probably it was during the years of miracle growth of the 1980s, it would have been an impossibility during the years of stalled hesitation of the 1950s and 1960s, but the Ancestral Spirits had once been here, throughout the 1980s Mona Rudao sat at the bar lost amid the chaotic atmosphere of wild dance and sexual abandon, the poets misrepresented the 1980s when they described it as age "devoid of poetry and song," I went around the door and climbed the wooden stairs up to the second floor, only when you are civilized to the point of ruin can a world devoid of poetry and song take the place of acid and speed, the second floor also had an empty hall, it was surrounded by a series of small rooms divided by thin planks of cheap wood, each room still had a neatly folded white blanket, toward the back were a pair of communal hot springs baths, looking out the window one could see the blurry mountains and forest in the distance, imagine the carnival-like atmosphere as they carried on until midnight or even dawn before taking a bath in the hot springs and crawling under the blankets together, they would sleep until dusk when the evening mountain mist would blow in awakening them so they could take another bath before going back down to the bar, there Mona Rudao would toast everyone with a shot of Misty Stream spirits, sounds of glee would ring out for yet another night of carnival-like ecstasy on the dance floor—in the name of the massacre or the headhunt, it is my understanding that in the old days sex after a killing wasn't some sleepy pigheaded affair instead it was a wild carnival of wine and dance, the carnivalesque had entered into the sex of the slaughter—wasn't this in fact the very reason for my decade of self-isolation? How could the army's "system" castrate anything? The whole time I was in the army we used the steamed buns they distributed for breakfast each morning as a means of counting down the days until being discharged, after midnight Mona Rudao would jump down from the bar, he would walk with the Ancestral Spirits all the way to the Mystic Valley, in any case he made sure to display all the proper courtesy a host should, the after-midnight carnival he would leave for the civilized world of Lu Mountain, it was Lu Mountain's, and not Mhebu's, I followed an extremely steep stone path up to the top of the building out back, which was an expansive area paved with cement, there was a makeshift construction built on the rooftop out of pieces of sheet metal, the structure was divided up into several small rooms by sheets of plywood, it was a chaotic mess around the structure with cement bags, piles of sandstone, a hotpot, a shovel, bottles, cans, miscellaneous cooking utensils, several piles of old books and magazines and an old Wild Wolf motorcycle, a single man must have been living there, there was a laundry rope with several shirts and pants hanging out, I climbed over the pile of cement bags and sandstone to enter one of the rooms, only then did I clearly see the images and writing scrawled on the plywood walls, someone had carefully used red spray paint to spray the words "the truth about the Musha Incident" in regular script on the outside wall, below was a series of images including photocopies and photos, on another wall was written "traditional Atayal life," most of the

photos were black and white, I had been searching so long and hard
to uncover the truth about the incident, and here it was not in some
development plan or history book but hidden on the plywood walls
of this abandoned inn, the first image I saw was of large planes flying
overhead between the canyons, beside it was a photo of two soldiers
dressed in their civilized uniforms with their arms akimbo looking
after a group of squatting savages with spears, I wondered how there
could be an original photo like this here since it didn't look like it
was simply a copy, could one of those soldiers with his hands on his
hips have left the image behind after the end of the war? moving on
the next photo was of three cannons in a triangular formation firing
from their strategic position atop a protruding peak, the fourth image was of several tattered corpses scattered around a breast-shaped
depression caused by cannon fire, the focus was on the horrifying
size and shape of the breastlike gaping hole while the dead bodies
were like scattered worms, when I saw this image my heart rate increased many times over, like that anthropologist in the 1980s who
came upon a group of dwarfs deep in the mountains of this island nation a pity they didn't bring a camera with them, or like the agent of
some detective agency that randomly stumbled upon a major lead in
a series of political assassinations that took place on this island nation a shame that he was shut up that very night while he was asleep,
could there be an actual photograph of what Mystic Valley looked
like back then? could there be a photo of Mahong and her elder
brother's "final banquet"? could there be a photo that reveals "the final
mystery behind Mona Rudao"? in the final row of pictures I caught a
glimpse of a photocopy image of a baby hanging dead from a tree
branch in silhouette, after that I squatted down to examine a frontal
photo of two children who couldn't have been more than three or
four years old dangling dead from a tree—I couldn't believe that this
person had primary photographic documents like this, he must have
even more inside details about the "truth," perhaps these details are

not terribly important to the major historical events surrounding the incident, but it is precisely those minor details that together make up the background of the incident as a living thing, I turned to another plywood wall where there was a group photo of the entire Mhebu tribe taken before the incident, another photo showed a bare-breasted Mhebu woman breastfeeding her child, I stared at that somewhat cone-shaped breast, which had a tough quality that was completely different from the 1980s and 1990s breasts of Taipei and Kaohsiung, those were Mhebu breasts from the 1920s ... perhaps when you come to the part about breasts in a novel you assume that one section is winding down or a new plot twist is coming, and that is precisely the case here, a pair of legs suddenly strutted in blocking my view of the breasts, perhaps in real life there would be a face-to-face meeting at this point where the two people would stare each other down, but that kind of scene is a luxury in fiction writing, in fiction this is the moment where the narrative must shift to whoever those legs belong to and there isn't even ample opportunity to express how unwilling I am to bring those breasts to a conclusion, "What the hell are you doing here?" the legs' owner spoke from the groin so in order to follow what was said you had to look up from his crotch until he came into sight, at times like this the best form of protection is to simply rely on one's natural reaction, "I'm here to do research," he moved his other leg so that now my view of the photo was completely blocked, "What the hell do you research?" naturally the truth behind the incident, but I couldn't be so direct with him or he might get defensive and be unwilling to talk, "I came up to the mountains to conduct research on the traditional lives of the Seediq people," he moved his legs away, "well then, you can start by looking at these pictures," the legs straddled that old Wild Wolf and with a few rumbles from the engine he was off, I carefully examined the photos surrounding those breasts, from that point on I turned my eyes away from those breasts, those breasts exuded a tragic "uncontrollable" sadness, during the

1920s in the very simple environment of the high mountains, there was a sadness that was uncontrollable, it was not due to that unpredictable incident that would occur a decade later, it was the living conditions themselves that contained this inherent quality of sadness that pervaded those breasts and spread out, never once had I felt that kind of sadness from civilized breasts, such a desperately uncontrollable situation, I don't want to spend any more time pondering the situation that led to civilized breasts abandoning the desolate beauty here, I instead turn my attention back to the truth of that group of photos, in good time Old Wolf came rumbling home, "Did you see anything interesting?" he seemed to be quite pleased that the incident had captured my attention, Old Wolf wanted me to come over to give him a hand, "Have a drink first, once you sober up we'll have something to eat," when he went out it was to pick up a day's worth of food and wine, I noticed that it wasn't even four o'clock, he said he only eats this one meal a day, the rest of his time is taken up with other important matters so his eating and sleeping schedule is completely out of whack, "My name's Daya," he started by finishing off a bottle of pure aged rice wine, "I was born in the 1960s," he handed another bottle to me, "Drink it all down if you can, otherwise just drink as much as you can handle, one bottle for each of us," this Old Wolf was still in his thirties, I was deceived by his graying hair and the crows' feet around his eyes, I told him I came up from Riverisle in search of Mhebu, he said he was also from Riverisle, he was born in Riverisle, later he scraped by in the city for a few years, before hearing about a homeland called Mhebu, and so he returned, he came back to manage this inn and create his own "Mhebu Utopia," His name was Daya and he was a member of the Seediq Daya tribe, by the time he returned to Mhebu the inn had already been closed for more than a year, he didn't have a place to live, so he asked for permission from the Ancestral Spirits and the tribal chief to stay here for the time being, by that time it was already the 1990s and while he was at the Indigenous People's Resource Center in the city he had heard that everyone should return to the site of their original tribal home and help rebuild the birthplace of their ancestors, Old Wolf figured he should return as well after all he had already had as much fun as he could in the city and spent all his money, he stayed in Riverisle for less than three days before leaving again, that's because ever since childhood people had been telling him that this was a condemned place, indeed it only took a few days for his bones to go soft, it felt like his tendons and veins were all backward and he barely made it out alive, it took him two and a half days to finally walk back to Mhebu, "Back when they were first exiled it only took them one day, they left in the morning and arrived at dusk," I told him with a laugh, he took another drink and said he didn't believe me, "The only reason for that would be that they were so terrified that all their courageous juices drained down into their feet," I kept out the part about the exiles riding part of the way on a light-duty cart and then on a light-rail train owned by the candy factory, his father never talked to him about "what happened in the past," he just wanted his son to work hard and make money, "I almost went overseas, I wish I had," he lit up the oven, asking me to wash the rice and vegetables, "As I see it you must be at least half Mhebuean, for the past two or three years no one has noticed the pictures hanging on the walls outside my room," That's right I said, I moved to Riverisle in order to return to my native home, everyone has a place they originally come from, even though I knew all too well that my native home was actually hidden away deep in my soul, I wasn't in the mood to talk too much or even ask questions, but one look at the empty bottle of rice wine was enough to tell me that Old Wolf was quite a talker, and goodness knows how long it had been since he had someone to talk to, I was willing to simply play the role of a good listener but not a so-called researcher, Old Wolf made a big pot of vegetable rice porridge and opened up a package of ground beef and a can of eel, after the chief agreed to allow him to look after the inn in his dreams, it was another full year and a half before the actual owner of the inn returned, his name was Old Daya and he had the aura of the old chief who had visited Old Wolf in his dreams with traces of the exhaustion of a man who had lived through war, Old Daya thanked the Young Wolf for his hard work taking care of the inn, he knew enough to preserve the original look of the first floor, the hot springs tubs on the second floor were all kept clean and the comforters were all properly folded neat and tidy, "I even take the blankets out to sun them on a regular basis!" Young Wolf said that Old Daya only stayed for two weeks, he spent every night at the bar, lost in deep thought as he gazed out over the empty dance floor, only after midnight would he find his way up to the second floor, he would sit in the hall drinking with Young Wolf, he asked Young Wolf to forget about having changed his name to Daya, and he called him Little Daya instead, the return of Big and Little Daya signified the return of the Mhebu people, after that he wanted to share all sort of stories with Little Daya "that must never be told to the outside," what Little Daya felt most unsettling was the very first thing Old Daya told him, "I am the grandson of Mona Rudao," for the first few days after the incident his mother, Mahong, tried desperately to escape by running into the canyon forest, in her arms she carried a child, and stumbling behind her was another child, this was a time that many of the Mhebu mothers displayed the great courage of Atayal women, for some reason many of them hanged their children from the trees, before running off deep into the forest, most of them did as Mahong, throwing their children from the high cliffs as they passed by Valleystream, the historical literature on this only provides one bland sentence to explain these actions: "In order to prevent themselves and their children from becoming a burden, the women wanted to leave all remaining food and supplies to the brave Atayal soldiers . . ." just as all the tribe members in Riverisle know, from middle age until late in life there were numerous times when Mahong would suddenly disappear, several times she was intercepted on her way to the place where the Mhebu people collectively hanged themselves, this was a breed of sorrow and depression that had accumulated to the point at which it builds up into a kind of hysteria, for her entire life she regretted not having followed her father and brothers to death in that dense forest, "My whole life I have been wondering if she ever regretted throwing her son off that cliff in Valleystream," said Old Daya, I suppose that the history books always record the side that is easiest to understand, facing the terror of death the mothers of Mahabo fled through the dense misty forest, as soon as one of them hanged herself or cast away her child, there was quickly a second, and then a third following suit, it was a kind of collective hysteria, it was this collective hysteria that led to the final collective suicidal leap from the cliff, the Ancestral Spirits arranged for Old Daya to land in a deep pool of water, he was pulled out just in time by Granny Atayal, "Even today I still don't know if I was the child in my mother's arms or the one running behind," Granny Atayal walked all through the night to sneak the child out of Valleystream, following the Mei River she evaded the search parties and made it to the home of some Presbyterian church members in Puli, the Presbyterians dressed the child in Chinese clothes, first thing the following morning the deacon brought the child to their church in Taichung, that very day the Taichung Presbyterian Church transferred him to the old Maxwell Memorial Church in Tainan, "So that's me, I spent my early childhood in Mhebu and grew up in the Maxwell Memorial Church," they trained him to one day be ordained as an Atayal priest, "The two main languages I studied at the Maxwell Church were my native tribal tongue and English," who could have anticipated that unrest would break out just outside the church in his eighteenth year, word spread that there was to be a public execution carried out in the small park just outside the church, the foreign priest forbade anyone from the church from going out to witness the execution of the "bandit leader,"[9] that very night of the bandit's execution, Old Daya was sent to a place called Section Seven or Section Eight near the sea, he took a small boat before transferring to a large container vessel, only after they finally disembarked did the deacon who had been accompanying him tell him, "We have finally made it to South America, we must be at least ten thousand kilometers from Mhebu," he began to study Spanish, that way he could still be a priest in his new home, but he could never submit himself to the discipline imposed by the Presbyterian Church, he drank, whored, read forbidden books, "Perhaps the Ancestral Spirits traversed the vast ocean to enter my body and bedevil me," in his twentieth year he married a rich Latin American widow, he was thrown out of the church the same year, and it was also in that year that his Latino Seediq daughter was born, he also began to freely traverse South America, the rich widow bought several large buildings, which she turned into apartments, she rented them out to new immigrants, the energy it took just to collect rent was already enough to make her forget which woman's bed her husband might have wandered off to, while he was in the United States he read some information about the Pacific War, he also went to Japan a few times to look up some information, even visiting a few Japanese who had "once been to Musha and Riverisle," he naturally did all of this because he was "possessed by the spirits of his ancestors," but it probably also had something to do with the many years of training and education he received from the Presbyterian Church, "—Was it Old Daya who brought all those photos back?" I asked, the drunken look in Old Wolf's eyes reminded me of the middle-aged Daya back in his days as a feisty wanderer, "they are part of his private collection, he had to pay for some of them," He couldn't ever figure out why in his later years the Ancestral Spirits would bring him back to Mhebu, as soon as he returned he saw this Japanese-style inn on the verge of ruin, it had been the home of his ancestors, that night from the rear window of the inn he could clearly see himself as a child being thrown down into Valleystream, Granny Atayal carried him on her back, finding her way past the inn to the Mei River, that night he cried as never before in his life, oh how he missed the mother who had tossed him away with her very hands, when he arrived in Riverisle, there wasn't a single person who didn't know his mother Mahong Mona, but no once accepted him as Daya Mona, by the time he returned in 1989, it had been many years since Mahong had returned to the Mystic Valley, because he could perfectly speak the native tongue the tribal elders treated Daya well, but most people on the reservation treated him like he was some maniac who returned to Riverisle after escaping from a nuthouse, he kept asking about Mahong, and people kept telling him the story of how she continually walked off in search of the place in Mhebu where the communal hanging took place, and each time he would cry until he had lost his voice, at first the sincerity of his tears moved many people and they cried with him, it continued until their cries became a kind of noise that "resurrected the pain of the past," the tribal elder publicly asked him to leave, because they couldn't spend all their time in pain, they still needed to plant the crops and raise the farm animals, and the most serious reason was that "children born unto pain are children that have been cursed by the Ancestral Spirits," they could not accept the thought of these children one day bringing about another "incident" among the Remains of Life here in Riverisle, He thanked the elder and bid him farewell, he returned the pain of his life to Mahong, it was Mahong's remarried daughter who supported him as he left Riverisle, it was clear that in all of Riverisle it was only this daughter of Mahong's who ever believed him, whenever he gazed at her, he could see Mahong staring back through her eyes, "I want to go back to Mhebu," were the final words he uttered through his sobs, and she calmly replied, "Mommy knows . . ." The first thing he did after returning was to have that Japanese-style house torn down, in its place he built a two-

story wood building, there was a dance floor on the first floor, and
the second floor was a hot springs hotel, he insisted that visitors
must climb up those three windy slabstone steps in order to finally
arrive at the House of the Elder, the reason for making it a hot springs
hotel was owing to the fact that the native home of Mhebu was
already quite famous as a hot springs resort, the dance floor seemed
to be inspired by samba clubs, but his original intention was actually
to have a place for people to brush up on or even reinvent traditional
Atayal dance, he publicly proclaimed himself to be the Grandson of
the Elder who had returned to carry on the family business, hardly
anyone knew who this Elder he spoke of was, he quietly went about
clearing away the trees and wild grass growing behind the inn so
there could be a large open tableland, someone from the Musha
Police Station came by once but they settled the case by claiming
what he was doing fell under "tidying up overgrown land," he planned
to add a projector and a large screen to the dance floor to transform
the space into an interactive memorial hall for the incident, the tableland facing the rear mountains was to feature a small-scale model of
what Mhebu looked like back during the time of the incident, the
dance hall was opened on October 27, 1992, he reserved a seat at the
bar for his grandfather, Mona, and on the second floor he maintained a small room that would always have a ready-made bed for his
mother, Mahong, the dance floor attracted the Generation Xers of
the 1990s, their dance steps were led by the Ancestral Spirits of the
Atayal but gradually transformed into a soul disco tango, the midnight racket could be heard from the nearby Lu Mountain Police
Station to as far away as Valleystream, the station was responsible
for issuing all land and construction permits in the vicinity, as the
conventional practice went they came and extorted money from the
hotel, in the end they demanded the hotel name be changed to remove
the word "Elder," they also made it clear that all activities would have
to cease before midnight, both were impossible conditions to meet,

changing the name from "Elder" would take away the symbolic meaning that he had for so long wanted to convey—this was precisely the age in which "symbolic meaning" was more important than reality, moreover in the hot springs resort area almost all of the major action didn't even get *started* until after midnight, he understood that the "Elder Dance Hall" had attracted civilized people north and south throughout this island nation and brought them to this Mhebu inn where they could live out a contemporary Musha Incident, once midnight came they would happily recount the past and head out toward the rear hillside and it was only then that they would begin to truly understand the traditional Atayal lifestyle of the Seediq people, the Police Station looked into Old Daya's background and discovered that although he was originally from Mhebu his legal status was in South America, he was ordered to leave Mhebu and expelled out of the country, the official document elaborated on his crimes of having "stirred up history, corrupted people's minds, and committed acts that have tangibly upset the peace and security of the hot springs resort area," Old Daya suspected that there must be people outside the Police Station who had a hand in this, he was reminded of what he read about the "Second Musha Incident," and he started to keep an eye on those Seediq people around him, perhaps this guy or that guy is the grandson of those who took part in the "headhunt" against the Mhebu people, Old Daya left in late 1994, he had only been back in his native land for less than two years, besides getting his inn business up and running during those two years he also completed work on a traditional Atayal watchtower overlooking the area, "I'll take you up to the tower in a little while, it looks just like what we see in those old photos," Old Wolf said, he had met the elder Old Daya Mona about a year and a half ago, Old Daya seemed to have returned specifically to seek out Little Daya for an evening chat, it was then that he asked Little Daya to continue on as the caretaker for his old ancestral home, Old Daya told him that

while far away in an alien land he had always been consumed with
the present and future of Mhebu, during this trip however he only
stayed for two weeks, and that was because his Latino Seediq daughter
was in the middle of a large-scale demolition and reconstruction
project, he came back to give a hand and make sure everything was
going okay, Old Daya promised himself, all the hard work and planning he had done for Mhebu would one day bear fruit, during his
next visit, he would start a true movement to "Return to Our Native
Land," to rectify those unjustly persecuted and allow those tribe members forcibly exiled all those years ago to return to their ancestors'
native land, he wanted Old Wolf to take care of himself, because the
moment he returned they would go straight to Riverisle and recruit
people to repopulate Mhebu as part of this movement, The Lu
Mountain Hot Springs Resort could be relocated to virtually any-
where on this island nation, but only the Mhebu people have the
right to claim their native land as the Mhebu Hot Springs, moreover
it would not be a "tourist" hot springs resort but an "Atayal Culture
Hot Springs" resort. I took my leave the afternoon of the following
day, Old Wolf had passed out drunk in the early morning hours and
was still in a stupor, just before I left I made sure to take a photo
of those plywood walls, naturally I didn't forget to take a photo of
"drunken Old Wolf," as I was walking out I noticed a carefully rendered model of a watchtower, behind the tower was a clean and
empty cement court, "the watchtower overlooks an empty village,"
I remembered someone saying but at the time didn't have much reaction, it was almost dusk by the time I got back to Riverisle, layers of
thin mist embraced the waist of the mountain, Girl's house was
quiet, I sat blankly before my desk intending to write some notes, but
my entire being was consumed with the words of Old Daya and
Little Daya, I didn't know what to write next, experience had taught
me that I needed several days to ponder things before I would be
able to digest Old and Little Daya, only then would it be possible to

commit something to paper, I avoided the kitchen and instead made
a hodgepodge hotpot, I thought back to my days at Rukai when we
used to make huge hodgepodge hotpots, "The entire Ailiao River was
the site of an ancient battlefield between the Paiwan and Rukai tribes,"
so my old Rukai buddy used to tell me between his sighs as we sat
around the hotpot eating, but there were no written records of those
battles, how many battles have disappeared with the passing of time,
forgotten with the passing of men, all that remains are hazy legends,
it is impossible to be certain about anything, but during my time in
Rukai I was never once disturbed by these "historical battles," "They
were completely unlike this Musha Incident," I muttered to myself as
I ate my small hodgepodge hotpot, actually there are many people
who made it through battle to live out their Remains of Life, "you
Han Chinese are the ones deserving of some real research," I suddenly
thought back to what Girl's cousin had said, that's right, from the
end of World War II to the February 28 Incident of 1947 and then on
to the White Terror of the 1950s . . . perhaps it was all too close, too
close, people want to avoid it in the same way one tries to avoid the
disgusting feeling of rubbing against the skin of a stranger sitting
next to you, why not let someone more appropriate face this history,
let those researchers do it, let them face up to the past, thank goodness history gave us a Musha Incident so I would one day be able to
come to Riverisle, it was with a warm quiet loneliness that I ate my
small hodgepodge hotpot, I fell immediately asleep that night even
without the sound of Girl's nighttime lullabies, the clattering footsteps I heard in my dream were those of Mahong Mona running
through the dense forest, behind her I could hear light footsteps that
would periodically stumble and fall, I woke up after the third rooster
crowed and all the other chickens awakened to talk about their
chicken-cawing world, perhaps they were exchanging stories about
their dreams from the previous night, the running footsteps from
that dream were probably so exhausted from running all night long

that the soles of her feet dragged along, making a dragging sound, they dragged all the way to just outside the curtain to the window of my dreams, as a child I also awoke each morning to the chicken clatter coming from our rear courtyard, the experience of waking up to roosters crowing continued all the way up through my teenage years, but after my mother took ill she no longer raised chickens ducks or geese, instead we planted tomatoes in the rear courtyard, above the tomato plants we erected a grape arbor, planting grapes in the city was quite a novelty back then and we really slept until the late morning sun warmed up our asses, none of us missed the chicken calls we had grown up with, If I hadn't come to the foot of this mountain in Riverisle and slept in listening to the ruckus of these chickens, I probably never again would have thought of those crowing roosters in our old house's rear courtyard as long as I lived, perhaps there are many other things I have forgotten, for instance as far as I can recall there was only one time in my life in which I heard roosters crowing a good while after dawn, all those years of my childhood and I never once heard midnight roosters crowing or roosters crowing at midnight, but now as I feel I've reached a point at which "my life is what it is," I clearly heard roosters crowing in the middle of the night on at least two occasions, at first it was the call of a single rooster to which seven or eight others from near and far all responded, after a loud exchange of chicken cries the night returned to its lonely silence, within a few days I had already grown accustomed to waiting for that first cackle in my dreams, when the cry came I would turn over to intently listen, then I would return to my dream waiting for the second one to come. . . . I never once pondered the reason or meaning of the third cackle, it all boils down to natural laws anyway, all you can do is accept them but there is no use in analyzing them, I recently came down from the mountains to return to Danshui, I stayed in a house built on a mountain slope not far from the river, around midnight I was awakened by a flood of frogs croaking, I turned over and once I was sure it was indeed the floodlike torrent of frogs, I fell back into a deep slumber, with the exception of cold rainy nights every night is like this, although nature can make an uproarious noise it never interrupts our clear dreams, it is made of the same quality as our unconscious, sounds and silence melt into each other in "nature," I never once had the urge to research what kind of frogs those were or what their natural habitat was like, better to become one with nature than to load yourself up with all kinds of knowledge about nature, in the morning, afternoon, and evening cicadas chirp, but in the middle of the night another breed of cicada whistles, we understand the meaning of the metamorphosis of ant-sized insects into moths, during the process we need only to carefully observe and listen, at the same time we accept the "completeness" of the entire process, people don't need to break their necks doing research and reeling silk from every cocoon, when our science teacher cuts open the cocoon, using her hands to completely pull apart the string of silk an insect has carefully spun, just what kind of an education are we giving to our children, the natural sciences have already developed to a point where such a question would be labeled as a "childish joke," but I still insist on writing: People must continuously reflect upon the fundamental nature of people and things—just that one sentence, now I want to go back to the cackling chickens around me, I had become clearly aware of the fact that I could not accept the massacre, decapitations, dignity, and ceremony that occurred during that "man-made incident" in the same way I accepted the chickens cackling, I must examine, ponder, and get to the bottom of its truth, and so I could not enjoy lying around amid the natural sounds of cackling chickens, not to mention the fact that those dragging footsteps had long left the window of my dreams and it was clear that they were now here right outside the window of my reality, I pulled open the curtains to look, there was Girl dressed in all black wearing shorts and a T-shirt and "energetically" pacing back and forth with her hands

over her face, "You're not cold this early in the morning?" I called out
to her almost shouting, "Want some coffee?" Girl turned around and
I saw two or three black-and-blue marks on her face, "Nope," the
marks were still a bloody red and were clearly recent, as I brewed my
coffee I wondered whether or not I should go over to see how she was,
but I didn't think my relationship with Girl had quite gotten to the
level where I could really talk about "serious" issues, moreover I had
to go for my morning walk amid the fragrant plum blossoms before
returning to my morning work of meditative pondering, I spent
about three or four times the normal amount of time pouring and
stirring my coffee, "Didn't you want to ask her about what things
were like for Mahong and her family in Riverisle?" I came up with
this excuse once my morning cup of coffee had been perfectly prepared, I went out the back door squeezed past the water tower and
made my way over to Girl's front porch, when Girl saw me she didn't
display even a hint of the "smile of a young Atayal girl," that was a
smile that had been forever associated with Atayal women in my
mind after I had seen it in a photo reproduced in an anthropological
survey book on the Atayal, "Have a seat, but I can't calm down," I sat
down on her front stoop leaning against the wall drinking my coffee,
Girl continued her hyperactive pacing, as she went back and forth
through the fragrance of my coffee I could see the top of Girl's head
higher that the mountain ridge one moment and obscured behind
thick mountain mist the next, extending down from behind her ears
were her dark and beautiful well-proportioned shoulders, wearing
those shorts her equally dark tanned legs went up and down as she
walked exposing the pure white flesh of her thighs, the white skin
of the Seediq Daya people verifies the "racial categorizations according to skin color" that anthropologists have made in their books, I
couldn't help but stare blankly transfixed by the white flesh on her
legs as it appeared and disappeared, had the white flesh of a Han
Chinese woman ever before flashed before my eyes like this? Or was

it a woman from the Cao minority with white skin that I saw back in my younger days, why do Han women always seem wrapped up with products like SK-II and worried about exposing their precious fair skin, Atayal women have absolutely no hesitation when it comes to letting the high mountain sun darken their skin, why after all these years does the memory of that young Cao woman's white skin still remain, ". . . there you are all fair-skinned and healthy, but besides pushing around women all you do is sit on your ass," Girl abruptly exploded with this harsh sentence, I was so shocked by the words "fair-skinned" "sit on your ass" and "pushing around" that I jumped up and asked, "Who?" "Who else? That Pimp-Bastard!" She asked me to come inside, I carried in my still-shocked cup of coffee and wondered who that Pimp-Bastard was and why she had exploded so suddenly, Girl said that she had been fucked so bad these past few days that her muscles were so sore she couldn't even sit her ass down on the stone steps, she slumped into the couch half-sitting half-lying, it was a good thing that there was a sofa chair across from her where I could sit and have my coffee, "It's not that I haven't been around the block before, I dealt with a lot of shit when I lived in the city," she grinded her teeth, "but I never imagined I'd get fucked so bad this time . . ." I had assumed that Girl had spent time in the city, otherwise where could that classical music I heard late at night have come from, anyone who could appreciate those classic pieces must have been deeply influenced by urban civilization, "After I got divorced I spent a few years in the city, I don't know why things were so bad this time when I went back," she walked around the city streets filled with anxiety, the sounds of traffic and people were so loud that she could feel her heart thumping in her throat, at that moment Pimp-Bastard who was off in an corner talking up a storm, immediately came over, the first thing he asked her was whether she needed a good job, and a beat-up black sedan took her away from the dark and seamy city, they would go to a "simpler place" to carry out the mission of their newly established social service enterprise, Pimp-Bastard told Girl how much they were in desperate need of mountain girls like her, "We mountain people have different physiques," Girl pinched the flesh on her arm, "we know how to get the job done," only after she went away with him did she learn that this grown man lived off four old whores who kept him plump and white, as long as Pimp-Bastard yelled and screamed, he never had to worry about not having enough food to eat and booze to drink, Pimp-Bastard ordered two of his women to take their posts outside, while the other two went in to drink with their new recruit, "I was so pissed that my hands couldn't stop shaking," one of the old whores caressed her trembling hands, as they gave her the first glass of rice wine mixed with golden sorghum, the flavor of the rice wine only came out when mixed with the sorghum, Girl was quite familiar with mixing rice wine with all kinds of other drinks, which they did up on the reservation all the time, and to think that they were afraid that all this Atayal girl ever drank was bowls of river water, Pimp-Bastard ordered his two old whores to get a few bowls of alcohol into her, after that the old whores held down her wrists and pulled open her thighs so that Pimp-Bastard could climb into her and start banging her over and over again, as he was about to cum whatever that was that came out of him he bragged to her that it would take seven or eight women to satisfy his pimp power, Girl could be regarded as the fifth external affairs officer to be offered employment by Chairman Pimp-Bastard of the Board, formal employment would begin after a free trial, afterward the other two old whores stayed behind to help Pimp-Bastard further hone his pimp power, they pushed Girl outside to take up the third post, it only took two or three minutes for passing clients to smell something different about this piece of meat, two or three men came up and surrounded her, it was then that she discovered just how much spunk Seediq women really had, it only took three and half minutes each to finish off three and half Chinese johns, one of them came as soon as his dick rubbed against her pubic hair and that's why he only counted as half, she tightly grasped the still-warm banknotes in her hand, she cursed a bit, which really made those other two old whores' eyes turn bloodshot, Girl then even went into the office to give Pimp-Bastard a good Seediq kick in the balls, it was a good thing that one of the old whores was riding him while another girl was feeding him her salacious juices, "Hell I took good aim just as his ass was moving up and got him right in the balls," Girl tilted her head and stared at me with her sparkling eyes, just as his balls were in agony and his mouth was filled with juice, Girl took advantage of this "moment of silence" to escape, she grabbed a taxi and arrived back at the reservation just after dawn, "How terrible that a woman from a good family should fall into a fire pit like that it sounded like it was right out of a novel," I felt angry but also helpless, "That's right!" Girl sat herself up straight, "how could I end up written into such a pathetically vulgar novel," we were both angry beyond belief at this most pathetic novel, according to Girl she paced around outside from first thing in the morning all the way up until midnight but didn't see any lights on in my room or smell the scent of my hodgepodge hotpot, as for how many times the chickens cackled during this time, that is something she never paid attention to in her whole life, she waited all the way up until she smelled the fragrance of civilized coffee in the mountain air, she was on the verge of tears, she walked even faster the Seediq Atayal people can't stand such insult and so she cried about wanting some coffee, I told her that I'd already asked if she wanted some but she declined, she said that she said, "No no no . . ." but not that she didn't want coffee, I immediately went back to my room to make her some coffee, I made a cup that was particularly rich, fragrant, and sweet, I also made sure to use the large china cup with floral designs, by the time I carefully carried the cup over to her, Girl was already asleep flat on the couch with one hand on her forehead and the other on her trembling heart, I carefully carried that big floral cup back, partly closing the door on my way out, I took slow tiny sips of that coffee all the way up until the afternoon, I didn't have time for any of my meditative pondering, I wracked my deranged brain but couldn't figure out why fiction always "directly appropriates" the vulgar and ugly side of reality when it comes to this dream Girl's return to her native home. Only a very small number of people from outer space know the secret about my "derangement," once my "derangement" kicks in it stays with me for several days and other times lasts for many months, I may look dignified and proper, but during my bouts of derangement I even speak in alien tongues, very few people pay sufficient attention to this secret, those few lock themselves up at home brushing up on their alien mother tongue, otherwise they will find themselves more fluent in earth languages than their native alien tongue, there was even a teenage alien who arrived crying, he said that after trying so hard to go back when he got there he couldn't even understand what they were saying, it is clear that time has run out on me and I'm at my busiest when I'm deranged, so much is about to be lost that is waiting for me to save, and yet I appear as someone who doesn't know what to do with himself, the secret behind why things secretly happen is a great secret, but no matter how secret the planet may be, there will always be other planets that know the secret of your existence, and look, penetrating the realm of the sun at this very moment, someone has come directly to my doorstep, "May I come in for a chat?" he spoke through the screen door, he was the size of an orangutan, without bothering to wait for a response he pushed the door open and only after he sat himself down on the sofa did I say, "Please have a seat," I started off by declaring that I was currently deranged because of my "deranged novel" and didn't have the free time to teach him alien talk, it was therefore a good thing that he also started out by declaring, "I live across the street, for the past few days things haven't seemed quite right at the house next door to you, so I came over to check things out," Oh, so there was something not sitting quite right about my fictional character living next door that was upsetting him, as far as a writer of fiction goes, compliments and criticisms are all useless, so I just told him, "Everything's okay," "Everything's okay," he turned his thumb and pointed it behind him, he was gesturing toward that fictional character that wasn't quite right, although he was a new arrival, he was also a fictional character so it wasn't my place to critique other characters from the novel, so I just said, "Everything's okay, I didn't know anything was wrong," "My name's Pihu, I'm glad nothing is wrong, I live next door to the house across from you, things are usually quiet here on the reservation, except when it comes to you missionaries and researchers," "I'm a researcher," I wasn't quite sure why I felt the urge to explain myself, "There used to be two missionaries—nuns—who lived in this house . . . you probably know what I am here to research without even asking," I was still lost away in my secret world, I had to be careful all the time of those lurking missionaries who were always looking to proselytize, there was no way we could have a real conversation, a good thing then that Mr. Pihu was one of the few "activist types" on the reservation, most of these types of people were natural public speakers, add to that their later experiences and the only thing they had to worry about was a lack of an audience, our island nation saw the rise of quite a few public speakers like this in the 1980s, and today I learned that there was also one hidden away here in Riverisle, the election had just ended and since Mr. Pihu didn't have anything else to do, he began talking about the "election on the reservation," upon returning to his hometown he had his heart set on running for village head, he was different from other young people, once he started running he ran in three consecutive elections, he ran as an independent, he had ideals, never took bribes, and was the kind of politician who had a plan, a roadmap for the future, during the last three political races in a row he lost the night before the election to Mr. Sun Yat-sen,[10] for this most recent election there were six candidates, he lost by six votes, that night he and the eldest disciple of Sun Yat-sen were the only ones laughing, but Mr. Sun's second and third disciples cried oh so terribly, although he laughed deep down he knew in his heart that those six votes could never bridge the "Sun Yat-sen gap" on the reservation, but he didn't blame it on the poor character or lack of ideals of the people on the reservation, "Just think about how many bottles of rice wine three bills with Sun Yat-sen's mug on them can buy," I was shocked, "Do they really pay that much? In the cities down in the plains people sell their votes for two or three hundred, if you get five or six hundred that's a cheap deal, but if they pay out more than one Sun Yat-sen then you've really got it made," Mr. Pihu laughed so hard his mouth went crooked, "That's right, that's why I'm always saying it's better here on the reservation than down in the plains, the special qualities of our tribal culture only reveal themselves on very special occasions, we don't flaunt and show off all the time like they do in the cities, that just ruins the mood," my sexual derangement gradually began to ease up, at least until I could sense it hiding in the cracks in the ceiling, amid the pile of washcloths in the bathroom, and in the piles of historical documents filed away in the cabinet or transformed into the triangle-shaped cactus outside the door, as soon as I heard Mr. Pihu talk about the atmosphere surrounding the election, I immediately understood that time would not wait to "proselytize," and I left with a secret unspoken pain, "Could you talk about the Musha Incident . . . from the perspective of the election that is," that question made it clear that my novelistic derangement had already recovered a bit of novelistic sensitivity, "Why did the reservation refrain from discussing the incident during the election?" I pressed him, "Ah ha," Pihu slapped his leg, he pulled one of his feet up onto the chair, I noticed his dark face, neck, and hands but extending out from his trousers were the pale white soles of his feet, "You are probably the only person on the entire reservation for whom the incident even crossed their mind during the election," the incident was out of style, it wasn't cool enough to make the election, "Otherwise had Mona Rudao stood up, Sun Yat-sen wouldn't have stood a chance," It was especially during election time that the incident couldn't be mentioned, otherwise the muddled complexities of the incident would give rise to a complex series of old scores from the past, "But don't think that means we have forgotten the past," the 27th just past and he and others from the reservation had gone to Musha to pay their respects to Mona Rudao, but beforehand they had suggested another memorial be held the following day in Riverisle, in order to "display the historical legacy and significance of this time and place," but nobody paid any attention to Pihu during the ceremony, deep down he was actually against any kind of hero worship, he felt that installing any single one person as the hero was unfair to their other tribal ancestors who had also taken part in what happened, for years he had been suggesting they establish a "Commemorative Hall to the Musha Incident" in Riverisle, far away from the site of the bloody massacre, far away from the homeland of those who should never have claimed it as home, "it should be erected among the descendants of the incident, so generation after generation of the Remains of Life may commemorate the past," This language is not the result of my literary manipulation, but these are almost the exact words used by Dafu, this was also the first time I heard someone from the reservation utter the words "Remains of Life," one can see that just as there is a "Memorial to the Remains of Life" erected in Dafu's heart so too it must also be standing high in the hearts of some of the other people on the reservation, but Pihu turned over his dark hands exposing his bare palms, "No one else ever voices support, I'm the only one who ever advocated building a hall," but that is no cause for worry, because Mr. Pihu has a ten-year plan, the hall will be completed during the coming decade, the next decade will correspond with the previous decade, Pihu couldn't help but talk about his past, he spent ten years as a bedeviled first sergeant before retiring, perhaps he looked back fondly upon his decade "in uniform," then again perhaps he hated it, he immediately returned to his homeland in Riverisle, there he took the two plots of level ground between the mountains that his ancestors had left him and turned them into fisheries, he only raised "national treasure fish," the type that people drive down from the cities in their Benzes and Chryslers to collect for their expensive fishtanks, even the small fish go for upward of six thousand NT, then one year on the eve before a major typhoon the Ancestral Spirits visited him in a dream and told him, "Let the fish go to lay their eggs deep in the mountains," he thought it made sense and agreed, the following day when he went out to his fisheries and discovered they had completely flooded over, the entire plot of land was a massive empire of water, the fish had indeed "been taken" deep into the mountains to propagate, after that he went with a group of construction workers to Taipei to work on the Taipei MRT, from there he worked developing the hilly area around Xizhi, he worked on the Lincoln City development and RSL Hotel and Resort project, he was also among those living in the cities who were deeply affected by the indigenous rights movement, he set his heart on returning to the reservation to help reconstruct his homeland, during the years he spent running for a seat as village head he established an organization to promote environmental education and protection, they monitored cases of fishermen who used electrocution and poison to catch fish, and they tried to maintain the purity of the riverbed, on several occasions members of the organization took a tour bus up to Taipei to participate in large-scale indigenous rights rallies, gradually his "Indigenous Rights Group" stopped taking part in the larger movement, that was after he witnessed firsthand his old comrades-in-arms' loss of ideals as soon as profit came into play, for example back when the Return Our Land Movement was in full swing, as soon as the village chief found out which plots of land could be leased, he would notify his relatives to register them before others could, "But that's exactly how things operate down in the plains," I interrupted, "as soon as somebody becomes mayor, his family business immediately gets a stranglehold on the entire city," and all of the expenses that the government allocates are "eaten" away at various bureaus at different levels until barely anything is left for land act reforms at the local level, by the time of the big election at century's end, there were still only two main streets on the reservation that had been paved, and so later his sole desire was to return home to look after the environment of his homeland, he wanted to make sure it wasn't lost, now he was redeveloping that area of land between the mountains, preparing to open another fishery, he had saved up some money and hoped to promote his ideas, including the concept of a self-governing region and ideas of environmental preservation and education, in another ten years he would run for a seat as a county legislator, "I often ask my wife if she knows what kind of a person I am—my wife says I'm crazy," his wife is a Taroko Atayal from Fonglin near Hualian. During my walks at dusk I delight in passing through the small path in the cemetery down to the ridge between the rice fields, sometimes I see the setting sun linger just over the point where the mountain peaks converge, looking around in all directions all one can see are the distant mountains in a thick layer of misty gray, it feels as though this mountain valley has been surrounded so utterly, so thoroughly, so meticulously, there is a feeling of such complete peace and quietude, the perfect place to live out a life of simple contentment, it was clear that Mr. Pihu was quite intent on spending his Remains of Life here protecting this mountain valley, it was also clear that the children of the hunters had passively piddled the remains of their lives away here in this mountain valley, waiting for Old Daya's "late-life revolution," when he would take them away from this place of exile back to Mhebu, but would those Remains of Life who had already settled on living out their days in this mountain valley be willing to leave? Would they be willing to devote their Remains of Life to developing a strange homeland they never knew just as they once developed this place of exile? I forgot to ask Pihu this question, would he participate in the "Daya Revolution"? Perhaps . . . perhaps the "Daya Revolution" is destined to be linked with the "Self-Governance County Revolution," perhaps Pihu and Old Wolf would be the two brave horses to lead the charge of this revolution, just as Old Daya's old dim-sighted eyes shone for the last time in his life with the beauty of revolution, I forgot to ask him about Daya Mona, and I remembered that he actually never directly answered my question about his true opinion concerning "the Incident," perhaps it was because I always asked him to talk about the election, but if I had directly asked him about "the Incident," maybe I would have just gotten a handful of superficial comments, but it was more likely that after some careful consideration he would have spun a bunch of elegant and lofty-sounding lies, does analysis after attack by innuendo still count as a form of research? I attacked Pihu and raised innuendos about Daya, which led me to analyze a series of "possibilities," from the fact that Pihu participated in the ceremony it was clear that he fully approved of the Musha Incident, his opposition to any kind of hero worship was rooted in his experience as a "fallen hero" in the indigenous rights movement, he bemoaned the injustices done to those citizens who had sacrificed so much, just as he had called himself out for having to cater to the wealthy and powerful during the election, his version of the Memorial Hall to the Musha Incident was to be on the scale of the Martyr's Shrine in Taipei, it is very possible that he would end up spending the remains of his life just researching the names and identities of those martyrs who took part in the incident, and wouldn't even have the time to realize his dream of self-governance, when it came to this Old Daya knew quite well that he was the one who could really help out, once he had tracked down all the names Old Daya would have

Little Daya rebuild each and every family home in Mhebu, the name of each martyr would be inscribed next to the name of each resident above the front door to each home, it would all complement the successful self-governance revolution, I anticipated the Daya Revolution to have a very high probability of success, although it would bring with it a massive human and environmental shakeup, but all things must take the "legitimacy" of their "nature" as the final end-all, is there anything more legitimate than returning the land of their rightful home to those who had been subjected to political exile? But after taking into consideration what I knew about the people in Riverisle I figured that less than half the people would actually leave, and so there would not be enough manpower and funding to build Pihu's memorial hall, instead the construction would probably continue all through the remains of Pihu's life, and then Old Wolf would have to ask Old Daya to summon back his Latino Seediq daughter to handle all the planning blueprints, legal documents, and everything else including the hiring of foreign laborers, all of this would carry on for the remains of Old Daya's life and possibly on through the remains of Old Wolf's life, naturally the Latino Seediq would go on to serve as the second magistrate of the newly formed autonomous county, she would expand the county territory up to the Tadu River, but then it is possible that "unable to provide proof of her Seediq bloodline" she would be deported, and back in Latin America she would establish the first Overseas Rescue Mission for this Autonomous County of this island nation, the real reason was that Old Daya never really examined "the Incident" he was instead blind-set on "full reconstruction," Old Wolf said that Old Daya showed him his "beautiful mixed-blood" daughter, but once this beauty became magistrate she immediately began sharpening her knife in order to swiftly purge the "Second Musha Incident" from history, however the limits of what "the powers that be" would allow was relegated to reparations and monetary resolutions, this was the price of both

justice and rape, this island nation had already successfully indoctri-
nated its people into this system of values, who hasn't benefited from
the reparations given to victims of the White Terror, as soon as the
reparation guidelines were posted more than two thousand people
had already registered, only the brave and just Latino Seediq stood
alone against "using money to whitewash history"—I neither oppose
nor support what the beautiful Latino Seediq did, the mission of my
words is but to explore the "possibility" of this Latin beauty, but
justice and courage do indeed lie within my words, otherwise how
could I have described the Latino Seediq as a beauty,—all that Old
Wolf ever did or thought about doing was maintaining the original
state of things whether that be clean or dusty, Old Daya was engaged
in some last-minute deliberations on the eve of the final revolution,
Pihu was busy raising his fish, and the only energy the children of the
hunters had left after working the land was to drink, dreamy Girl was
still asleep, dreaming that Bakan wanted to get her drunk and fuck
her, according to Priest, Mona Rudao would have been baffled by
a solely romanized version of the Atayal language, the tribal elder
cursed the fact that he had lived long enough to see yet another
one of those people researching "the Incident" visit the reservation,
hadn't Girl's cousin gotten a taste of what great Chinese chauvinist
pigs are like, the owner of the general store shook his head and said
that based on his many years of experience living in this island nation
he understood that the success of the "Daya Revolution" didn't add
up to much, his wife was the only one who thought to ask why the
people of Riverisle didn't organize a group to go to Daimaru in Tokyo
to protest, they should request a historical reappraisal of "the Musha
Incident" with reparations being the main objective, even comfort
women get to ask for reparations, they received their reparation
money so one would think that they should pay at least four million
for each person who lost their head, Danafu Toda was in such a panic
upon hearing this that he was constipated for three whole days, He

explained that four Chinese pounds of silver was the reward paid for the strength needed to take a head, a skull especially one taken during a headhunt was a priceless treasure, how can one start bargaining for prices now that a new age has come, in private he attacked the general store owner's wife accusing the old lady of having served as a "Taiwanese volunteer comfort woman" and after returning without a scratch after the war went a few years ago and got herself a comfort woman reparation, that's the only reason she's now bringing up comfort head reparations, acting with the utmost speed the following day Danafu went to the media and proclaimed "life is priceless so how can we possibly put a price on a head," only Heaven could have anticipated that the Latino Seediq would meet up with Danafu Toda online from across the seas and they immediately established an Internet "Musha Incident United Front" for while they had their differences, they were after all both savages, all my life I have written by hand and most despise Internet writing, I really felt like walking away from "the Incident" and going home to take some drugs and pass out, but then, the contemporary known as contemporary history reminded me that I can't allow suspicions or other opinions about the incident to become forever locked in the "past tense," I needed to take them down and dry them out under the contemporary sun until they were in the "present tense," and so just like that, the past history comes alive and transforms into a branch of contemporary history, only when the "contemporary" is as plump and full as the breasts or buttocks can it be called contemporary, and so "the contemporary Musha Incident" or "the Musha Incident in the contemporary" is not there just to scare people away, it is not only the theme of this novel but also a pertinent historical perspective, when I first entered into the contemporary Musha Incident, I immediately sensed that "the injustice of the massacre" could do battle with the "dignity of resistance" and the "ritual of the headhunt," this alone is possibly enough to overturn the "legitimacy" of the historical Musha

Incident, however, I heard the first cry of the rooster cackling, isn't the process of overturning like the hasty virgin rooster cackling from the beginning of time, I heard Schubert coming from Girl's room, after a short battle I discovered that the main problem had nothing to do with the battle itself, indeed the embrace of the mountains has the ability to sooth pain much better than any human embrace, the problem was in how to respond to "dignity" and "ritual," I needed to remember to have a cup of bedtime coffee before the second cackle of the rooster sounded, the difficulty of which was almost unfathomable: the disappearance of dignity and the meaninglessness of ritual, before my cup of bedtime coffee I needed to report to "the contemporary." I dreamed of the moment that Ms. Latino Seediq and Mr. Danafu Toda shook hands online, I was awakened by a sharp scream, a series of curses followed and I murmured through my dreams that I had never heard Girl yell at anyone like that, with dreamlike speed I froze the date and location on the computer screen and saved the file, I then rolled out of bed and rushed out the door without even putting on my shoes, under the sun Girl was standing in front of the chicken coop near the rear mountains her shoulders so dark and strong, "Are monkeys that strong?" Girl's uncle and cousin who lived next door came over, her elder uncle squatted down next to the broken bamboo coop and surveyed the damage, measuring the size with his hand, "They were roughly two and a half times the size of the palm of my hand . . . it was around the size of a male monkey?" inside the coop were two decapitated chicken heads and a bed of scattered feathers, the other hundred or so chickens were all pacing around in search of food, "It must have been that son-of-a-bitch Pimp-Bastard's pet monkey, he always lets him eat whatever he wants," Girl cursed, "I'm the one who feeds them twice every day and even I don't give in to the temptation to eat any of them," her uncle was more practical, "It has been a long time since monkeys came down from the mountains, were there any strangers on the reservation last night, the dogs barked for a while, but I didn't hear any voices," I remember it taking Girl's brother two or three weeks to make that chicken coop, "Your brother," I suddenly asked, but Girl interrupted me with a sharp look, "Who knows where the hell he flew off to," and then she added, "who cares about him at a time like this," she was trying to tell me how stupid my question was, her uncle was experienced enough to know without asking, "I've never heard of a person with such a large palm, it's been quite some time since that Pimp-Bastard-Monkey of yours had to deal with someone that tough, could it be that . . ." "Hey, Pimp-Bastard's coming . . ." Girl cried as she leaped to her feet, her face contorted almost to the point of tears, she waved her arms as if to grab on to something but there was nothing to grab on to, her uncle's family seemed to be unmoved by the arrival of this so-called "Pimp-Bastard," instead father and son diligently maintained their silence, "Black Bear," her cousin spoke first, "That's right, it's Black Bear," her uncle affirmed it was him, "Black Bear would never . . ." Girl stamped her feet and continued waving her arms until she finally grabbed hold of her own hair, "It *is* Black Bear, but I wish it wasn't him . . ." her uncle and cousin looked upset as they went home, "nothing's going to happen, don't blame everything on old Black Bear," Girl gave me a solid belt on the back, that was for being so useless that I didn't even have the balls to say anything to stick up for her, I let the momentum of the blow to my back take me down the slope and it only took a moment before I was back in bed to catch up on some sleep, from the warmth of the sun I could tell that it was definitely not yet nine o'clock, no need to feel regret for not being a specialist in black bear research, but I seem to have a faint recollection of there being a page in one of my existing files entitled "On Black Bears," just before I drifted into dreamland I located the section on black bears and sent it to DimBaby over the Internet: the accurate name to refer to the grizzly bears of this island nation that have a V-shaped pattern of white hair on their chest is "black bear," during the journey down the mountain the black bear is famished, eggs they find in bird nests on their way down the mountain provide ample nourishment, they are too lazy to get the chicken eggs out of your coop, with the exception of course of those rare occasions in which birds stop laying eggs and chickens stop shitting, all they can do is stumble down along Valleystream to catch some fish, but just a few days earlier all of the fish in the stream had been shocked stiff and poisoned dead, so there really was some woman on the reservation who saw a big black bear stealing chicken eggs in broad daylight right from her kitchen as she was throwing diced chicken cubes into her wok, the iron bars adorning the doors and windows on the reservation are all to protect against "possible" black bears, but that's not true—since ancient times bears have been looked upon as holy creatures in the eyes of the tribal hunters, looked at as equals with the spirits of the tribal ancestors, feared and respected they are normally not hunted, naturally the bears don't even give a second glance to the hunting rifles the tribesmen carry, let's not forget, the palm of the bear can knock down half of Half-Screen Mountain, it was only the "Han Chinese race" with their taste for medicinal foods who knew to boil bear palms in order that their own little birdies could stand erect as long as a bear paw, Girl also rushed over in the dream to explain a bit more about who this netizen DimBaby was: only when Mama Bear abandons Grandpa Bear for death is he finally shattered to the point where he eats anything or has no idea what it is he is eating, and having lost all "conception of love and sex" can't find his way and ends up at someone's doorstep 300 meters above sea level, the people on the reservation all take pity on this lost soul, and so they allow him to wander without disruption, at least until he disappears into the medicinal cauldron of some Han Chinese . . . sometime in the afternoon I suddenly awakened to write a file "On the Life of Daya Mona," the waning mountain sunlight combined with the small lamplight on my desk made me feel like I was going blind, a pair of bright lamplike eyes suddenly blazed through my window and I really did go blind, it was only then that I heard the rumbling sound of a jeep, once I regained my sight I saw that the hood was open explaining why the engine noise was so damn loud, someone was bent over with his head buried under the hood of the rumbling engine, at almost the same time I saw a shadowy figure run over and after a moment or two of shock utter, "How the hell did you find this place?" the voice was soft and surprised but it was the joyful tone that made me unable to believe my ears that it was really Girl talking, the guy remained silent amid the rumbles for a good ten minutes, Girl stood erect beside him for a good ten minutes, the guy silently slammed the hood shut silently patted Girl on her black-lotus ass and shut off the rumbling engine and high-beams before walking over into the light shining outside Girl's door, he had fair white skin and a small pale face, it was pathetic to see this guy from the plains unable to stomach the twisty mountain roads, there were a few times when he almost lost his ass down a cliff, that's why he had such an deviously cowardly and ruthless look on his face, Girl was so stupefied that even though they were only a few inches away she had no idea what else to say and of course she couldn't yell, she wouldn't want to broadcast the "dark secrets from the plains," the guy went straight inside and from near and far one could hear the sound of him throwing all kinds of things around, a good thing that all there was inside were some stones, pebbles, sticks, and branches, seeing her babies being thrown around the courtyard she let out an arsenal of curses followed by tears, all the neighbors came out to see the action some even rode their motorbikes over to catch the show, a pity then that Girl made up most of her own curse words, so although the people on the reservation knew she was upset, they couldn't understand just what exactly she was upset about, but after all Pimp-Bastard really did have the air of a pimp bastard as he slowly stepped out to give Girl two good slaps in front of the crowd, "I feed you, give you a place to sleep, and then you just walk out with my money," once he announced that Girl was his new girlfriend all the women started asking her what was wrong in their native language, all the Seediq men stood there with their fists clenched and arms crossed, after more than six decades of living under subjugation that was all they could do, Girl seemed to be really knocked for a loop by that pair of slaps, she dragged herself in from the courtyard, it wasn't long before the elongated rhythm of one of Debussy's minuets broke out, meanwhile Girl's new boyfriend lectured to the crowd about how difficult it was being her man, everyone listened patiently and it wasn't until strains of Mr. Chopin's "Nocturnes" sounded that they began to disperse, the strange thing was that the instant Pimp-Bastard went back inside Mr. Chopin immediately stopped playing his evening melody, for the next four nights we were without those soothing notes, instead floating through the reservation's nighttime air there seemed to be something more akin to a panting boar in heat, Girl borrowed some money to buy alcohol from the lady next door before taking her smileless face out back to fetch a chicken from the chicken coop— she used half of it for a dish of sliced cold chicken and the other half for soup, everyone on the reservation seemed to think that if anything shady happened it must have something to do with Girl, no one ever asked too many questions, during the daytime Pimp-Bastard wasn't one to stand on ceremony as he blasted rustic Taiwanese pop music from his jeep's custom sound system for the entire village to hear, from time to time screams and moans could be heard, "Oh, Mr. Wang..." "Uh, you're all mine Mr. Wang..." for the group of tribesmen sitting together drinking the sound of those cries was castrating, there was a rumor secretly circulating around the reservation that in the middle of the night a man started quietly sharpening an old rusty fish-tailed hunting knife, he was preparing to take the head of Pimp-Bastard: the tribal tongue overtook Riverisle, who among the Seediq could bear such insult, who could stand it, perhaps the Ancestral Spirits convened in the Mystic Valley of dreams to debate the legitimacy and appropriateness of this current headhunt, it was then at that moment that someone went to the Police Station to file a complaint about Pimp-Bastard for public intoxication and racing around the reservation on a motorcycle, he even grabbed a woman's ass and got off his bike to curse, "Fuck you!" Leaving only a single officer at that station the rest of the policemen on duty all went down to Girl's house in full riot gear and took up an offensive position, they refused to even look at his ID and instead took a hard-line stance accusing him of being an illegal immigrant from the mainland trying to hide out in the mountains, they ordered him to immediately put on his pants and leave, Girl ran out to the courtyard wearing nothing but a pair of black panties and a black camisole crying and cussing, one couldn't really tell exactly what she was cursing, it took less than one minute for Pimp-Bastard to get dressed and without a word he disappeared into the evening colors of the mountain mist, the officers even had a few choice words for Girl, "Take a look at yourself, stay off the bottle, and stay away—you've made everyone in the tribe lose face!" after this battle, those strong, lonely middle-aged men on the reservation seemed to have a sudden realization, no matter how strange Girl might be she was still their Meimei, "It is only when we don't look out for her that we end up fucked over and pimped out by the plainspeople," the sharpening of the knives quickly came to an end, they seemed to conspire together about "Meimei's Situation" and once a decision was made they immediately began carrying out their new plan, in some ways "Meimei's Situation" was quite similar to "the Incident" that occurred all those years ago, it is just that there was some difference concerning the final result of what they conspired to do, after all, historical traditions have to come from somewhere . . . and so every Sunday after church, the "mysterious intercourse" would be ceremoniously carried out, the ritual was to be completed amid the celebratory atmosphere of cigarette smoke and rice wine mixed with Whisbih, there were also young men with slick shiny hair who came home once a week for church, after Sunday services they would secretly observe the rite and try their best to emulate it, when the time came, Girl would put on a march or some other song appropriate for this ritualistic transaction, newcomers were required to present an outfit that represented the cutting edge in urban chic, and during the ceremony Girl was required to wear an outfit that displayed the latest popular fashion, the entire ritual usually lasted until just past four o'clock in the afternoon, after which time silence fell over Girl's house and the mountain mist would begin to blow into her courtyard, the most gentle melody of clanking glasses would rise up as the newcomer cleaned up the empty bottles, oh how soft and gentle it was, until it finally disappeared amid the cold misty air of the midnight mountain forest, "And what of our dream of the return?" I secretly snuck in and asked her one day when the man had gone out to buy alcohol, Girl was lying on her flowery bed with her feet up in the air smoking a cigarette, "Have you ever done any research about the sexual habits of the men here?" Girl retorted with a smirk, it was in this her thirty-fifth year, that she finally learned to give back to the reservation that bore and raised her, although there was some question about the "legitimacy and appropriateness" of her method, it was certainly practical, "Let's put it off for a while, my dream journey," Girl rolled her black silk ass over, her eyes squinting through the smoke, her smile tainted by wine, her white breasts squeezed erect between her arms. I'd been suffering from insomnia for several days, neither before nor after the moment I heard that melody had any "man-made" sound entered my ear, quietude of such an extreme form made reflection an impossibility, I crudely thought, I had to admit that over the course of all these years I hadn't done any research into sexual habits on the reservation, nor could I think of anyone on this island nation who had carried out any research in this area, in contrast so much has been published on the sexual habits of civilized people that it can't even be contained under the term "research," I suspected that the tribe's men naturally inherited their magical "*qinggong*"[11] powers from the blood of the hunter that runs through their veins, therefore no need to overanalyze it, but tribal women on the other hand went from several thousands of years of primitivism to less than a century of civilization only to find themselves without a voice amid this "transition," without practical experience it was very difficult to formulate any more nuanced reflections on what it must be like, just thinking about being unable to "reflect" was already quite exhausting . . . I once reflected about the civilized people residing in the west coast cities of our island nation, and then I thought I should try moving east into the central mountain region, I instinctively knew that there were many forests still unknown to me here in this island nation, "what lies in those forests" is the kind of thing that no amount of reflection can uncover, only by getting close to it, understanding it, living it can one substantiate his personal experience, while simultaneously enriching the existence of this island nation. . . . I thought back to the way the screams, moans, and adoring cries of civilized women during sex can shake the foundations of nearby high-rises not to mention what they can do to people's ears, to the point that a few years later those high-rises start to mysteriously crumble, and people are left with only a fraction of a fraction of their normal hearing, then what of the primitive bedroom cries of those primitive women whose screams must have ripped apart countless mountain chains on this island nation and turned them into those enormous boulders and tiny pebbles scattered along the twisty path of Valleystream, I couldn't help but also think about how civilized breasts can be restrained by a bra yet still be bursting with sex appeal when they get outside, what then of those primitive breasts whose unbridled radiance makes each peak admire them to the point that mountains resemble breasts and peaks resemble nipples, why is it that I ponder "the contemporary history of the Musha Incident" and never once even considered "the contemporary history of sexual habits in Musha," could it be that sexual practices are hidden within the incident itself, not in a surface or superficial way, but "contained" deep within in a most primal way, thinking about it this way brings me back to my original reflections, I have a brief reprieve from my insomnia, I sleep, but I cannot escape from "the sexual habits of people during the incident" but that will have to wait until later in the novel. . . . One day, I arrived back in Riverisle from the city, it was already nearing dusk, exhausted from the journey up all those windy roads, my mood seemed to be one with the gray hazy mountain air outside the window, there were always relationship issues going on with me while in the city, once things would come to a temporary conclusion, I would always go back deep into the mountains, but deep down remnants of what had transpired lingered in my heart, at times I would gaze out upon the layers upon layers of lonely mountains and wonder what was lying hidden deep within, knowing all along that that hidden place was somewhere I would never see in all my life, the "loneliness" of these two realizations combined was much more than words can ever adequately describe, I sat on the porch step gazing off to the left, watching the peaks of the distant mountain gradually become swallowed up by the thick mountain fog, to the right layers of rouge clouds dissipated like falling flowers in the sky, I suddenly felt like I needed to drink something, I quickly walked over to the convenience store and grabbed a bottle of red label rice wine off the shelf, and it was at that very moment that I suddenly came to the realization that I was indeed here on this reservation deep in the mountains, it was also at that same moment that I began to feel the depressing nature of the reservation's aged rice wine, at some point I also got into the habit of leaving the lights off at dusk and just sitting alone in the living room as the colors of night crept in while I took sip after sip of that aged rice wine, actually even when I lived in the ancient capital city of Tainan, unless I had a deadline and had to write, I would otherwise leave the lights off, that was a continuation of my lifestyle left over from the many years I lived in the small town of Danshui, I'd grown accustomed to sitting inside on clear evenings watching the colors of night move in on the nearby mountain and river, as for what I was thinking about all those nights during those years, today there is absolutely nothing left as all those thoughts have been erased, all that remains is that posture and sentiment that lingered on leading me to face those remote mountains with a glass of aged rice wine in my hand—suddenly I saw a shadowy figure of a person that looked like a walking pickled vegetable flash by my door, before he even made it to the screen door I could hear him chittering and chattering, chittering and chattering, until he pushed open the door and walked right in, "Mr. Weirdo," I softly greeted him, I figured he would understand the meaning of my greeting, but he didn't understand my pronunciation of "Mr. Weirdo," just as I didn't understand two thirds of the things coming out of Mr. Weirdo's mouth, but we nevertheless had no problem sitting around for serious two- or three-hour conversations, after which time I would spend another two or three hours thinking back to our conversation and trying to unravel whatever mysteries of the universe he might have inadvertently let slip out, Girl's little brother was the only person on the reservation who understood what it means to be a drifter and Weirdo was the only person on the reservation who understood the art of going for walks, he would often disappear on those walks, just as Girl's little brother would drift off until he disappeared, but here was Weirdo chittering and chattering, someone must have taken him out and gotten him drunk, I wondered what was so important for him to come straight to me to talk about, I poured him two thirds of a glass of rice wine, "I love this one the most," and he downed it, I understood that sentence clearly enough, perhaps he had heard more than his fair share of popular urban phrases like "love this one the most," I poured him another two thirds of a glass, as he raised the glass to his lips, "Take it slow," I told him, and he took a small sip, he smiled and tried to mimic me, "Take, it, ah, slow," he took another sip, he held his cup with two fingers and twisted it around as he kept repeating the same short sentence, I leaned in with my left ear, I leaned in with my right ear, I edged in even closer, but just couldn't figure out what he was saying, "What did you say? What?" I wasn't anxious, I was just afraid that after twisting around the rice wine would dance right out of his glass, nor was he anxious when he realized that I couldn't understand even that simple sentence, and a strange smile appeared on his face, he was hinting at the absurdity of the fact that a bookworm writer like me couldn't even understand the most simple of sentences, after a period of silence that lasted as long as it took to drink half a glass of rice wine, Deformo went on the attack again, this time using his hands to sign his meaning, it only took one look to realize he was talking about something that all of humankind does every day: eat, and then he waved his arms around pointing to the slope outside the door as he kept stuttering, "fam—fami—family" as his right hand kept pointing to his nose, I tried my best to put together what he was trying to say, "You want me to eat with your family?" He violently nodded his head, "eat," "eat," it finally became clear that he was trying to invite me to partake in this most fundamental of human activities, it was getting late and I noticed that all the houses on the reservation had already turned on their lights, I thought that showing up at someone's house for dinner at the last minute would be a bit too rude, according to the "relationship of understanding" between Deformo and myself, I suspected that he only thought of inviting me for dinner after he came over and saw me sitting alone in the dark, there is no way his family could have prepared for a guest, although I had never been to his house, "We'll do it another time," I spoke slowly enunciating each word with a pause, "Tired, me," and then I repeated, "another time," "We'll do it another time," I was afraid that refusing an invitation to dinner went against their tribal rites, in the same way refusing sitting down for a drink when invited was considered improper on the reservation, "Tom—tomo—tomorrow," Deformo squeezed the words out, I quickly nodded my head in agreement, "Tomorrow I'll go to your house for dinner," a smile lit up Deformo's face, and he took several more sips of the aged rice wine, I was afraid that the two of us would again slip into another long period of silence, but then, Deformo's acquired silence couldn't hold a candle to my innate silence, it was as if we were engaged in a Zen Buddhist meditation contest, on one occasion we ran into each other on the ridge overlooking the fields at sunset, we both quietly sat down to watch the sun as it prepared to set behind the mountain valley in the west, in the end we sat there until the waning moon appeared behind the mountains to the east and rose into the sky, we gazed there at the waning moon until we eventually parted ways in silence, only when I got back to my rented room and looked at the clock did I realize that our Zen silent meditation contest lasted a full six hours, accompanying us was the fragrance of the rice fields, the smell of betel nuts and kidney beans, and the sound of trickling water as it ran through the irrigation ditches, I got up, opened the door, and as soon as I went outside, Deformo rushed up to me, grabbed hold of my left elbow with his right hand, and led me away, we passed through Girl's courtyard and walked past several other homes, I silently allowed myself to slip into a completely powerless state as if I were floating through the universe in a dream, completely powerless, willing to let others take the lead and make decisions for me, perhaps Deformo would lead me to the cemetery where we would visit the grave of a young Atayal girl who died in childhood, or to a cave near the plum garden behind the mountains, but more likely we would end up helping each other climb up a massive ancient tree that had been petrified after being struck by lightning toward an eagle nest on the side facing the mountain, all of

those were places where Deformo would seek out temporary respite
from the world, any one of those places was much closer to nature than
the cement-brick room that I was renting, living in nature one can
naturally observe all kinds of unnatural phenomena, perhaps one
could still fight one's way out and stop some of the Ancestral Spirits
passing by to ask them if Mr. Mona was doing okay? Mahong isn't
still crying, is she? May as well also do Girl a favor and find out if there
are any shortcuts to Mystic Valley, Deformo took the lead and dragged
me to the easternmost residence on the reservation where there was
a courtyard surrounded by a dense bamboo forest, Deformo brought
me in through the kitchen, Wife was preparing dinner for her husband and Granny, everyone smiled and silently nodded to welcome
me, but Deformo was the only one who looked excited as he chit-
tered and chattered, I went into the living room to show my respect
to the old man who was staring at a Japanese sumo match on television, the Seediq Grandpa couldn't stand that they never delivered
fatal blows and just kept getting up, his three grandchildren were
wrestling on the floor in front of the TV displaying the old Japanese
spirit, that true Seediq wrestling was no half-ass show, Deformo
took me by the hand again and led me back into the kitchen, he
pushed my shoulders gesturing for me to sit down at the dinner table,
Granny and Son also told me to eat with them, Wife brought me a
bowl of rice and a pair of chopsticks, I didn't feel the need to stand on
ceremony or become self-conscious I just expressed my thanks and
joined them for this Atayal dinner, they had prepared three dishes;
white cut chicken poached in fragrant soup, stir-fried cabbage, and
simmered butterfish, along with a bowl of loofah soup, Weirdo
moved a chair over to sit diagonally behind me and watched everyone eat, just as before he was all smiles as he sat there giggling, I don't
know what Granny said to him but he didn't respond and just kept
giggling, Granny helped herself to another bowl of rice, Son was
handsome and refined, much different than the striking contrast of

his Granny's beautiful chiseled features, "You just arrived?" he asked, "Used to it here yet?" I said I was doing great, I came from a city in central Taiwan and liked the scenery in Riverisle, Son laughed, "If you have spare time, come by in the afternoon and hang out with my dad, he knows quite a bit about what happened back in the old days," Granny explained, "Son's surname is Yongya, which means brave, his father's family was recognized for their achievements, which is why they earned the name Yongya," Son took on small contract jobs as an electrician and plumber, he was also in charge of taking care of the mountain goats, chicken, ducks, and geese that grazed out in the passion fruit garden on the slope of the back mountain, and he was the one who looked after those two old dogs, I was unsure what would be the appropriate way to show my respect, "Next time I'll be sure to come by to seek advice from Daddy Yongya," I finished my bowl of rice with the "appropriate speed" got up from the table and took my leave, I told Granny and Son to take their time eating, the grandchildren followed me out to the courtyard where they wrestled with Deformo, I asked Deformo why he didn't have anything to eat, "wine—rice, wine—rice," he was taking on wrestling opponents coming at him from three sides, as he explained that he had eaten wine made from rice, Wife stood at the screen door and called the kids inside so that they wouldn't hurt their cripple uncle who only ate rice—wine—rice, my silence had given Deformo the opportunity to lead me into another house, I don't want to waste more time talking about wine and rice, since rice can be eaten then once it is distilled into wine it can of course be eaten too, moreover it will be even purer, when silence debates silence there is no winner or loser only silence, Deformo brought me into an abnormally clean room in the house, the atmosphere in the room could be summed up by the words "compulsively clean," all of the furniture were large "meticulously maintained" items, the marble glowed with its original stone luster and the logs gave off their natural shine, perfectly centered were two hanging scrolls of calligraphy in a cursive style, but I couldn't figure out what deep philosophical ideas were written there, the calligraphy was hanging above the kind of samurai sword display stand that you typically see in antique stores or in Japanese costume dramas on TV, it was displayed exactly in the center recess between the two frames, it was at that moment that the man of the house solemnly walked in, the strange thing was that Deformo didn't say a word after he went inside, the samurai sword display stand must have sensed our presence and magically transmitted that information to the master of the house, he was probably not quite sixty, his jet-black hair was neatly combed and slicked back with oil, it was more perfectly maintained than even those smooth old players working the city nightclubs, he sat down and starting speaking a bunch of Japanese, and then explained why it was that he so enjoyed speaking Japanese, he had received a Japanese-style education all the way through elementary school, and so he had a deep understanding of how the samurai spirit of the great Japanese nation captured the very essence of life, "wine, there's some here," Deformo was suggesting that we should start drinking in this "compulsively clean" room, but the master sternly rebuffed this suggestion and apologized for being unable to accompany us, "Go back home if you want to drink," He didn't drink, the only thing missing was for him to admonish us not to have any inappropriate contact with women, it was clear that after fifty years the "Japanese spirit" was powerfully manifested in this certain man in this certain room deep in the mountains on this reservation on this island nation, we had practically been "invited to leave," he didn't even ask me what I did, after several years on indigenous reservations this was perhaps the only time I had "experienced something like this," I couldn't fathom why Deformo would want to bring me to the samurai's house, it was obvious that this samurai had a distinctive spirit that stood out among the other families on the mountain reservation, as for what that represented perhaps the people on the reservation didn't really know they just knew that he was different, I thought about it for a while and after my thoughts had gone round and round in my head I decided that I would find a time one day to come back to this House of the Samurai and ask the master, 1) from where had he inherited his samurai spirit, 2) about the whereabouts of his samurai sword, 3) did he usually eat sushi and if so did he use rice grown in Riverisle, 4) do samurai really exercise restraint when it comes to relations with women, or perhaps better to phrase it as, 4) are female relations a major taboo for all samurai or something they loath to part with but must or something they are "obligated to give up but refuse to let go of," and let's not forget, 5) I must get to bottom of the meaning of what is written in cursive script on those two pieces of framed calligraphy, 6) I would also like to get his own appraisal of what kind of meaning and value are obviously "embodied" in a "samurai that appears to have never fallen" on a reservation deep in the mountains of this island nation, all of these questions are very important, for this island nation during the 1990s and not just Riverisle the last question was the most pressing, at last I found myself being led to Deformo's house, it was a Taiwan-style three-room brick house, in the living room was a few old crudely made bamboo chairs, it was really an utterly destitute house but at least they had a television set in the middle of the room, when his old man saw that Deformo had brought someone over he turned off the variety show he had been watching and disappeared out the door, he didn't say a word to me and he never returned, once he got home Deformo started to behave like a little boy acting up, he kept chittering and chattering until his mom brought out two bottles of rice wine, some dried fish, and a dish of stir-fried potatoes, Deformo's mother could speak amazing Mandarin, she must have known that I had a "compulsion for careful listening" and so she sat beside me and started to tell me her story, sometimes Deformo's chirping would end up leading to a fight between him and his mother, but his mother's

mother tongue would of course always quickly smooth things over
and he would have no choice but to "humph" "humph" before going
back to his rice wine and television while monitoring what was going
on, Weirdo's mother was born in 1932 in Riverisle, the year after the
survivors were exiled there, her birth was filled with happiness and
sadness, happy because after the great calamity life was continuing
on for the Seediq in exile, sad because her arrival came at a time when
labor was needed for the cultivation of this new land, she wasn't
upset when she thought back to her childhood, she probably felt that
having something after starting with nothing was better than still
having nothing, after the end of World War II a new government
came to power, the economic hardship lasted many years, she didn't
know the actual reason why, but suspected it had to do with the new
"officials" in power having a different way of doing things, now her
home is beside a river a bit farther away from the reservation where
she has three rice fields, just planting the rice was almost too much
for her and her husband to handle, at least today they have all kinds
of equipment that can take the place of manual labor, there was one
thing that had been tearing at her heart, she realized that the amount
of arable land in Riverisle being wasted was gradually increasing,
how she wished she could grow ten more arms to save that land from
turning into a wasteland, "Where have all the people who used to
work the land gone?" I asked, one family moved to the foot of Reunion Mountain to grow tea, another family moved to the city and
are living near the Veterans Hospital, their daughter is working as a
caretaker and gets $1,000 per day for each person she takes care of,
"and the others, they all disappeared," his mother was overcome with
melancholy, they say the back mountains are under the jurisdiction
of the Forestry Bureau and there are some people from the plains
who are renting a plot of land near the summit to plant plums, ginger,
camellias for oil, betel nuts, and some other kind of red fruit, "betel
nuts, Amer- Amer—American, red" Deformo was explaining that

they were planting imported red betel nuts from America, his mother was convinced that local green ones were tastier than those imported red ones, Deformo declared that when he was in America he had tried "Grade A" betel nuts, his mother said that Grade A America makes her want to throw up, it had taken her perfectly normal son and turned him into a Mr. Deformo, he refused to go back to school after his sophomore year of high school, instead he ran off to Taipei to rig some scaffolding up, "There was—a lot—of things to rig up—in Taipei," not much happened during his three years in the military, but when he was twenty-six he got a job on a fishing boat and set off on the high seas, four months later his vessel came to port in Argentina, and the first mate dragged him off to go drinking, outside the bar he was assaulted by someone from who-knows-where who beat him so bad he ended up with a brain injury that also damaged his spine, it was said that he got drunk and made a move on someone else's girlfriend, when the story got to this crucial juncture Deformo became much more animated than normal chittering and chattering to the point where his brother stopped watching the variety show and just stared dumbfounded at Deformo's wild arm movements, his mother said she had heard thousands of terrible stories but never seen an American woman viciously slam someone's head against her own set of rock-hard breasts, Deformo told his variety show brother to stop pretending to look shocked everyone knows that American breasts have the power to change from soft to hard, when they are soft and hard simultaneously you end up with cerebral palsy, once paralyzed you end up being sent home on a boat, you can't speak or recognize people, your limbs grow stiff, the doctor said there wasn't anything he could do, and so he just went home and gradually became the Mr. Deformo that he is today, his mother knitted her brow, "I wonder if it could have any connection to that girl he fell for when he was young, she went off to work in a factory in Taichung," one day he went to Taichung to visit the girl and found her "thrusting it in and out" with another man, he was so shocked by the sight that he turned into a demented weirdo, "The sea—the sea," Mr. Deformo was objecting to the notion that he had once sailed the distant seas, and not for one second did his mother believe that American tits could ever beat out Atayal tits, according to actual fieldwork conducted by the Japanese colonizers Atayal breasts ranked first in this island nation even surpassing Japanese breasts in their size and strength, it wasn't that she didn't know that large breasts were typically soft, "I can't believe it," even if the nipples were hard I still can't believe they would be hard enough to knock cerebral palsy into someone, "There's a time and place for nipples to get hard," she had a really hard time facing what had happened to her son, Deformo took notice of the women's breasts who'd just appeared on the variety show and asked me about Mahong, his mother told me that Mahong used to have a family back in Musha, amid the crisis that broke out in the wake of the incident her husband threw himself from a cliff and one after another she tossed her children off the precipice into the river below, "Daya Mona is still alive!" I said, Deformo's mother said she had hear about him but never seen him, for her whole life she always thought it was strange that Mahong didn't also jump from the cliff with her family, was it in case her sole surviving son should one day return in search of his family? After being relocated to Riverisle Mahong remarried, she married a man from the tribe but they never had children, the girl here who claims to be related to her is actually her adopted daughter, "adopted daughter—that's not possible, she concealed her birth because her ex-husband was the father," Deformo snapped out of his variety-show-breast induced daze to dispute the fact that she had been adopted, when it came to the Musha Incident Deformo had his own take on things and he stubbornly stood by his own opinions, he didn't agree with either history's narrative of the events or that of his mother, he was certain that at the time of the relocation there were 292 women and 91 men, these were the people who made their way to Riverisle when the fighting broke out in Musha, no need to discuss what his mother said but his debate with history got so heated that he looked utterly miserable—how could the other side be so stupid, in order to spare Deformo from further misery I decided to take my leave, "Din–dinner," the bottle was empty and Deformo wanted to open another one but his mother wouldn't let him, "Tom—morrow—dinner," I agreed to come back over the next night for dinner again, Deformo forgot all about the bottle he wanted to break out and instead broke out in a smile, the following day at sunset I went to Deformo's house for dinner, his mother was sitting under the eaves chatting with another woman, she said that Deformo had gone out for a walk in the morning, she had no idea where the hell he had walked off to or when he might be back, who knows where Deformo might be walking by the time I finally leave Riverisle. The first time I got a true taste of what "human dignity" means happened in a classroom when I was in the fifth grade, it occurred during the second of two after-school crams courses I was enrolled in, it must have been late autumn or early winter and the classroom was already a bit dark and hazy, the routine of the "ulti-mate purge" had finally come, from a young age I had the misfortune of being in a class where the cut-off for outstanding student perfor-mance was at 99 percent, my grades were usually just above average, I had grown accustomed to sitting there silently watching those stu-dents who got called up to the teacher's desk, they placed their hands on the chalk holder under the blackboard with their butts facing the class as they awaited the rattan pointer receiving one strike for each point they missed, I usually noticed that after receiving their punish-ment and returning to their seats they would either have a look of bitter resentment or a twisted grimace, on the day in question I only earned a score in the 80s, when it was time for me to be called up to the teacher's desk I could barely recognize my own name when it was called, I mistakenly put my hands directly on the blackboard and the rattan pointer corrected me to put them on the chalk holder, just as I was thinking about how embarrassing it was to have my butt facing all my classmates, the first strike came down, in that moment the pain went directly to my heart and I lost track of how many times I had been hit, as I returned to my seat I kept my head down so that my classmates wouldn't see the mixture of shame and hatred on my face, but even up until today I can still see that face ever so clearly, it was only a few years later I realized that was what it is like to have one's self-respect trampled on, one's human dignity, owing to this "injury" I began to grow rebellious during my teenage years, that rebelliousness continued and can even be seen in my writing today—writing is itself a form of rebellion, I really despise endless rebellion, I have spent many years reading countless books and experiencing everything there was to experience, reflecting on rebellion from another perspective, I know that there is a way to bring an end to this rebellion, but the key to resolving this issue lies not in suppressing rebellious actions, it lies in truly facing up to this thing called "dignity," those who rebel against something and those who fight to safeguard something are simply expressing two sides of the same coin, what they both fight for is dignity, most of humankind's energy is spent safeguarding and rebelling, fighting for and against things, we suffer for our dignity, moreover "standardized" education goes even further in demanding that we continually fight to safeguard and stand up for "our dignity as a people, a race, a nation," If I ever run into Deformo again, I will ask him the question I have been most wanting to ask him, "Where is your dignity as a person?" Deformo smiled in silence, during that moment when he walked into that room where he saw them "thrusting it in and out" he must have used all the energy in his body to snuff out his own dignity in order to allow himself as Mr. Deformo to freely stroll through the rest of his life up until the end, otherwise he would have probably picked up a knife and thrust it in and out of them in order to safeguard his own dignity, or he would have rushed out of the room and spent the rest of his life rebelling against this and that without ever seeing that at this moment he was actually caught in a cycle of "rebelling with dignity," naturally the "utter destruction of Mr. Deformo's dignity" as I imagined it is a special exception, if indeed one needed an exceptional case such as this to "destroy one's dignity," that wouldn't qualify as true destruction, it was simply a case of him still having a childlike innocence and not having found his dignity simply because he was just so absorbed in himself, once he had pulled himself together, he would have matured enough to see himself through others and find his dignity, I have been observing the historical Musha Incident within the contemporary Riverisle, both the remote and immediate causes touch on the theme of "dignity," going into the distant past, it was during the third year of the Japanese colonizers' occupation that they arranged a "sightseeing tour of Japan for the tribal chiefs," together we can imagine what it was like for these "untamed savages" from a remote mountain tribe when they first saw a man-made battleship and all the toys of death that it was equipped with, it was the first time they had even seen the vast ocean and it was a sea specially made for their colonizer's warships, for the first time they witnessed the myriad wonders and marvels that civilization had brought to everyone under the Meiji Restoration, the dignity that the tribal chiefs were shown at home was shaken to its core, to the point that "what was once a mountain no longer felt like a mountain," later this type of "education by way of shaking one's core" continued for many years, especially just before and after each act of resistance, from the contemporary perspective the benefit of these types of "sightseeing tours for tribal chiefs" is debatable, but even though the unconstrained power of mighty civilization wants to shake and unravel the tightly bound roots of the primitive, it can be difficult, especially when men and women travel to a distant place and see even more beautiful men and women and then go home and aren't interested in their own men and women, moreover they start to have all kinds of sexual fantasies, many took indigenous men and women as their own property, this started back in 1896 during the second year of the Japanese occupation when a resistance movement began that lasted almost ten years, that was because the Japanese treated them like animals tying them up and severely beating them to the point where their "dignity" to even move freely was damaged, in 1911 a war broke out resisting the Japanese order for tribesmen to turn over their rifles because rifles were the most prized possession for heroic hunters, how could they possibly hand them over because of some "political" excuse the government came up with, this continued until the Japanese bombs ended up on their doorsteps and they finally unwillingly turned over their rifles, but ever since that time the tribal hunters' "dignity" suffered a terrible blow, the same year they also resisted the order to hand over their collections of human skulls, because they were important sacrificial objects in their rituals, they were left to later descendents as a public display of their own power and strength, giving them up was like handing over their "dignity," and once it was later forbidden to display skull racks there wasn't even a place to put their "dignity" anymore, tattooing was prohibited in 1917 and the following year they started instituting short hair for men and outlawed the practice of *otching*, a tribal rite that disfigured the front teeth,[12] after all of this that and the other the Japanese may as well have dictated the length of the tribespeople's ass hair, but then how would their asses have the "dignity" to sit down, in 1916 arrangements were made for a group of Atayal to "tour" Taipei where opium had just been outlawed and they could get a look at "dignity growing moldy" on the faces of the people there, that night the group made a collective request to return to their home in the mountains the next morning, in 1920 the Slamao Anti-Japanese Incident[13] broke out, politics couldn't enforce the ban on headhunting, members of each tribe cut their "dignity" back and forth in an attempt to headhunt their "dignity," which was still very dignified, in 1922 indoor burials were done away with, if the "dignity" of the Ancestral Spirits couldn't be preserved how much "dignity" could the living really hope for, within twenty years dignity had gone from being shaken up to becoming a rare commodity, the rulers established a youth club, a women's association, and a parents' association in order to replace all those primitive rites and customs that were wiped away and promote a civilized new life in their place, in September 1926 "dignity" fell all the way down to the bottom of the valley, the Atayal tribe had "peacefully given up" 1,319 rifles and 8,086 bullets, by 1930 the rulers had carried out the "collective relocation" of several tribes in order to better manage and keep an eye on them, by this time the fate of their "dignity" had been reduced to that of a stray dog, the same year history brought forth Mona Rudao, who could not bear the sight of "stray dog dignity" and launched the Musha Incident in order to help the strays regain their "great dignity," shocking everyone on the island and beyond, not long after there was the "dignity of the cliff jumpers," "the dignity of the hanged ones," "the dignity of those who shot themselves," and "the dignity of those who hunted each others' heads," this climax of dignity achieved new historical heights, reaching the height of 3,261 meters above sea level high in the mountains, one can't resist the temptation to leave something behind, massacres and violence carried out in the name of civilization have determined the historicity of "dignity," but looking at things from the contemporary perspective, the fixed nature of this historicity was only temporary at the time, later with "Sayon's Bell"[14] and the "Takasago Volunteer Army"[15] we could see "dignity" wavering back and forth in the mountains as it struggled to find its way, looking at things from another perspective, the Musha Incident elevated the "dignity" of the Atayal Seediq people but at the same time it ran the risk of delivering "dignity" its fatal blow, jumping from the cliffs, hanging themselves, committing suicide, being decapitated, in actuality they all died without dignity, leaving the surviving Atayal tribe members to see "dignity" stripped naked before their eyes in the face of the rulers' extreme violence, and just like that the tribe that had been regarded as this island nation's most valiant and dignified was tamed under the heels of their rulers, when a person or group loses their dignity, their foundation is shaken and they start to buckle, suddenly a few more girls like Sayon, and a few dozen or hundred more volunteers for the Takasago Army don't seem strange anymore, for once things start to buckle and lean and eventually they fall, perhaps it was a response to what one of the first Japanese colonizers to set foot on this island nation said, "If you want to colonize the island of Taiwan, you must first tame the wild savages," and so in the context of the Musha Incident "the dignity of resistance" or "to resist with dignity" carries with it both a positive and negative meaning, but I'll bet that Mona Rudao, who once sailed the seas to Japan where he witnessed civilization firsthand, never imagined any of this, was it only because of the direct causes excavated by historians that he decided to "resist"? in order to construct a Buk-Tik Palace[16] in Puli, everyone down in the plains who had money donated, the mountain people didn't have money so they had no choice but to donate their labor, they cut down ancient trees, the rulers didn't want to damage the massive logs by dragging them through the forest so they demanded the savages carry the "natural logs" on their backs, utilizing their own wisdom gained from life experience, the Seediq had developed their own method of transporting logs using ropes to guide the massive logs as they rolled down the mountain, but the rulers couldn't bear the sight of natural logs being damaged so barbarically, they must be shipped back to the colonial motherland "perfectly intact" as tribute to the imperial family and the imperial people in order to construct Shinto shrines or toilets for women's asses to sit on—but the uncivilized didn't understand the meaning of words like "primitive" and "perfectly intact," no wonder then that the whips of civilization kept letting off steam by coming down on the flesh of the wild savages' backs, the Seediq could withstand the pain in their backs, but they couldn't withstand being treated like "second-class citizens" and being paid just forty cents a day, at the time they didn't know better to negotiate with them because the property rights rested with them, and the rulers were also obligated to pay a hefty fee to purchase the lumber, but rulers always know how to use their authority to twist words like "nationalization" and "public land" to resolve the issue of not having enough capital to achieve their goals, and as for the women, ever since ancient times there has been the assumption that clever and beautiful women are sexually attracted to "power," it's not clear if it is power itself that attracts them, or if men's bodies that have been tattooed by some power or authority attract them, perhaps at first they were having sexual intercourse with "power," but as time went by it became harder to separate things, the tribespeople started to look at these women differently, now they were women with power, accessories of power also have their own impressive aura, that phenomenon was a product of the occupier's strategy of "Japanese-Indigenous Intermarriage," naturally there was no shortage of volunteers, it was also fairly common to see some cases where women were forced into marriage and eventually gave in after a show of reluctance, after an exhausting day of hard labor the Seediq men most despised the sight of seeing their tribal women they so admired walking through the hazy mountain mist at sunset and into the Japanese station house— twenty years later, even more aboriginal young women would start marrying another occupying power that would come over the sea to this island after suffering a great defeat, one after another those youthful bodies comforted those defeated and panic-stricken souls, by the time they had seen the true face of the brutality and crudeness that years of protracted warfare had left on these men, a second generation of mixed-blood children had already been born, perhaps it is a good thing that that those Seediq who took their own lives during the "Musha Incident" didn't live to see this tragedy unfold, or then again perhaps we should call it a deceptive farce, the way tribe members bowed down toward power was like a flood washing away an embankment, it was a woman's betrayal of the womb that gave birth to her—as for whether or not the "primitive defiled hands" of the savages accidentally sullied the pristine white gloves of the civilized during a toast, or the civilized white gloves rudely pulled away from those "primitive and pristine hands," in the end both sides were infuriated after they felt they had suffered a great "indignity," leading to the most direct underlying cause for the incident,[17] but this hypothesis is awaiting further verification from a collaborative effort between contemporary psychologists and psychiatrists who will need to appraise the historical research, I can accept both the immediate and remote causes behind the Musha Incident, but at the same time I also realize that all of these causes are related to their "dignity being left intact," but in real life, the phenomenon of individuals having their dignity damaged, nibbled away at and stripped away has always existed, must people choose to take their own life when a part of them is stripped away? even if it is something as central as their dignity? I don't agree, the contemporary also calls its legitimacy into question, and that is simply because "survival always outweighs dignity in terms of its legitimacy," before all forms of existence everything must first come into being, even a flicker of a life-force still burning is enough to ensure that one's own life doesn't wither away to ashes, in the process of coming into being one can observe dignity being damaged and eaten away before it is reborn and crystalized, as for the Musha Incident, contemporary history has used "survival and the process of coming into being" to refute "the legitimacy of dignity." One day, upon returning from my morning walk, I could hear the chickens chattering, but all was quiet at Girl's house, she must have still been sound asleep after having performed her nightly rituals, I suddenly decided to go check out the rear mountains on the reservation, when gazing at the reservation from a distance, one can clearly see that each of Riverisle's rear mountains is taller than the next one, no wonder that the cold mountain air comes in through the kitchen window each night as soon as dusk falls, I really wanted to go for a walk on the "isle" in Riverisle, the flat surface of the isle is sandwiched between tall mountain slopes on either side, one look and I could tell that any large flood would make the Bugan River rise over the riverbed and flood the rice fields, the tribespeople would quickly climb onto the isle in the center of the river, which protects them from even the most destructive floods, and Heaven can feel at ease, I rode my bike past the "Memorial to the Remains of Life" and then on past the nearby homes on the west side of the reservation, next came a graveled path that ran alongside Waterhead Stream on the right, on the left was Valleystream, which started off very narrow but gradually widened as you went along the path, as I pedaled along I would periodically stop to listen to the sound of the trickling water and gaze at the features of the mountains, I turned back to look at the reservation as those lofty and lonely mountain peaks loomed over it, it didn't at all resemble the carefree distant mountains that I normally gazed out at from my porch on the reservation, the mountains near the reservation looked like the back of a tame housecat, it was only after I'd been riding for quite a distance that a small pickup truck came up from behind, I pulled my bike over to the side of the path to let the truck pass, as it drove by I saw seven or eight women wearing straw hats, bandannas, and elbow pads in the back, soon after the truck turned right down an asphalt road just in front of a Forestry Bureau sign, the sound of the engine was eventually swallowed up by the forest, I thought back to the nursery on the mountaintop that Deformo's mother had mentioned, I decided to make a right turn and follow them over the bridge and onto that asphalt road, I thought those must have been women from he reservation hired to do odd jobs, the asphalt road ran amid an increasingly nar-

row valley canyon and on the left was a small stream just one third of
a meter wide, no direct sunlight could shine down into the valley
canyon, the walls of the mountain were covered with green moss and
fallen leaves, the thick dampness extended to the branches and leaves
of the foliage around the stream, which were all covered with dew,
from there I went uphill and then even farther up as the road wound
upward, I thought about how good it would feel to cruise down and
turned my bike around, the cold moist air indeed gave me the refreshing cool feeling of being far "removed from the world," I immediately thought about coming out to this valley canyon stream again
for a little camping trip, only after I had experienced life in the back
mountains could I say that I had truly seen all of Riverisle, before I
knew it I came to the end of the asphalt road and had reached that
sign again, the three words The Forestry Bureau were written largest
and the remainder of the sign was devoted to various cautionary "ad-
visories," years earlier a sign like this would have long been chopped
down by the Seediq and used as firewood to barbecue with, it took
the Remains of Life nearly thirty years before they quietly erected a
short little "Memorial to the Remains of Life" in the place of the
former Shinto shrine in the rear center of the reservation, the laid-
back nature of the Remains of Life bordered on inferiority and naturally no one dared lay a finger on that official wooden sign, if I hadn't
been a non-Seediq guest here or if I had been a guest long enough to
become a quasi-Seediq, sooner or later I would have borrowed Girl's
savage knife to chop down The Forestry Bureau, what the hell did
they mean by "This is designated public land under the jurisdiction
of the Forestry Bureau," and what the fuck did they mean by "destruction of government resources is subject to severe punishment," here
we are almost at the end of the twentieth century, the opposition
party is still fighting for the "throne" and squabbling over "seats," yet
there seems to be absolutely no plan to reopen discussion about the
actual meaning and limits of this island nation's policies concerning

"government resources," "public land," and "national property," it reminded me of back when I was doing my compulsory military service and we were stationed at the foot of a mountain, as soon as the
battalion designated the natural area surrounding the rear mountain
as under the control of the barrack, no one could enter the area at any
time without being interrogated and searched, it's already the fin de
siècle for heaven's sake who the hell cares about interrogations and
searches anymore, I didn't give a second thought before trespassing
into the area under the jurisdiction of the Forestry Bureau, I rode
along that difficult path for a long time all the while Waterhead
Stream was not far off on my right and Valleystream continued to
widen on my left, the shape of the mountains twisted to the right and
the peaks extended out evenly resembling the seemingly never-ending panoramic background curtain used in classical theater, when
nature created this low ringlike wall it certainly had no intention but
to attract people to "circle inside," I circled around for a long time
and had a marvelous time almost losing myself in the circle until
I suddenly caught sight of an obstructive object beside the road, as I
got closer I discovered that it was a freight container with two makeshift sheet-metal structures attached on each end, if I wasn't mistaken I seemed to hear the sound of someone reciting scriptures, I
suddenly felt goose bumps all over my body, deep in this secluded
mountain as the midday sun shone down only the sounds of nature
were appropriate, a bald woman wearing a long gray gown who must
have been a Buddhist nun emerged from the freight container and
gave me a good hard stare, she uttered some kind of greeting or in-
cantation before going into one of the sheet-metal structures, I made
sure to carefully set my bike down to avoid inadvertently scratching
the new paint on her freight container, I walked past the freight container door, which was covered by a pair of hanging bamboo curtains,
I leisurely strolled inside the makeshift sheet-metal structure, Nun
apologized that she couldn't invite me into the main hall because it

was closed for their afternoon break, the sheet-metal building I was in was actually the kitchen, "the kitchen is great," I said, Nun could tell that I wasn't from the Forestry Bureau and hadn't come to inspect whether or not she was violating any land laws and began to relax a bit, "It is thanks to the kindness of the people on the reservation that we have a place to settle down," "settling down in a freight container," Nun smiled, probably out of awkwardness because I had been standing there awkwardly for so long, I was used to it, after all I often would awkwardly hang around the cities where civilization and civilized people would make fun of me and so I learned to tune them out and pretend that I was in a different world, "That's right freight containers are also places where one can settle down and put down roots," Nun laughed, freight containers usually come and go empty or get tossed back and forth on the waves, I inquired about the possibility of Nun actually putting down roots in a freight container, she explained that she was with a research class from one of the larger temples and she had come here with some other nuns as part of their course of study, after completing their studies some of the nuns would remain at the temple but most would be sent to different places where various Buddhist rites are performed, those who remained at the main temple would periodically have to go out and chant scriptures for the deceased, and during set times each year they would all work themselves to death preparing for the Great Dharma Convention, most of the sites where those rites were to be performed were beside homes in bustling areas, charitable men and women provided for them but besides all kinds of various tasks, the nuns had no choice but to elucidate the most basic and popular Buddhist principles so that "ordinary people could enjoy them," Nun explained that she and others who had taken the Buddhist vows had achieved enlightenment, we all understand the principle of "cultivation through action," but they were after all still young, they still hadn't quite reached the point where they could live a life of quiet cultivation with a peaceful mind, "Can you understand all of this?" Nun handed me a cup of plain tea, the tea leaves still had their stems attached, it was a good thing that during my ten years of isolated living in Danshui I had boned up on my Zen philosophy from the debates between Hu Shih and D. T. Suzuki all the way back to classical writings on Zen from the Ming and Qing dynasties,[18] "It all sounds good to me," I took a sip of tea but tried not to say too much, but all Nun needed to hear to continue her story were the words "sounds good," there was one occasion when all of the nuns returned to the main temple for a cultivation meeting, everyone at the meeting shared their various suspicions, but none of them could fend off the feeling of guilt that they might inadvertently "speak ill of Buddhism" or "speak ill of the dharma" and not be able to face up to the consequences, one of her sisters in the order who had been selected to serve as the resident abbot of Freight Container Hall convinced them that Buddhist teachings also have a secular side, she didn't criticize her for that view but was also careful to guard against falling too deeply into secular Buddhism for fear that she would never come out, she quoted her sister in the order who said that those who go against the teachings of the group often go on to become founding members of a new sect, among the sisters in the order there are eight who dared to present their dissenting views to the Master, who was also the abbot of the main temple, at the same time they begged Master for his mercy, "Master's face was expressionless, but I could tell he was very angry," "You are able to read the heart of your master?" "I don't know, but I could tell," it took Master less than three seconds to respond: Your fates are no longer aligned with the dharma, it is time for each of you to take your own path, "Was Master trying to show his mercy?" Nun took another sip of her plain tea, I replied, "His response was somewhere between mercy and mercilessness," among the eight of them, their specialties included literature, math, accounting, and even business management and civil engineering, I sighed as I thought about this new generation of marginalized alternative subcultures that had somehow risen up in the wake of this island nation's economic miracle, pooling their money the eight of them had enough to purchase a monastery, but the former business management major who had studied abroad in Europe and the United States insisted that purchasing a "freight container" would be the best option for them, the literature major thought that with a freight container as their base they could move around and wouldn't have to spend the rest of their lives stuck in a monastery in some mountain canyon, the math major agreed that that way they could save some of their money for future living expenses, "Have another cup of tea," I had been drinking alcohol all the time since arriving on the reservation but hadn't had a single cup of tea, I could taste the wonderful aroma of the unrefined tea leaves, the nuns began traveling around this island nation on foot, avoiding the holy mountains where all the large temples and small monasteries were concentrated, instead they searched for a quiet and pristine place in nature where they could shut out the world and practice self-cultivation and meditation, they arrived by foot in Riverisle not long after the checkpoint had been shut down, walking along the river they too were enchanted by the way the river "circled in" and they followed it all the way, later they purchased a freight container, hired a tow truck to transport it, and "then we ended up here," another nun came in holding a purple wildflower, they were about to begin their afternoon meditation and they could use the flower as an offering, I just told her I was from the reservation, and had just come down to look around, I'm not a big fan of talking about Zen and dharma, but I despise reciting scriptures even more, it looked like they had no intention of inviting me in to see their Freight Container Hall, so I said my good-byes and got on my bike to go back, it was a long road and I went back the same way I'd come, in my mind the only thing I kept thinking about was how "strangely wonderful" it had all been, besides those two words there wasn't much else I could think of, the glow of the mountains and colors of the stream surrounded me but I was busy thinking and had no time for nature, people on the reservation always talked about a huge tiger lying in wait somewhere in the rear mountains, as I rode back to the reservation I kept my eye out for any tiger heads or tiger tails, at dusk I went to the general store to buy some alcohol, I asked about the group of nuns I had seen earlier that day, the Seediq with the beard who worked there said they had already been there for three years, they had to pay $30,000 each year to the Forestry Bureau to rent the land, and they even had electricity and running water, people on the reservation looked at them as long-term campers, they don't contribute to the reservation in any way but they also mind their own business, "anyway the checkpoint is now gone," it was a good thing that everybody got along and that there were no problems, whenever they pass through the reservation they always wave and say hello, everyone on the reservation knows they are here to practice strict Buddhist training and they know it is best to leave them to their own devices, I asked him what the local priest thought about all of this, he said he didn't know, but when would he have time to go to church on Sunday morning since that's when everybody comes to his store to buy alcohol, "It's strange, it's as if we Seediq intentionally break the prohibition on alcohol," that's especially true on Sundays when everyone seems to get out of bed and just start drinking, "That's only natural," I said that they were trying to make up for not going to church, those who did go to church were falling over themselves by the time they got there, "but anyway don't waste your time worrying about all that stuff, investing in land is what's most important," the owner of the convenience store offered his conclusion, "Even those nuns know about the government's rent-to-buy program, in a few years' time that whole place will be all theirs—" after three parts rice wine and seven parts Whisbih I felt like religion was invading primitive nature "like a freight container" and I couldn't help but feel how utterly strange and unthinkable the whole thing was, nature knows no thoughts it has no desires and it does not recognize land rights, those cultivating the Way must learn the true meaning of the classics they must act in accordance with the dharma and they must recognize land rights, the cultivated ones must have misused the word "nature" when they came to a place where land was not recognized yet they still saw it as land, the air was clean the water and soil were good there was a mountain stream before them a mountain behind them there were birds singing insects chirping the wind was blowing through the wild grass, one's true essence can be seen through nature who needs enlightenment from the freight container's shining aura, those who see can the light will come from all around in an endless flow following the aura to descend upon this reservation, the freight container will be expanded into a major temple, the local Seediq will all give up their jobs and start selling strings of paper money, incense, and flowers to the pilgrims who come here, after a few more years they will even change the name of the reservation, they would call it Rivertemple or Squatting Tiger Temple, the "Legend of the Freight Container" would rewrite history and I would forget all about "the Incident—Musha—History," after downing a few glasses of seven parts rice wine and three parts Whisbih I started to pray that the nuns were indeed a rare treasure that had come down to this world, otherwise how did they know to come to this place at this time, and to forever embrace this "grassroots" wisdom, the core nature of holding fast to religious cultivation lies in fully devoting oneself to cultivation and cultivation alone. It wasn't yet midnight, the sound of a motor scooter came breathing down my front door, that rice wine-Whisbih mix hadn't brought me completely down and I could clearly see the hazy shadow of a man in a jacket standing outside my screen door, he peered into the darkness of my room and said, "I'm your neighbor next door, I had to come home unexpectedly,

I don't want to disturb my sister, can I crash at your place?" Oh so it was an ever-drifting Seediq spirit that was passing by my door, I turned on a light and invited him inside, Drifter only drank un-boiled water that had come directly from the source he didn't give my rice wine-Whisbih a second glance, "You do research and I'm a missionary," but he said that he wasn't a properly ordained minister, he just drifted around different reservations spreading a silent teach-ing, the boys and girls enrolled at the local boarding school were his spiritual disciples, they each had a set of gentle deerlike eyes that ac-companied the restlessness of their youth, at dusk each day and dur-ing days off from school the kids would be bused back to their reser-vations in the area, he would drift from one reservation to the next, waiting beside various bus stops, when he gazed deep into those deer-like eyes all of the kids' troubles and restlessness would immediately dissipate leaving behind only a docile softness and static beauty, this mutual gaze upon each other's static beauty would sometimes last only a split second at other times it went on for several minutes but in that time an intangible mutual understanding rose up in each of their souls, he brought a peace and serenity to their youth, embracing his magnanimous teachings of generosity the youth also rewarded him, "Are you someone from the age of Mona Rudao?" I asked with a silly grin, Drifter retorted with a smile, "If Mona Rudao were alive today do you think he would go around trying to convert people the way I do?" "I do," after experiencing the Musha Incident, Mona Rudao would teach the next generation generosity and give them peace and serenity, "You really think so? Perhaps..." Drifter told me that it had been many years since anyone had mentioned the name Mona Rudao to him, when he and the deer eyes exchanged their gazes the "Musha Incident" never appeared, "But they talk about it in our textbooks," he said coldly, all the Seediq boys and girls read about how Mona Rudao was the "Atayal people's hero," and how the Musha Incident was a "glorious page in Atayal history," Drifter's bright alert eyes met my drunken hazy eyes, he couldn't care less about this guy named Mona Rudao, he didn't object to the way that Mona Rudao has been transformed into a hero for the people, and he didn't know if the Musha Incident's place in history was glorious, painful, or shameful, but he knew that most of the men in his family had been decapitated during the incident, he didn't know how his father had managed to escape to live out his life in pain and shame, up until the day his father sprayed chemical fertilizer in his face, Drifter took the family hunting knife and drifted away from the reservation, for the next several years he kept exacting revenge on everyone who was a part of his imaginary headhunting ritual, this carried on for several years up until the moment that he noticed that first set of deer eyes on some reservation and suddenly he realized that the hunting knife that he had carried with him for all those years had at some point gone missing, "Your sister said that you hid the knife somewhere," Drifter laughed, "My sister loves me, but she's not young anymore, she lives in the adult world now, I'm just her useless little brother who never grows up," Drifter asked if I had a room for him, he wanted to lie down and wait for sleep to come, just as he usually lay down on a bed of leaves in the bamboo forest in late autumn sleeping in wait, as he awaited sleep I asked him to explain a bit more about the teachings he was trying to spread, he lay down and his gaze pierced through the ceiling looking off to some distant place, "Those deer eyes go straight to your soul, after staring into them over and over, I transmit a kind of mutual trust—research the history of our headhunting rituals, the repeated wars between our tribes, ever since primitive times there was never any such thing as mutual trust among different Atayal tribes—" After spending almost two years deep in the mountains of the Atayal, I too had seen those children's innocent deer eyes, at first I simply felt that those beautiful deerlike eyes had a "unique quality," the soul embodied in those deer eyes didn't care about history, the so-called historical heroes have been locked away in a prison of

legends, but youth lives in the contemporary and not in history. . . . I
didn't need to wait until I fell asleep and could already hear myself
snoring, but as I was snoring I couldn't help but feel like I'd forgotten
something, it was only when I heard the sound of Drifter snoring
from the other room that I remembered: I had forgotten to ask Nun
about how the Musha Incident fits into the Buddhist view of causes
and effects and karmic retribution for sins carried out in previous
lives. . . . In my dream I saw the deer eyes of several young girls embedded on the face of Nun in her holy robes, they were quietly giggling beside the stream as they skipped rocks and played games, after
that a priest with salt-and-pepper hair and a red swollen face arrived
he kneeled down beside the river and prayed to the Heavenly Father
to drive the devils from His kingdom, after that we noticed large and
small stones divided into two separate piles, the water in the center
of the river was swelling up into a flowing water dragon that slid
down Priest's throat, this continued until a desert road appeared hori-
zontally between the two mountains of stones, after Priest complimented the Heavenly Father on his limitless power, he led the demons down the desert road out of the realm of the demons and into
the realm of the Heavenly Father, the deer eyes and Nun were probably so utterly shocked by this scene that they periodically forgot all
about their Ancestral Spirits and spiritual masters, a pity then that as
soon as they began their voyage down that desert road, Priest's Heavenly Father-size belly got stuck between those two mountains of
stones and no matter how hard he tried to suck in his gut they just
couldn't get through, Nun whispered a suggestion, "Perhaps peeing
would help" that might indeed be an option, at a loss Priest looked
down at his crotch and saw that it was already bloated beyond recognition yet the pee just wouldn't come out, though the deer eyes were
experienced in these matters she was a bit embarrassed to show
it, "The bigger it gets the harder it is to pee," Priest concentrated so
hard that he even muttered "motherfucker" under his breath, Nun

couldn't stand to hear those words and said that when she went home
she would have to put on a tape of recorded scripture chants to clean
out her ears, the deer eyes had already agreed it would be more fun to
return to their reservation to play with the younger deer eyes, It was
still a long way from morning coffee time and I saw Priest concen-
trating so hard that he probably forgot today was Sunday and he had
to prepare for services, Drifter didn't make a sound all night, I'm
sure he wet his bed thinking that he was still sleeping on a bed of
bamboo leaves, the motor scooter he drifts around on was still outside but he was gone, thinking about it he must have been summoned
at the last minute by Priest to preside over the silent prayer, because
the silent sheep didn't need to hear another predictable sermon, all
they needed to do was sit quietly on their long stools until they were
given a silent signal that the service was over, Hallelujah, the sheep
were particularly happy that this week's donations could be used to
buy booze, Drifter didn't return until three or four o'clock in the afternoon, I was writing down some short sketches in my notebook, as
it turned out Drifter ran into a whole slew of his childhood buddies
who had come home to relax for the weekend at the service, they gave
him a bottle of mineral water and the rest of them drank alcohol and
sang songs, "We sang the songs of our Ancestral Spirits, it was only
during the past few years that one of the elders started to remember
some of them," I asked him whether he might be willing to spare a
little time to help with my research, Drifter said that he had originally
intended to rush off before sunset to see the deer eyes in the weekend
dusk, but he was willing to make this sacrifice for the sake of "Atayal
research," I busted out two bottles of pure mineral water, I had filled
the bottles myself from the water tower on the slope beside the "Memorial to the Remains of Life," I thought for the amount of time it
takes to drink three sips of mineral water before opening my mouth
to speak, "Is it possible to go river trekking from Riverisle to the
Great Cave in Mhebu?"[19] Drifter was dumbfounded by my question

and it was only after the mineral water swished around his mouth several times that he finally responded, "If you drift up on a motor scooter and then go on foot you can make it in two hours, as for river trekking hmm I suppose you'd first have to do some research about the river," Drifter said, when you go river trekking you are going against the current, one look at the source of the upstream river and he was "convinced by the flow of the river," in all of Drifter's life he never once thought to go down to the creek to play in the water and certainly never gave any thought to going river trekking, nor did he ever trek a person's face downstream to their thighs, that was the kind of thing civilized people did, a "shady psychological game," primitive people go directly from the thighs upstream to enter that dark unknowable path but perhaps they would catch a glimpse of some light to guide them upstream to the fountainhead of life, although I did not approve of his stance against river trekking, I must confess that all the roads I have traveled in my life have been a "journey against the stream" and they have held fast to the earliest most primitive journey, which is to repeatedly "go upstream in search of the fountainhead of life" or perhaps it is some kind of eternal return, when the wanderer finally returns home he often feels like it is a journey of pursuit that takes him upstream back to the very beginning, although he didn't know what he was in pursuit of, Drifter felt that though he was a missionary who had encountered a "scholar doing research" carrying on an actual conversation was quite exhausting, he did his best to discuss the basics of my research topic, but if our probing long-winded conversations were to become a habit it might hurt his "silent teachings," beginning upstream even before Riverisle at the Northport River, as a researcher I corrected him on the Northport River, the Southport River was a name haphazardly given by Han Chinese, since there is already a very well-known civilized place on the western coast called Northport I felt a "primitive disgust," the proper name for the Northport River should be the Bukan River, at the upper reaches of the river there is a very well-known primitive place called "Pinsebukan," haphazardly changing the name Bukan River to Northport River is the same kind of trick that Confucian Han scholars have been playing throughout history since Southport matches Northport, let's just call it Southport, Drifter agreed that the source of the Bukan River was in "Bukan" and since it was originally an Atayal word from now on the correct name should be the Bukan River, starting out before Riverisle and going upstream from the Bukan River, passing through the tribal areas of Center Plateau and Brow Plateau and flowing deep into the mountains in Valleystream then after flowing on for a full day and night it merges with other streams, half a day later it merges again with Nine Fairies Creek, which originates from South White Dog Mountain, after passing Nine Fairies River it bends southward and in less than a day reaches its summit at Southbend, leaving the summit the Bukan River flows southeast as it heads through the ridge between the northeast and southeast sides of the Eye Mountains, or it would go through Valleystream and converge with Brow Stream, on foot it would take three days at the least and four nights at the most to complete such a journey, heading alongside Brow Stream for one day and the stream arrives at Musha before heading into the Wanda Reservoir and then on upstream into Muddy River, in a single day it can pass through the spot where the Truwan River merges with the Mhebu River and Muddy River, from this final intersection it flows upstream into the Mhebu River and the river eventually trickles into the dense forests but only "history" knows for sure if it even makes it upstream to the Great Cave, as a drifter he never caught up to history and wasn't fated to learn any of "history's secrets," I was busy trying to calculate how long the entire journey would take, this "historical journey upstream" should take at least nine days, "Nine days isn't that long," I sometimes close myself up in my workshop for three weeks straight without ever going outside then I spend the fourth week out and about, "A few days is no problem," Drifter smiled, "the main challenge comes in the degree of difficulty, do you know how many people ended up paralyzed or nearly lost their lives trying to make it through the pass between the northeast and southeast sides of the Eye Mountains, we each took a few sips of mineral water, we imagined the unimaginable, I imagined that all of this must be recorded in the river's book of happiness and the main challenge lies in passing through the mountain range and it doesn't really matter how high the mountains are you can experience this kind of thing in your everyday life the time it takes to go from one mountaintop to another, the stars had children by the time I got an answer from him, "Let's talk about the other option," but just as Drifter opened his mouth he heard his sister calling him, "Hey Didi, the food's ready little brother," Drifter invited me to join them, I told him that I had something to eat prepared in the fridge already, if I stayed home I could take some notes while I ate to make sure I didn't forget what I wanted to write down, "There's nothing wrong with forgetting," Drifter said jokingly, "Have a good lunch," when his sister pronounced Didi, or little brother, it was the softest and warmest word to come out of her mouth, I asked Didi to come back over after lunch so we could continue our research, he said that for the sake of research he would be there, I didn't have time to make a small hotpot and didn't feel that hungry anyway so I opened up my notebook and drew a diagram of the first potential route, it was a good thing that I had a lot of practice drawing maps in middle school I drew a map of all the provinces in some country, I even drew all the railroads and highways not to mention all the rivers, though I'm getting older my drawing skills are still there in the same way one's cultivation of the Dao will still be there after they are dead but not for their whole life that's enough, Didi strolled in with a wry smile just as I was drawing Brow Stream, his sister had stewed him a free-range chicken, which is supposed to be very nourishing, but for many years he had grown accustomed to eating raw fruits and vegetables with bamboo shoot soup, when I heard him mention bamboo shoot soup I couldn't contain the cry that emerged from my stomach, "Tender bamboo shoots are my favorite," whether I was in the urban jungle or the wild jungle, I would always instinctually notice if there were any bamboo shoots around "form pre-dates existence," tasting the soft tips of fresh bamboo shoots allows you to experience "the now" and comprehend "how eternity can be contained in a single moment," it was a good thing that Didi drifted right over after having some of his sister's stir-fried cat whiskers fern, for the second potential route we would most likely set out from Riverisle, traveling alongside the Bukan River and heading upstream past Nimble Tail and Nine Fairies meandering around the bend in the river to "Pinsebukan," after taking a quick look at the Sacred Stone we would continue upstream to arrive at the convergence point at Rueiyan River, traveling upstream along this route would take at least five days, continuing eastward along the Rueiyan River toward its end and passing over the valleys of Reunion Mountain and Qilai Mountain in search of the source of Muddy River, Reunion Mountain is 3,416 meters Qilai Mountain is 3,559 meters and the river valleys are steep and treacherous it's unclear just how many days it would take to pass, going upstream from Muddy River you pass three or four reservations before converging with the Mhebu River, two days should be enough, "I can't figure out how many days altogether," "Well if we lose our way between Reunion Mountain and Qilai Mountain, the number of days won't matter," Drifter smiled, "It's not so bad . . ." there is also a shortcut, there is a shortcut for almost everything in life, otherwise why would there be so many ever since ancient times, if you go from the Bukan River near Riverisle down to where the Ganzai Forest meets the Southport River, and then follow the Southport River back up until you reach Puli it will be much more relaxing and enjoyable, there are a lot of people and cars along that route and it should only take one day to get there, going from the Mei River upstream toward Musha where it meets the Muddy River, which shouldn't take more than a day, although the Mei River was once quite enchanting today the banks overlooking the river are lined with cheap sheet-metal shacks and human-skin huts, you have to pass by quickly so that the word, the essence of the word *mei* isn't further degraded, you can make it from the Muddy River to the mouth of the Mhebu River in a single day, from then on whenever running into historical problems like this I knew that they would never see the light of day, "Uh oh!" I exclaimed, "It's been less than three days and we are already at the point of seeing the light of day, and we got to take the shortcut too," "If you follow alongside the river there will be a lot of small shops, so you don't need to bring along instant noodles," Drifter completed his journey along the river and downed half a bottle of mineral water, I broke out a new bottle of water filled to the brim, "So there are these three routes," for many years Drifter had drifted all over on his motor scooter observing the surrounding land from the great heights of the mountain roads and although he never paid much attention to geography he probably had a basic understanding of the lay of the land, if you want a clear picture of the terrain you had better get an aerial reconnaissance drone or hire a group of aeronautical artists, "Which road do the Ancestral Spirits take when they return to Riverisle?" I lowered my voice and asked in a hushed tone, Drifter bent over and looked at the bottle of water in his hand as a sly smile appeared from the corners of his mouth, "That all depends upon which generation of ancestors you are talking about," before the end of World War II the Ancestral Spirits never would have taken the pass between Qilai Mountain and Reunion Mountain, that's because they never would have been able to make it through "Pinsebukan," the Ancestral Spirits of the Sekoleq tribe never would have agreed to let the spirits of the Seediq Daya "pass through" the realm of their Sacred Stone let alone steal a glance at it, "That other path would never work either," not only was the "atmosphere all wrong" on the route

from Brow Stream to the Southport and Northport rivers but it was
likely to lead to the spirits being discovered by the Chinese gods and
devils down below in the plains, that was the road they took many
years ago when they were first forced into exile, the Ancestral Spirits
would never willingly walk that "path of shame" again, I also heaved
a sigh it wasn't easy trying to find a path amid overgrown grass, not to
mention trying to find a path in Valleystream, which was filled with
all kinds of lingering demons from the past and a dangling uncertainty about the future, "So I guess that's it," Drifter muttered after
three sips of his water, and with that he offered an answer to the
question of which path the Ancestral Spirits would take: leaving
Mhebu, they would follow Muddy River to Musha where they would
take a look at the small battlefield over Emerald Lake, from there
they would go upstream along Brow Stream, passing through the
north and south East Eye Mountains on to the Southbend area of
Bukan, continuing on downstream it wouldn't be long at all before
they would arrive at Riverisle, "Given the speed that the Ancestral
Spirits travel, they should be able to make it there and back in a single
day," "And what path would they take during the postwar period?" I
asked, Drifter looked up and laughed aloud, "This is the age of assimilation," he knew that there was only one path the Ancestral Spirits would like, it allowed them to wade through the streams over long
distances while also leisurely exploring the scenery on Qilai Mountain and Reunion Mountain, they could go from the high mountains
and deep valleys back to their original home—it wasn't quite midnight, but Drifter took his leave of Riverisle, his sister heard the rumble of his engine and rushed outside, "Didi! Didi!" she told him that
she had already set up his room for him, "Sis, I'm leaving because I've
got something first thing tomorrow morning," Sis grabbed hold of
his handlebars and refused to let go, I helped Didi pry Sis's hands
off his motorbike, and off Drifter went puffing down his drifting
road, "What the hell kind of research do you researchers know about

researching, don't you have any decency?" Girl was screaming at me, "He's my brother for heaven's sake!" she began to bawl and ran away from me. My thoughts were running all over the place, at the same time I took out my notebook and drew sketches of the "River-Trekking Journey," I used a red pen to mark the important sites on my map, by the time the second rooster crowed I suddenly realized that the cold mountain evening chill was getting stronger each and every night, Drifter never once asked me "why" about anything, for example he never asked why I wanted to research these different paths, people here had probably grown accustomed to seeing researchers all over the reservation, this wasn't that odd considering that only after the war and after all the chaos has passed was it time for research, but the reason Drifter never asked probably has to do with the fact that for many years his heart was no longer in Mhebu and certainly not tied up in that "Great Incident" that had occurred many years ago, the beautiful deer eyes not only used their youth to create form they were also embedded with clear sparkling hearts, my choice to go into the mountains first thing in the morning two days earlier was not a spur-of-the-moment decision, those mountains behind the reservation were along the route that I always suspected the Ancestral Spirits had been passing through, following Waterhead Stream down to Riverisle where they turned off Girl's CD player and tucked her in, Nun's knowledge of "the Incident" was extremely limited but she could certainly help fill in some of the gaps when it came to awakening people to how karmic redemption and the Buddhist principle of primary and secondary causes fit into the incident, I had to be sure to show Elder my sketch of the map so that he could verify the "path of choice" taken by the Ancestral Spirits, It was a good thing that the Ancestral Spirits didn't hail from the rear mountains, otherwise for the past two or three years they would have been running into those nuns and they would have been forced to wake up to the reality that there are people living like this now, when would be the "appropri-

ate" time to discuss my map of the "Quest" with Girl, at the same
time I should decide when was the "appropriate" time to set out, I
saw that the leaves on the various trees growing on the slope behind
the cemetery were the first to turn red, the season had come when the
people on the reservation would drink even more, it was almost that
time of year that marks yet another year "lost" in exile, the "beauty of
the deer eyes" can only be found in their original home those eyes that
go from a young girl to a young woman to old age up until the very
end, how I regret that this is the "age of assimilation," while passing by the Sacred Stone the Ancestral Spirits can now spend some
time having a few drinks with the Sekoleq and still make it back on
the road in time, but don't underestimate the connotations of the
term "assimilation": at the appropriate moment "the contemporary"
always reminds us, sunrise was coming, I lay down in bed in a daze
letting the Ancestral Spirits of the Atayal "assimilate" me just as
the first ripples of autumn arrived—was it "assimilation" that hurt
Mona Rudao's "dignity as an Atayal man"? in primitive cultures the
word for "man" almost always carries with it a meaning that goes
back to "the very beginning," man sees "himself" as being unique,
and this may be the origin of "dignity" at the very beginning, from
that very first moment of recognition where man saw his own unique
selfhood who would have imagined that centuries later he would
suddenly be thrust into a position where he was forcibly assimilated
by "others," overnight they suddenly became "the other" and everything was turned upside down, the sense of losing one's own most
primitive and earliest sense of self is not able to be carried or contained by any one man's sorrow, it must be the collective sorrow and
anger of an entire race, some anthropologist or ethnic studies specialist once put forth the theory: assimilation is a gradual process, there
is a mutual commingling as the primitive merges with the civilized
and the civilized simultaneously merges with the primitive, it is a
peaceful remolding, no, remolding is a bit too strong a term, it is almost

like a natural transformation, and during the process of this natural transformation the weaker race gradually accepts this change without even realizing it . . . in order to analyze this passage we need to first point out that this text is a wolf in sheep's clothing, it is indeed a fact that assimilation is gradual, after all you can't rush someone when it comes to adapting their diet to eating rice cakes made from polished glutinous rice and giving up "millet lacking in civilized nutrition," as soon as they were forced to eat it their stomachs would immediately revolt, whoever observed assimilation as "an almost natural transformation" must have been blinded wearing a pair of glasses covered by sweat and shit, for lurking behind assimilation is the pressure of political power, it uses the force of cultural power to order "the primitive to blend itself into civilization," no, it's not a case of blending itself in, the primitive is *pushed* into civilization, and you certainly can't call this a "mutual commingling" after all just what specific aspects of primitive society has civilization adopted? peace is a means of remolding, but in the process of remolding civilization dumps all of its "primitive garbage" out along the way, native tribes lacking in political and cultural power have no choice but to believe the saying "what cannot be seen must be pure" and "gently without even realizing it" they accept this long-term swindler known as "assimilation," during the years following assimilation violence resulting from self-destructive drinking and fighting began to appear on the reservation, and people began to realize that they were using this to resist "assimilation," naturally as long as the violence didn't result in any of the "assimilators" being killed, as had happened during the Musha Incident, then no matter how bad the violence and self-destructive behavior got it was always *their* business and outsiders left them alone, I often wonder about what happened so many years ago in one small corner of this island nation: during that final night, what exactly was Mona Rudao thinking as he sat gazing into the bonfire, what was the breaking point that led to his final decision—it was quite possibly the anger and sadness of assimilation that became the gravest reason for the uprising, the lifestyle, beliefs, clothing, language, and customs that had been with them for hundreds of years were all suddenly labeled as backward, dirty, and unsanitary, all of a sudden the kimono was the most elegant form of dress sushi was the most delicious food Japanese was the most beautiful-sounding language emperor worship was the most lofty system of belief for which people could even commit *seppuku*, only decapitating someone wearing a kimono could show that the kimono was actually not the most elegant form of dress, the most elegant form of dress was a traditionally woven Atayal garment worn by a young Atayal girl, cutting your head right off was the only way to show that neither Mikado nor your Shinto gods could care less whether or not you committed *seppuku*, after all *seppuku* was only a way for you to show the emperor that your own "masochism" had reached a kind of "ultimate state of spiritual emptiness," using this kind of method to learn about "others" or your own imagination of what civilization is, if you forcibly remold an entire race with thousands of years of its own "primitive civilization," how could it be anything but a "violent assimilation," how could it not inflict serious injury to the intrinsic dignity of this "primitive civilization," Mona Rudao put everything he had into this one powerful assault against "assimilation," it represented his rejection of and resistance against "assimilation," in the historical progression of assimilation, the "Musha Incident" highlighted what was the "most extreme example of an antiassimilation complex," at the same time historical records openly commended the meaning of this "antiassimilationist" stance, although ten-odd years later there would be a new group of rulers wielding an even greater degree of political force and cultural power who would mindlessly speed up the pace of assimilation, up until this point I still feel sorry for Mona Rudao and those who sacrificed themselves with him, supposing—even though history doesn't allow suppositions—but supposing a more advanced civilization had taken up rule, perhaps they would have been shocked by what they learned about the Musha Incident, suddenly they might reflect deeply about what had happened leading to a reevaluation of the indigenous people's intrinsic cultural traditions, they might allow them to retain and protect their own people's culture under an autonomous system, instead of "tripping up like the great samurai" who then felt obligated to swiftly obliterate the "savage natives" who had made them stumble, at the same time they utterly failed to reflect about the "assimilation" they had tried to carry out, when it comes to Mona Rudao and those from the six tribes who lynched themselves with him or threw themselves from the cliffs the one thing that I can't bear to face is that after the Musha Incident "the tide of assimilation" did not even temporarily stop, instead it picked up speed as it headed toward the "Kominka Movement,"[20] Riverisle would be deliberately singled out as a model reservation by the Japanese, who knows just how many young lives from the reservation were sacrificed in the rain forests of the South Pacific in the name of "the Emperor" or "courageously volunteered to Serve the Empire," pushing history forward to the 1970s and 1980s if you went to the Baodouli whorehouses in Taipei you would see girls lining up outside as soon as night fell, the most eye-catching and beautiful women were all young Seediq girls, just what kind of "assimilationist education" is this, just how does this display respect for their tribal dignity, did I once see Mona Rudao in the eyes of a young Seediq girl in Baodouli?—I have expended so much energy and written so much trying to protect Mona Rudao, but in the end I need to say something on behalf of "the contemporary," I was born into the contemporary, raised in the contemporary, educated in the contemporary, I have spent my entire life in the contemporary, and I can only speak from the perspective of the contemporary, while "the contemporary" has not officially refuted it, "nor has it affirmed" the legitimacy of the dignity of resistance in the Musha Incident, the contemporary's consideration of this thing has already gotten to the point or perhaps even surpassed the level of "nonconsideration," its logic has already surpassed the point of the illogical, the speed of "commemoration" has already surpassed the speed of light and by now even aliens from outer space know what happened in Musha, "Generation Y" negates "Generation X" while at the same time affirming the new as a "simultaneous transition," this is something that Generation Y has in common with Generation X, as ideas and vocabulary can go out of fashion in the blink of an eye, I must again stress the fact that "coming into existence" is the foremost meaning of the contemporary, the contemporary believes that on one level Mona Rudao misunderstood the "necessity" and "immediacy" that dignity called for, those who sacrificed themselves during the incident could not use their dignity to achieve absolute redemption, the contemporary has affirmed the place of Mahong Mona and Obin Tadao[21] but has expressed suspicion about Daya Mona, they avoided "immediacy" and continued to live on in order to provide firsthand-witness accounts of what happened during the incident, which balanced out the official government accounts, with the exception of Mahong most of the survivors of the incident carried on in hope for the future but were not willing to have their "Remains of Life be buried alive" in the name of the incident, Daya Mona whose life was spent carrying out the foremost meaning of existence gave the best explanation, in the same way that "the contemporary" never officially negated the historical Mona Rudao, they also never affirmed the contemporary Mona Rudao, "the contemporary" no longer embraces heroes, only grassroots activists like Pihu, brimming with energy and zest for life, they allow the contemporary to come into being and persist, and so the statue of Mona Rudao that stands beside the official memorial may be a historical hero but he is also a contemporary puppet, contemporary officials also realize that perfunctory commemorations are just a waste of everyone's time, and so gradually they abandoned their puppet hero, who knows just how many copper statues and monuments to past heroes are buried in garbage dumps and beneath graveyards all over this island nation today, but Daya Mona can still have Latino Seediq produce cute little Mona dolls, they can distribute them to every Seediq family so that each newborn child will have a little national hero to play with. Obviously, no person thing or event would be happy settling for just being "written down in a notebook," just a few days after I had sketched out the Ancestral Spirits' path from their homeland to their place of exile they started acting up again, during the day I would sit down to write at the large kitchen table, the kitchen table faced the window, my apartment on the reservation wasn't any worse than my apartment in the city both had large kitchens, and my kitchen window opened up to Granny's vegetable garden who lived diagonally across from me on the right, there was a row of betel-nut trees fencing off the garden, looking up I could see loofah stems crawling everywhere, the pure yellow of the loofah flowers would bloom as the sunlight faded, even farther off in the distance were the mountains, at the foot of the mountains was a well-maintained betel-nut garden, with dusk a thin layer of mountain mist would enshroud the area, but before the sun even set the mountain chill would already descend upon my desk, I would put down my pen and take a few deep breaths of that cool mountain air, imagining that it must have come from the afternoon mist at the peak of Reunion Mountain, it followed along the edge of the mountain ridge to arrive just before dusk when it would pass through my window, and into my heart, those are the moments when I would often reflect upon what it was that I was searching for in life, could it be something as simple as this twilight mist, as the mountain air penetrated the window into my heart I could barely bring myself to pick up my pen again, the action of what they call "writing" is superfluous, but later that night as I lay in bed yet still awake I heard the sound of pages turning coming from the kitchen, I had the habit of only leaving a

notebook and a few pieces of paper on my desk, why was someone so
anxious to leaf through what I had written, and if they were how
come they didn't have the common sense to do so quietly, I figured
that Drifter's fingers probably didn't know how to be quiet and nimble, the sound of pages furiously turning followed me into my dream,
this lasted all the way up until the rooster cackled for the second
time waking me up to the fluttering sound of pages turning, at that
exact moment the sound abruptly stopped and after the rooster cackled all fell under a blanket of silence, the second cackle was actually
to inform the Ancestral Spirits that it was time to return home,
I could stand the fact that the Ancestral Spirits might be worried or
even be getting into arguments about the "notes and memorandums"
I had been writing, but I was more concerned that my notes and
sketches might be faded or even erased by the hands of the hunters
thumbing through my notebook, and even more worried that they
might get lost deep in my "memorandum" and not hear the rooster's
second cackle, or what if they happened to depart in a fluster taking
the "memorandum" with them so that they could carefully research
it, any of that is possible, my notebook is written in a free style that
combines observations with my own imagination, the entry for any
given day might record "the writer's" imaginative musings or sexual
fantasies all of which lie somewhere between fact and fiction and are
not intended for the eyes of others, attempting to research just this
single notebook of this "writer" might take someone's entire life, the
way I write is hard to read and even harder to understand, and if
the Ancestral Spirits should be at a loss and just read it as an example
of the "Neo-New" they would be making a very grave mistake let's
not even mention the changing colors of the mountains and rivers I
can't even sit still at my desk in the kitchen, I thought about it and
decided I needed to seek out Girl in order to help me quickly get to
the bottom of all this, otherwise the sound of them leafing through
the pages was bound to get louder each night, If I really did wake up

to discover my notebook had been taken I would have left my tooth-
brush, comb, and other personal hygiene effects behind, in that instant I would immediately set out for the Mystic Valley of the Great
Cave no matter where it may be hidden, I must preserve my face and
get back my notebook, I wouldn't ask them any other questions or
carry out any "on-site research," the Ancestral Spirits would notice
my long shoulder-length hair and realize that my facial features were
quite similar to the Seediq, perhaps they would negotiate terms and
offer to return the notebook if they could rip out the "memorandum
page," I would of course agree and take my leave of the Mystic Valley
vowing never to return, and never to speak a word of what I'd witnessed for the rest of my life, actually I had once considered carrying
out an individual research project on the Great Cave of Mhebu and
the legendary Mystic Valley, but betraying Girl and just focusing on
my research would go against my nature and "the contemporary"
would never agree to that, although the development of research is at
the core of "the contemporary," there is no limit to the scope of what
most researchers study, it could be as small as worm eggs to something as big as black holes in outer space, that being so "the contemporary" has its own set of rules regarding research, the first rule is to
"treat life with dignity" or "respect life," I took my "memorandum"
and gently knocked on Girl's half-open door in the most dignified
way, the door creaked open in response to my dignity, I was aston-
ished to see Girl sitting on the sofa with a cigarette dangling from the
corner of her mouth, I opened up to the "memorandum" and placed
the notebook on the front of her knees, "please take a look a these
couple of pages," Girl raised her head and exhaled some smoke, in
an instant the smoke had passed through the courtyard in another
instant it had passed through the mountain ridge across the way
another instant and it arrived at some distant unknown place, and in
an instant I realized that Girl was only wearing a sheer one-piece silk
dress, there were a few large black tulips growing on the dress to

cover up all the important areas, the dress was low-cut exposing her back and shoulders, "It's not time for that yet," Girl said with an absentminded smile, she was apparently in the middle of one of her "Giving Back Ceremonies" and it was still going on, I closed the book on my "memorandum" and Girl asked me to have a seat and stay a little while, she said that she'd been drinking from the time she woke up until the afternoon and 60 to 70 percent of the time she felt really good, she was willing to give me something worthy of research, "Do you know where we Atayal people come from?" Since I respect the Atayal I honestly replied that I had read about that in some historical documents, "That's okay," Girl took a sip of her mixed drink—champagne-brandy-rice wine—"Even though you're passing through you're like one of our own, let me tell the story again special for you, it'll be different," Girl poured me a cup of champagne-rice wine and handed it to me, "Go back and write this down and I guarantee it'll be way different than those shitty documents," "Of course it will be different, that's only natural," Girl's confidence got me excited, I immediately prepared myself to get into "research mode and carefully listen," but before Girl started her story there was still time for me to turn off "research mode" and just focus on enjoying the pleasure of "careful listening," "You civilized Chinese down in the plains really fucking crack me up, you've got fathers fucking their daughters, crazy huge things happening all the time, people stare holes in the newspapers reading about all this crazy shit," I never imagined I was in for such an enticing opening, Girl's drunken eyes squinted as she laughed, she said that primitive Atayal women couldn't help being so slutty fate had damned them to seduce their teenage sons; husbands would be out hunting deep in the mountains going from one mountainous area to another and by the time they would finally return they would discover that their wives had already given birth to their son's son, after spending a few days with their son's son the hunters would always go back to the mountains to hunt saying they were doing it for their newborn sons or grandsons, you could see that kind of thing all over the reservation and nobody ever said a word, women love bedding their own sons, and occasionally they would sleep with their heroic hunter husbands, a few years down the line and they'll start sleeping with their son's son's son, "those primitive Atayal women had it good," I was quite taken by all of this and could sense the incredible charm and magnanimity of the primitive, after a period of silence Girl took another drag from her cigarette and a sip of her drink, she squinted as she gazed out at the distant woman from the primitive Atayals' past, "We Seediq are born from the semen of trees, by nature we are not supposed to stray far from the mountain forests, when we move into apartments down in the plains we always go through a lot of trouble to plant all kinds of potted trees and plants, most of them are even taller than a person, my mom used to always say don't worry about not having enough food to eat, as long as you have tree semen," Girl leaned in to let me see her more clearly, "I grew up drinking tree semen," it was a large beautiful tree, who knows how many tens of thousands of years it took for it to begin to produce semen, half of the tree was dried wood and half of it was fossilized it was the only one like that on this entire island nation, the year the wood portion of the tree came of age it was overflowing with love, and couldn't help but "drip semen," the dripping semen creates a concave indentation penetrating the vagina and congealing in the empty womb, inside the womb is a "stone egg" that has been there waiting for countless years, when the sperm of the wood initiated "intimate relations" with the stone egg the first Seediq girl was born and then came the second child a Seediq boy, the boy was as "stone-cold cool" as his mother, which became his bravery, the girl was as "hard and strong" as her father, which became her suppleness, "The semen of that beautiful tree must have tasted wonderful," I took a big sip of my rice wine-champagne, "A shame those people upstream had to grow up eating rock powder," Girl knitted her drunken brow, "How is someone supposed to eat rock powder," she was talking about the Sacred Stone of Pinsebukan, the stone is actually made up of two rocks with one massive stone resting on another tiny stone, there is a hairline crevice between the two stones, "Liquid comes out of the crevice," Girl made a special point to emphasize this, the liquid that comes out is either sacred semen or sacred water, once these two kinds of liquid start to come out the stone is ready to produce children, probably because the material of the rock is so very dense, when the children emerge they are full-grown men and women, moreover there are two men you can imagine what it was like for the three of them to coexist within the Sacred Stone during those "stoney days" and still live in harmony, this alone is yet another example providing ample proof that the primitive is more advanced that the civilized, it was probably due to the fact the outside world is so coarse and bright and inside the Sacred Stone it is dark and damp that after pulling his torso out the third man scurried back into the rock, those left to take on the difficult task of living in the world go on to raise the children and grandchildren of the Sekoleq, I listened to her story up until this point and began to wonder just how many people since ancient times have hidden out in this Sacred Stone eating rock powder, ever since I learned of the existence of the Sacred Stone I started to understand why this island nation has so many stone freaks obsessed with collecting stones, but of late my heart had been "very dry" because while clearing out the riverbed an excavator knocked down the Sacred Little Stone leaving behind the Sacred Big Stone to sit there all alone, that crevice that contained the sacred semen and sacred water was reduced to ash, we often sigh at the fact that the people on this island nation lack culture and refinement "and that's also how it is deep in the crouch of the mountains," civilization knows not whether it has any responsibility to drive the people out of the Sacred Stone so they can see just how "colorful" the world really is, "You're crazy," Girl jokingly cursed me, "Where the hell are they supposed to come out from?" I felt lost, such a magical work of natural beauty and even it was carelessly damaged and destroyed, what else is there to say, but Girl had something else to say, "All of us eat rock powder and we never fought or had any contact, if you lose your weapon there's no rush to find it, just paste it back up, see if you can still use it, otherwise just take a fake one and try to make it look real, after a while the fake one comes back to life as the real one anyway, oh fuck, how could we Seediq be so damn lazy," I felt that Girl was really quite reasonable, especially when she said "oh fuck" which sounded so pretty the way she said it, Girl might have spent even less time on indigenous reservations than I had, otherwise she would have really been even more angry and disappointed, many years earlier I had visited the only reservation on this island nation where all of the homes were made from stone, each stone house planted a wall of triangular cacti around their courtyards to serve as a fence, above the highest slope on the reservation was a flat area where there was an elementary school that stood between a massive tree and a bed of flowers, towering behind the classroom was a mountain peak shaped like the cone of a women's breast, at the foot of the slope in front of the reservation was a broad and pristine riverbed opening up to a valley, "This place is another hidden paradise in this world," but how many hidden paradises like this are left on this island nation, at the time I went there I had heard that they were getting ready to relocate the entire village elsewhere, they were to move to a low-lying area close to the highway because "the closer you are to the highway the closer you are to money," a year and a half later I returned to that hidden paradise, it was overgrown with weeds and wild grass vines had crawled over everything the entire place was enveloped in a deathly silence, it felt like it was on the verge of completely collapsing, "Adopt this place!" I silently screamed to myself amid my excitement, "Adopt this place!" all I would need to do was band together with five or six friends and get the permission of the former village head, the point of adopting that place was to preserve and maintain the reservation's original character, preserve one of the few remaining hidden paradises left on behalf of this island nation—I went back to the city, got high, and passed out for three nights and four days, when I came to I convinced myself that if I couldn't even take care of a "fucked-up reject" like myself how was I supposed to preserve an entire reservation? Later I visited two or three other abandoned sites up in the mountains, comparing the naturally created scenic beauty with the neglected ruins left behind by humankind, although I am aware that the human heart is also a natural creation, it still can't hold a candle to nature itself, all the human heart cares about is what's practical with the occasional show of mercy, it has no heart to preserve what is not useful to itself, there are gods of legend, but it is obvious that after being corroded away by the practicalities of civilization they too are useless, so let them rot too, with the word "too" I downed the last drop of my rice wine-champagne, Girl gave me a fresh glass of mixed rice wine-brandy, "What do you say about going up to Daba?" Girl was married off to Daba when she was nineteen and quickly discovered something peculiar, all three of her children were born of pigs and dogs, or speaking more precisely, they were all conceived by way of standard doggy-style or piggy-style intercourse, nine years after marriage there was still never any variation to this doggy-piggy-style, she thought it was peculiar because her intuition told her there must be other ways to do it, but her intuition also told her that everyone in Daba had been preserving this position for thousands of years with no change, it was only after she moved to the city after her divorce that she experienced the closeness of doing it face-to-face "missionary style," "In ancient times Daba stood by a woman," when she felt an itch she had no choice but to grab hold of a pig or dog to scratch it for her, eventually the male dogs and pigs learned to climb up onto her back by themselves and scratch her itch, and she gave birth to one, and then another, "The peculiar thing is that now . . ." I heard what sounded like a massive belch coming from the bedroom, "Oh, just ignore him," I had turned toward her bedroom before turning back around, ". . . so the peculiar thing is that nowadays I have to have it doggy-piggy-style," in order to conceal what she had just said she took a couple frantic drags from her cigarette, so she could hide in the cloud of smoke she exhaled, "It's the same for men and women, they can't cum unless they do it doggy-style, missionary-style is just for fun anyway," Girl wondered, "Maybe it's because we aborigines are so primitive, although we've been civilized, deep in our bones we naturally revert to the primitive," I picked up the conversation from there, "Primitive positions are the only ones that get the job done," Girl smiled but didn't say anything, I heard more sounds of someone moving around inside the bedroom, perhaps that guy hadn't heard enough and was going to come out to tell us what he thought, Girl quickly nudged me to go outside, once in the courtyard Girl said that if I was able to teach her research skills, she would spend the rest of her life researching "A History of Changing Sexual Habits Among Indigenous People" on this island nation, I didn't have a chance to respond and went back to my apartment, I started by brewing myself a cup of coffee to help get the alcohol out of my system and then I prepared a hodgepodge hotpot for myself, as I was cooking I thought about Girl's thesis regarding primitive sexual positions of this island nation and couldn't help but feel she had made the mistake of taking the part for the whole, I thought back to a girl from the Pangcah tribe, she only liked to do it "human-style," navel-to-navel, eye-to-eye, mouth-to-mouth, tongue-to-tongue and each tongue should continually frolic and play without the other never straying too far, that was the only way she could really enjoy making love, her mind and body were connected with her partner's mind and body, even the bedeviled moans of her climax would wind their way through her partner's mouth, "Now that's a woman who really knows what good sex is all about," I told myself, memories of that Pangcah girl always lingered in a place deep inside me. It was around seven or eight o'clock, television miniseries time in this island nation, Elder was probably watching with his Daughter-in-law, he doesn't understand the Mandarin Chinese inherited from the Manchus that is spoken in the miniseries, I thought I could take advantage of the opportunity to ask Elder what he thought about my "memorandum" during the boring parts of the series, tonight in my dream I will appear in dialogue with the Ancestral Spirits as the spokesman for the Elder, I will express my thoughts and share what I have learned from the memorandum, who knows it might even lead to unimaginable consequences, I strolled past the memorial along the small path in the rear of the reservation, the colors of night shone down upon the "Memorial to the Remains of Life," the motley of shadows from the surrounding trees waved and swayed, I imagined that when they had nothing to do the Ancestral Spirits probably loved to gather around the memorial and chat together, when they were happy they could even circle around the sunken area surrounding the memorial singing and dancing for the "Remains of Life," I stopped and gazed at the "Remains of Life" as it stood enshrouded by the colors of night, I stared until what I saw burned an image into my soul, It was Cousin's husband who came out to open the door for me, Cousin yelled hello from the living room, and then she and the kids continued with their miniseries, I thanked Cuz-Hub for the flying squirrel soup and the free-range chicken they'd served me the other day, he said that this was the time of day when he usually cooked out in the courtyard and then went for a walk after dinner, "You don't like to watch the TV miniseries?" I was a bit surprised, Cuz-Hub laughed, I told him why I had come, Cuz-Hub wanted me to hold on a minute before going inside, at that moment the entire family was drowning in the tearful atmosphere of the miniseries and topics unrelated to the plot weren't open for discussion, he invited me into the courtyard for a stroll and chat, he inquired as to whether or not my research was proceeding smoothly,

"Superficially it's easy to put in the effort, but deep down it is sometimes hard to find a focus," I said, Cuz-Hub nodded and replied flatly, "What happens inside you is always harder," I asked Cuz-Hub to tell me a little bit about himself, back when we met during the flying squirrel get-together I had noticed that he was the calmest one among the group, Cuz-Hub told me that he was an elementary school teacher, the school where he worked was located in the adjacent village, all the Seediq children were required to attend the Chinese elementary school in the adjacent village, "That's one phenomenon that I've already grown accustomed to seeing, a main scenic highway is opened up a few kilometers away, and then they pave a small public road leading to the nearby reservation, suddenly the speed with which people from the reservation move away dramatically increases, there are fewer school-age children, leaving residents no choice but to start closing down schools and merging campuses," I told him that I had seen the same thing happen on the Rukai and Paiwan reservations, a well-working school in the beautiful mountains abandoned to lie in waste, one particularly painful sight for me was when I saw a classroom amid the ruins of an abandoned school high in the mountains, there still hanging on the dilapidated wall was a blackboard, and the chalk writing was still there, you could only peek in from behind the prickly lantana that surrounded the school, "Rotting away with the passage of time," Cuz-Hub sighed, that was the kind of image that has a real impact on one's life, and it wasn't just a melancholic feeling that it left me with, I thought, "A little bit of new technology comes into the reservation it brings television miniseries, variety shows, and before long we are destroyed, assimilated," Cuz-Hub said that he couldn't accept that, but he couldn't help but accept what was happening before his own eyes, "I'm really not willing to use words like 'invade' or 'assimilate,'" if we talk about invasion then we must also reflect upon why we didn't resist invasion, and if we talk about assimilation we also must ask ourselves why we didn't resist assimilation, "I simply feel that we were 'disturbed' while innocently minding our own business," we strolled through the courtyard under the glow of the night, in that moment I suddenly wondered whether or not the Ancestral Spirits were there beside the "Remains of Life" intently listening to our conversation, "Before there was time, there were the Heavens, the land, our Ancestral Spirits and our own native lifestyle, we were first disturbed by the material goods of the merchants, our hunters originally only used hunting knives, bows and arrows, and spears but later we came to rely on the rifles supplied by the merchants for hunting, after that we were severely disturbed by the politicians, they even made us suspicious about whether or not the very land upon which we had been living was even our own, they made us question if our traditional way of life was appropriate or suitable anymore, not long after that we were disturbed by a religion that negated our view of the Heavens, land, and our Ancestral Spirits and brought with it a new figure to 'look up to,' it was at this point that those unwilling to be tamed began to fall into a state of uncertainty, they felt the pain of being excluded, and finally it was civilization that completely took over, disturbing us by completely remolding our lifestyle, today we are no longer the Seediq Atayal from the time before time, here in this process you can see the tragedy of our people, the pain and sadness of our lives, it is deep and hopeless, did those people things and events that disturbed us have the right to do that? And still we don't know how to protect ourselves, we don't have the ability to resist these disturbances, looking at it from this perspective, I think Mona Rudao was a wise man of courage and insight, he needed to resist these disturbances, and was willing to sacrifice his life to do so, when we teach children their native tribal language in school, we define Mona Rudao as a 'great hero of the Atayal people,' I cannot accept looking at him from any other perspective than that, if we did so many things would suddenly become uncertain, if the Musha Incident itself were to come under suspicion, then those survivors who came here to live out the remains of their lives would end up suffering for the rest of their lives in uncertainty and pain—" Cousin came outside to say hello, the kids came out with her, the miniseries was over for now, she said that she was going to give the two kids a bath, Cuz-Hub said he wanted to take me over to see Elder, Cousin urged me to come earlier next time because she wanted to "do some good research about your race," she reminded her husband not to forget to bring a ruler, a setsquare, and a scanner home after school, "When the Japanese arrived they researched us as if we were a new form of human being," Cuz-Hub explained as he led the way, "in the end, they discovered that we excelled over them in every category, whether it be physique, height, or even the size of our brains," government documents that recorded academic investigations from the time all officially acknowledged this, and that is why they implemented a policy to cross-breed Atayal and Japanese, but this policy was later done away with by other politicians who had alternate plans, it is hard to say if it was a good or bad thing that history would never see these "cross-breeds," "Oh, the researcher," Elder was just having a few small cups of carefree booze to loosen him up before bedtime, but as soon as he saw me he called out to me in Chinese, "Hey, its the researcher," with the exception of wine worms, Elder must have seen more researchers in his life than anything else, Cuz-Hub interpreted and interpreted, speaking a mix of Chinese and his native tongue, Elder couldn't make heads or tails of the map I drew in my notebook, he even joked, "Where did you copy this treasure map from?" for my final question I had Cuz-Hub ask him what route the Ancestral Spirits take when they visit Riverisle, Elder looked surprised for a moment, his carefree glass was suspended in the air as he responded, "Underground, of course they come from underground, there are many natural paths underground, they arrive in a split second, but how could you among the living know anything about any of this—of course I know." I walked past the houses on the front end of the reservation and took the long way home so I could stop at the convenience store, I could see the light of the flickering screens in all the dark houses, my detour to the general store was so that I could pick up some bedtime booze, who knows when my bedtime cup of coffee was replaced by a bedtime glass of white spirits, as I carried the bottle home I thought about my assimilation and how I had already become at least one-third Atayal by now, I felt just a teeny tiny bit, just a little shred of happiness about this assimilation, but I couldn't feel or even find even a shred of sadness about the fact that I still didn't have the dignity to sweep the floor, perhaps before long I will be half Atayal, it would be best if I settled down, took an Atayal wife, had a bunch of Atayal children, and "celebrating in the happiness of assimilation" became an out-and-out Atayal, I planned to go home and close the door and drink white spirits in the dark like a true Atayal, while at it I would reflect upon the "dignity" of all the friends I'd met since this novel began, and I would carefully mull over the things Cuz-Hub had said to me, a final effort to try to get "dignity" to stay, looking out at the houses in the distance I noticed one home with all the lights on, the brightness shone through the windows and floated out over the eaves of the rooftops, if that had been in the city there would certainly have been three games of mahjong going on in that house, but among the world of the Atayal we have long grown accustomed to dark lighting, even on nights when a family is mourning a dead relative there is no need for extra lights to give them the courage needed to have a dead body in the home, ever since ancient times we have been comfortable with death which is to be celebrated, but now the lights of our Atayal homes have been assimilated, yet our souls continue to walk the path of the dark night, those living in that home with all the lights on must be cowards afraid of the dark, I stopped for a few seconds to figure out whose house it was and, indeed, the lights were coming from Samurai's house, on this night we must summon our strength and take up our savage blades to kill his empty samurai sword, "—no not kill, but a duel to the death," Samurai wears his gray kimono, sitting Indian-style on a circular mat before the samurai sword stand, "Atayal stranger whom I know not, upon completion of my Zen meditation, I shall teach you the art of the duel," his sharp words made me break into a cold sweat, I immediately regretted stashing my bottle of white spirits away in a ditch before going in, otherwise I would have taken a few swigs on the spot and then done battle with this "sharp-tongued foe," before I even entered his house he could sense that I was a stranger who had self-assimilated into an Atayal, and then he refuted the kill of my savage blade, instead affirming a samurai duel, what was happening was entirely on a psychological level, we could research and debate this all night long and still not exhaust the matter, in my excitement I broke into a cold sweat it was the first time in my entire life that I had seen a samurai doing Zen meditation, the way Samurai practiced his meditation seemed to be different than normal Zen meditation he didn't have his eyes closed and head hanging, instead his sharp gaze seemed to pierce through everything: the Atayal Stranger, the moonlit courtyard, the tile rooftop of his neighbors, the shapeless wind blowing over the rice fields, the shape of the mountain cliffs beyond the river, all the way off until it arrived at some unknown emptiness beyond the mountain ridge, his gaze stayed fixed on that shining emptiness for a full three minutes, now return-ing to gray-garbed Samurai's eyes they carried the gaze of a revving engine ready to go, "Please don't take offense at me addressing you as a stranger, during our last meeting we did not have the opportunity to properly introduce ourselves to each other, you young Atayal sir have just recently joined the ranks, my name is Miyamoto Saburo," "Mr. Miyamoto, did you have your kimono specially made for you in Japan?" "Please do not stand on ceremony my young Atayal gentle-man, ask not questions that your heart truly wants an answer to, speak not words that your heart truly wants to say, I sense that what you truly want to ask is: Are the actions I normally engage in all in the name of displaying my dignity as a samurai?" Again I found myself so excited that I broke into yet another cold sweat, "Normally the samurai have the highest order of dignity, but in the end a true samurai will be left without an ounce of dignity," "Can someone live, work, and have success in life without dignity as they normally would?" "It is only once your dignity is gone that you can truly live and work, and true success comes when it comes—taking the founding master of my school, Miyamoto Musashi,[22] as an example, during his life he accepted many invitations to do battle all in the name of preserving his dignity, he one day abandoned his dignity, at the same time he abandoned his sword and left society taking with him only a wooden blade, he lived a normal peaceful life, up until the day that Sasaki tracked him down, he requested a final duel to the death and the winner would have the final success, this was the moment that true success finally came, with only a wooden sword master succeeded over Sasaki in the end," this may be a story similar to others you have heard but please remember that living in solitude deep in the mountains Mr. Miyamoto doesn't have many opportunities to share it with the young Atayal, "The Musha Incident was entirely unwarranted, Mona Rudao misused dignity, and the Japanese soldiers at the time were nothing but third-rate samurai, and yet they put their samurai swords up to those savage knives, it was a duel carried out on two completely different spiritual levels, the result was a pathetic battle, both sides suffered miserable defeats, staining history for both, and in the end all of them were *baya yaka*[23] bastards," Mr. Miyamoto hoped that I would understand the pain he felt being forced to speak Chinese instead of the language that he truly loved, "My apologies, after I arrived here on the reservation I really started to regret that I never studied Japanese," Mr. Miyamoto flashed me a sparkly smile, he was completely different from the reserved manner he'd displayed that first time I met him with Deformo, "On one level

I feel that you and I should have a good face-to-face duel, a pity then that your heart is consumed with the Musha Incident and Mona Rudao, actually what you are really searching for is yourself, you need to turn yourself around and face the question of your own dignity, let me ask you Young Atayal, if you were in Mona Rudao's shoes, how would you have faced what happened?" "Should I face Mona Rudao, or face the meaning of dignity, or face the final decision leading up to the incident?" "All three are tied to that same critical juncture, just look at it as if you were Mona Rudao," I had never tried to approach things from this angle: But supposing I was Mona Rudao—actually let's get rid of the supposition, I am Mona Rudao—I would have chosen to be a Mona Rudao without dignity, unburdened of dignity I wouldn't get hurt, if I didn't get hurt my pain would never transform into the anger and hatred that led to resistance, and there would be no "incident," today I would be an old grandfather living in Mhebu, my eldest son and his wife, my second son and his wife, my daughter Mahong and her husband, and my grandchildren would all be working at our family-run hot springs resort, I wouldn't have to stand as a statue in front of the memorial, it's so lonely just standing there, too many of my old friends all died during "the Incident," I used what little dignity I had left to shoot my wife and my two adorable grandchildren; did they understand why? Do I even understand my own death? For the sake of dignity I had no other choice, I wish I could be a Mona Rudao without dignity. . . . "There's no need to be that kind of a Mona Rudao," Mr. Miyamoto's eyes lit up as he spoke, "Dignity is only a temporary thing, if you pay too much attention to it or overemphasize it you will misunderstand what it is really about, in the face of a superior power, dignity sometimes needs to get down on one knee, it's actually about getting down on one knee before the 'practical realities' you are facing, but you never lose your dignity, if Mona Rudao had done that he would have gotten by, there would have been no need for a Musha Incident, but it wouldn't be appropri-

ate to expect Mona Rudao to give up his dignity, he wasn't that kind
of a person, there is no such thing as those kind of innate conditions, or acquired manners, he would never recognize those things,
when you get to that level, this is the kind of person that I would expect Mona Rudao to be, when facing grace and beauty he would
never just look at the good qualities of others, when facing the grace
and beauty of others all of his energy would go toward submitting
himself to them, as he submitted himself he would learn about this
graceful beauty and absorb it, and he would quietly wait for the opportunity to be reborn, when the time came for him to stand up
again he would be an Atayal who had absorbed this new graceful
beauty into the old," But would this really be achievable? And what
if the opposite should happen and instead of the old absorbing the
new, the new absorbed the old? "I somehow perplex you, your confusion about me as a person has made you uncomfortable about my
theories, so I will start by answering a question about my personal
life, you seem to be quite interested in what kind of relationship
samurai have with women?" Mr. Miyamoto once had a wife—but in
order to save Mr. Miyamoto from having to speak too much Mandarin Chinese, I will use Chinese to narrate his story—Mr. Miyamoto
was married to a typical Atayal woman, back when he had first begun practicing samurai-style Zen meditation, he had once asked his
master this very question, his master responded with one simple sentence, "never completely prohibit yourself from anything, prohibit-
ing yourself is itself an obstacle to be overcome," and so Samurai
and the beauty spent the rest of their days together supporting each
other through difficult times the only thing missing from their relationship was children, but after a few years he started to hear rumors
that his wife and a plainsman who had come up to the mountains to
"reap from the savage" by farming land rented from them were doing
it doggy-piggy-style out on rear mountain, yet he didn't say a word
nor did he lose his temper, he didn't have an ounce of what would

later be called "dignity," this went on all the way up until the two lovers ran off together, the local police station heard about what happened and we're planning to arrest them, but he asked his master to step in in order to prevent any unnecessary actions being taken, it was from that point on that he arranged his house as it is today, after World War II he immersed himself in the cultivation of samurai-style Zen meditation, there was nowhere else that he wanted to go, and no one to truly understand him, today he is simply just another a "clean and friendly" old man on the reservation, it's quite possible that he is "the only man without dignity" on the entire reservation, "and so there is no such thing as doggy or piggy problems, my young Atayal," Mr. Miyamoto corrected me, "there are only relations between men and women," I felt ashamed that my Atayal Chinese was no better than a dog or a pig, "I make my sushi with local rice growing right here by the river, I have two plots of land on the eastern end beside the river, I farm half a plot myself and rent the rest of the land to other farmers," the key to being "clean" refers to the fact that he doesn't drink alcohol, "friendly" refers to the fact that all the tribe members feel that this is a man who has achieved nothing in his life and has not an ounce of prestige or dignity, "the picture frame and samurai sword were both left to me by my master after the war, Master felt he no longer had any need for a sword and felt better if he could return to Japan empty-handed, Master never explained to me the meaning of the calligraphy that was framed, he only said that the 'flying cursive style' calligraphy in which it was written represented the entirety of the soul, as for the actual meaning of the words that is only incidental," not long after the end of the war Mr. Miyamoto's samurai sword was confiscated by the government as a prohibited item, but for me there will always be an invisible sword there on that stand, Mr. Miyamoto nodded his head and smiled, with the utmost sincerity he tried to explain that never in his wildest dreams did he ever imagine that a person like him would end up protecting a spiritual idea, living a life of his own choosing, and the several decades that followed since the end of the war, he thankfully did not bother others, and he never imagined that the spirit encapsulated was somehow representative of a certain era, or that he himself was the embodiment of a person to take on an entire era, for his entire life he never strayed from the samurai path of Zen meditation, it was only through the way of the "samurai" that he was able to truly appreciate the beauty of Zen, it allowed him for the first time and from that point after to feel this thing called "beauty" in everything, he was fond of wearing a kimono because he could feel its beauty, he loved speaking Japanese so that he could feel the beauty of language, he ate sushi because it is simple and filling moreover it's the kind of food filled with an artistic beauty, Born an Atayal, he will die as an Atayal, he was different than those political and cultural figures who publicly declare that they hate the fact that they weren't born Japanese, and It wasn't that he didn't care about his fellow tribe members, but all he could do was use his feelings to observe them, he knew that his fellow tribe members would never be able to understand the beauty of Zen, "such a pity that they live such dull and monotonous lives," Mr. Miyamoto expressed the deep regrets he felt for his people, as I faced his bright piercing gaze, I could sense the exhaustion of a defeated man, deep down I felt ashamed that during my first visit to Mr. Miyamoto's house all I saw was the face of the samurai, I didn't sense the Zen within him, I sensed a kind of extreme loss, "Forget the liquor you left out in the ditch," Mr. Miyamoto showed off his sense of humor as he saw me off to the door, but it was just humor there wasn't an ounce of anything satiric about the way he said, "Let me tell you something, it might have something to do with your research into 'dignity,'" Mr. Miyamoto walked me out to the front end of his courtyard, his legs spread out naturally as he stood before me tall and erect: there was once a Japanese man, he was a retired county clerk, he came back to Riverisle and ended up staying more than a decade, he lived in that

Japanese-style house behind the police station, he often drank with the old-timers on the reservation, he wore a bandanna on his head and a Japanese-style thong, he still had the air of the colonizer about him, he spoke frankly, and when he drank he became assertive, and when he drank too much he would start ordering people around, just like in the old days, we called him Aini Hala or Stubby Rice, he had probably spent time in Riverisle before the end of the war, after retirement he started to get nostalgic about his days deep in the mountains and came back to the reservation to live, the older generation, including Elder, we're all polite and warm to him, once bitter enemies engaged in bloody struggle now they were like little kids blowing bubbles together, drinking he would sometimes talk about his experience during the old days, one thing that made everybody admire and respect him was that after a long period of time he would always go home to visit his relatives back in Japan, when he passed through Taipei on the way, he always made sure to visit North Zhongshan Road, he'd launch "critical strikes" from Alley 3 down to Alley 7 of Taipei's Japanese district, he would always visit on his way back home and again when he returned, according to what I know that was back during the days when the Japanese used their economic power to deliver a "critical strike" to this island, the older generation admired and respected him to the point that they would all flock around when he showed up, middle-aged members of the tribe didn't pay him too much attention, at the very most the younger generation would just occasionally give him a "*hai*," it was as if they had no common language since they did not share the same "memories of the bloody war," he was chronically ill and often dragged his sickly body away on these trips, after he died I even heard the tribal elders forbid his body be buried here in this place of exile. . . . I almost forgot about the bottle of liquor I had left in the ditch, thank goodness that the aluminous glow of the darkness helped me find my way back to my dark room, I forgot about the booze and lay down falling into a deep sleep, throughout the night I tossed and turned according to the plot details of my dream, by the time the rooster cackled for the third time I woke up to find my dreams forgotten, I drank my morning cup of coffee, and went out the back door for a walk, as I strolled down the small path through the cemetery I couldn't help but begin to unravel all the details that had occurred "the night before," naturally I began my work by running the narrative backward, Miyamoto Atayal used "beauty to destroy his dignity" while at the same time expressing true beauty through his everyday life, the last thing he said to me seemed to touch upon the way "life comes into being," in which human nature subsequently allows dignity to oscillate between a state of existing or not, moreover, no matter how wild my imagination may be I never would have imagined that Elder would think that the Ancestral Spirits would take an underground tunnel, I don't think that Cousin was joking when she said that she wanted to research me, she is after all one of the reservation's big feminists, perhaps she wants to do some research about postwar interactions between the Han Chinese and Taiwan's indigenous people, but the heaviest thing that I learned was, the elementary school teacher faced history with modesty, speaking in defense of Mona Rudao as one of the Atayal people's great leaders, he had no choice but to use the "Musha Incident" to resist the "long-term disturbances to his people's dignity," but the "incident" itself was of an "unquestionable nature," otherwise the survivors would have no place to put their "dignity, whether it be national or tribal, where would they put it—" I was thankful for the morning freshness in the air at the cemetery, my nose could smell the fragrant plum blossoms in the morning dew, and the white pointy tips of the cogon grass gently swayed in the wind, before the morning sun even had time to shine down on my face the atmosphere there had already helped me figure out what had happened during the evening spoken drama from the night before, I returned to my apartment that was surrounded by betel-nut trees, it was only after

I got home that I realized that night had fallen and it was time for bed, I could smell the fragrance of the betel nuts, I realized that there was a branch of betel-nut flowers right outside my window, I came to completely understand what Miyamoto Atayal meant by the "Beauty of Zen" and the "Beauty of the Dao" having the power to destroy dignity, but this type of characteristic is tied to an individualistic understanding, wouldn't really be possible to expand it into a "communal understanding," are there any historical precedents for this? I must search the electric mind of my computer for "contemporary" files on this in order to figure things out, if I were to use my human mind to try to contemplate all of this the level of difficulty would far surpass the height of even Jade Mountain, which stands 3,996 meters above sea level, the communal is concerned about "internal solidarity, joining forces against outsiders," they don't recognize any kind of "individualistic understanding," over the long course of the brutal struggle to survive on primitive reservations, "individualistic understanding" is something that never existed, so how can you even talk about its development, perhaps what "destroyed dignity" during the Musha Incident was not a matter of individualistic or collective understanding, it was rather the result of exhaustive contemplation regarding the "practical situation," this is also the primary reason those six other Seediq tribes did not participate in "the Incident," the ironic part of all of this is, those who took these practical factors into consideration probably would have only strengthened the "dignity of resistance as a Seediq," during the secret meeting of the twelve tribal heads before the incident the main players were "dignity" and "practicality," it is possible that over the course of their debates and attempts to persuade one another that dignity was destroyed, but the issue of whether what they were facing was some sort of fortunate event or an adversity was something on a completely different level, naturally neither side could persuade the other, by this point the "Musha Incident" was already inevitable, however the "legitimacy of dignity" is still open to doubt, there is no person thing or event in this world that exists in a place "beyond all question and doubt," I do not endorse the views of the elementary school teacher, there is nothing wrong with historical incidents existing within the contemporary, moreover it may very well be necessary that they "are called into question," one must leave behind the emotions of the people involved, "the contemporary" calls the historical Musha Incident into question, going one step closer "does not affirm" the dignified legitimacy of those who resisted during the incident—if there is still enough time, I promised Cousin that I would use my own race as a primer for another research project, that topic would be postwar interrelations between the Han Chinese people and Taiwan's indigenous population, I suspect that "the contemporary" would most certainly call the authority of the Han Chinese into question, a laissez-faire political and cultural invasion, and a "across-the-board assimilation policy" carried out completely naturally without an ounce of reflection or examination—I glanced at the bottle of white spirits that was still sitting on the couch from the night before, I immediately popped it open and took a swig, I drank just like that Atayal woman I saw the very first time I went to the general store she had just finished up her work in the fields and grabbed a bottle of red label off the shelf popped it open took a swig and then proceeded to wipe away the sweat that had dripped down her cheek toward her mouth, I wasn't about to let my fight for "dignity" stop here, and that wasn't because of the research theories or methodologies of "the contemporary," I have always been a person living on the brink of "the contemporary," moving to Riverisle and facing the "Musha Incident" and its Remains of Life is an intrinsic living part of my own life experience, I won't talk about it in terms of its "meaning" only in terms of its "experience." I collapsed on the living room couch, spread out on the coffee table were the books and magazines I brought with me up the mountain, I used small cups to control the amount of white spirits that I was drinking, a pictorial biography of Georgia O'Keeffe[24] and a collection of photographs of women's faces were the two books I found myself thumbing through most frequently, I kept all of my materials about creative writing in a shameful place I'd rather not mention and only looked at them when it was absolutely necessary because the more of that stuff you read "the more con- strained your writing becomes," there were two paintings by Georgia O'Keeffe that were so good they deserved two glasses of white spir- its, she not only captured the essence of form but also adorned her paintings with the beauty of flowers, it's quite different from a certain famous writer who wrote about her vagina so nakedly that it was almost to the point of genital worship, there is also a artist with the grand ambition to paint several hundred large-scale hyper-realis- tic paintings of vaginas, which has all now gotten to an utterly dis- gusting point, all objects in the world that we worship end up inspir- ing countless forms and portrayals, you can't simply point directly at the actual object, otherwise you'd get sick of it in less than three days, even a great ass or an outstanding set of breasts could only last three and a half days or four at the most, female genital worship has been all around us since ancient times, it takes less than an hour to get to the countryside from the city where I usually live, once you get out to the country you can see enticing temples dedicated to female genitalia all over the place, there was wisdom in the ancients, they knew enough to use small and mid-sized pottery vessels to represent the vagina, in the 1990s Taiwan's indigenous communities started a resurgence movement aimed at preserving their traditional culture, and suddenly female genital worship activities began to come back to the mountain villages, the only difference was that they now used new terminology for it, so nobody could figure out that what they were actually talking about were vaginas, actually the primitive belief system of the Chinese plains people on this island nation also calls for female genital worship, after women have been forced to kneel for half their lives it was finally clear that vagina worship goes all the way back to our most primitive belief system and this is worth a toast of three or four small glasses, those female genitalia temples deserve at least three or four pottery vessels, Georgia O'Keeffe self-identified as a Mexican American, well I'm a Pingpu-Siraya-Han Chinese, of all the faces in that photography book not one of them could compare with the image of Georgia O'Keeffe's ninety-eight-year-old face, the difference between that and the other images was not one of beauty but one of courage, it was the beauty of courage and confidence when facing the camera, and for this I toasted her one small drink, there was a row of books on top of the cupboard, one of the heavier volumes was *Portraits of the Island Nation's Indigenous People*, I bought a copy and put it up there but still haven't read it, because here on this island nation I have the opportunity to see the real thing firsthand, it was only when exhausted to the point where I could barely move that I finally picked it up to see if the photographs were really worth their weight, all that matters is that the vagina enjoys herself she probably doesn't even think about being worshiped, as I shrugged my shoulders at the boredom of life the research that I must research was not enough to bring an end to my worship, when I think about all the various forms of worship out there the one I admire most is "female genital worship," one of the reasons I so admired Georgia O'Keeffe is that she banished civilization for more than fifty years to live the Indian life in New Mexico, she banished her civilized vagina to live the life of a primitive vagina all the way up until the time of her death, in the name of this "banishment" I toasted her two glasses, ever since the moment I saw Georgia O'Keeffe, I started to imagine the Latino Seediq as resembling a middle-aged O'Keeffe, a mixture of beauty and rebellion, and in the name of this "mixture" I would finish all the remaining liquor . . . the early winter sunlight was warm and affable, I had said good-bye to white spirit liquor for quite some time, the white spirit bottle was empty but carrying the empty bottle around seemed to be a "symbol of life," I went outside down the path into the waves of rice growing in the paddies and kept going all the way until I reached the edge of the Bukan River, I searched for a spot where I could make it down the slope directly to the water using my empty bottle as a cane along the way, "See, not hard to make it down to the river at all!" I said to the distant mountains, "Let's see where you can run off to, I'll find you by following this river and bring you the white spirits," the current wasn't terribly strong, I walked alongside the sandbar passing the two reservations on the inner mountain, the back doors of the homes alongside the river opened up directly over a cliff overlooking the water, I didn't see any garbage or abandoned items, the young boys and girls with the deer eyes must've been looking after this place, after passing the reservations the river turned and I came upon the first gorge, the river water flowed over a bed of small pebbles, the white spirits and river water passed over the rocks, fronds were growing from the moss on either side of the riverbank, looking up you couldn't see the sky as it had been sealed up by the looming mountain crest, there was a gentle wind that brought with it a feminine darkness that was like a silent vagina in wait, I pulled the tips of my feet and the bottom of my balls up into my heart, I was afraid of disturbing the vagina, I looked down at the pure emerald water on the fronds and immediately thought about how long it had been since anyone had been in this vaginal opening, as I continued the crest of each mountain I passed seemed to get higher than the last, yet the river valley remained just as narrow, in the distance I could see where the river curved and the valley narrowed to a sliver, I imagine that as soon as I made it through that sliver I would emerge into the broad riverbed, these are the kinds of games that nature plays when creating images, the hero relies upon his white spirits yet feels sorrow for this vagina, the broad riverbed was filled with boulders of all different sizes making it difficult for anyone to find even a thin passage to slip through, I'll probably have to learn to jump like a leapfrog to make it through, but if the river valley turns out to be narrow and the river water is as clear and pure as a pristine lake, then I would need steel stakes and ropes and I would have to learn about rock climbing in order to figure out what kind of rock-climbing equipment I would need to buy, or perhaps I should prepare a small inflatable raft, but you need to have strong arm muscles to row those things otherwise the current will just take you right back to Riverisle, I deeply regret that I didn't study science otherwise I could just use an individual propulsion engine to shoot myself past the river and fly straight up to the summit of the mountain, a shame just how much primal energy I have expended on this vaginal cavity, I couldn't even make it through this long narrow valley, the sky darkened over the vagina, I left the canyon and saw the rosy clouds of late dusk floating somewhere between heaven and earth, I felt the lightness of letting go of the heavy burden in my heart once I decided to only focus on my work I felt settled and carefree as I did when I faced the quiet vagina in wait, I threw the empty bottle of white spirits down on the couch, and the first thing I did was jot down a memorandum entitled "A Little Adventure Before My Quest," I heard that there are some people who just throw their empty bottles of white spirits under their bed when they're done drinking, this would go on for a few years up until the time when the bottles would start making a strange clanking under the bed sound and everyone would know that this guy still had what it took to get the job done in the sack, I should probably cross out the word "Little" from the title of my memorandum, there are actually two or three houses on the reservation that use empty bottles of white spirits to decorate their houses and courtyards, besides the aesthetic value it also shows that their family knows something about the current state of "ready-made installation art," An Adventure Before My Quest is really much too wordy, perhaps I should instead use "My Adventure Quest," normal people usually return their empty bottles for a one-dollar recycling refund, below my revised title "The Search: An Adventure" I clearly wrote out the different types of terrain I might encounter on my voyage, different levels of river water, for that I have to be sure to wear plastic boots because there's no way I could get away with wearing white spirit flip-flops like I did today, I would have to figure out what food to bring based on how many days the journey might take, naturally we would have to bring hats, sunglasses, and sunscreen lotion, the other supplies that still need to be confirmed include materials related to my recent research into "rock-climbing studies" and "river-trekking studies"—these were all things that needed to be done in preparation for Girl's search, but it wasn't at all about my own tribal adventures, it was only once Girl's Atayal-led Quest had been settled that I was able to establish a clear theme for my work, it was only after Mystic Valley reappeared that imagination could again become a possibility. I went into town in hopes of buying some books on "rock-climbing" and "river-trekking," while I was there I thought I would also see if there happened to be any recently published studies about the Musha Incident, as I set out from Riverside into town, all along the road I could continuously see the mountains in the distance beyond Musha, it was hard not to look at this without feeling a complex mix of emotions, wasn't it understood that we would try to be firm and unwavering, how could anyone know that ever since ancient times the mountains of this place where man has fought man, man has fought beasts, and beasts have fought other beasts such is the way of war, there is the old saying that "the benevolent enjoy the mountains" but what the fuck is there to enjoy? that's just some sick psychological fantasy about the mountains that the great Han Chinese have come up with, since there are no written records of what those battles in the mountains were like no one talks about them, but when writing finally did come up the mountain there was a "Major Incident" that broke out, this has forced people of today to look at the Musha Incident and its hero Mona Rudao in a completely different light, when I got to town I realized that it wasn't the same place I had visited twenty years earlier when I been stationed there in the army, the small town had taken a note from the cities on how to carry out "small-scale urbanization" but this is also probably the shared fate of most small towns on this island nation, all humans have their fate, the fate of things is sometimes controlled by humans and sometimes not, objects actually have their own fate, it's a shame that this island nation went from a state of impoverishment to a phase of rapid economic development up until its current state of postprosperity , the characteristic of "working hard" that so many people on this island nation share is still in place although it is now on shaky ground, and so over the course of these past few decades, the massive transformation of material things by the hands of man can be seen everywhere, and it is also owing to man that everyone on this identical island nation has an identical disposition, the transformation of physical objects is also carried out in an identical fashion and after a while even those objects begin to look identical, those who grew up here during the 1960s and 1970s have seen what the simple and quiet downtown districts, small towns and rural farmlands on this island nation used to look like, they always sigh when they see what the cities of this island nation look like, by the fin de siècle they look like they are all part of the same chaotic and disorderly mess, the small towns have all become semiurbanized losing all of their character and charm, you would think that the rural fields should be a part of nature but they too seem to be in a contest over who can hang up the most red lanterns and silk ribbons as they rush toward touristization, most terrifying is the way that the men and women from these pristine fields deep in the mountains have sold their flesh and prostituted themselves to those cities and small towns, gradually increasing to the point that it has gone from something fashionable for a time to now simply something that everyone is used to, the government occasionally clamps down on prostitution, and the media always eat it up in their reporting, no one ever thinks about why they use the word "yellow" when referring to prostitution, and certainly no one has put any kind of deep thought into this by asking isn't this island nation of ours a free-market economy? You can slaughter a living chicken in public so what's the big deal about "renting out some human flesh by the hour," those free-range chickens must be laughing their asses off at us, McDonald's has naturally moved its golden arches into the small towns, and 7-Eleven signs are so ubiquitous that elementary school students think that 7-Eleven is a life necessity, the most talked-about store names have also become increasingly postmodern along with the city itself: "Old Flame New Love," "Action First, Consequences Later," "Partners Unlimited," "Dominating Knockers," such literary creativity swept the cities, making me feel that there are indeed many more "new possibilities for writing," I bought a few books on "river trekking," "rock climbing," and even one on "outdoor survival skills" at King-something Bookstore,[25] I thought back to when the incident in Musha happened, back then all the people in this small town must have been terrified that the "untamed savages" might fight their way down the mountain, thank goodness the rulers sent several divisions of soldiers on horseback to set everyone's mind at ease, of course it was also necessary to offer "bonuses" to those who helped them, back when they first built the Buk-Tik Palace the townspeople donated money while the savages donated their labor, there were 2,420 laborers who came to town from the surrounding mountains in the northeast to cut down trees, transport logs, and build structures for the Japanese, one year and five months after the incident the survivors who were exiled got on a bus that took them down to Puli and were then transferred on to Riverisle, in October of the same year the "great purge" began, twenty-three strong young men were tricked into leaving Riverisle— added to that number are the thirty-eight who were rounded up in in the mountains around Musha—in March of the following year they were all driven to kill themselves after being repeatedly tied up and beaten while in custody at the Puli Detention Center, according to the official line the cause of their death was listed as a series of serious illnesses such as beriberi and enteritis, three years after the incident a Toda hunter discovered Mona Rudao's skeletal remains in the forest, officials had the body moved to the Buk-Tik Palace and asked Mahong to come up from Riverisle to identify the body, later it was publicly displayed in the newly completed Prefecture Service Building, Mona Rudao was open for exhibition, this is how the Musha Incident is connected to this small town, and that is why I haven't been stingy when it comes to how much I have written about this subject in this section of my "memorandum," I did it in order to preserve the historical memory of this small town because besides being famous for its red sugarcane and Shaoxing wine, this town also has a place in history as the "great base" of the Musha Incident, for those who believe that "fame is 100 times better than anonymity," this is something for the people who live in this town to feel proud about, I thumbed through the book on outdoor survival skills on the way home, that small minority of people able to survive the incident all had strong natural skills, "surviving in the city is no easier than surviving out in the wild" those are the famous words spoken by a good friend of mine from the Rukai tribe upon moving back to his hometown after thirty years trying to make it in the city, he was extremely concerned about the future of this island nation as they faced a choice between "all-out urbanization" or "all-out national parkization," he didn't want to end up as part of a national anthropological park like the Bunun tribe, if you were to ask him what the difference was, he would provide a meticulous answer explaining how extremely different it was, but the psychological feeling attached revealed an even more "radical difference," I returned to Riverisle, I sat down beside the abandoned plastic shed on the ridge near the fields, and continued reading about outdoor survival, I even tried

some of the weeds and fruits that were growing on the ground beside
my feet, "the most colorful and attractive ones are the most poisonous" is a natural law but it is also a fundamental principle for people to
follow when seeking a mate, "when you encounter a dangerous
area, you must not attempt to pass, instead rely upon your confidence to get you through," this is a line stolen from some philoso-
pher's manual on the art of war, an elderly Atayal woman leisurely
strolled by, she asked in Taiwanese if I had had lunch yet, her daughter-in-law was from Xiluo and she had just had Xiluo food for lunch
and had come around to check on her rice crop, which was almost
ready for harvest, I stared at that elderly Atayal woman as if in a daze,
her face still had traces of a young girl's adorably delicate features, her
pretty charm almost made me feel like I must have mistaken her for
someone else, snapping out of my daze I responded by telling her that
I had had a good lunch, I got back home to my living room and decided to sit down and finish reading that book on outdoor survival,
in the event it was necessary for me to carry out further research, the
terrain and vegetation surrounding the rear mountain cemetery was
the perfect place to practice my survival skills, you never know perhaps these new skills might even come in handy in my dream tonight,
it was at that moment that a man called out to me from behind the
screen door, I said hello what can I help you with please come in,
from behind the screen door I could already smell that he had just
crawled out of Girl's bed, "it was the smell of primal Atayal scents
inter-tangled" that's the only way to describe it, any other description
would be too graphic or inappropriate, "Nothin's up, we all know
that you came here to do research and we welcome you, you wanna
come over for a drink, let's try to have an emotional bond man,"
while on the reservation there had been many times while on a walk
that I'd been invited to join impromptu gatherings of people drinking in a circle, but never had I received such a formal invitation as the
one that day, an invitation to establish an "emotional bond" can't be

refused especially when it comes to tribe members who are all emotional animals, the guy said that his name was Moxi, the drinking party would be over at Boss's house, I didn't bother asking him who this Boss was, up in the tribal mountain land bosses are fairly quiet keeping an eye on things but not causing too much trouble, "What does your name, Moxi, mean?" I asked him on the way over, the old folks all call me Moxi but I don't know what the hell it means either, but in his teenage years as he was starting to feel himself out he grew to like the name, "and so I eventually just settled on Moxi," so even though it doesn't mean a damn thing I never worried about its meaning, Boss's place was located on the central west side of the reservation, his courtyard was one and a half times the size of everyone else's, a row of cockscomb flowers surrounded his wattled wall and two large triangle-shaped cacti stood like pillars beside his store, "I actually went over to invite you first thing this morning but you weren't home, where the hell did you run off to?" The voice came from a man sitting in front of a picture of the Holy Mother breast-feeding the Holy Infant, so that was Boss, "I'm so sorry, please accept my apologies, I went into town to do some research and just returned," looking at the leftovers strewn all over the table I knew that the five or six of them had been drinking for hours, "Moxi," Boss ordered, "Pour him a drink, and go inside to make a few fresh dishes for him," they drank a mixture of rice wine, Whisbih, and Mr. Brown coffee, which according to legend could make you strong and powerful like Mr. Brown,[26] "Cheers!" Boss asked everyone seated to drink a round in my honor, the taste of rice-Whis-Brown was better than whiskey-brandy, "Tell us next time you need to leave the reservation, Boss has connections with people out beyond Reunion Mountain and on the other side of Muddy River," I didn't dare ask them whether they got in touch with those people they had connections with using messenger pigeons or the Internet, instead I just said, "Thanks a lot," "We invited you here today concerning Sister," it was a good thing that

Boss didn't beat around the bush when it came to the matter at hand, and he made sure that *he* was the one always doing the talking, "We would like you to use your research skills to convince Sister of something," now this really had an academic air to it, everyone at the table was in their upper forties or fifties, it turns out that Girl had proclaimed that she would bring her "Giving Back Ritual" to a close on Christmas, the ceremony to end the ritual would be held on the afternoon before Christmas, by Christmas Eve Girl would return to her life as a free agent who had returned to her hometown, "She might be satisfied to bring all of this to a happy close, but that doesn't mean we are," so spoke a man wearing a particularly loud and colorful shirt, it was at that moment that Moxi came in and placed two dishes on the table, Moxi's entrance cut off Mr. Colorful Shirt and Boss had no choice but to say, "Please don't stand on ceremony, help yourself," I took a bite of dragon whiskers stir-fried with gem-faced civit and then tried some of the cat-roasted river eel, Boss lowered his voiced and explained that they were not what some people would call "throwaway men," for instance the man who had spoken earlier was once the number one playboy on the reservation, he married the most beautiful Atayal woman on the reservation, he was even greedy enough to then go after the number two beauty, "You must know how tender and shrewd our Atayal women can be," I had never experienced sweetness and cruelty together, but I could imagine how much passion and affection must have been raging within each of them and as they battled for one man's affections, neither was willing to give up or lose to the other, but eventually one of them left the mountain and the other one followed, and for many years thereafter Lonely Playboy remained alone on the mountain, "Let's drink," I said, "I'd like to toast each of you," Boss analyzed the situation for everybody, 1) Back when we were classmates all the boys and girls left the mountain to look for work down in the plains, we all planned to meet up again after we had made enough money, but how could we have imagined just how many pitfalls there were waiting for us in the city, eventually everyone finds a spot to put down roots, but by then we could no longer find each other, 2) When the men finally did return home, none of them had thought about getting married in advance, it was only after they returned to the reservation that they realized that all the young women were gone, and once they left almost none of them ever returned, 3) Every young woman still on the reservation was already married, "Our Atayal tribal rules about these things are very strict," 4) There was no way they could leave the reservation to seek out prostitutes, there was too great a risk of sleeping with a tribal relative, moreover just think about how many bottles of white spirits you could buy for the cost of a single encounter with a prostitute, 5) There were a lot of STDs in the city, they had a responsibility not to infect Riverisle—Everyone at the table nodded in agreement, they all had a responsibility toward Riverisle, they all went back to drinking, Boss's tone of voice changed, "We can't afford to collectively pay a woman to service us, so we use chicken fights or draw lots or draw up a ballot to choose someone," That change in Boss's tone of voice hinted at the fact that he had been forced to give up whatever special privileges he once had, "Why don't you set her free for a while?" I tried to bargain on behalf of Girl, "You have no shortage of gunners, but there is only one cannon for you to use, why don't you give her a little break," "We could consider that," Boss nodded, as did the others, "but if we let that Sore Meimei go free for too long, she would quickly become a dangerous person on this reservation," everyone laughed, thinking about that "My Oh My Mr. Wang," "Do you mind if I ask you a question?" I never give up a good research opportunity, "Of course, please go ahead," this time they each nodded at different times, "Why do you insist on always doing it doggy-piggy style?" I put on my serious research face, "Doggy-piggy style?" Boss's eyes widened, everyone else was eating and laughing, but Boss immediately understood what I was trying to say,

"C'mom, let's drink! Cheers!" Boss drank and laughed until he was almost out of breath, "That is the natural position we are born with, it is only because you civilized people can't fathom its profundity that you were forced to invent face-to-face style, but all the different species of higher animals do it this natural way, this position surpasses you civilized people in terms of its power, position, force, orgasmic potential, and level of satisfaction ten thousand times over—" Boss indeed knew something about the world, he got right to the heart of the question, at the same time he was able to display an impressive academic vocabulary when it came to the subject at hand, I promise to research this matter with Girl, "Set her free until spring!" I proposed, "Spring may bring a change," Boss asked me to research things with Girl first and they would decide on a course of action later, he then ordered Moxi to see me home, he also prepared some food and drinks to drop off at Girl's house, just as I was going out the door I could hear Playboy complaining about something, "Remains of Life deprived of sex are like the walking dead living without a soul." Toward the end of 1990 I decided to leave the semiurbanized small town where I had been living, I ventured deep into the mountains of this island nation, at the time I had read a few books, but my intuition told me that there must be things here inside this island nation that I had yet to see, things I had never imagined, let alone come close to understanding the inner meaning of, I continued to live deep in the mountains, all the way up until now the spring of 1999, my senses have helped me understand the fact that there is indeed a rich inner meaning lurking inside this island nation, this inner meaning has not only led me to understand that "the city is a stranger," but even more importantly, to discover that it is possible that there "exists a primitive force coming into being" within this tiny island nation's civilization as the fin de siècle approaches, from a distance its inner meaning is powerful enough to contend with urban civilization, and ultimately become the representative force of this island nation, later the contemporary era I was in asked me to move closer to the "Musha Incident," I didn't approach it with the presupposed stance or predetermined framework of most researchers, I am actually a novelist by trade, the perspective, feeling, and thought process of fiction is necessarily different from that of a researcher, just as all artists have their own independent "imaginary reality," I took a cue from the way anthropologists conduct fieldwork and live on site, besides the limited "historical materials on the incident" that I brought with me when I first arrived, in my heart I had only a faint confusion concerning the "legitimacy and appropriateness" behind the incident, as a novelist, I have long naturally fostered an approach by which I try not to think of my fiction and there is no place for the novel in my heart, people events and things do not exist so I can write about them, but to actually experience everyday life, and those random moments in our everyday lives that move me, like Deformo, like Mr. Miyamoto, and when I occasionally hear things like "This stream is the place of my dreams," or "Remains of Life deprived of sex are like the walking dead living without a soul," no matter what kind of lifestyle they have, or where the vocabulary they use comes from, you can be sure of the fact that it is all coming from the tribal souls of people who have lived for many years deep in these isolated mountains, what moves me is the authenticity of their everyday lives, which is as en-chanting and moving as the distant mountains eternally enshrouded in a layer of mist, my contemporary age gave me the job of thinking through what happened during the "Musha Incident," but my soul and everyday emotions are moved by the natural state of life itself, and that is perhaps the critical element that allows me to enter and understand those things I see here deep in the mountains—Before moving on to the second challenge I face in my work, "attempting to explore the legitimacy of the headhunting ritual," I must make an emotional confession, I am an artist who writes novels, I believe that emotions are the primal force behind my work, my writing represents all of the emotions I have accumulated from my many years living deep in the mountains all the way up until my experience now in Riverisle, it has driven me to carry on to face another possibility and what may very well be an even more difficult challenge, but I never do it for feeling any sense of "accomplishment about my work" or any other "work-related reason," as for where this work will eventually take me, as of now I have absolutely no idea, just finding the proper angle with which to address the question at hand has cost me several days of hard thought over heavy liquor, the right amount of white spirits can inspire me to break through or tap into the excitement of my work, it can help me feel like I am that much closer to the state of "walking side by side with you" and "coexisting in harmony"—The most primitive origin of "headhunting" probably evolved out of the huntsman's hunter instincts, hunters have the custom of preserving the skulls and jawbones of wild animals and hanging them all over their guest room as a means of displaying their greatness as a hunter, the heroic names of the tribes' great hunters would stand alongside those of the tribal leaders, once they had the experience of preserving animal heads, they were only one step away from preparing human heads, the motivation behind crossing that line must have come directly from the hunters themselves, for if they dared to decapitate another human and preserve it what else was there in the realms of heaven and earth that these hunters could possibly fear, this was the hunters' means of pushing themselves forward, while at the same time announcing their terrifying fearlessness to all his fellow tribe members, I imagine that when the ordinary tribe members first witnessed the act of decapitation and the preservation of the skulls they must have stayed far away and avoided it like children today who see a dead cat hanging from a tree,[27] but the great hunters brought together all of the powerful forces in the tribe to force the other ordinary tribespeople to face these skulls before and after being preserved, they simultaneously emphasized the fact that this was a "skull of revenge" that used anger to replace fear, and so the great hunters began to decapitate and preserve the heads of their victims, which over time gradually became "routinized" into a headhunting ritual, in a tribal area where disputes over hunting grounds and farmlands had long persisted, the "headhunt" became the most fashionable, threatening, and heroic action a hunter could undertake, especially once the headhunt had been elevated to the primary precondition to "become a man," teenagers who had not partaken in a headhunt were not allowed to drink wine during tribal festivals, those who had not taken a skull and commemorated their feat with a chin tattoo could not take a wife in the tribe, and certainly could not be allowed to have children and start a family, historical records show that headhunting activities flourished among the indigenous people of this island nation for a very long time, this was particularly true among the fierce and brave Atayal, different sects of this tribe would often carry out headhunting expeditions against one another, this was quite unlike the Rukai and Paiwan tribes in the south who "never went after their own people's heads," I suspect the reason it flourished so was not because of some "necessity to headhunt in and of itself," but rather owing to the practical "conditions" that came with headhunting, "conditions: benefit" here the inherent primitive nature can prove that they are in no way pseudo-modern, at the same time amid the crazed passion of the headhunt, what had become routinized gradually becomes "ritualized," before everyone's eyes headhunting activities begin to carry with them all kinds of taboos and prohibitions, once taboos are broken you naturally need another headhunt to resolve the "fear of taboos," so in the process of implementing prohibitions, the need for more headhunts is ironically increased, I began to reflect upon what was entailed in "the completion of a headhunting ritual" that had lasted for hundreds perhaps thousands of years, how they collectively went from seeing it as a taboo to carnivalesque celebrations of it, and how individuals went from a state of hero worship

to gazing alone face to face at those skulls, there are perhaps anthropologists from the end of the last century who had witnessed headhunts and the carnivalesque rituals that followed, a shame that none
of them left behind any photos or written records, I once saw a photograph of the Slamao Incident from 1920 where I could see women
from Musha holding decapitated heads, they were lined up in a circle
in front of the Musha Police Station, dancing a celebratory dance
during a "ritual headhunting sacrifice," one can only imagine on the
night of the Second Musha Incident, the carnivalesque scene that began in the early morning hours and carried on until past midnight after the Toda tribe decapitated 101 people, the "level of involvement"
of such a carnival went from frenzied dancing to a trancelike state
to wild intercourse I'm afraid that there was probably not a single
Han Chinese party held on this island nation for the next hundred
years that could compare with that carnivalesque scene—There is actually some basis behind me writing about the transition "from frenzied dancing to wild intercourse," there is not a single primitive race
whose carnivalesque rituals break from this pattern, historical records
attest to this, naturally this is how human nature operates, after
humans became civilized Western carnivals also inherited or learned
from this pattern, academics might read this phenomenon as "a means
of letting out all the stress of primitive society, and the ritualistic nature of the event legitimizes it," I somehow naively thought that
"wild sex" and " wild incest" were both a fundamental part of humankind's primitive nature where "the individual doesn't know who
he is" can find suitable release, even a quiet observer would be moved
by the sight of that kind of "inhuman involvement," as the carnival
reached its climax it was not the human heart racing but rather the
pulsation of the earth itself, the historical records have a lot to say
about the various rituals of war but they seldom focus upon headhunting, in the history of warfare there are many examples of warriors
consuming their enemy's organs and flesh, when it comes to that, we

should be thankful for "the headhunt," for thousands of years deep in the mountains of this island nation there have been large-scale carnivalesque rituals, these carnivals are important for what they inherently represent, they not only wipe away the shackles of "a fledgling process of societalization," returning everyone to the bosom of primitive nature, they are like a volcano erupting, releasing hot lava to freely flow, today when we admire the natural beauty of the river valleys, there is no reason for "headhunting" to even cross your mind, but we must never forget that all of this beauty arises out of the "carnival" of the universe, the planet, and humankind. Along the small path through the cemetery where I go for my walks, I often notice a small tomb shaped like a little room, perhaps because it is located so close to the path, or then again perhaps because what it contains is so unique, above the tombstone is a picture of a middle-age man wearing a Japanese-style suit in a porcelain frame, the suit is buttoned all the way up to his chin, beneath the picture is the square cement tombstone, leaning up against the bottom of the tombstone is a photograph of him wearing a kimono and holding a samurai sword, in front of the tomb is a long rectangular table made from cement flanked by cement benches on either side, the most peculiar detail are the two wooden bookshelves beside the cement table, on the bookshelf are copies of *The Analects, Mencius, The Annals of the Eastern Zhou Dynasty, The Biography of Saigō Takamori, Biography of Tokugawa Leyasu*, and *D. T. Suzuki and Zen*,[28] there is also a pile of magazines, most of them are copies of the Japanese literary magazine *Bungeishunjū* or local annals, after strolling past that tomb two or three times I decided to look more closely and only then did I discover that only *D. T. Suzuki and Zen* and the magazines were real, the others were all bricks that had been painted to look like books, the Ancestral Spirits had probably borrowed all of the other books, temporarily leaving those bricks behind as placeholders, from the titles of the books I guessed that on a spiritual level this man must have inherited a combination of the great Chinese and the great Japanese national traditions, but the Japanese tradition was probably more important to him, after all *The Analects* and the *Mencius* were also politically important for the Japanese, neither the positioning of the tomb nor any of the items including the photograph of him wearing a kimono had been disturbed, I suppose that he was once a highly respected intellectual on the reservation, it is a pity that I never saw anyone from the reservation having tea and engaging in philosophical debates before him at his table, instead it was empty and covered with dust, later during my strolls I would occasionally go inside to have a look, I would thumb through the magazines and especially that book about D. T. Suzuki, I would squat down and carefully examine how the samurai sword went with the kimono and that face in the picture, I suddenly became interested in "the percentage of books read on the reservation," I had visited several families on the reservation but had not seen any books, then again perhaps they had them hidden away in a back library somewhere, I still remember not long after first arriving on the reservation, the owner of the general store had proudly said to me, "The cultural level here on this reservation is one of the highest around here," at the time hearing those masterpieces of classical music coming from Girl's house each night made me believe him, amid the overgrown grass and weeds of the graveyard was an ancient tree towering out into the sky but probably having been nourished on the flesh of man, this ancient tree had a dark serenity, the dejected nature of the people on the reservation also nourished an atmosphere of dark serenity, I can't put my finger on the exact spot but sometimes when I am walking past certain places on the reservation I can sense it, I don't feel that darkness when I'm at Girl's house, the hubbub there instead feels a bit manic and crazed, even the softness of those famous classical pieces at night can't sooth the unrest, I wanted to go over to Girl's place to ask her if the person who used to read Saigō Takamori had been a native from here, if she didn't know I would look for an "appropriate opportunity" to ask Mr. Miyamoto, perhaps that unusually talented sensei he studied under also began to miss Riverisle in his later years, "Don't speak on behalf of others," Girl saw me entering her courtyard and took a few steps outside, her words were as coarse as her shoulders were broad, "Just work on researching yourself, whoever said you were half an Atayal anyway," perhaps the Ancestral Spirits had come to her in her dreams to warn her about the Young Atayal Stranger living next door, otherwise Mr. Miyamoto must also be a member of the secret Giving Back Club, he just didn't show up at the meeting the other day, "Do you think I'd really be able to get you to change your mind about anything?" I only needed to offer that single retort, Girl immediately laughed because she knew I understood her, after all for how many nights had I listened to those sorrowful classical melodies coming from her house, "I'm not here to change your mind about anything, nor do I want you to help me research myself, just tell me some stories about yourself or life on the reservation," the lazy part of writing is always listening, if you don't have the ability to intently listen then there is no way to see the beauty of the deep and profound world hidden behind words, when Girl tells stories she needs some hard liquor to really get to that deep place of dark serenity, for an instant the dark serenity of the graveyard flashed before me, in another instant Moxi came outside to bring us a few bottles of white spirits before scurrying back inside, we sat under a betel-nut tree on the far end of her courtyard, I asked her about that guy's tomb in the graveyard, Girl said that ever since she was little she never went to the graveyard, all the way up until today she still has no idea what the reservation's graveyard even looks like, "Don't you dare mention that place," Girl popped open a bottle of white spirits, she then reached out her arm to pick a ripe betel nut to chew on to go with her drink, "Say, if I talk about when I was married off to Daba, can you write about that in your research, in your own research?" When she was close to eighteen Girl left her hometown and went to Taichung and from there on to Taipei, the first night after she left Girl met Yongfu Daba, Yongfu had showed up at the guild hall to look for his friends, while he was there he also wanted to try to recruit a few new workers to help on his scaffolding crew, he said that his bright eyes took one look at her and he knew that he would be with her for all eternity like the moon to the stars, he stared into eternity for half the night, he explained that his scaffolding team was really hot and they had a great future ahead of them, "We're so busy that we don't even have time to get wasted," she looked at his sturdy dark tanned muscular body, his muscles were quite enchanting, but she had come to the largest metropolis in this island nation in order to experience all those things she had been looking forward to ever since she was a child, "I wanted to taste all those things civilization had to offer me in life before I was ready to settle down," Yongfu understood what she was trying to say, but he frankly told her that it usually only takes a few days for young indigenous girls like her to lose themselves amid this evil city, they end up thrown into the fire pit and don't even know if they're living or dead, as a Brave Warrior he wasn't willing to see another one of the girls from the tribe end up in such a terrible situation, "So my brave warrior, what should I do?" Yongfu said, you can do odd jobs for our crew and make some money, if you save your earnings for a few years you can buy a small apartment and it still won't be too late to experience the city, the next morning she was taken directly from the guild hall to the construction site, in the early morning hours the city felt like a shadowy dream passing before her eyes, it "looked like an old lady wearing a pair of colorful panties that were now old and faded," they were working on a large construction project in a hilly region on the outskirts of the city, once the crew arrived they ended up staying there two full years eating sleeping and living in a series of makeshift sheet-iron shacks, besides taking on various odd jobs at the construction site Girl also cooked

for all the guys from the Daba tribe, it was a good thing that before
too long Yongfu was able make a small sheet-iron shack for himself,
that made it more convenient for him to give Girl massages at night,
"After that I of course massaged that sheet-iron body of his," it was a
good thing that besides knowing how to make money Yongfu also
knew how to spend money, on their days off he would take her to all
those happening places in the city, she realized that they seemed to
be spending more money than all those city people around them, yet
she still felt like "they didn't really fit in," each time they went into
the city they would splurge on food and drinks and then go shopping, Yongfu bought her anything she fancied and then they would
go back to their little sheet-iron shack on the hill, after two years the
scaffolding crew was getting ready to move on to another hillside
region to work on a new development site, it was then that Girl decided
that she had had enough, she thought about leaving, but wasn't sure
where to go, she just decided to head to the city and figure the rest
out later, "I didn't want to be a fledgling anymore," but who would
have imagined that the Brave Warrior had figured out his beauty's
plan, and so during a banquet dinner with his crew to celebrate the
completion of their construction project he took the lead by announcing that the Brave Warrior of Daba intended to take the woman from
Reunion Mountain as his wife, the announcement took everyone by
surprise and the whole crew gathered around them as they danced
and drank the night away, she drank a lot that night, yet she clearly
remembered, the moment she got stuck with this new label, the
"Woman from Reunion Mountain," "So I'm the Woman from Reunion Mountain, am I? Is it that all women are by nature destined to
unite with someone?" All of a sudden she became the center of a big
marriage bringing together Reunion Mountain and Daba, she went
to Daba for the wedding and stayed there, Yongfu also agreed that
staying in Daba to raise the kids would be much more important than
her rejoining his crew in the city, in three and a half years she gave

birth to three children, by the time she had her last son she was so weak that she couldn't even remember whose it was, or who had given birth to him, "Daba Mountain is much higher, and the people there are more primitive, they don't know anything about privacy, men and women hook up as casually as taking a piss," although Yongfu returned to Daba whenever he could, Brave Warrior couldn't always be there up in the mountain to warm her cold bed each night, she often would just pass out at night, there were many times when she couldn't tell if it was dusk or the middle of the night, "I swear I really have no idea who fathered that last one I had, but he is certainly a child of the Daba," up on the mountain there are just two things to keep Daba women busy, mahjong and gossip, their mahjong games could go on for four or five days—the record was five and a half days—most of the men had left the mountain in search of work, so there was no one to stop the women from their unbridled gossip, once they got going they would talk about how the Daba mountain resembled a man's prick and they would "debate from which angle it most resembled one, starting from the angle with the most girth," there were so many women in on these gossip sessions that they could have formed a Daba army, and then they'd gossip about "why that Seediq woman always kept her door closed," in the process she was stripping away her own Seediq virtue, they said that because the women of Daba were used to keeping their doors open to each other, after that she left her door open and people started to barge in all the time, when it was men who barged in they would always say they had just come back from the city and asked her if she needed anything, often when the door was closed she would be shocked to discover two or three men's faces staring in through a hole in thin wooden wall of the adjacent room, when she told Yongfu about it he just responded by saying, "That's just how things are in Daba," One day early in the morning five years after she had gotten married, she took the first morning bus off the mountain, she left her kids with her mother-in-law and aunt, she bought a newspaper while waiting to transfer to another bus in Daxi, she circled a few ads in the paper while on board, and when she got off the bus she went straight to a sex café, the owner was sitting at a desk in a back office smoking a cigarette, the first thing he did was ask her to lift her tight skirt so he could see her thighs he then asked her what size skirt she wore and finally had her remove her top so he could check out her breasts, "You're a bit old, but you've taken good care of your face," the owner was straight and to the point, our clients are always curious about "unique races," "You can't let your waist get any thicker than a 25, and don't get any heavier than 108 pounds, if you do we'll put you on probation for a week, and if you don't get rid of the extra weight you'll be asked to leave," each day when she went in to work the first thing they did really was to have her go into a special room where they would take her weight and measurements, but they did make exceptions, they would let it go if the extra weight went into your breasts but you were able to keep the same waistline, "Back then my skin was so fine and white, I got my waist down to a 22 or 23, I kept my weight between 103 and 105 pounds, and made sure that when I went over all the weight stayed in my breasts, everyone wondered how my thin waist could even support my breasts when I walked," it was a good thing that it was a high-class café, they had an expensive menu and took both male and female clients, there were actually much fewer men than women, one of the guys working there was called "Black V" and he was one of their red label service employees, the first time she laid eyes on Black V she knew he had some indigenous blood in him, she was also thrilled when she too made red label status after only a few weeks on the job, once you make red label you can earn more money and the work isn't as hard, in order to please Black V she put on a few pounds weighing in at just under the limit of 108 pounds while maintaining a 23 waistline, all of her clients looked at her breasts first and were then captivated by her "unique

facial features," none of the women who came to hook up with Black
V had "qualities" that could compare with her, one day Black V asked
her out and that night she sampled "the incomparable taste of gentle
sweetness and wild brutality that this Civilized Savage had to offer,"
I asked Girl to hold on for a moment while I ran into my room to
get my notebook, I had heard of "incomparable masterpieces" when
discussing literature but never had I experienced an "incomparable
taste," after hearing so many colorful stories about her life in the city
I was afraid that the white spirits we were drinking would end up
spirited away, I wrote the words "incomparable taste" down in my
notebook, and as I did I imagined whether or not something of incomparable taste was more valuable to the world than an incomparable masterpiece, while I was writing this down Girl stepped out to
pee or perhaps she went into the other room to let Moxi cop a quick
feel, the taste was incomparable being both fresh and mind-blowing
at the same time, there is no reason to say much more about the story
of Black V from the mountains and the Mountain Beauty, at least up
until one day when a super-duper sophisticated-looking man in his
fifties—perhaps he was close to sixty—showed up and after only a
few minutes asked Girl to leave with him, they went into a room in
some big hotel that had an amethyst BioMat mattress where the guy
removed just his suit, but he left his tie and underpants on, the first
thing he did was examine her mountain pussy, and then her grasslike
pubic hair and on to her lakelike belly button, and her beautiful erect
nipples, at last he used his middle finger to carefully feel her forehead, the area around her eyebrows, eyelids, nose, and lips down to
her chin, and then his finger felt its way back up outlining her face,
with the exception of when she did it with Black V she always kept
her eyes closed with other men, she gradually grew a bit uncomfortable by the way his middle finger danced across her face, but at that
moment she heard him speak in a faint but perfectly clear voice,
"After our ancestors spilled so much of their blood in Musha, who

could imagine that their descendents would one day sell themselves in the bed of this hotel," by the time she had figured out what was going on, the man had already put his suit back on, there was a strange look on his face that resembled a smile but it wasn't a smile, he opened the door and left—I took a deep breath of the Riverisle mountain mist, Aha, at long last the plot of this drama had finally connected with my "research about 'the Incident,'" the way of the world is such that I didn't waste my time inviting Girl for a drink nor did the white spirits flow in vain, everything you experience leaves something behind, at the right time everything comes back like the moment Girl's memory came back recounting the exact sentence that man had said to her—she even remembered how to punctuate that sentence, for the rest of that night she just lay there on that amethyst BioMat mattress trying to figure some things out for herself, the next morning she went back to the apartment she was renting and changed into a black pair of shorts and a black T-shirt, she didn't go in to work or even bother saying good-bye to Black V, instead she took a public bus and then walked the rest of the way to the construction site where Daba was working and asked him for a divorce, she imagined that he'd give her two good slaps across the face to show off his warrior spirit and display his authority as her husband, but seeing how good she looked Daba couldn't bring himself to hit her, all the guys from Daba also gathered around to check out how tight her ass was, she calmly recounted the details of her life working in the sex industry after leaving the mountain, she kept going until Daba realized he had to do something to preserve his face as the crew leader, "You fucking bitch!" Daba cursed like a real Chinese, "We the Ci'uli people don't give a shit about sluts like you," they had to sign the paperwork three times before they got it right, she took the forms to two notaries who had an office beside the courthouse and had them complete the paperwork at the Taiyuan Resident Administration Office, and then went straight back to her home village, the only thing she had in her suitcase was a radio and some CDs, "Where did you learn about Chopin?" I asked, Girl explained that the place where she worked as an escort was actually a very classy Western restaurant, "Oh!" I cursed myself for being so stupid, I had forgotten all the different ways the world works: Chopin has his uses. . . . If I may digress for a moment, I would have liked to have offered a detailed comparison of Girl's life in Daba and her life in the city, drawing on experience and imagination I am confident that I would have been able to capture the taste of "gentle sweetness and wild brutality," that way just as readers were being swept away in a moment of passion they would get a shot of sexual stimulation as a catalyst inciting their everyday selves to reach new heights never before achieved, that would be a true form of self-experience, "incomparable" is after all just an empty adjective, but if I may digress a bit further, I would temporarily take leave of Riverisle, I would seek out that classy Western restaurant, I would search for that man called Black V from the mountains she left behind three years earlier and in whom I had now grown so boundlessly interested, Girl said that all of that happened three years ago and in the time since the sun had darkened her shoulders and legs, yet I suspected that Black V was probably there because once he came down from the mountain that was probably the most suitable urban nest he could find for himself, I would find a way to get close to him, observe him, and see what I could sense, at the same time I would ask him: Can the "unique races" of this island nation truly satisfy the men and women of this city? Or is it just a temporary curiosity, as they say, "Good things only come around once, and there is no going back," I especially wanted to find him so I could figure out if he had more male clients than female ones, I suspected that there must be, when this high-mountain man engaged in his spiritually empty high-mountain fucks was the physical sensation really that different? I always thought that it was the spirit that excited the body, and interest in this kind of spiritually devoid sex would wither rather quickly, in the end the mind is indeed quite important for sex, was he thankful for his unique physique and physical assets or was he often wallowing on the margins of regret or was he living this life as a means of mocking himself and others, abusing himself and others, fucking himself and others, one thing for sure was that he would never return to his home village, in the future he would still be hidden away in some urban nest somewhere, but the future wasn't a problem all that mattered was "feeling good in the now," If I could be allowed to extend my "research" with Black V as a research specimen, the first thing I would do is have him do some reading, I'd have him look at some materials, and then ask him whether or not he had any kind of physical or even psychological "complicated complex" when it came to him "penetrating" or "being penetrated" by different races, did this complicated complex ever include a momentary urge to "cut off his partner's head"? a group of crying mourners passed by on the small path outside my back door, I came back from my daydream fantasies about searching for Black V to the parade of mourners before my eyes, a coffin made from thin pine was leading the parade, following behind were twelve or thirteen people, it was that old man who was always serious and reserved who had passed, I suppose he was of the same generation as the tribal elders, but when he drank to a certain point you couldn't get him to stop laughing, he wandered around the reservation aimlessly with a bottle in his hand and whenever he ran into someone he would ecstatically yell, "Do you know how much I love a good drink—" the kind of pure ecstatic joy he exuded was contagious it moved me and it moved my booze, when booze runs into someone who understands it so profoundly you can't go against it have to just take a chance in this human world of ours, as the cold and cheerless funeral procession saw off this ecstatic man, tears and sadness were not necessary, there was the cold and refreshing mountain air and the fragrance of the betel-nut flowers, and later there was the aromatic smell of the plum blossoms, the grave they dug for him was quite shallow that way it would be convenient for him come out and go to the general store when he needed to, it would have been perfect if they had a carnivalesque drinking ritual just before interring him in the ground, a shame that most people don't understand how to live and that isn't just the case here on the reservation, as they lowered the coffin there was one guy who cried so hard that he needed to put his head on my shoulder, through his tears he kept repeating the same thing, "I wasn't born to work on a scaffolding crew, you knew that," perhaps he was the son of the deceased, he felt hatred or regret over the fact that he had wasted his life working on a scaffolding crew, later a woman came over to support him as he left, they were followed by two children around ten years old, the family of the deceased thanked me for attending the funeral, originally I had wanted to hang around the cemetery a bit longer so I would have time to go over some things in my mind, that's when a woman with typical Atayal features walked over to me and gently said, "Let's go back, the dead are never lonely, we don't want to leave you all alone here," I followed her back to the reservation, when we parted ways neither of us said good-bye, we just exchanged a silent glance, I went home and sat down quietly on the front step of my apartment, I thought that the reality of death was perhaps missing the sentence, "Do you know how much I love a good drink!" That is why deep down I feel such pity and affection for Girl, Little Daya, Black V, and the young deer eyes, I would like to give them all an economically stable family, with a good learning environment, with their natural gifts and good looks they would probably surpass the achievements of most young city kids down in the plains, of those who really make something of themselves in society, these "unique races" would account for a huge proportion of those who excel here on this island nation, many years earlier I had encountered a young girl from the "Cao minority," a Pangcah girl, that's when I first had this thought, more than ten years later I was living deep in the mountains of Dawu when I ran into Mr. Rukai Kadresengane,[29] that experience made me even more convinced that I was right, for decades, the semipolitical society of this island nation intentionally overlooked their potential and discriminated against their rights, by the time the privileged class began to self-reflect and curse themselves or others as "male chauvinist Chinese pigs," indigenous groups had already been at the very bottom of the social ladder for so long that it was virtually impossible for them to reverse their situation, for the sake of celebrating with a close friend so drunk that he was about to enter a state of ecstasy, filled with thought I strolled to the general store for some white spirits, there were a few middle-aged men hanging out drinking under the veranda at the general store, when they saw me they all called me over, "Since you came here from the city to do research, we need you to set things straight for us," one of them with completely white hair and salt-and-pepper whiskers all over his face spoke loudly, "We are all the same age and always hang out and drink together, we just don't want to be corrupted by those Chinese variety shows, we don't wanna end up varietized, look at the younger generation they've all been varietized, don't ya think it's strange that it took less than thirty years for this to happen, varietization has already destroyed 60 or 70 percent of our original Seediq culture, but not one of our political candidates ever takes 'de-varietization' as a political position, so for this current election, we are just collecting money but not voting," at that moment a cold voice interrupted, at first I couldn't tell who it was, "What's all this garbage about the great cultural melting pot they're talking about? They put straws in their shitty fucking variety shows, expecting us to suck it all up until we're all fucking brain-dead idiots!" I felt dizzy just listening to him, it was a good thing they gave me a glass of Mr. Brown's with some hard white spirits to keep me from completely passing out, weren't they here to celebrate the white spirit fairy? So how did they end up talking about varietization? This is a topic for Academia Sinica's[30]

Institute of Sociology and Research Center for Information Technology Innovation to collaborate on and they would also have to borrow materials from the Institute of Ethnology, Do I need to varietize myself by pretending to be an idiot in order to get them to laugh as a means of apologies on behalf of "our popular variety shows"? Let me repeat once again, "I never watch any variety shows, even down in the plains, if I find myself catching sight of one on television in a shopping arcade or while in a store I always quickly shut my eyes," all the middle-aged men applauded my bravery, and only after toasting me with several glasses of rice wine mixed with Mr. Brown did they finally let me go, this variety show intermission made me forget what I had gone to the general store for in the first place, I stood beside the bamboo forest for a while before I finally remembered I had come to pick up some celebratory wine for Mr. Ecstatic, but by then I didn't dare go back to the convenience store, what if they started asking me about the structure and content of different variety shows, about which I wouldn't have a damn research-worthy thing to say, anyway there were more than enough drinking buddies on this reservation, even if I couldn't even reach the point of that place of ecstasy it was at least enough to console Mr. Ecstatic, "People always drink for a reason, or they use drinking to escape from something," Mr. Ecstatic had only just now been laid down to rest and yet he was busy instructing everyone on the reservation, "If you ask why one drinks, you will never achieve that state of drinking into sublimity," I started to self-reflect on why I chose white spirits as my liquor, I made my way out of the bamboo forest, not far off in the distance was Mahong's house, they day before I had made a special trip to the police station to ask an officer where it was, he took out an illustrated map of all the houses on the reservation and pointed it out to me, perhaps it was only owing to the power of Mr.Brown-rice wine that I was finally able to get so close to Mahong, even though she had died so many years earlier, but ever since I started reading historical records about the incident many years before, every time I encountered Mahong's name a strange bewitching magic seemed to come over me, Mahong's adopted daughter opened the door, instinctively I could sense that the blood of Mona did not run through her veins, she was probably sick of people knocking on her door doing research or asking about Mahong, she seemed a bit flustered at first but then invited me in to sit down on a rattan chair in the shade, she began by making two things clear all the while her face absolutely expressionless, the first thing was that she wasn't going to answer any questions, and secondly she could only talk about Mahong's later years, "My mother lived to be quite old, but in some sense she died with 'the Incident,'" everyone in the tribe knew that she would often go missing during her later years, she would go off walking alone in the direction of Musha, she was searching for Mona Rudao's final resting place, she wanted to hang herself from a tree, to hang over the spot where her father took his own life, that way she could give her father some shade, "Even after 'the Incident' Mahong was still stuck living in 'the Incident,'" she was unable to forget 'the Incident' or leave it behind, even though all kinds of people said and did all kinds of things to calm Mahong down and help her live a normal life, but in the thirty years after 'the Incident,' all the way up until the time of her death, never for one second could she leave it behind, the reason I am stressing this is because I want to show you the extent to which the blood feud of our Ancestral Spirits completely dominated Mahong's life," the oppressive weight of this blood feud made her lose her mind, she began to do all kinds of peculiar things, "Mahong never accepted God into her life, and she taught me never to accept him too, Priest did everything he could to convince her to come to church hoping that she could serve as a model for the entire reservation, but my mother said that God's 'love' had nothing to do with her 'blood feud,'" Each night at dusk the Ancestral Spirits would cross Valleystream and enter Mahong's dreams, when she awoke from her dreams all she cared about was what the Ancestral Spirits had ordered her to carry out. I lost myself in Mahong's dreams, there were a few clear images that tied together Mahong's life, thank goodness that Mona Rudao had a daughter like Mahong, his Remains of Life wandered for more than four decades after his death before arriving at their final resting place, I have always strongly suspected Mahong of intentionally misidentifying her father's body after it was discovered, history only records superficial facts about the incident but it is unable to face all of the minute details, but I believe Mahong wanted her father to forever rest deep in the forests of Mhebu never to be discovered or disturbed, the rulers were eager to shower Mahong with praise and hastily went through with the identification of the remains, so every year on the anniversary of the Incident when everyone pays their respects at the memorial who knows who is really buried there, perhaps only he knows, I told myself that I needed to go out for more walks, otherwise just sitting at home drinking white spirits all day would end up drowning out all this "historical suspense," otherwise how can you explain the fact that even in her later years Mahong continued to sneak out in the early morning hours each day and head toward Mhebu, the final resting place of her father and brother, she must have known that they were still there, and thank goodness that Mahong Mona brought a bottle of White Crane rice wine deep into the forest in order to induce her brother Da'ou Mona to surrender, only in our imagination can we witness the celebration of death that took place during "the Incident," beneath the branches from which they planned to hang themselves they first lost themselves in the pleasure of dance, singing the songs of their ancestors and dancing the traditional dances of their ancestors, drinking their enemy's wine, they were to use this unbridled carnivalistic celebration to bring their lives to an end, history only records the actions of these historical figures but is unable to penetrate their souls, Mahong surely entered the forest intent on convincing her brother Da'ou to surrender, after all there wasn't "anything" that his life was worth throwing away over, it wasn't that she wanted to turn Da'ou into a brave warrior, but did Mahong ever imagine that even after Da'ou surrendered, it would still be death that awaited him, his only option for survival would be to become a "puppet for propaganda," but would his "value as a puppet" be enough to allow him to service the great purge that would come a year later? And even if he were to escape with his life, his life as a puppet would force him to face Mahong's tears, and he would be harshly judged by history along with his contemporaries, I would have approved of Da'ou hanging himself at the end of the celebration, actually no, I probably would have also helped Mahong persuade him not to do it, for even if there is only one path left to take in order to stay alive one must take it, being reproached by one's contemporaries and censured by history are all quickly forgotten "in time," life is only bright and vibrant if you are alive, if Mr. Da'ou could have survived as a puppet until the end of World War II, right now I would be paying a visit to an elderly Da'ou and Mahong, and not her adopted daughter, "Can you reach a state of ecstasy if you drink in the name of celebration?" I asked from a distance as I strolled down the small path near the cemetery, is drinking in the name of celebration the same thing as celebrating in the name of drinking? I would have gladly held a crazed celebration for the siblings Da'ou and Mahong had they lived to see out the century, Daya Mona would have showed up with Latino Seediq on his arm all the away from South America to be a part of the festivities, if only Mahong hadn't spent her later years lost in "the Incident," I walked to the end of the plum garden and continued on along the slope of the rear mountain, at times you couldn't even make out whether or not there was really a path, I then followed a small path arriving at an open betel-nut garden, the beautiful betel-nut trees near and far stood at different heights and the graves that were scattered around nearby and in the distance resembled bonsai plants, the rich fragrance of betel nuts filled the air, combining with the sweet distant smell of plums, I felt that it would be okay if my path in life were to end right here—I brewed a pot of strong coffee in my teapot, it was the kind of strong coffee I needed before getting to work, today in Riverisle I needed to face "the interactive relationship between hunters and their heads before and after the ritual," Granny in the house diagonally across from me was outside in her garden pulling weeds and watering the plants, the flowery pattern from her shirt and the deep yellow of the back of her shorts kept flashing before my window, she was born in Mhebu and was exiled here when she was only three years old, her son and grandchildren visit on the weekends and they told me that the farthest she ever goes from here is to Puli to pick up medicine from her pharmacy, so she never witnessed a ritual headhunt, those hunters still living who have taken part in a head-hunt must be over 100 years old by now, that is with the exception of a few Toda men in their nineties who may have taken part in the Second Musha Incident, during my second visit to Nadafu Toda, he was already less welcoming than during my first visit, perhaps it was because I didn't have the credentials of having a "national level" orga-nization vouching for me, or perhaps it was because he felt that he had already fulfilled his duty of "fully divulging everything he knew" about the incident to me last time, over the course of my Musha Inci-dent "fieldwork," I discovered a common tendency, those living at the site where I was carrying out my fieldwork and even those who had some personal connection to the Incident all felt it was "in the distant past" even though in reality it was less than seventy years ago, they felt it was their duty to go through the motions and share what they knew about what happened, most of what they said was quite similar and all very limited, it was difficult for me to acquire the kind of details not found in historical records that one needs for fieldwork, I sus-pect that dark shadow of the "blood feud" that Mahong spoke of still lingers in people's hearts, I asked Nadafu if he could introduce me to a member of the Toda tribe who had taken part in the Second Musha Incident, "There's almost none of them left," Nadafu knitted his mountain river brow, I immediately latched on to the world "almost," "There's almost none, but there must be a few who are quite old?" "I despise the shrewdness of you civilized people," Nadafu smiled, "It's not that we don't know how to be like that, we simply don't want to, ever since childhood our parents taught us to never lie and to never steal," among the three Toda tribes there is certainly someone with headhunting experience that is still alive, but who knows maybe that person moved to Hualian, Nadafu wanted to know what I planned to ask about if I found someone, he was quite reluctant to intrude by bringing a stranger to call on him, "But this person took part in a headhunt," I was trying everything I could, "That's true, and that's a fact that has somehow become very important to some people," history has already interrogated them, but now it was time for "contemporary history" to interrogate them again and provide a judgment, Nadafu finally agreed to take me to someone, because "these days there aren't many people who still care about our past, when people from our tribe try making it for themselves in the cities it is as if they are a people without a past," we went from where we were and followed Muddy River upstream as far as we could go until we arrived at Placid Reservation, "I used to live downstream at Chunyang, but as far as I know there aren't any old people there like the ones you are looking for, and I certainly don't have any relatives in my family with that kind of experience," Placid Reservation was built on a flat plot of land on the mountainside along the banks of Muddy River, it is surrounded by mountains more than 2,000 meters high, there were only three rows of houses, we walked a lap around the street, Nadafu asked an elderly woman weaving something in their native language, the woman shook her head and smiled, "They don't have any tattooed men on this reservation!" Nadafu said, and so we immediately set out for Tranquil Reservation, "Women her age know everyone on the reservation, and old women like her don't know how to tell a lie," Nadafu explained to me in the car on the way there, Tranquil Reservation was quite expansive, houses were built practically on top of each other along the slope of the mountain, in front of the reservation there was a dirt sports field, it even had a 200-meter running track, Nadafu told me that for the past few years they had been holding many of their traditional festivals and celebrations at Tranquil Reservation's sports field, "the Toda people all feel that this reservation has the best natural scenery and the houses here are also the most unique," Nadafu went straight into the police station and spoke to them in his native language for a while, he even showed them his work ID so they would know he was the kind of Toda they shouldn't ignore, after that the officer in charge said something, I saw the way the veins in Nadafu's nose twitched on his placid face and I knew that we had something, "There's an old man here after all," Nadafu knit his brow as he smiled, "However for a long time there have been orders in place, unless it is for truly important matters he is not to be disturbed, there used to be a few old guys like that around, but now he is the only one left," it was clear that the people in charge were wavering about whether or not to let us visit, I suggested to Nadafu that we buy a gift and pay him a visit to show our respect, we'll just shake his hand that way we won't have to waste his time or energy, Nadafu passed this on to the man in charge, he immediately agreed, he even gave us instructions in Mandarin, "For the gift, just buy him two bottles of rice wine," Old Man was sitting outside getting some sun, he was wearing a jacket made from the skin of either a panther or a leopard cat, he had ritual tattoos on his forehead and chin, he popped open a bottle and gave us each a betel nut, Nadafu waited until Old Man had drunk three glasses before saying anything, Old Man took one listen and violently shook his head, after that he started to rapidly say a bunch of things I couldn't understand, "I just directly asked him whether or not he had ever removed the skin from a head," Nadafu explained as he chewed on his betel nut, "The old man said that he never did, he said that all the heads decapitated during the Musha Incident were confiscated, he actually turned in some heads for a reward," Old Man said he was ninety-six years old as was clearly written on his residence card, I did a quick calculation and figured out that he was already thirty years old and an elite member of the tribe when "the Incident" broke out, he definitely played a significant role, and there was indeed a policy whereby heads could be exchanged for a cash reward, but did he take part in any headhunts before "the Incident"? Perhaps, "The old man stands by the fact that he himself never did, he only did it during "the Incident" but then so did everybody, he said that the authorities were quite strict on headhunting and anyone caught would have to pay with their life, this was an official policy," Old Man started to hum a song, he drank six or seven glasses of the rice wine, "The old man says that is the headhunt song they sang the night before the headhunt, it doesn't mean anything, but that's the melody of the song," I could tell that Nadafu himself was actually quite interested in this "research," but his normal job limited how much time and energy he could spend on it, "The old man says that his memories about what happened that time in Musha are still quite clear, he was responsible for taking three or four heads, three at the least, the third was the most difficult to sever, it took so long that he almost lost his own head in the process," I wanted to ask him what it felt like to cut off someone's head, frankly speaking I'm quite curious about what the process of "severing a neck" is like, "severing a neck is just like severing a chicken's neck, you have to first sever the carotid artery, and you have to come into the neck at a straight angle otherwise it will be very difficult to cut off, the old man says that the feeling one gets from cutting off a head is an incomparable happiness, it is indescribable—" in the distance we could see the head of the police station coming over, Nadafu stood up and gave Old Man a good long handshake until the officer got close, then it was my turn to shake Old Man's hand before we bade him farewell, as we walked away we could hear the old man mutter a few more sentences and he started to hum that headhunt song again, the station manager explained that Old Man lived alone and was under state protection, usually it was very difficult to understand him when he spoke, and he certainly never sang any songs, "Next time you visit things will be a bit smoother if you can bring an official letter of introduction," we followed the road that ran alongside Muddy River down the mountain, due to his work Nadafu had been living in the large town of Puli for many years, "It's not that he was difficult to understand, it's just that no-body bothers taking the time to talk to him," Nadafu sighed, "Almost every reservation has a few old men and women like him living on their own, they can't bear to leave behind their old homes or the old environment that they are used to, if they moved to the city they would never be able to adjust and they probably wouldn't live as long," I sat in silence as I chewed on that sentence, "The feeling one gets from cutting off a head is an incomparable happiness, it is inde-scribable," when we were almost back to the small town Nadafu laughed and said, "Actually if you want to know how to skin a person there is no reason to go so far, all you have to do is ask me, all the men in my family from my father and grandfather on back all took part in headhunts and knew how to skin a human head," I said good-bye at the bus station of the small town, and I thanked Nadafu, Nadafu also thanked me for caring about his people "even if I was motivated by other factors," He was certain that the Old Man from the Toda tribe we met had a delightful time chatting with us, which was quite rare for him during his usually quiet days, on the way back to Riverisle I figured that whatever Nadafu knows must be from leg-ends passed down from father and grandfather, whatever I know is from legends passed down from other people's fathers and grand-fathers in addition to various printed historical materials and I proba-

bly knew just as much as Nadafu knew, yet I needed to leave home
and go deep into the mountains to see for myself a real live "head-
hunter" sitting in the sun and humming a headhunt song, I shook
the hand that he had once used to sever heads, I felt the blood pulsating through his wrist, only by doing that can my writing surpass
"research" and surge forward—He was there waiting on the white
snowy mountain slope, waiting for his beloved, the snow came down
heavier, yet he insisted on waiting for his beloved, a tall young figure
appeared on the mountain slope, standing beneath a petrified pine,
"My beloved, the one I love, the one who loves me," "Finally we can
be together never to be separated again, come home with me in happiness!" Oh beautiful girl, beautiful girl Oh . . . it must have been an
indigenous high mountain love song, the snow was pure white like
the snow on Qilai Mountain and Reunion Mountain, this island
nation's pop singers can take a timeless high mountain love song
like this and sing it like a fin-de-siècle rock ballad, you can just see
the thousands of asses in the audience swaying in unison to the melody, but this is actually a "headhunt song" from the beginning of the
century or perhaps the end of the previous century, he lies in wait on
the mountain slope waiting to decapitate "his beloved," waiting until
"the one who loves me" appears, and after a battle in the snow, he cuts
off the head of his beloved, and at last he who loves and he who is
loved are together never to be separated again, the beloved goes home
with him in happiness, this is a scene that can only be expressed by a
beautiful young girl, the beautiful girl is pure and innocent, the lyrics
were not composed by a primitive Atayal poet, they came from the
beautiful snow-white soul of an Atayal woman, she transformed
the act of brutal killing into an act of pure and beautiful love, like the
enchanting song of a witch summoning the spirits of the dead, and
capturing the wisdom and humor of life, when readers encounter a
"headhunt song" like this, the contemporary will know that this is a
race with a mature "primitive civilization," they know how to take

knowledge and wisdom and make humor of them, the contemporary should consider how to adapt these songs into a retro-style power ballad without losing their original meaning or flavor, as a means of deepening our island nation's inherent cultural worth, when he brings his beloved home, he loudly announces the joyful news as he nears the reservation, and indeed all the beautiful young girls come out to welcome him, they surround his "beloved head" singing and dancing, this continues until sweat soaks all the way down the cracks of their asses and into their souls and until their trancelike state reaches the point that they completely lose themselves, at this point something leaves their bodies and something else enters their bodies, they become one with their Ancestral Spirits, heaven and earth, and their beloved, they unconsciously continue their crazed orgy of dance and song until dusk when the sun falls, the hunter ignites a pine torch and carrying the head enters the reservation, at that point an even larger welcome ceremony begins, everyone in the tribe comes out to surround the precious head, wine is passed around among all of the "true men" as all the women sing and dance, the children run over to get a good close-up look at the head, the women's dance reaches a frenzied state, and the men drink with abandon, the high mountains silently watch as those people who are usually so quiet push their bustling clamor as far as they can take it before giving the mountains their silence back, only that hunter stands apart with one hand grasping his prized head and the other hand wrapped around the waist of his wife or one of the dancing young girls as he starts to walk toward his house, he sets down the head facing the window, and opens the closed eyes prying the eyelids open with his fingers, or for those who "died with their eyes open" he forcibly pulls them open three or four times their normal size, his excitement continues until he enters the body of his wife or that young girl at which point he realizes that having his beloved watch him have sex is naturally at least three or four times more exciting than normal and so he contin-

ues until the shady gray light of early dawn sketches out a fresh new
face with all its features inspiring him to bravely fight on until the
final climax when he comes and finally falls fast asleep, I really have
no idea nor can I even imagine whether or not that beautiful young
girl would truly fall in love with the head that witnessed her having
sex, perverts have been around since ancient times and abnormal
psychology is not just a modern phenomenon, but once this can be
confirmed it will be between the hunter and the head, the next night
the wife will need a good night's sleep, the first reason is she had been
singing and dancing so hard the previous day, the second reason is
after bravely fighting on all the way up until dawn her vagina was so
swollen that it hurt to walk, you can imagine that if he had sex with
that young girl she would need to lie in bed for three nights and four
days, only after she went home would she realize that a part of her
body was swollen shut, the first thing the hunter would have to do is
figure out a way to close the eyes of his beloved head after it had witnessed the all-night carnival of "centennial sex," that should after all
feel that what it witnessed was worthy of its eyes, after that he would
present a bowl of rice and a glass of rice wine, as his beloved ate he
would keep him company by talking to him, "Thanks so much for
coming, at first you might not be used to it here, but I'll take good
care of you, the Ancestral Spirits are also quite happy that you are
here," or "Thanks for staying, everyone here on the reservation knows
I have you my dear, and neither the young nor the old will every look
down on me again, we will be eating and drinking buddies, I hope
you continue to bring me good luck, please tell your relatives and everyone from your tribe, we provide food and drink here, we'd love it if
you'd bring more of your friends next time," you can imagine how
boring things were for the hunter when he wasn't hunting, but now
he had a beloved head to keep him company, and plenty of handiwork to keep him busy, who knows how much of his primitive time
would be spent just on plucking out his Beloved's hair one strand at a

time, he also needed to frequently wash his Beloved or else his wife wouldn't let him lay a hand on her, gradually the skin on his Beloved's face would start to rot, at this point the hunter would have to decide whether or not to just bury it or continue on with his handiwork, if he wanted to bury it he would have to find a secret love nest for his Beloved, and he would still have to bring his Beloved three meals a day and spend time chatting with him, if he continued his handiwork and removed the skin then he would have to first find a piece of the treasured Sacred Stone from Valleystream, it would be used to gently shave away the skin from his Beloved's face, this stage of the work needed to be completed alone in secret, his wife and everyone else on the reservation would pretend that they didn't know what he was doing, occasionally the Sacred Stone would hurt his skin and the Beloved would have a tantrum refusing to eat or drink and that night the Ancestral Spirits would come to warn the hunter not to be disrespectful to the Beloved, who knows how much of his primitive time would again be spent on this stage of the process, it must have taken at least two years, during this time the hunter was the only one to see the head face to face, you can imagine that over the course of keeping the head company and talking with it they established quite an "interactive relationship," if there had been a tape recorder to record the conversation between a hunter and "his beloved head when he was keeping it company" it not only would have had great research value for contemporary academics but also would have surely been a best-seller throughout the centuries, finally after two years, a beautiful skull would emerge, two years of handiwork would make his Beloved's skull a gorgeous beauty, after all that hard work the overwhelming sense of accomplishment he feels during the ceremony where his Beloved finally joins the other skulls on the tribal head rack is such that he actually secretly sheds a few tears. . . . When I was nearly forty years old and participated in the rite of shigu,[31] where I excavated my mother's bones to rebury them, only after I saw her skull after it had been buried for nineteen years did I genuinely discover how dear and adorable skulls can be, just as mainland Chinese immigrants from southern Fujian to this island nation have a "complicated complex" when it comes to the site of *shigu*, the Seediq Atayal's "interactive relationship between hunters and their beloved heads" is also riddled with a complicated and tangled complex, on the reservation women and children, the young and old all went from being terrified at the sight of these bloody heads to gradually feeling close to them and eventually they came to see them as just another part of their normal everyday life, we should give credit to the natural education program designed by the primitive, for it allowed headhunting to become an important honorable and perfectly ordinary affair, it enabled the entire tribe to transform into an integrated "headhunting community," and they used this to protect themselves while threatening and sometimes even invading other tribes, amid a cycle of never-ending tribal warfare, this powerful headhunting community managed to protect themselves and ensure their survival, at the same time they were also awarded certain benefits, the "wonder" of humanity is revealed not only through the brutal violence of war, this wonder is also revealed when a great hunter brings food and wine to his Beloved head each day and takes the time to chat with it, but is this a kind of "self-redemption" or just a "primitive game"? Speaking on behalf of the contemporary I cannot be certain, because these ideas and terms were all only adopted much later, the actions of primitive man were always much more simple, much more in line with their natural instincts, but even after "primitive civilization" has matured, "When I cut off your head, it's because I love you, and you shall always know that there is someone who will love you until death, and that is the only reason you walked over to that petrified pine on that snowy day, you barely resisted, you died for love, let us sing and dance in the name of love until our hearts break, you are the love of my life, only I truly understand you, so many things I said to you, I shall never utter those words to another, only you understand my heart, the love I feel for you even if you should one day end up on my skull rack, whenever I get close I immediately recognize you just as you immediately recognize me, tomorrow I shall bring you fresh food and wine, and you know that when I hold my wife in my arms each night, it is you that I think about, it is you that I am holding—" I think these true-to-life words would serve well as a monologue from a 1980s Little Theater production,[32] during the ceremony marking the transition from the end of one century to the beginning of another, I recommended that "the contemporary" use this very passage to serve as the opening remarks to be delivered on behalf of Generation Z, it was both dialectical and antidialectical at the same time, and it has both postmodernist and anti-postmodernist connotations. For several days now I have been lost in my notebook and writing, sometimes by the time I decide to go out for a walk it is already dusk, it is even more common for me to wake up so late that I don't even hear the third cackle of the rooster, I stay up so late so I can enjoy that moment when the cold mountain air comes in through the window and penetrates inside me, even at a very young age I realized that deep inside me was a kind of indifference, not just indifference, but a coldness, after I got older I seemed to naturally adjust to spending time alone, whenever I was with friends or a group of people for a while I would always start to crave some time alone, best if I could scurry back to my own lonely nest, after my student days, I had almost no friends, "Aren't you lonely?" people would ask out of concern, I would just laugh, solitude knows nothing of loneliness, perhaps it was that cold mountain air that somehow struck a chord with my solitude, the next time I went back to Riverisle was during late autumn of the following year, I told people I went back for the Remains of Life who had survived after "the Incident," in actuality it was because I missed sitting in front of my desk at dusk, I missed the cold air that enshrouded my mattress at bedtime, that cold mountain air, it had the same feeling as my solitude, the same aura, as I took down my notes I skipped over Black V, when it comes to characters like Black V who "accept both men and women" I can directly write about them from the inside, but it was instead what was said to Girl while lying on that hotel's amethyst BioMat that led her to turn herself around, that threw my memorandum into disarray, that sentence was a line right out of an erotic historical drama with a rotten modern ending, it had an overwhelming melodramatic force while at the same time being completely hysterical, does anyone even talk like that in real life? Even in this island nation's number one metropolitan city I doubt you could ever find anyone sophisticated enough to utter those words, In that kind of a setting, uttering those words must have been his way of expressing his laments about life, his mockery of history or his compassion for the world, or perhaps he just couldn't get his cock hard enough to penetrate her, or perhaps he realized that no matter how he penetrated her he would never be able to "move" her, and so in the spur of the moment he decided to use a single sentence to penetrate her and get deep inside her, I'm willing to believe that it was that one single sentence that moved Girl to the point that it penetrated deep inside the core of her being, I don't accept the fact that Black V abandoning her suddenly made her see through all the darkness and lies of the big city and drove her to return to her home in the bosom of the high mountains I don't buy that trashy plot for a second, that sentence touched upon "the Incident," it also tied in to the Remains of Life who continued on in the wake of "the Incident," I felt quite awkward for a while, I wrote down that sentence exactly as I heard it, I didn't miss a single word because I wanted it to be an accurate record of one's life, at some point I'm not sure when, I heard the sound of someone at the front door calling my name, I listened again, it was Girl, she knows that I often sit at the desk near the rear window writing, yet she never comes to the back door when she's looking for me,

and when I awake in the middle of the night and see the shadowy
images of betel-nut trees reflected on the wall I never have to worry
that there might be someone standing there, "I want to go for a stroll
down to Valleystream to have a look," she asked if I had time to go
with her, "This time I'll teach you the names of all the fish," as I put
on my shirt I asked her why Moxi wasn't going, she said that he was
still in bed and needed more sleep, "He loves to caress me, every night
he strokes my body until I'm sound asleep," Christmas was less than
a week away, I shook my head, Girl's "days of sleeping soundly were
numbered," Girl wore a hippie handbag over her shoulder, a short,
tight black silk skirt, a short cream-colored undershirt, all of her
clothes looked brand new, "I left my old bathing suit inside, along
with my old stuff," she could read what I was thinking just by looking in my eyes, with the utmost sincerity I told her how her cream-
colored undershirt really brought out the dark beautiful complexion of her shoulders and back, Girl told me that Atayal girls all
have naturally broad shoulders, but in the four years since she'd
been back home they had grown even broader, Girl reached up and
put her hands behind her neck, her think underarm hair stood out
against her cream-colored undershirt, "We Atayal women seem to
have really thick underarm hair," without even looking Girl seemed
to notice where my gaze was falling, "Let me tell you a joke," whenever those hostess girls in the city raised their arms she noticed that
they were all perfectly smooth and shaved, and for the first time in
her life she started to feel embarrassed by her underarm hair, but that
day after the boss "inspected" her he made sure to tell her, "Whatever
you do, don't shave your underarms, that's a special rule for you,"
later she realized that one of the main reasons she was so popular had
to do with her thick underarm hair, women think that men like
smooth clean-shaven underarms but that's all too common, thick underarm hair like hers was itself the ultimate manifestation of sexual
desire, I never imagined that I would get sidetracked by underarm

hair, Girl also started to sense that I had gone on too long about it, "Look at me, just because you're a researcher, I totally let my guard down when it comes to research," Girl smiled, I said, "But your under-arm hair is indeed quite pretty," we cut through some small trees and a bean garden and arrived at the riverbed, "Even if it's pretty, the per-son still has to invite you to look," Girl walked straight out into the water, "The river water isn't as deep as usual," she stood there gazing upstream looking out toward the mountain in the distance, "When I was a little girl I always believed that one day I would walk all the way up to the peak of that mountain," "Me too, when I was a kid I could see a series of tall mountains far out in the distance from our front window, I often imagined that after I grew up . . ." for Girl that was a real possibility, but I don't think I ever would have ever had the stam-ina to make it, "after I grew up I realized that those mountains were part of the Reunion Mountain and Xilai Mountain chains, what about your mountain?" "It's in the Jade Mountain range," I walked into the water wearing my flip-flops, the river water was cold and crisp, "Jade Mountain Reunion Mountain Xilai Mountain, we're practically neighbors!" "Of course we're neighbors!" Girl said that one day when she was around twelve or thirteen years old she snuck out of the house during her mother's afternoon nap, with a bamboo basket strapped to her back she headed out past the rear mountains toward Valleystream with the sole intention of walking all the way to the very end and who knows perhaps she would never return, un-der the stars she tripped and stumbled several times, she had sev-eral cuts and scrapes from her falls yet she kept going, eventually she started crying for the end to come soon how far would she have to walk before she would arrive at the distant mountains, she remem-bered how strict her mother was, she never dared to go outside with-out asking permission first, I would often sit in a secluded corner of the back courtyard digging with a small drill bit, among my other tools was a shovel and the sharpest knife from the kitchen and I

could sit there digging all afternoon, "I wanted to dig into the deepest part of the soil, and then go deeper to see when was down there,
my greatest ambition was to dig to the very bottom, until I could find
a cat face or a human face on the other side," "How could there be a
cat down there?" "Cats are the most clever and mysterious of all the
animals, with the exception of my mother, I always believed that I
was born to a cat, I would start digging over here, and our cat would
know to start digging with me over there—don't you often see cats
digging in the soil?" Girl laughed, one afternoon I woke up and
decided to just hang out in bed, outside the window I noticed Girl
sitting on the stoop outside the front door feeding a cat a handful of
wild vegetables she had picked, the cat was clearly eating the vegetables, at one point Girl's eyes met the cat's eyes as she held a piece of
lettuce between them and that was one of those moments in my life
when "everything stopped," during my time living in seclusion in
Danshui, there were usually at least a few cats that I took care of,
around three of four o'clock each afternoon I would often get hungry, I
would pick up a half a loaf of bread nearby and sit on the doorstep
facing Danshui's Goddess of Mercy as I ate my bread, all the stray cats
in the neighborhood would immediately surround me, "Kitty," I
would say, "have some bread!" the cats would sit there watching
me, I tried to break off a few pieces to feed the kitties, I never imagined that they would like it, from then on every day there was afternoon bread time with me and the cats, "I have raised both dogs and
cats, I never differentiated domesticated cats and stray cats, the dog
was my brother's, but he asked me to take special care of him," I wonder
how stray cats up in the mountains feel about life, are they more
enlightened than those stray cats in the city who feed on garbage,
we waded through the water for quite a ways before arriving at the
Great Rock that Girl spoke of, the flat platform on top of the rock
is where Girl would often sit and fish, the area behind the rock is
where Girl would change into her swimsuit, she wore a brand-new

orange bathing suit that she hadn't yet worn into the water, she left the barbecuing to me, but she couldn't wait to get into the water, beneath the Great Rock was a pool that was like a deep cave, I didn't hear a single peep from Girl about how cold the water was, after a while I faintly made out her voice, "The water's so cold, so cold, it hurts, but it kind of feels good," I didn't turn around and instead just quietly flipped the sausage, meat, and sweet potatoes on the portable grill, I put the taro roots off to one side, before long Girl climbed up to the top of the Great Rock to sit down, "There are less fish in winter, there is a kind of fish called the bitter melon fish that has completely disappeared," the bright orange against her dark skin was an almost perfect combination, once the river water washed over her skin she had once again returned to nature, I gazed at her bare curvy legs, back, and shoulders, how refined and exquisite are nature's creations, it is only natural for people to lean toward refinement, when I write for instance it is only natural for me to enter a "refined state," I have to occasionally remind myself to "relax, relax," after all it is impossible to achieve perfection, perfection is nothing but a fantasy constructed by human consciousness, but refinement is a possibility and humans adore refinement however the human heart cannot tolerate too much refinement, refinement must occasionally take a break from itself with a bit of crudeness, or create some space for crudeness, only then can refinement sustain itself and become the leading force of civilization, which had originally been the "will" or "unintentionality" of nature, "I want to return to Valleystream, today I'll start by having a look," Girl opened up half a sweet potato to go with her shredded meat, her breasts were competing with the mountain peaks for my attention as they revealed their form through her wet bathing suit, "You like the view?" Girl laughed, "just don't take *me* as part of your research," I asked her if they started getting that big when she was a teenager? Girl said they were about the same size then, but after she had her kids they became engorged and later they seemed to get even bigger after wearing tight lingerie every day, "once back home on the reservation I did a lot of manual labor, and that seemed to help them naturally get back to the size and firmness from when I was young, "That's because there's nothing between us," there were a lot of things that Girl couldn't help but say directly to me, naturally I could also ask whatever I felt like asking, "Nothing between us," I said, as I passed Girl another piece of sausage, "Our bodies and behavior are both too far removed from nature," by bodies she was naturally referring to men's bodies, but behavior she was probably referring to how men handle various situations, but Girl couldn't express herself in too much detail using Mandarin Chinese, instead I needed to try to understand the deeper meaning behind her simple sentences, "Men never made me feel disheartened, only their bodies did," I'd seen Atayal men trying to flatter Girl by complimenting her on her looks, I imagine that they were not doing that "in the name of sex," but it was instead part of their nature, it was their innate good side, but changing times had transformed the meaning of their lives, and with this change in meaning so too their tribal spirit transformed, it had been seventy or eighty years since Atayal men had used the term "brave" to describe themselves, seventy or eighty years is almost an entire lifetime and more than enough time to erase any remaining imprint of their tribe, it took only five decades for this island nation to ask for a new and independent symbol to capture the new spirit of this island nation, Atayal men's bravery was naturally eaten away until they ended up "normal just like everyone else," it is this normality that helps maintain harmony among men, from a "contemporary" humanistic perspective Atayal men won't leave women disappointed, but my contemporary has trouble understanding the following sentence, "Men's bodies should be natural, but when they're supposed to be natural they never are, at the most they're only 60 or 70 percent natural," Girl's timely explanation left open the possibility for further interpretation, reflecting on

Girl's past, she and the men from Daba were stuck in a messy sexual relationship, she naturally accepted the sex that Daba deep in the mountains had given her, but there wasn't much else, Daba wasn't just a place it also represented the people there, but even if she had stayed in the city things still wouldn't have been simple, Girl may one day forget but her body will always remember, after that she went back to the city and worked in the sex industry there for two years, she saw every trick in the book when it came to sex, the sexual civilization she experienced in the city may have temporarily stimulated her but it could never compare with nature's primitive ways, "City-boy Black V" may have gotten up to 80 or 90 percent but he had to rely on his addiction to sexual enhancement drugs, by the time Girl went back to her hometown for three years and had gotten herself back in shape, pure primitive natural sex once again became the only kind that satisfied her, a shame then that just as Atayal men's bravery had been eaten away they simultaneously accepted "civilized sex," civilized sex taught them many new tricks for the bedroom, but at the same time it gradually ate away at their "primitive sex," all that was left of their primitive sexual positions was doggy-piggy style, but that single primitive position wasn't enough to take them to that "pure natural state" that was once theirs, I pretended to think "perhaps too many tricks in the bedroom takes energy away from doing the deed," "Exactly," in her excitement Girl threw a piece of taro down on the rock, "they even use this and that all kinds of toys as if women are toys, heaven knows that I've known for years that women don't need any of those things, all a woman wants is a man to really fuck her hard, and pray to God he doesn't cum too fast," I was afraid that in her excitement Girl's words might go beyond the standards of my novel, although "the contemporary" has long taught me that there are no standards when it comes to contemporary literature, "Research has shown that premature ejaculation is a common phenomenon," "You're right about that, some guys cum as soon as their pricks touch my pubic hair, but even more of them can only last twenty or thirty seconds once they get inside me," "It's a good thing that they invented Viag-whatever-you-call-it for men," "In nature no one needs any Viag-whatever-you-call-it, it is only the civilized that think they need Viag-whatever, Vito-whatever and all those other drugs," I was finding it difficult to continue with this topic, many of Girl's problems were common sexual issues faced in civilized society, but she was the one who mentioned "being sexually satisfied by the natural and primitive way," which was quite unique, so much so that I'm afraid that typical civilized ears wouldn't even understand what she was trying to say, I was able to understand and get close to the state she had described, but since I had never actually experienced it, it didn't make sense for me to try to say anything more about it, "Have you ever had one of those truly unforgettable sexual experiences?" Girl lowered her head for a long time and drew a circle with her finger on the ground, "Never, there was never a single time where I felt like I was truly satisfied, but I know that if I ever had one it would be like a surging flood, it would be like an exploding volcano, I'd give my life for a feeling like that," I was silent, I peeled the other half of the sweet potato to eat, I also believed that such a thing must exist, but humankind had already lost their capacity for sadness, I tried to change the subject, I asked what a typical Atayal's sex life was like on the reservation, Girl said that as far as what she had seen from her father's and grandfather's generations, they were all quite faithful to their partners, "It was always one man staying by the side of one woman, one woman staying by the side of one man," if anyone wanted to get married, get divorced, or get remarried they had to go through a public ceremony, it was almost impossible for anyone to have an affair, where were they supposed to go to hook up on this tiny reservation, ever since ancient times the Atayal tribe has stood by the principle of monogamy, those days and nights of carnivalesque abandon were an exception but the nature of "the carnival required it," "During the Japanese colonial period we Atayal women were pretty good about maintaining our chastity," but for the twenty or thirty years after World War II it was like the levees broke, wanton sexual abandon quickly drowned out the concept of chastity, "Among all the indigenous groups in Taiwan, our tribe was probably assimilated the most quickly," one of the practical results of assimilation was the loss of sexual chastity under the weight of power and money, Girl said she was starting to feel cold and went around to the other side of the Great Rock to change out of her bathing suit, when she emerged I once again saw a beautiful and glowing Girl decked out in her black silk short skirt and practically busting out of her tight cream undershirt, some of the phenomena that we discussed had previously been covered in the investigative calculations and research reports of various researchers specialists and scholars, but the Girl standing right there before my eyes was fresh and rejuvenated having let the river water cleanse her body, Girl asked me to finish all the leftovers still on the barbecue rack, "Next spring and summer I'll bring you out here for grilled fish and shrimp," I asked her what was going on with that whole Giving Back Ritual, Girl said that she had barely had any sex in the three years since she came home, she had almost forgotten about sex, she felt that she no longer needed it, "But Pimp-Bastard started to turn on my primal sexual desire," It was only after that that Girl accepted the sexual recommendation made by Boss and his buddies, Boss made her two promises: one, she would always be their "Meimei," two, Boss would take care of any "moral issues" that might come up on the reservation regarding their arrangement, she never had any interest in the affairs of men so this promise didn't mean shit to her, "Boss and his buddies are really good to me, they take good care of me, they listen to me and don't force me to do anything I don't want to do, I understand what men's sex lives are like here on the reservation, and I provide them with some sexual comfort, there is nothing exchanged between us and there is nothing to feel shameful about, they only give me gifts to try to get on my good side, but now I feel like I have given enough back, when I first returned home this wasn't the way I wanted things to go, but you can imagine that Boss wasn't going to be having any of that, but the ever-reasonable Elders Council here on the reservation made him see the light . . ." "So the real reason you want to bring it to an end is—" "The desperation of that untouchable unknowable black hole of human desire." I thought that I could understand Girl's desperation, in my teenage years sex was something that I yearned for, among the unknown things awaiting me in life it carried with it the greatest enticement, but once I had my first sexual experience, "Is that it?" I began to question myself, and so I did it again, and again and again until sex was reduced to a scab on a sick dog's skin, all those workaholics are trying to forget about sex, all those who take the path of a monastic life are trying to use monastic discipline to cut off sex, most people accept their "so-so half-assed sex lives" in the same way that they accept reality, they look at sex as one of many trivial matters in life, for that split second you cum and feel good, you have an orgasm that lasts thirty seconds to two or three minutes at the most, if you live surrounded by the best local restaurants it's not a big deal if you don't eat all those local specialties, the question is does such a state where one reaches ecstasy to the point that feels like a "surging flood or an exploding volcano" even exist? during my life journey I have often been suspicious of such a thing, during the time of my own remaining life I still don't know how "real" this question is, perhaps it doesn't need to be answered, my only hope is that life reveals truth and doesn't simply hastily write itself off, gradually one comes to a point where that voice deep inside asks you to let go of your hopes and expectations, and when things come to simply use your heart to experience it, and then there will be nothing to feel desperate about as nature has a way of providing consolation for life's sadness and losses, whenever I stroll through the mountains or gaze into the river nature always brings a feeling of peace and tranquility to me, peace and tranquility have the power to dissipate those feelings of sadness and loss, if only thoughts of these mountains and rivers could bring an end to Girl's desperation, but something inside tells me that these feelings of desperate longing actually began here among the mountains and rivers, the black hole of sexual desire has been around since the beginning of life itself and existed here in the deepest recesses of the mountains and rivers, at its most primal level life is always waiting for the volcano to erupt and for the floods to be unleashed, this kind of pulsating desire, this feeling of our naked bodies trembling as we cry out, has been drowned out under the ugly clamor of civilization, my earlier suspicions were only finally verified after I learned about the black hole of desire that Girl had been living with, Girl had been fortunate to be born and raised here in this primal land of mountains and rivers, she experienced the false pride of civilization and abandoned it, only after returning home to this natural world of mountains and rivers did she truly come to understand the black hole of sexual desire lurking within her, perhaps during her Remains of Life she would never be able to touch, stir, let alone satisfy that desire, the fact that the true primitive nature of this kind of naked physical sexual desire can only be understood through "a meeting of hearts," is that itself not a commentary on the absurdity and tragedy of life?—I woke up late for the next two or three days, each night around midnight Chopin's Nocturnes circled through the cold mountain air, I sat at my desk in front of the window or lay in bed thinking crazy thoughts, I couldn't help thinking back to my time of seclusion in northern Danshui,[33] besides the most basic daily necessities I threw everything else away in a big plastic garbage bag, cooking utensils, those beautiful plates and bowls were really beautiful, those artistic photos hanging on the wall, my dirty clothes, sheets, old letters, stale emotions, moldy books, piles of manuscript paper, during the past few years all that was left on the front of my

bed was the most generic radio and two cassettes of Chopin's Nocturnes, night after night I fell asleep to the Nocturnes, I never thought
about the meaning of my own life, I just instinctively felt I needed
to experience new things, at the time I didn't understand what was
going on night after night with those Nocturnes, not until a decade
later when I heard those same Nocturnes here on this reservation
deep in the mountains, by relaxing and carefully listening to the
notes one can dance freely through the mountain air, I still don't
know just how those times and places are connected, or what kind of
personal meaning they might carry—after my cup of got-up-late
coffee, it was already time for everyone's afternoon nap on the reservation even the chicken and dogs were having a nap, I felt like going out
for a walk, under the heat of the blazing sun the only cool path was
the one through the bamboo forest to the general store, I had gotten
into the habit of browsing through the aisles of the general store
when I had nothing better to do, I would look at the packaging and
names of all the new products, I liked to see what kind of tricks the
advertisers were using to deceive kids, often I would buy a can of beer
or a bottle of white spirits and sit down to listen to people screaming
along to the karaoke machine, I could hear the whispering sound of
the wind blowing through the bamboo forest, which would mix
with the eerie groanlike sound of branches brushing up against each
other, the convenience store at nap time was completely devoid of
customers, I read each and every word printed on those product
labels, "Ah Q Instant Noodles" really captured my attention, "Lifelong
Tenderness" for a brand of tissue wasn't bad either, I thought that
"Pure Native Beef" did a really good job at putting Pure and Native
together, when I saw "Chanel Mild Face Soap" I wondered if mild
was also popular here in this secluded mountain reservation, and
even an elementary school student would be able to tell that the
"120% Nourishment Elixir" was at least 20 percent better than anything else out there, When I read the label "Drink ComeBest Before

You Do It" I couldn't help but ponder the difference in implied
meaning between that and "Drink It Then Do It," but at that moment someone suddenly patted me on the shoulder, "Hey old buddy,
long time no see," it was the owner of the convenience store, "You
haven't been drinking lately, how's the research going? Have you decided to buy some land here and settle down yet?" If I were to buy
land and a house without a wife and a son I would just end up a lonely
old man, "Oh c'mon, you've been here enough times to know how
things work around here, once you've got land and a house I can
guarantee that there will be Atayal women interested in you," I
thanked this Atayal man from the bottom of my heart for so warmly
welcoming me to immigrate to the land of the Atayal, he grabbed
two cans of beer and invited me to sit with him under the kiosk and
have a drink, he said that there was something he needed to talk to
me about later, "What's your take on the Musha Incident?" I tried to
ask him in the most clear-cut way, "If Mona Rudao had emerged
victorious," Mr. Owner stuttered as he swished some beer around in
his mouth, "I would have opened up my basement to everyone on the
reservation and let them all drink until they were dead drunk," it was
a miracle that his father had survived the Second Musha Incident
and somehow escaped to Riverisle where he eventually fathered a son,
"If Mona Rudao had emerged victorious," I tried to imitate the way
he spoke by swishing the words around in my mouth, "Let's talk about
how your father escaped, perhaps Mona Rudao might learn something," I couldn't tell whether or not the joke was inappropriate, but he
wasn't laughing, not a whisker moved on that full beard of his, "Mona
Rudao didn't need to escape, none of us businessmen could even hold
a candle to him," for several generations his entire family all did business on "the border between the savage land and the civilized world,"
ever since he was a child his father would teach him one word of his
native tongue and then one word of Chinese, no wonder then that
the first time I met him I thought he was a plainsman who had settled

here among the Atayal, his Chinese was even better than college-ed-ucated Bakan, and the elementary school teacher Cuz-Hub, early in the morning two days before "the Incident" broke out his father had taken a bus from Musha down to Puli to purchase some wholesale liquor, "my father knew that something big was about to go down on the reservation, and that made the need for alcohol even more pressing because we businessmen don't meddle in what's happening, we just make sure to bring in enough goods and alcohol for people's needs," the big wholesalers in town had a relationship with his father and grandfather that lasted more than two generations, they often re-ferred to themselves as the "Puli Savages" in order to ensure that there would be no conflicts between these different groups of savages, once his father picked up the wholesale goods he was preparing to return home, but his wholesaler ask him to stay for lunch, as they were eating his father mentioned that "something big" was brewing on the reser-vation and he needed to get back quickly with the alcohol, the whole-saler was a shrewd man who had seen a lot during his years, he im-mediately asked the waiter to exchange their wine for something stronger, "My father probably realized that what had been happening was no simple affair, and there was no telling when he might be back to purchase more alcohol," the wholesaler encouraged him to drink and he did, "I suspect my father drank too much that day, the whole-saler kept asking him one question after another, and my father pro-ceeded to tell him everything he knew that was going on in and around the reservation," as the store owner spoke his long beard made him appear solemn, "I'm sure that the wholesaler had some kind of secret intention, it was a good thing that he was indeed a savage from Puli, and not some guy who had the Chinese up his ass, or even worse the Japanese up his ass," his father drank so much he passed out, they laid him down in a room in the back, the wholesaler even hired a street-walker to look after him, the next day when his father awakened the wholesaler only had one thing to say to him, "This time you listen to

me, you will do exactly as I say, otherwise consider this close brother-
hood of ours over," his father spent more than two weeks there in
town, and only then did the wholesaler finally allow him to leave,
"My father took a bus to the Pass of No Return, where he was sent to
a detention center, which they said was to protect him, Drodux,
only when he arrived at the Drodux tribal land did he learn what had
occurred," I asked him why his father didn't wait until everything
had completely calmed down before leaving, "I think that given the
circumstances at the time there was no way for him to remain there
down in the plains, moreover we Seediq have a hard time staying away
from home," he laughed, "Seediq back then were really attached to
their tribe, it took a lot to get them to leave home, whenever my father
went to Puli to purchase goods he would always set out first thing
in the morning and be back in Mhebu before nightfall," the shop
owner took out two bottles of beer, I turned around and noticed
that his wife was sitting behind the counter minding the shop, "My
father hated him and all the way up until his death never forgave the
Drodux for what they did, there was absolutely no hint of what was
coming, he thought he was being protected, it was only when they
were awakened in the middle of the night by the sound of gun-
shots that he realized he had been betrayed, men with rifles and
knives wantonly slaughtered the sick, elderly, women, children, and
wounded soldiers who had been detained, I feel deep shame as a people
for the Seediq's actions that day, regardless of whatever 'rules of competition' our ancestors once had, if that kind of senseless slaughter
of one's own people is not savagery I don't know what is," the owner's wife shouted something to him from inside, he picked up his
beer took a long sip and continued, "My wife doesn't want me to get
too worked up, but there's nothing for me to get worked up about,
but that certainly wasn't the case for my father, he used to stamp his
feet until they hurt, he cursed them so hard that his teeth fell out,
and even in his old age he never went to church, he also tried to avoid

any contact with Priest, and that's because he had spent time in the Drodux detention center," Shop Owner tried to get me to see if I could differentiate which part of what he said was his own view, and which part was actually his father's view, he told me to try to look past the emotional side of what he had said, his father's perspective was that of a firsthand observer, "There was a mother and daughter that my father was trying to help out at the detention center, they screamed out in the darkness, there were many terrified screams when the slaughter began, my father grabbed the mother and daughter and just as they made it to the corner of the room they saw the flash of a Savage Blade drawing near, in a fluster my father yelled at that Savage Blade in Chinese, the way he cursed was fueled by true anger, that Savage Blade thought that Father must have been a Chinese soldier sent there on guard duty, so he figured it was pointless to kill him since he wasn't after Chinese heads—Even after my father went to Riverisle he continued to curse them for many years, he would curse what kind of a fucking headhunt was that, where is the honor in taking a commemorative photo after a headhunt when all the victims were unarmed and locked up, an underhanded attack like that where they just chopped off 101 people's heads, it was even more pathetic than the tradition of publicly beheading chickens during local elections,"[34] the Great Purge didn't fully purge away his father, everyone knew that he was a businessman, he didn't know anything about anything except how to buy and sell, a few years after World War II he passed his business down to his son, unless he had business to take care of he never left Riverisle and he certainly never went farther than Musha, he could no longer stand the sight of Seediq from the Toda tribe, "My father left me with one important lesson: businessmen must always remain neutral, this is a principle our ancestors left us with," that's why his general store always served as the center for exchanging information on the reservation, it was a place where people could go to release their pent-up emotions through song, it was a place where people could get together and have a drink and have a good conversation, but he always remained neutral never joining them in song and always scrupulous when it came to public and private matters, he just focused on supplying goods for them to enjoy, "Nobody on the reservation has ever objected to anything I ever did," he took me over to the other side of the bamboo forest to see his storeroom, there were cases of rice wine stacked from the floor all the way up to the ceiling, they were secured by steel shelves and wire, "Why don't you settle down here, you can marry a good Atayal girl, I bet she'll give you three sons within the first year, after she gives birth all the booze is on me for a month," looking at his beer gut I asked him why he didn't drink rice wine, "My wife won't allow me to drink any white spirits, she said that if I drink a single drop of that stuff she'll chop off my balls and pickle them in rice wine, then she'll auction them off to the wealthy tribe members as a special medicinal tonic," Atayal women are really cruel I joked, "She wasn't joking," the serious appearance of his beard made it clear just how cruelly funny Atayal women could be, through the bamboo forest you could see glimpses of the mountains in the distance, the mountain ridge had been tortured by that bamboo to the point that it was screaming out, "Shit, fuck me in the ass," you rubbed me in that spot that fucking hurts, "I allowed you to stay so that I could secretly tell you," we returned to the edge of the kiosk, Beer Belly popped open another can of beer, "If anyone starts fighting around here over these next two days, I'll just pull down my iron gate and ignore them," that's Girl's business, it's an open secret around here, most of the people on the reservation didn't know all of the details, but now Boss's gang had split into two factions and they were unable to work things out, one side refused to let the matter go, the other faction insisted that they let it go, after all they were all doing just fine before Meimei came back to the reservation, but how were they supposed to get along without their Meimei, the two factions had already come to blows once over this matter, the police came out to investigate, Boss just explained it away by saying that they had gotten drunk around Christmas and got into a little scuffle but it was nothing, the Tribal Elder had clearly instructed Boss to respect the wishes of the individual involved, as long as they didn't stir up any trouble the "moral issue" could be overlooked, but if we want to handle this affair on the basis of "morality" then we would be in for trouble, the Tribal Elder asked Boss to carefully weigh the gains and losses at stake, who was exploiting whom, "And what should happen if Girl decides to report all of this to the police," the Tribal Elder didn't continue, Boss still hadn't taken a clear stand on the matter, but all Boss had to do was say one word and it would turn into all-out war, "If this thing really explodes, there's nothing the police will be able to do to stop it, it would have a terrible psychological effect on everyone on the reservation, think of how many husbands and wives would lose sleep over this," "Ah," so it appeared that Girl had quite a lot of pull, here in this semi-isolated reservation deep in the mountains she indeed did, I would often see those wives living in multistory homes with fair skin, they hardly ever ventured outside, and when they did they always went by car, only occasionally when I passed by on my walks would I see this one woman occasionally sunning herself each time she would be wearing a different style bra and panties. Each night at midnight everything was cradled in a lonely silence, the cold mountain air would start to spread and saturate the reservation, sometimes Chopin's Nocturnes are superfluous, I awakened from my dream and felt a gentle light coming in through the window, I got up amid the gentle light but realized it still wasn't time for the cocks to crow, I turned on the kitchen light and made myself a cup of coffee, ordinarily I liked to take my time slowly sipping my coffee, daylight gradually filled the sky and the cock began its final cackle of the morning, on that day it was only after I had finished my coffee that I realized there was still a gentle light coming in through my window, all around everything was encapsulated by a perfect silence, I opened the front door and walked out onto the porch and looked up to see the bright moon surrounded by a massive lunar halo, under the light of the moon Girl's courtyard was bathed in a silver white glow, when that glow entered my window it transformed into a gentle light that continued to light up my dreams, it was after all "Bright Moon Alley," that's what the street sign said on the alley where I lived it was called Bright Moon Alley, I realized that I was standing close to the very center of this island nation deep in the mountains under the bright moon of the lunar halo surrounded by perfect silence as the cold mountain air slowly penetrated my body and soul, the mountain ridge was right before me, under the bright moon the peak of the distant mountain was even clearer than daytime mist, I made myself another cup of coffee and sat down on the porch step, I gazed out upon the reservation that had experienced so many days just like this, perhaps this is what it really means to be among the Remains of Life, at the very least this is the backbone of the Remains of Life, once all of the sadness, unrest, fear, and confusion has been eliminated, I sat there until the rooster cackled for the second time, and in my notebook I jotted down the following sentence: "It's not necessarily a bad thing to be tricked into being awakened by the moonlight," during the following day I planned to carry out "an investigation into whether or not the Musha Incident was a headhunting ritual," I sat at my desk staring out the window as the gentle light shone down on the backyard and up onto the mountain slope, continuing along the mountain slope and bearing left through a small densely forested canyon and just a few steps away is the "Memorial to the Remains of Life," I picked up my pen to write the following sentence "The Musha Incident was a planned insurrection, the scope of this plan was on the margins of 'the political,'" the Ancestral Spirits surrounding the "Remains of Life" came over to see what I had written, let them return to the dense forests of Mhebu's Mystic Valley so they can discuss which path to take along the valley, from 4 in the morning until 6 in the afternoon, they carried out surprise attacks on twelve police stations, they cut off the policemen's heads and took their rifles, and they went even further when it came to wiping out the Japanese rulers present at the primary battleground of the Musha Elementary School, this was a united effort on the part of the six tribes led by Mhebu, if you claim this was not a "political insurrection" that would indeed by an insult to the original intention of those who rose up to resist the Japanese and the political significance of the event, two days later the colonizers mobilized their army "along with a united military and police central strike force" responded by force to the Musha uprising, some of the weapons they used included machine guns, grenades, cannons, airplanes spraying down machine-gun fire, and in the end they even employed poison gas sprayed from airplanes, this response was completely in keeping with how one operates when in a state of war, but behind the scenes the true mastermind of this war was politics, it was a political war striking out in response to a political insurrection, and there is nothing more that History can say about this, at the most it can only criticize the rulers for bullying the weak and being excessive in the casualties they inflicted, but as the uprising is confirmed as a "political insurrection" the protestors simultaneously confirmed their stance against tyranny, Mona Rudao has been politicized to the point where today he has become the Atayal people's "National Hero Against Tyranny"— but from another perspective, the principal means by which the instigators waged war was a traditional "headhunt," later the colonial rulers discovered that their civilized weaponry was unable to completely eradicate these resisters, they in turn used a combination of threats and coercion, recruiting members of other subtribes of the Seediq to "headhunt the headhunters," this was the most effective form of battle to be waged in the dense mountain forests, the strange thing was that both sides seemed to accept this, in reality the civi-

lized army needed only to display a show of force on the outlying
perimeter of where the real battles were taking place, the true life-
death struggle and headhunt between different factions of the Seediq
tribe all took place deep in the woods, at each stage the battles were
all small-scale headhunts, no wonder that Nadafu held fast to the
belief that the Musha Incident was "a large-scale headhunt," there
were many elderly Seediq tribe members who other than its place as a
"headhunt" couldn't care less about any of the other meanings that
have been attached to the Musha Incident, all of their interest was
focused entirely upon the completion of the "headhunt mission,"
and that is why people like Nadafu's father felt such joy when they
cut off a head, you could even say that this kind of joy and excitement
in life had always existed in the headhunt from primitive times on
down, the Second Musha Incident was an even more typical headhunt, putting aside conspiracy theories concerning the Japanese
rulers for a moment, those members of the Toda tribe who participated were completely and utterly invested in exacting revenge from
the Mhebu tribe for those heads lost in battle deep in the forest, according to principles of headhunting it doesn't matter whether or not
your opponent is armed, they carried out headhunts against two
detention centers filled with unarmed resisters, it didn't take much effort to capture 101 heads, it must have been one of the highest-ranking
head counts in the history of all recorded headhunts, the vast majority of Seediq tribespeople had no political consciousness thus as far as
they were concerned, the Musha Incident was simply a "large-scale
headhunt," it was quite rare for them to be able to "headhunt their
hearts out" during one of these large-scale rituals, this was especially
so for members of those six tribes that had not participated in the
original "Incident," for them the headhunt was different as it was
only undertaken so they could be provided food, later they were su-
pervised by men in uniform, they were rewarded with two taels for
each head, the actual struggle the tribe members engaged in during

the headhunt was no different than the traditional headhunts that had been carried out since primitive times, but what I think they were actually concerned with was "the native ability of life itself to take another's head," but at the time they didn't necessarily understand the "political meaning" of the six tribes' headhunt, even today they don't have the same respect for Mona Rudao as others, at the very most they look at Mona Rudao as a "Hero of the Headhunt" the same as they do countless other nameless headhunting heroes ever since primitive times, even today when they come and go from Musha they never even give a second glance at the statue of Mona Rudao erected in front of the large memorial—this has led to two questions, should the nature of the "Musha Incident" be summed up as "political" or as a "headhunt," history records what it knows to be "fact," the political powers that be affirm their own "political nature" on the basis of these "historical facts," while at the same time adjusting them to match the political consciousness of the day, secondly, ever since primitive times civilized education has refuted this important aspect of tribal life known as "headhunting," today there is virtually no one researching the Musha Incident from the perspective of a "headhunt," there seems to be a consensus among everyone middle-aged and younger that "the Incident" was a "political struggle against tyranny," these two questions thus truly exist, but the political has its side, while simultaneously utilizing all of the resources at its disposal to suppress the other, I must make a tentative conclusion, it is a good thing that this historical debate has not fallen into an outside ideological clash, care must be taken so that it remains an internal debate between those with a "conscience" and those who remain "unenlightened," and so it goes on and on, in reality the "political struggle against tyranny" and the "primitive headhunt" simultaneously coexist within the incident, at the same time the "struggle against tyranny" and this "headhunt" are forever locked in a never-ending dialectic, by the time they finally come to a "temporary concordance," the most accurate definition of the Musha Incident is: A Politicized Head-hunt. By the time I wrote down the words "A Politicized Headhunt" it was already past noon, I prepared a hodgepodge hotpot with sardines and flowering cabbage and hastily ate before crawling into bed and passing out into a deep sleep, after I woke up I sat down in the living room, the mountain mist felt like it was right on my front doorstep, in my daze I seemed to still be stuck on those "two questions," I already forgot if there was anything I had written that could destroy one's dignity, but I know that strong white spirits can destroy one's awareness, I paced back and forth in front of the kitchen cabinet, rummaging through all of the items inside, until I actually did get my hands on a bottle of some kind of hard liquor, it only took one look to see that it was 66 proof, probably one of the Ancestral Spirits secretly stashed it there before going home, after all there is nothing wrong with preparing for an emergency, I'll be sure to give it back to him a little later once it is dark when he comes back with his bag full of white spirits, I took a sip and the primitive flavor wasn't bad, by the time I took my second sip a well-dressed woman with long black hair and a cool gaze had suddenly appeared outside my screen door, I waited for her to say something but after three seconds she was still dead silent, I had no choice but to sip my way over to the screen door, the woman with the long hair grinned and I immediately recognized that it was Girl and she was wearing a tight dark-green dress, she was so well dressed, all so that her breasts would really stand out, I raised my cup to her but she shook her head, "I came over to invite you to observe the ceremony the day after tomorrow," her breasts were pressed right up against the screen door, I told her to be careful not to get her shirt dirty, "It's okay these are my pajamas," I almost wanted to tell her that it was no big deal, my birthday suit is my pajamas, "I'm going to Christmas morning prayer and joining the church choir, you wanna come," wearing your birthday suit to bed is much more convenient as you can wear it both summer and winter, "I'm not going to church, I've been a bit tired lately from all my writing," "You get tired writing? Come out and get some exercise, that'll wake you up," Girl said that since it was still early she could take me out to see the plot of land that she and her brother owned, "Wow, you own land!" I had thought that she was a lifelong member of the proletariat like me, "We have six plots of land, we set them aside to let the weeds and wild grass grow freely," "Can we walk there?" it was already getting late, Girl pushed open the door and yanked me out onto the porch, on the way out the door I put my cup of white spirits down on the grass beside the steps, we passed through the west side of the reservation on our way there, Girl's pajamas attracted quite a bit of attention along the way, that dark green color was deeper than the green mountains, Girl seemed to only know how to take shortcuts she cut through the plantation garden, the betel-nut garden, and the kidney bean trellis watching her step all along the way, "Watch out for snakes on the ground," we finally came to a small cement bridge, Girl stopped to gaze down into the river water below, "We used to divert water from this river to irrigate the fields," from there we took a small path on the other side of the cement bridge, we kept going until we almost ran into the side of the mountain, Girl stopped in an area where the wild grass was up to our waists and made a circular motion with her hand, "From here all the way to over there is the plot of land that my brother and I own," "How come you don't plant anything here?" "There are six plots of land here, we'd lose money just trying to hire laborers to work the land," "So why don't you just sell it?" "Take a look at how far off the beaten path this is, who would want to buy it, the owner of the general store once offered my brother $300,000 for each plot, but my brother said that even if he was offered $3,000,000 a plot he still wasn't selling, I heard some of the guys drinking say that the going rate should be at least $500,000 a plot and the price is still going up," Girl told me that when she first returned to the reservation she would often come here and walk around, all the while pondering what to do with this land, "At one point I suggested to my brother that we plant imported fruit, we could develop a fruit farm and open it up as a tourist destination, my brother said he was fine with us raising fruit but he didn't want anything to do with raising tourists," I also couldn't figure out what was wrong with raising tourists, Girl told me that all the color she got on her shoulders and thighs was from this garden and the Valleystream of her dreams, If I had six plots of land I would of course build a large log warehouse workspace, naturally I would emulate the Seediq of old by cutting the wood down from the large mountains surrounding the city, and carry the logs on my back, "I'd use 10 percent of the room as a writing space, 25 percent would be devoted to a painting studio—I can actually paint in the style of fauvism—the remainder of the space would be devoted to a dance hall, I would sleep and eat my hotpot meals on the hardwood dance floor," "Wow! That's awesome!" Girl gestured up to the heavens with her Wow, "I'm an expert at Crazy Dancing!" "Wow! So am I!" We made our way back to the reservation along the small trails, by the time we passed the Memorial to the Remains of Life it was already getting dark, I turned around to look at the "Remains of Life" but all I saw was the milky white of Girl's skin showing through her silk pajamas, I went home and as I made myself a small hodgepot hotpot jotted down "Remains of Life Milky White" but I felt it didn't sound as good as "Remains of Life Breast White," I wasted a lot of time pondering whether to use "milk" or "breast," I can't even remember what I ate that night let alone how it tasted, "Breast-White Remains of Life" wasn't bad either but not as good as "Milky White Remains of Life," I suddenly remembered the cup of white spirits that I had left on the doorstep, but just as the cup touched my lips and I was about to take a sip four words suddenly flashed before my eyes: Remains of Breasts Life, ah, that's it let's settle on "Remains of Breasts Life," that could not only be a great title for the book but also be used as the name of a store, once I finish this novel I'll open up a "Remains of Breasts Life Workshop," I'll figure out later what to do with the place or what to sell, Ah it was just at that moment that I heard the sound of something hitting the ground coming from Girl's courtyard, I looked out the window and saw a large pillow and a canvas suitcase on the ground, a few seconds later I saw a man silently running out of the house barefoot, I rushed over to the front door, "That's how she is when she doesn't get enough booze in her system," Moxi said with a frozen smile, "From the time she got home last night until now, she already burned through all the alcohol we had on hand, and then she even kicked me out," "Don't blame her," I tried to appeal to both reason and emotion, "Hasn't she been through enough these past few days? You'll be getting off easy if you can settle everything with a few extra bottles of liquor," Moxi said that he was going to bring back two bottles, I asked him to return an empty bottle for me while he was going, Moxi said don't mention it he actually wanted to give me a bottle, even two bottles, if I could go over and try to smooth things over between him and Girl by talking to her, he didn't want her to throw him out again when he went back, I walked over to Girl's courtyard carrying a near-empty bottle, there was a light on in the living room, which illuminated part of the courtyard, I slowly picked up the long pillow off the ground and set it down on the living room sofa, I put the suitcase up against the sofa, I turned off the living room light, as I went out I left the door halfway open, the light of the full moon lit the courtyard so brightly that I could barely tell if it was day or night, I turned and went back to my place and sat down on the front stoop, I seemed to hear the phantomlike sounds of Chopin's Nocturnes floating through the cold air on this moonlit night. I thought back to a bar girl I once know, she wasn't one of those flirty elegant ones who likes to play the needy girl role, she had a strong brow and piercing eyes, extra meat on her bones, and would prop up her high heels and look me right in the eye, the main role of a bar girl is to keep you company when you are drinking, and from the very beginning she gave clear signals that men had no right to buy a bar girl's body, on one occasion I witnessed firsthand as she tried to politely refuse some guy's advances, but when he didn't listen she stood up and raised her voice, "So you wanna buy a piece of meat, that's easy enough, take your ass over to the 543 pleasure house and stuff your face with meat until you fucking choke!" that guy stood up but he only came up to her chin, the manager and receptionist both came to smooth things over before things got out of hand, everyone could tell that Sister Phoenix knew how to handle a situation, as it happens Moxi really did bring two bottles back with him, he brought them over and thanked me, I told him that all her lights were out, but he said that's okay, he was used to feeling his way around in the dark, the origin of Sister Phoenix's sadness comes from when she fell madly in love with a man when she was thirty years old, "There was indeed such a man," even after getting drunk Bar Girl still wouldn't reveal his real name, she never talked about that man's background or appearance, the fact that her sadness was due to men didn't prove anything it was just because she had worked as a bar girl that she "didn't have any options," Bar Girl said that she had lived the bar life for seven or eight years, for all that time she never let a man take her body or her mind, yet her whole life was taken by the stigma of the label "bar girl," her method of revenge or self-punishment was quite melodramatic, whenever Bar Girl slept with a john, she only did so on the condition that he first drink with her until she was 90 percent drunk but still able to walk with some assistance, Bar Girl didn't remember or wasn't that clear about just how many men she had slept with, there was only one image that stayed with her, perhaps because it kept recurring it ended up imprinted in her memories, occasionally some of the more aggressive things men did to her would make her open her eyes, each time she would see herself stuck to the ceiling looking down at herself, at first she thought that there must have been a mirror installed on the ceiling, but she quickly realized that wasn't the case, she had floated up to the ceiling where in her loneliness she gazed back down upon herself, it was only when the woman on the ceiling became skinnier and skinnier to the point that she looked like a sickly little girl, only then did she finally leave the kingdom of bars behind, she used the money she had saved during her many years drinking with men and selling her body to live a simple life, she passed her days drinking glass after glass of wine, numb to the past present and future. . . . Breathing the night air here deep in the mountains my thoughts somehow drifted off to that distant Bar Girl, of course what made me think of her was Girl's own crazy taste for alcohol, I wondered if Girl also floated up to the ceiling when she was drunk, the most benign form of sadness—which can also be the most profound—can be cured with the proper dose of "time," but no one asked the Remains of Life how they carried on once they had recovered, the reason that "time" couldn't cure Mahong Mona was that her sadness was not so simple, the kind of deep and complex wound that she carried with her was something that "time" was unable to heal, yet in her later years Mahong lived a happy life, she didn't have the problem of try- ing to figure out "How to spend her Remains of Life," "the Incident" went from being a wound to injecting her life with the energy to carry on and with that power Mahong repeatedly attempted to re- turn to "the past," the site of "the Incident" that the real Mahong had actually experienced, thus "the Incident" enriched and completed Mahong Mona's Remains of Life, I went inside with my two bottles of white spirits, and the lonely quietude drowned out the sound of the Nocturnes, I stashed one bottle in the cabinet behind all the other stuff and placed the other bottle beside my bed, "People feel rooted in life once they are attached to a piece of land," I'm afraid that this saying is rooted in a particular era and represents a particu- lar ideology, People feel settled in life once they buy a condo, the plot of land that Girl and her little brother own seems so disconnected from their lives, the Nocturnes drifted into the dreams of the deer eyes perhaps what our lives need more of are freedom and dreams, I wasn't quite sure what to jot down in my notebook, freedom and dreams are two things that don't need to be written down but when they come together they are the soul of our lives and creative work, I sat amid the blue-green glow of night intently listening to the lonely silence, it was only after a long time that I finally turned on the desk lamp and jotted down a memorandum for myself, "Don't forget to pay a visit to the head of the scaffolding crew tomorrow," I turned off the lamp and sat for a bit longer, the cool mountain air had already gone from chilly to cold, as I got into bed and pulled back the covers there was one sentence I couldn't get out of my mind: The remains of one's life are passed in lonely silence—Crew Leader told me that he was considered to be at the bottom of the social ladder on the reservation, many people like him had a common dream of going off to the faraway cities to earn money and try to make it in the world, before the 1970s the men who had it the worst had to work on fishing boats out on the high seas, those who stayed behind did worked on highway projects doing hard physical labor, many of the girls ended up having to marry old retired soldiers from the mainland, others went to the factories where they worked long shifts, more than a few couldn't help but fall into the world of sex work where they became playthings for the male customers, "If I had been born few years earlier, I probably would have ended up out on the high seas," Crew Leader's face, hands, and feet were all dark from a life working out in the sun, he was only around fifty years old but his face carried the scars of a man who had weathered the storms of a difficult life, he invited me for tea and told me that he had been using the same tea set for over twenty years, I told him that this was my first time since I came to Riverisle that I had been invited for tea with a full tea set, "There's others," Crew Leader explained as he washed the tea cups, "The cultured people on our reservation often drink tea,"

After five years he had worked his way up to crew head, it was then that he started drinking tea, he let his brothers on the scaffolding team continue drinking alcohol, but he made sure they drank less than before and he really let them have it if they stirred up trouble after drinking too much, he left the reservation in 1975, the second half of the 1970s all the way through the entire 1980s was the "golden age" for this island nation, there were at least three different scaffolding teams from the reservations surrounding Riverisle, most of them worked in the vicinity of the larger Taipei metropolitan area, they were paid just as well as other skilled workers, the projects they worked on were long-term and stable, before work on one site wrapped up they already had everything set up for their next job, for more than twenty years they lived in temporary shacks and construction trailers, some of them brought their wives along on the condition that they agreed to help take care of various daily chores around the site like cooking and cleaning, if they were able to save their wages in ten years they would have enough money to go home tear down their old house and build a new multistory one in its place, "My dad said that he was used to living in his Japanese-style house, so I'll wait until he dies before tearing this down and building a new house, instead of tearing it down, I just fixed it up here and there, if you look around the reservation you can see there are quite a few old-style Japanese houses mostly occupied by the elderly, who knows perhaps I'll also end up living my entire life in a Japanese-style house, and it might be the next generation that finally tears this place down to build a new modern house," Granny who lived diagonally across from me lived in one of those typical Japanese-style country houses, the front of her house was decorated with checkered wood patterns, the large planks of natural wood on the side walls were supported by tall blue-green pillars, when I first arrived I thought it was strange that they had preserved so many old Japanese-style houses on the reservation, later I realized that the reason for this was rooted in history,

"People say 'the good days never last long,' but as far as I can tell we have used up all of our good days, they've been squeezed dry, workers like us don't understand politics, but just thinking about the simple fact that the government seems to have no cap on the amount of local capital it allows to flow outside of Taiwan, how much money could possibly be left to invest in this island nation," a few years into the 1990s, capital investment in this island nation dramatically decreased, investors started to demand lower costs, "Our salaries were reduced, we had to cut back on the size of our crews, at its largest my crew used to have thirty-four guys, we were forced to cut back to fifteen, and that went on for two or three years," the government never took any steps to stop this, and foreign workers from Southeast Asia poured in, working for less money and longer hours they ended up taking away all our jobs, "Sometime we really can't understand what the government is thinking, it's as if all they care about are elections, but they don't even do anything to protect their people's jobs, they just let these foreign laborers in, of course those city people don't want to do those tough jobs that require manual labor, they think that we indigenous people don't want to do them either, that's really how it is and when these companies decide they don't want us anymore, they just send someone to inform us by which date we need to leave the premises, when the time comes they give us one to three months of severance pay, and that's it, all the temporary worker housing we built on site ends up being used by those foreign workers, in my twenty years doing this job I never imagined any of this could ever happen, it's not like we enjoyed living a primitive life in those temporary trailers," when he smiled several dark wrinkles appeared on his face, he took his fifteen-person crew and started working jobs in central and southern Taiwan, foreign workers needed to rely upon "middlemen to open doors for them" and they started following everywhere they went like flies, they continued moving south taking on any small construction project they could get, they took jobs in

Fenggang, Hengchun on the southernmost tip of Taiwan, "The final battle took place on a large recreation resort that was just being developed in Manzhou Township," at first the developer couldn't find any foreign laborers to hire, so he was really kissing up to them, but the foreign laborers eventually showed up in Manzhou too, by then they knew that the entire island nation was lost, "We were fired halfway through the job," the investor's representative told them that the concessionaire said he would be willing to keep them on if they would accept the same pay and conditions the foreign workers were offered, a handful stayed behind deciding that they needed to "temper their bodies and minds" in order to adapt to this new reality, "But I told myself it was time to say good-bye to this chapter of my life!" in the past he only went home during the lunar new year holiday, but this time he intended to stay long term, "The most important thing is that I remembered to bring my tea set home," back home there were more idle young people wandering around the reservation than before, then there were some men in their thirties and forties who just stayed inside all day drinking, "I tried to get on their good side, I urged them to try their hands at a different career before it was too late, and not to drink so much," one young guy who was around twenty-seven or twenty-eight years old actually listened and ended up going out to sea on a fishing boat, a few of the middle-aged guys in good shape went down to the Department of Environmental Protection to help collect garbage from the cities "which they looked at as a kind of garbage calisthenics to do either first thing in the morning or right before they went to bed," he himself had also been all over Ren-ai Township and Sinyi Township where he worked on virtually every small construction project around, there were at least twenty days each month where he could get a full day's work for himself and a couple other young guys, "This isn't a bad lifestyle, it's much different from before when I would be away from home for years at a time, of course I don't have to mention how happy my wife and son are with this new arrangement, I can even see how much happier my father is," he adapted fairly well for someone who went from being a big boss on large construction sites to a day worker, "It is probably because I'm a big tea drinker," he drank a kind of green tea that still had the stems attached to the tea leaves, and he ate stir-fried potatoes as a snack, he was always keeping up with all the latest information so he could be prepared if he decided to change his profession, "I figure I've got at least a decade left where I can still expect to be in good shape, so it's not like it's impossible for me to change my profession, but no matter what happens now that I'm back I don't plan on ever leaving my hometown again," He knew that I had come to do research, "Although sometimes I feel unaccustomed to the whole thing, after all I did tough work in the city for so many years, but I hope the next generation will get a better education, if they are able to I'd like them to keep studying and take it as far as it can go, that way they will have more options in the future, the age of working on a scaffolding crew or out on a fishing boat is already behind us," I told him that I was doing research on the "Musha Incident," he looked shocked for a moment, only after taking a few sips of tea did he say, "The only thing that people of my generation think about is going out to the cities to make money, we've almost completely forgotten the traditional legacy that our ancestors have left us with, my father lived through the Musha Incident, he never says much about it, he keeps most of it inside, but I'll ask him what he remembers about the Musha Incident for you," It was clear that it had been quite some time since anyone had mentioned the Incident to him, it had also be a long time since he had even heard those two words, I gazed out past the betel-nut branches in the courtyard and to the distant mountains, as I listened to father and son speaking to each other in their mother tongue, the old man's voice was weak but clear, his expression didn't seem to change when he spoke of the Incident, "My father said that he never complained when he was forced to move out to Riverisle, the hard times were behind him by then, what he felt worst about was the sheer number of people injured and killed during the Incident, at the time they were living each day in fear even though they didn't realize it, but later when he thought back to what had happened he felt increasingly sad, so many had died, my father says that he didn't oppose the 'headhunt' it was like a big ritual sacrifice, but such a large-scale incident where both sides slaughtered one another could only happen if you were mentally deranged, my father says that no one has mentioned the Incident to him in a long time, our culture is nearly gone now, it is time for people to start talking about what happened, we need to commemorate what happened in our own way, how much of our culture even remains anymore, we should take some time to think about these things, we should save as much as we can, think about it, we are the Seediq Daya people." Before I made it back to the lane where I lived I could hear the sound of Girl cursing, as I approached the front courtyard I could see Girl outside facing her house as she waved her hands in the air admonishing someone, inside I could make out the flickering silhouette of a person, and I could hear Boss's crude voice even though he was trying to keep it down, Girl was going on and on about something in her native language and I only understood the sentence "What kind of man are you, you fucking dog, you fucking pig!" after that Girl flashed him a look of disdain and paced around, but then as if she suddenly remembered something she stepped forward again releasing another rapid succession of curses, my guess was that Boss had come for a final discussion and the others had come along to hear what she had to say, the sound of Girl cursing went from her bedroom straight through the wall and into my kitchen where I could hear it sitting at my desk, I jotted down the words the father of Crew Leader had said, "the headhunt was like a ritual sacrifice," "we need to commemorate what happened in our own way," "we should save as much as we can," I underlined these three sentences in red, among them I lingered on "we need to

commemorate what happened in our own way" for a particularly
long time, I underlined it in red twice and decided that I would need
to come back to face this sentence at some later date, I heard Boss yell
something in his loud voice, which was immediately followed by Girl
screaming back, "Why is it my duty, I was only feeling sorry for you
guys!" Spoken in Chinese, this sentence must have been of particular
importance, but Girl was probably a bit too harsh on him, she should
have said that she "felt compassion" for him instead of "felt sorry" for
him which would have been a more appropriate choice of words, I
went out the back door and walked around Granny's Japanese-style
house, and from there went off on my usual walk, I decided to let the
parties involved worry about that other matter, as an outsider there
was no way I could have understood all the intricacies of what had
happened anyway, even a psychic couldn't have hit the nail on the
head, besides even if Boss were to suppress himself he still wouldn't
try to embarrass Girl in front of everyone, there were a few people
on the reservation who were growing tall poinsettias in their back-
yards, ever since I arrived it was a rarity for me to hear man-made
noise, with the exception of the ruckus made during local elections,
the only hope for that pair of dreams expressed by Crew Leader's
father to be realized would be if his son really took them to heart
and planned everything out and then spent the rest of his life trying
to carry them out, Crew Leader was the kind of man who had the
ability and vision to see this through, but he would also need to feel
an "unwavering sense of mission" toward his tribe, otherwise he
would end up quickly losing hope just as Mr. Pihu did about the indigenous rights movement, once I passed the slope where there were
people raising sheep, chickens, and ducks the path opened up to reveal the expansive world of the mountains, for those living here who
might have lost hope in the reservation, it was still easy to continue
on, all they had to do was keep their mouths shut, just like the vast
majority of people living down in the plains on this island nation,

wild straw whipped back and forth in the wind as the sky overhead grew dark, when I gazed over in the direction of the cemetery I noticed more red than before, one of the more endearing things about the tribal followers of the Heavenly Father and Jesus Christ was that the their tombstones were all decorated in Christmas red, it was quite different than the cold desolation of local cemeteries surrounded by weeds and yellow earth, once while on the Rukai reservation of Kochapongan I met an old Rukai man who had a natural talent and prayed before he took on any task no matter how large or small, once the job was complete he would get everyone who worked on it together to stand in a circle and lower their heads in prayer, that is precisely the kind of grassroots religious devotion that could bring reassurance that Jesus Christ and the Heavenly Father had indeed truly arrived here on this island nation, one of my favorite things to do was to stand on the trail that leads through the plum garden and look up at the mountains that abruptly tower above, that kind of vigorous beauty is so powerful that it weighs down on you, there are many more scenes of beauty like that lurking in secret places throughout this island nation, different kinds of beauty cannot be compared to each other and discussing beauty is all about the feeling that it gives you but our hearts never wait for the word "beauty" to be spoken, I had better wait for Christmas vacation so I can have an opportunity to discuss matters concerning "headhunting" with Bakan, does the brutality of the "headhunt" also include a kind of beauty? I'm sure it must, the shudder one feels in that moment that a head is severed, what truly stirs the heart is the transformation of that beauty, it is not about being twisted or having a perverted love of violence it is all about the transformation, most of the crops in the fields have been harvested, left behind are the dark scars lingering on the burned fields, ever since the very first time I came here the sound of the water trickling through the irrigation pipes has always been so vigorous and abundant, even before the setting sun arrived at the edge of the mountain valley the fields were already enveloped in the mountain mist, the thin mist allowed layer after layer of cloudlike patterns to form displaying a soft haze, this was very different from sunsets near the seaport where the entire sky is filled with clouds bathed in sunset hues, from the ridge overlooking the fields down to the river was quite a distance, I suppose that a field of such size would have been enough for everyone once exiled here to live off of, I walked along the ridge toward the west side of the reservation where the gray colors of the falling sunset and rising night held court, I still had a faint recollection of the path that Girl had shown me, but I couldn't tell exactly which direction Girl's Valleystream was in, while I was passing through the west end I thought about stopping by the general store to pick up a small present for Bakan, but Mr. Bakan is the kind of guy who seems to already have everything he needs, I went home via the small path that runs behind the reservation, stopping for a while near the Memorial to the Remains of Life, it was surrounded on both sides by tall cedars, the memorial was on a level platform cut out from the mountain slope, because this was once the site of the local Shinto shrine there was also a pair of thick lantern poles, only more than a decade after the glorious light of the "Son of Heaven" had retreated[35] did someone finally silently erect a "Memorial to the Remains of Life," he was a young man with the physique of an elementary school student, what he did was innocent and quite moving, there were no cries of inequality or ostentatious displays of celebration accompanying its erection, It wasn't an accident that brought me to Riverisle, but it was those words I saw written on that memorial "Remains of Life" that made me stay, I wanted to truly understand the "Remains of Life who had survived the calamity" and "the Incident" was simply a cause I had to explore in order to get there, as for Girl, just thinking of her makes me quicken my step, I could already hear the rumble of Girl's motor scooter coming from Granny's courtyard, I already mentioned the fact that people on the reservation have long since lost any interest in "going for strolls" or perhaps they never had that habit to begin with, so when they go from the east side of the reservation to the west side and back to the east side they always go on their motor scooters, I looked out my window and could see that Boss was the last one to get on his motor scooter, there were four motor scooters and they all took off, "Moxi, Moxi," I could hear Girl running after them calling, "Moxi don't forget to come back tonight to scratch my back!" I called up Bakan at his house, Mrs. Ba's Mandarin Chinese was supple and sweet, her pronunciation was at least three times better than my own, she told me that Mr. Ba had not yet returned, but that he would be home early tonight, I asked whether he might have some free time over the Christmas break, Mrs. Ba laughed and explained that he was usually even busier during the holiday, Mrs. Ba asked me to leave a number, don't stand on formalities, please, she would have Mr. Ba called me back when he got home, I prepared a hodgepodge hotpot and was halfway through eating when the call came to, "Come on over here," it was Mr. Bakan's cheery voice, "Don't stand on formalities," I wanted to get ready, but didn't know what to prepare, when I visit people to interview them I make it a point never to bring my notebook or a tape recorder, after thinking about it for a moment I had a few more quick bites of my hotpot, rinsed my mouth out, wiped my face, and went out the door, Girl was standing in the shadows beside the door, "I've been exhausted all day, I was going to go to sleep, but I came over to see you," she had probably decided to come over after she heard the phone ring, "Get some sleep, you've got things to take care of tomorrow, don't you?" I waved good-bye, telling her that I had to go over to Bakan's house to go over some things, we can talk more tomorrow, under the dull green light I couldn't make out Girl's expression, Bakan emerged from the main hall to receive me in the library of the western chamber, he lived in a traditional rural-style Taiwanese courtyard home, the only difference was that they had modified

part of the eastern wing to serve as a parking garage, the first time
I had seen him was in the backyard of his brother's large two-story
house, "Would you like tea or something stronger?" "I will let the
host decide," "Okay then," he had just returned home from a wedding in town, he smiled as he said that I had dropped by at just the
right time, he always set aside one night each week for himself and
that night was tonight, I wanted to apologize, "It's okay," he waved
his hand, at that moment Mrs. Ba came in to ask if I would like
some tea, Bakan laughed, "We're okay for now, we'll just talk," one
look at Mrs. Ba and I could tell that she was a city person from down
in the plains, she still had the air of a city girl, and her facial features
were not as sharp and refined as Bakan's or the Atayal old ladies that
I would often see out in the fields, "Why do you think the first generation of intellectuals from the reservation all look at 'headhunting' from such an extremely positive perspective?" face to face with the
first person from Riverisle to earn a postgraduate degree, I sensed that
it was okay for me to expand my vocabulary a bit, "Nothing in this
world is simple, but sometimes you look at complex problems from a
simple perspective," Bakan didn't seem to need to stop to think,
the words just flowed out, many of these questions were things that
he had already meditated on for many years, he articulated each
word calmly without showing emotion, and his spoken Chinese was
such that I could later directly write down everything he said without having to revise his words and rearrange his grammar, "As for
this practice of 'headhunting,' according to primitive belief systems
it is a common tribal rite, the historical perspective on 'headhunting'
has been such that in the process of recording the act, they probably
also built a historical criticism into their narratives, and that comes
from the perspective of civilization, seeing it as one of the primitive
and barbaric customs of the savages—but I don't believe that history
and civilization have the right to speak first when it comes to deter-
mining the meaning and value of the practice of 'headhunting,' the

tribe members should speak first and have the strongest voice on this point, especially those tribal elders who are still alive, if one truly wants to face the reality of 'the headhunt,' then I suggest holding a meeting with the tribal elders, this is something that can still be done today, but I'm afraid that in another twenty years there won't be anyone around qualified to talk about 'headhunting' anymore, all they will be able to do will be to quote from legends or historical records, they will be able to cite others but not offer any firsthand accounts, let alone offer any firsthand evaluation of its place in our society, but there is no way we could hold this meeting now, and that is because nobody cares about 'the traditions of minority ethnic groups,' and that's because the government has already established its meaning and value for us, and I don't see much chance of such a meeting being held anytime in the next twenty years, people in Taiwan don't have a strong sense of historical consciousness, and indigenous people here are even more likely to care only about the here and now, after going back and forth between the city and the reservation have you noticed that the period of the 1990s when the anti-assimilation movement was heating up actually corresponded to the period of the most rapid and thorough assimilation—I'm what you call a civilized tribal man, I utilize primitive perspectives to examine primitive people, events, and things, looking at things this way bring me closer to the truth, history is often guilty of misunderstandings due to the perspectives and methods with which it observes the past, civilization carries with it an ideology of criticism, 'headhunting is a traditional practice shared by primitive tribal societies, and it carries meaning as a custom and ritual,' this is the meaning and value I assign to it," I was so wrapped up in listening to him that I lost myself, as I intently listened I melted into his words, and through this process each and every one of his words melted away as I absorbed it, we sat in silence for a while, sometimes you need a comma after talking and listening, for a while, commas are like empty cracks, they represent pure silence pure inaction, they do not reflect on the past nor do they think about the future, Bakan slightly raised his head and closed his eyes, without realizing it I drifted over to the books on his bookshelf, the first thing I saw was an entire set of the Japanese Shinchosha Library collection the old pages were already turning yellow, there was a complete collection of World Literature Classics standing erect on the shelf of this house deep in the mountains of this reservation even though the publisher of the set had gone out of business a long time ago, there was also an entire set of The History of the World's Civilizations next to a copy of *The Decline of the West*, the volume on Edvard Munch was sticking out from a complete set of Early Modern Paintings from Around the World, and then there was a pocket edition set of the Knowledge About Nature series, I couldn't make out many of the other books on his shelf, "Of course you can also look at complex phenomena from a more complicated perspective," I noticed that Bakan's eyes seemed to be a bit bloodshot, "You can certainly take 'headhunting' as a research topic, you can start by examining all of the details, although you will find that there are limited materials to go on, but your research methods should help you in trying to tease out the causes and development of the practice from those small details, the difficulty will be in trying to avoid making too much out of those finer details, if you pay too much attention to these details once they are magnified and jump to conclusions, you will end up distorting the entire thing, but if you just give up and look at the whole instead of the parts, for instance one of the results of researching the Musha Incident was the discovery of headhunting, later people began to focus their attention on the practice of headhunting, but they were unable to get a complete perspective on the Incident that way, during the Musha Incident headhunting functioned as a means to an end but it was not the motivation or the objective behind what happened, both the motivation and the objective were

'political,' Mona Rudao did not launch the Musha Incident in order
to stage a massive headhunt, but the political resistance he stood for
called for political justice, large-scale decapitations occurred during
the Incident, but that was because that was the appropriate action
the Atayal tradition called for, later the 'headhunt' was used to ne-
gate the 'political aspects' of the Incident, but research that argues
for that view is twisting reality, 'the Musha Incident was a case of
civilized weapons giving a good lesson to the barbarous practice of
headhunting' is precisely the kind of argument that makes us upset,
I do not approve of looking at headhunting as a primary factor in the
Musha Incident, it is too easy to blow the importance of headhunting
out of proportion that way, we need to get a good grasp of the entire
situation, the Musha Incident occurred in 1930, even then the seeds
of civilization had already begun to take root and germinate in indigenous high mountain communities, the Musha Incident itself
even had a 'civilized' aspect to it, it was certainly not just some primitive tribal headhunt, it was a civilized revolt against an unjust war,
so it was only to be expected that it would incite the vengeance of
the civilized war machine, I'm a Atayal-Seediq living in the 1990s,
there is no way I can speak for the decisions my ancestors made in the
1930s, but when people at that time faced those specific circumstances I'm sure that they considered all aspects of the situation, and
in the end they decided to resist, knowing full well that their blood
would be spilled in the process, I imagine that it must have been a
heart-wrenching decision for them, once I was a bit more mature I
became reluctant to exaggerate 'the Musha Incident as something
that belongs to us,' you probably know that after 'the Incident' there
were also voices of dissent against the Japanese among the Taiwanese
down in the plains, I'm afraid that those most vocal in their support
were members of the proletariat who formed a united front in support of their indigenous compatriots from the mountains in order
to 'resist the Japanese imperialists,' we really don't particularly care

about whatever honors those currently in power give us, all of that is just 'political,' I would prefer for that to come from the hearts of our children and grandchildren, I hope that when later generations of Seediq people commemorate the Musha Incident they also understand its meaning, and I hope they are able to share a common heart with us in understanding that 'the Musha Incident is something that belongs to us' . . ." "Do you believe it was appropriate for Mona Rudao to launch the Musha Incident?" "I'm not willing to make a precise appraisal about the Musha Incident, perhaps there is an emotional level at play here, now that it is over historians and critics can discuss whether or not 'the Incident' was justified all they want, but they will never be able to return to the actual site of history to truly feel, analyze, judge, and make a final decision, I respect Mona Rudao's decision, perhaps he paid a higher price than was necessary, yet I still stand by his decision, he stood there 'on site' took in the situation and made a decision," I thanked Bakan for sharing his thoughts on the matter with me, Bakan said that he had great respect for every researcher who took the time to come all the way up to their home in the mountains, Bakan said that he was not really worried about "matters concerning history," because there were many members of the younger generation including several young people from the reservation who had devoted themselves to historical research, he also intended to leave behind some materials that "might be of relevance" to future historians, but he was frustrated that his position as the "chief official" kept him so busy that by the time he got home to Riverisle each night he was already exhausted. "today is the only exception to that, one day a week I have some free time," as I went outside I thanked Mrs. Ba for her hospitality, "It was our pleasure," Mrs. Ba held Bakan's hand, "It's not often that people talk to him about those things—" By the time I got home it was already past eleven o'clock, Bakan and I had spoken for more than three hours, my body and soul were struck with a deep feeling of utter exhaustion, perhaps

I had been going for too many walks lately, or maybe it had something to do with the things that Bakan said, then again perhaps it was all because of what was going with Girl and the Quest that lay ahead, perhaps the way "the Incident" seemed to silently cling to every person thing and event on the reservation constantly distracting me and leaving me feeling perplexed was all but a figment of my own imagination, I lay down in bed opened up a bottle of white spirits and took a swig, this was the same drinking position of all those legendary Buddhist arhats, with the exception of a barking dog all was perfectly silent, in my mind I went over all the things that Bakan had said, he had affirmed the meaning and value of headhunting, his recommendation that the elders hold a conference to discuss the meaning of "headhunting" was quite interesting, and could indeed work, after all don't we have all kinds of international academic conferences in the cities these days, we could even apply for a government conference grant to subsidize funding, he didn't subscribe to the idea of the "Headhunt Proclamation" that headhunting somehow stood out independently from the Musha Incident, he instead believed that the Musha Incident itself contained its own notion of "civilization," no one can return to the actual site of history itself, and thus all research carried out in the wake of the incident is simply pure talk dressed up as something else, it's all just inconsequential bullshit. I sat down under the betel-nut tree that was growing just outside my bedroom window, I watched as the "End of the Giving Back Ritual" was being carried out, the elders sat in the center of the courtyard, Girl was sitting to their left, sitting a few feet across from them were five men facing Girl's house, Boss was sitting in the middle directly facing the elders, there was a stack of gifts behind each person, there were two gifts behind one of the chairs in the front but the chair was empty perhaps that person hadn't yet arrived or something important had come up, between the elders and Boss was a stone placed flat on the ground, it was the size of a watermelon, from the historical materials I had read I was able to figure out that this was a traditional Seediq "Bury the Stone Reconciliation" Ceremony, the ceremony was carried out in the Seediq language, the tribal elder presiding over the ceremony spoke many words to Heaven, Earth, and all of those people present, I figured that the stone might have been the same "Buried Stone" that was used in the forced reconciliation between the Toda and Mhebu tribes after "the Incident," I wondered which sneaky Ancestral Spirit had dug it up when everyone was sleeping, he rushed over and left it beside Elder's bed while he was taking an afternoon nap, Elder woke up from his nap and figured that he better bring it along since there was a ceremony today, when Elder placed his hand upon the stone a look of terror appeared on the face of everyone present at the ceremony, Elder pressed down on the stone as he asked each and every one there a question, each person responded with a simple one-word answer, Elder then picked up the stone and rose to his feet, his grandson revved up on his motor scooter and whisked both Elder and the stone away, Girl continued to sit there facing the other men for another two or three minutes but it was hard to tell who was looking at whom, Elder must had rushed home to bury the stone under his bed so that Boss wouldn't go back on his promise, Girl got up and went inside, the men then all stood up and shook out their arms and legs, This fin-de-siècle "Bury the Stone Reconciliation" Ceremony lasted a full fifty minutes, forty minutes of that time was devoted to Elder's admonishments, it was a shame that Boss had likely cleared the area beforehand, I was the sole person to observe and listen in on the ceremony, however it doesn't take much to figure out that the most important witness was actually that stone, how many people attended wasn't terribly important, Moxi recently told me about a farewell banquet being held and invited me to attend, "I don't think that would be appropriate," I tried to refuse, "I'm not even . . ." As I got up to go back inside I caught a glimpse of Boss leading the others inside to say a final good-bye, I figured that I'd better give up on my afternoon nap for the day, once they got a few drinks in them the sounds they would make during their good-bye would be enough to keep me awake, I was just about to make myself a cup of no-afternoon-nap-coffee when I heard someone calling me from outside, "Sister has locked herself up inside and won't come out," it was Moxi, "Boss wants to know if you might be willing to go over and act as a go-between," with a cup of fresh-brewed coffee in my hand I thought about it for a few seconds and decided to go, that way I could rest assured that my subsequent "strolls on the reservation would be uneventful," as soon as Boss saw me he called out to me just like last time, and then with a wave of his hand, someone motioned for me to sit down beside Boss, Boss leaned over and whispered to me asking if I could get Meimei to come outside, I knocked twice on Meimei's door waited a second and then knocked again, Meimei cracked open the door, I saw that she was still wearing the same thing she'd been wearing during the ceremony, a pair of black shorts and black faded T-shirt that wasn't even as dark as the skin around her neck, Meimei shook her head no, the one eye that I could see through the crack in the door looked particularly calm, I figured that she must have said her prayers and sung her hymns that morning that way she wouldn't have to bother with saying good-bye in the afternoon, "Meimei said that she is tired," I whispered in Boss's ear, Boss then popped open a bottle of white spirits and a bottle of brandy, and everyone started in on their farewell banquet, I noticed that all the men were wearing dark slacks and white shirts—the only thing they were missing were ties—Boss didn't eat anything instead he just drank a mixture of white spirits and brandy while the others sat silently and drank beer and spirits, Boss poured me a glass of pure brandy to go with the "white cut chicken" I was eating, it wasn't long before some of them started to get drunk and began smoking, crossing their legs, and spitting on the ground, "Why don't each of you say a few words of farewell to our Meimei," Boss suddenly suggested,

when I heard him say "words of farewell" I almost spit out my brandy
chicken, but to my surprise someone immediately stood up, everyone
else started to applaud, "I would like to thank Meimei, although I
messed around with other girls when I was younger," Oh my with
that white dress shirt I almost mistook him for a playboy, "but that
was only because I lacked confidence back then, so I couldn't commit
to anyone, back then I figured that I'd just end up hanging around
this reservation my whole life like a zombie, but I want to express my
gratitude to Meimei for restoring my confidence," it was obvious that
Playboy was amplifying his voice, he clearly wanted Sister to be able
to hear his confidence from inside her house, "I have decided that
first thing tomorrow morning I will bid farewell to my hometown
and go to the city where I plan to spend the next few years, I have
confidence that I can make something of myself, and I owe all of this
to Meimei," before Playboy even had a chance to sit down, another
big tough-looking guy was already on his feet, "Originally I had
wanted to just leave without saying a final good-bye to Meimei, but
now I'm determined to stay, let's see what Mei . . . Mei . . . Meimei can
do about it, I . . . I . . . I'll bet my last breath on it, Let's see what Mei
. . . Mei . . . Meimei . . . can do about it," Boss slammed his fist down
on the table, the guy who had been speaking immediately shut up
and sat down, he went back to silently drinking his beer and spirits,
"I might leave here too, I'll probably first try to find a job, and then
I'll work on finding a woman to marry," Moxi's voice was clear, it was
a shame that he was trying so hard to suppress his emotions, which
made his arms and legs jump around, one simple sentence and he
went through several different poses and positions, "These hands of
mine have gotten too used to feeling her body, if I don't have my
hands on her before going to bed I always wake up before dawn, then
I feel exhausted all day yet I still think about touching her, and this
isn't the kind of pain that a simple drink will take care of, Meimei
told me I should go find a mother pig to cozy up to, but I think I'd

better find a real partner," people applauded, Boss nodded his head
in approval, there was one guy who looked like a skinny monkey who
had a sullen look on his face the whole time, when he finally got up,
Boss told him to speak in Chinese, because I was there as Meimei's
representative, Skinny Monkey must have been at least 70 or 80 percent wasted, he had his feet propped up on a bench, and with his
head buried in his knees he somehow managed to mutter, "If Meimei
is gonna get married she should marry me, I'll take her swimming
down by the river, if Meimei doesn't marry me I'll marry her, Meimei
can carry me on her back and we'll swim all the way to that lousy
place—" Boss threw down his paper cup, it splashed all over Playboy's white shirt, Mr. Playboy smacked Skinny Monkey's propped-
up foot making him fall over, Boss stood up, so did I, "I'd like to
thank everyone for all your concern," Boss left immediately hopping
on his motor scooter and speeding off, everyone still remembered
their presents they all hugged each other good-bye as they drunkenly
zigzagged off on their motor scooters, "I'll clean up," Girl opened the
door the second they left she had a smile on her face that seemed to
hide a sadness, at dusk I sat down in the living room, I tried to clear
my head of all thoughts, I'm not sure where my heart drifted off to, I
saw Girl dragging a large plastic garbage bag over her shoulder,
I opened the door and Girl flashed me a smile, "I'm cleaning up the
gifts that they left in the courtyard, I'm going to take them over to
Elder's place to store them," I stood on my front porch and looked at
Girl's black shorts, black T-shirt, and black garbage bag walking
slowly in the thick mist of dusk, at that moment the distant sound
of the church playing Christmas songs over their loudspeaker came
through, I took a few more sips of my old cup of no-afternoon-nap
coffee, and here in the nighttime air of the mountain wrote of the
"Remains of Life," the Christmas music was over by nine o'clock,
I felt a bit nostalgic as I thought back to my time on the mountain
reservations of the Rukai where their Christmas dance parties would

often carry on until two o'clock in the morning, I suspected that tonight I would probably hear some "Pathetique" Tchaikovsky, not
long after I got into bed I heard the sound of Girl's door squeaking
open and closed, she must have just returned from caroling, in the
wee hours of the morning I heard the sound of ICRT's Taipei broadcast, that's right, ICRT, if it had actually been "Pathetique" now
that would have been so perfectly appropriate that it would've felt
contrived, I never imagined that the "appropriateness" of something
could be tied to anything but timing, on the contrary perhaps the
artificial contrivances of humans are precisely what decides timing
in the first place, I quickly hopped out of bed and jotted down a
memorandum about the problem of timing when it comes to appropriateness, at the same time I had another cup of bedtime coffee in
order to fight off ICRT, but then in my dream I suddenly remembered that I had been sleeping in the wrong room. The winter sun had
already ascended high into the sky, I looked down at the refracted
shadows stretched crooked across the ground, it was still a long time
until noon, I went out to the rear mountain for a stroll, ever since I
woke up I had been itching to get outside and go for a walk, nature
doesn't bother with the affairs of man, but just think of how many
white-collar urbanites are always dreaming of running off to experience nature, I don't think I've ever heard of anyone becoming disil-
lusioned with "nature" and running back in dejection to the city to
live out their Remains of Life there, perhaps this is because before
they got a chance to "become one with it" they already "became disil-
lusioned by it," I would love to pay another visit to those Shipping
Container Nuns but this time I would bring along two bottles of white
spirits, the smell of alcohol in that place of cultivation would mix
with the scent of incense curiously resulting in a great breakthrough,
otherwise they would just spend all their time reciting passages
from dead books, while their eyes "saw not" the natural beauty before them, I'm not sure if two bottles would be enough, a good thing

then that the Shipping Container Nuns had taken their cultivation to such depths, If I keep walking at my current pace I wouldn't get there until dusk, I suspected that they probably adhered to the practice of "fasting in the afternoon," but last time I was there I'd noticed that nun I spoke to having tea even though it was well past noon, white spirits can of course also be used as a "medicinal remedy" or a late-night snack, if someone were to get up in the middle of the night and "display their true nature" on account of the white spirits I wondered if the Ritual of Displaying One's True Nature would disturb the nature of the mountains and streams, eventually I turned around on the path and my feet carried me back to the reservation, of course I made sure to pick up a bottle before going home, only when you let yourself loose and just fucking do what you set out to without the slightest hesitation can you clearly see your original intentions a true expression of one's mind a naked display of one's true nature, I'd forgotten to ask Girl if I could borrow a traditional headsack, otherwise I would have brought them a hundred bottles of white spirits, that way they wouldn't run out, they would even have some extra to water their vegetables with, I stopped for a moment when I got to the police station, I realized that there was something that I had to take care of with the police and figured that I might as well take care of it now, I must have stood there zoning out for at least ten minutes before I remembered Mrs. Ba's soft hands on that dark night, as Mr. Bakan squeezed her soft hands he said, "There is an old wounded veteran from the war that you could visit, it's hard for me to give you clear directions to his house, but they'll be able to help you out at the police station," Bakan's voice was just as soft as his wife's hands, "I feel embarrassed that you refer to us as the first generation of intellectuals on this reservation . . ." as soon as the guy in charge at the police station heard who I was looking for, he began to shout, "Oh, what a pain in the ass, how come you're always looking for these difficult people," several years earlier they received a report in the middle of the night and immediately set out in their patrol cars along the mountain road in search of Mahong Mona, but when Mahong saw their headlights shining though the darkness she immediately hid in the bamboo forest, only later did they learn that Mahong mistook their headlights for the torch lights of the Japanese army's search teams, the person I was looking for was named Sapu, he didn't spend much time with others, since the old man lived alone, it was decided during several reservation meetings that the police should occasionally check on him and make sure he was doing okay, "Who suggested you meet with him?" the station manager asked, I wasn't quite sure what his intention was in asking that, so I decided to answer honestly, "Mr. Bakan," the station manager nodded and immediately ordered a young officer to take me over to see him, "Since you're going over there, bring him something to eat," the police officer circled back to the general store and had the owner prepare a vegetable egg-fried rice lunchbox to go, it was thirty dollars, "They'll reimburse me for twenty dollars, I'll pay the other ten myself," I must have looked quite surprised, the officer just laughed, "It's a good thing I'm single and don't have any other expenses," Sapu's house was on the far west side of the reservation, it was a low Japanese-style house built on a flat area that had been carved out of the hillside, the house was old and in disrepair, it didn't have the same flair as my next-door Granny's Japanese-style house, "Sapu, Sapu," there was no response, the officer suspected that he might be in the back working on his blockhouse, the officer walked around back and called out to him projecting his voice toward the mountain, "Sha-Ah-Bo," shortly after that we saw a human figure climb out of a recess on the slope, "That's how he gets his daily exercise," the officer didn't even wait for Sapu to come down but simply handed me the lunchbox and said he had to get back to the station to take care of some things, Sapu came straight for the lunchbox, he took it and went over to sit down on the rattan chair in front of his house and started eating, "The old man must have been

famished," I walked over to the betel-nut tree and grabbed a stool
to sit down on, the old man ate half his lunchbox before carefully
packing the rest up and putting it inside, he came back out a few
minutes later, "Did you eat?" this was probably the first time he'd
really looked at me, but then he really surprised me by addressing
me in Taiwanese, "I already ate this morning," "That's good, so
what'd you come all this way for?" "How come you speak Taiwanese
so well?" it is often easy for the elderly to go off on tangents, I was also
afraid of asking direct questions that might upset him, "I speak au-
thentic Taiwanese that I picked up living in the market district of
Dihua Street in Taipei," after the war the old man spent twenty years
"idling about" on Dihua Street, all the store owners and wholesalers
in the market district saw how savage he looked and hired him to stay
on as a "security guard," he would listen to one line of Taiwanese and
silently repeat it to himself a few times before speaking it out loud,
everyone complimented him on how smart he was and how quickly
he learned, during those twenty years he never wrote letters home,
the only thing people on the reservation could say for sure was that
no one had ever sent his ashes back, but Sapu was missing, he idled
through the 1950s and 1960s seeing Dihua Street go from a bustling
market district to a state of decline as one after another all the bars
and restaurants shut their doors until Black Beauty[36] was the only
one left, as times changed men like him were no longer needed, after
a drifting life he ultimately decided to return home, he never imagined that the moment he originally left would end up being a turning
point, he had spent his time on the streets and alleys of the city living
a nearly destitute life yet not completely penniless, all the while Taiwan
raced to open up twelve-lane highways and eight-lane highways,
which all became clogged with traffic, He returned to Riverisle in
the early 1970s, his parents had already passed, and all that was left
was the family house, ever since that time he hadn't set a single foot
outside the reservation, he didn't have a single electric appliance, and

everything in the house dated back to the end of World War II, naturally he was also oblivious to all the changes that had occurred in the
world beyond the boundaries of Riverisle, "Is the Pavilion on Dihua
Street still there?" "Uh huh," "What about the Xia-Hai City God
Temple?" "Yep," but those old bars are no longer in fashion, these
days it's those high-scale restaurant bars that have taken over, all the
old wholesalers on Dihua Street have long gone global, they all re-
invented themselves as distribution agents for various name-brand
manufacturers, after seeing all the changes there over the course of
twenty years he probably assumed he would never see the changes
that had come during the twenty years since he left, just like those
who died that year in Mhebu had seen enough of that place and
thought that they never could have imagined the hot springs resorts
like Lu Mountain and Crimson Peach Blossom that have popped up
there today, "Were you injured during the war?" the old man snick-
ered, he raised his left hand to reveal a lone thumb, the rest of his
hand was smooth like a ball of flesh, the old man got up took a few
steps and asked, "What's the difference anyway?" "There's no difference," as soon as he started to relax I noticed that he swayed to the
right when he walked, his legs were straight but his body pulled to
the right with each step, "Back when I was on Dihua Street in order
to keep a steady job, I learned how to stand up straight and force
myself to walk normal, but as soon as I relax my body goes crooked
again," one third of his pelvis bone was smashed, later he had surgery
to put in an artificial hip, he ended up in bed at the Taipei Military
Hospital for three years after that, "The first time I snuck out of the
hospital to check out the city I ended up finding my way to Dihua
Street, I did my best to walk tall and hide my limp, and eventually
someone there hired me to be a security guard," He had already grown
accustomed to covering up his limp in front of other people, until
that moment I hadn't noticed his limp either, "I joined the army in
1942, I was among the first wave of volunteers for the Takasago

Army, we were all shocked when we first boarded the battleship, there were more than five hundred of us and every one of us was as strong as a bull, the ship went to the Philippines, stopping along the way at different islands, before long the five hundred of us were scattered all over, and I didn't even know where I was," "I think they called that place the Batan Islands," "Anyway it didn't matter to me if that place was the Batan Islands or the Tanba Islands, all that mattered was working and shitting, what, you don't think that mattered? What, do you think that eating and sleeping matter?" I asked him what his thoughts were about his life during those two years, but Sapu turned the question around to me, "I did hard labor for two years, during that time I never had enough sleep and never had enough food, what kind of thoughts do you expect me to have?" "But there were comfort women?" "I heard there were those kind of women who came to our camp to work, but I didn't pay much attention, I didn't have any experience with that stuff, sometimes in the rain forest I would run into those scantily dressed island women but they never left any special impression on me," Sapu flashed an innocent smile, "It's not that I was somehow less able than the other guys, I think we are all born about the same, we just felt kind of numb, day after day we were subjected this 'hysterical form of discipline' that killed our appetite for life, so who in their right mind would still have an appetite for women, I think those women must have been provided for those of us who were truly 'hysterical,' they needed to push their 'hysteria' as far as it could go and release it," I suddenly thought back to Mr. Miyamoto and his "Miyamoto Spirit," "The Takasago Army, explosives strapped to their waists, sent to the front lines, charging into enemy territory—" "That's all bullshit," Sapu interrupted me, "To put it in simple terms, we did volunteer, but you could say that we only did it half-willingly, we signed up in a semicoerced state, we had no choice but to agree to serve as the 'workhorses' for the Japanese rulers, but it never really went to the point of 'loyal until death,'" Sapu laughed at me for being so naïve, "That was all propaganda, they wanted to sell the fact that even third-class citizens were willing to sacrifice themselves for the nation, who could imagine that the descendents of our high mountain people could be so naïve, it's all because the new government that came to power after World War II started to tell their own version of what had happened, once you repeat the story a hundred or a thousand times people believe it as if it was true, but that too is propaganda," everything I knew I had only read in historical documents, so I didn't want to press the issue, "But one thing is true, there were indeed urns and urns of ashes that were sent back to the reservation from the front lines, I think the majority of the people who died had been sent to Honjima Island, they died during the landing operation there never knowing who or what they were dying for, I also came pretty damn close to being sent back in an urn, but somehow ended up spending two decades on Dihua Street, it was there that I clearly saw the reality of 'birds dying for food, people dying for money,' and it was at that point that I realized those people whose ashes got shipped back home never even knew who or what they died for," Sapu got up to take me up the rear mountain to have a look around, I noticed that he was standing erect as he climbed up the mountain slope and I couldn't see any trace of his limp, "In the end we just dug holes like this one in the palm forest beside the sea," the mountain slope was covered with holes, they were all different sizes, Sapu was quite comfortable walking around the holes, but I ended up falling in one, "At the time the holes we dug were used to set up machine guns, they needed to be big enough for two people to squat down inside, just think about how much effort it took to dig out those holes all over the island, during the last year before the end of the war we were out there digging every single day, one day at dusk I found myself a bit lightheaded after digging all day, I threw my iron shovel aside and took a step toward the ocean, but then I heard the sound of cries mixed with screams, I had set off a land mine buried under the sand," after a long silence, I asked, "So what are you digging these holes for?" "That's a secret," Sapu smiled, "For several days, I stood in my backyard staring at the mountain slope, I don't know why I was looking at it or what I was doing I just stood there staring, I kept doing that until one day I picked up a hoe went up there and started digging, later I found that my hands would get antsy if I didn't dig, I would start digging a new hole before I even finished the previous one, anyway I could always go back to dig more, a few people from the reservation came by to see what I was doing, some of them even threatened to send me off to the loony bin, the only one who complimented me on my holes was Mr. Secretary-General Bakan, I complained to him that I felt all antsy if I didn't dig, and when your hands are antsy your heart is antsy, Bakan he understood what I meant, so later nobody bothered me about it anymore, one time even the manager from the police station came over and told me that there was more than enough land on this island for me to dig up," "That's right, there is plenty," I agreed, "You're just as smart as Little Ba," Shaba was standing amid a sea of countless holes that he had dug up, he patted me on the shoulder with his left fist, "Who knows when the third bomb will drop, but when the time comes everyone on the reservation will understand the benefit of the holes that I dug." I managed to escape with my life from Sapu's hole, I walked through the west side of the reservation cutting through the bamboo forest near the general store, I picked up a can of Whisbih and safely made it back to the east side of the reservation, this long voyage home was similar to Sapu's supply ship that made numerous stops yet managed to avoid getting sunk by an enemy attack, after a perilous journey like that one needs a good can of Whisbih to soothe the soul, I really need to find time to warn that nun about this, "Better not to drink too much white spirits," from what I know about the historical biographies of famous monks not a single one of them attained enlightenment after drinking heavy liquor, but this was a view that would be easy for the nuns to refute, after all the number of people who have achieved enlightenment throughout the ages far exceeds the number of famous monks we know about, "whether or not drinking hard liquor can lead one to enlightenment" will ultimately be up to the nun's individual destiny it is something beyond my ability to predict, I wonder if some of the more perceptive individuals on the reservation like Mr. Bakan ever noticed that the psychological state of that old man living alone here was actually a topic quite deserving of real research, loneliness can eat away at an old person's strength of mind, it can warp their mental state, I had seen other elderly people living alone on other reservations and their eyes all looked like stars it was like discovering a flicker of light amid a vast nothingness just before it is extinguished yet those stars are already dead, it is no surprise that we can't understand the old man Sapu's holes, after all we can't even understand the games a small child plays when he is playing by himself, one day someone will probably discover the old man hiding out in one of those holes refusing to come out, actually "this isn't the first time something like this has happened," this has nothing to do with differences between the city and the country, the metropolis and the reservation, the civilized and the primitive, it is probably more just a phenomenon that is true to the human experience, loneliness is something that must be addressed early on otherwise once you are older you will end up like a little mouse waiting to be eaten by the big cat of loneliness, I crawled back to the little hole-in-the-wall place I was renting, and in my loneliness faced my can of Whisbih, I sat there until dusk came the sun set and the cold mountain air came down along the ridge from Reunion Mountain to see if I was home, to check whether I had had my hodgepodge hotpot dinner yet, and to make sure I had enough blankets to stay warm, I took a deep breath of that mountain air, I held it inside me, I let it play there for a while before letting it return to

Reunion Mountain to report back, "That long-haired madman is still there, he's still going strong, in Riverisle," did Mr. Bakan send me to meet Sapu in order to get an education in what it means to "escape with one's life?" Sapu managed to escape with his life from an even larger battleground, he only experienced one war in his life, I never once resisted during battle, the individual is helpless amid the hysteria of the collective, this "helplessness" extended into his post-war life, he spent the 1950s and 1960s idling away in the old market on Dihua Street just like he had idled away his time on the islands watching the sunset each day, but there was a disconnect between those things and himself, whether or not the sun set down over the sea, and whether or not it was a bad day for business down on the market street, none of that had anything to do with Sapu, one of the most infuriating things was that the Takasago Army's "volunteer suicide corps" was completely refuted by one former volunteer soldier, he didn't have any idea what his native land of Mhebu was like, he went home to Riverisle and lived "a completely individualistic life," he had no contact with the world outside the reservation, none of the news from civilization where new things seemed to be happening every day ever reached him, at the same time he virtually cut off all his ties to everyone else on the reservation, Bakan wanted Sapu to show me that "life is filled with all kinds of differences, but if we were to unify them under a single perspective" or "according to your opinion, take Sapu's life as a special case to be examined," both sides would be ridiculed, because both sides are completely meaningless to Sapu, it is a good thing then that I am a writer, Bakan didn't realize that the eyes of one who illuminates are different from the eyes of a researcher, due to this and that factor the eyes of the researcher become fixed, the eyes of the illuminator are always changing due to this and that factor at the same time because of this and that factor they never change, it would be utterly meaningless for me to put a satirical spin on Sapu's actual life events at the same time putting a satirical spin on Sapu's real life would be fucking incredible, "You've had too much Whisbih and beer, haven't you?" the big cat of loneliness was still somewhere in the dark lying in wait, "Why don't you go to sleep, if it's cold use two blankets, I'll be there looking after you throughout the night," I petted the big cat's tail, he licked the tip of my nose, he was completely at ease, "the contemporary" had something else to say, there were four points on which "the contemporary" disagreed with Bakan, 1) the contemporary inquires into all possibilities including the primitive, and contained within the process of inquiry itself is already a form of criticism, that is because there is no such thing as "pure inquiry," that is because criticism has a quality that is constantly moving and never stagnates, 2) the contemporary always pays a lot of attention to details, it is the details that make up the whole, sometimes you can even catch a glimpse of the entirety from a small detail, the contemporary opposes anything that stakes a claim to "comprehensive meaning," it instead advocates painstaking investigation, each minute detail might have immense importance for the whole, 3) the contemporary opposes the perspective that "those standing too close to history don't have the right to voice their criticism," otherwise there would be no such thing as "historical existence," those who write history must be the illuminators for "the site of history," it is only because they criticize that they are able to illuminate, 4) posing a supposition about a historical site or attempting to re-create a site of history are methods derived from theory, without that, it would be easy for the contemporary to overlook or lose all kinds of historical facts,—I got under the covers with the big cat of loneliness, because I'd had too much Whisbih I'd forgotten my bedtime coffee, the big cat squeezed inside a pair of pants that were somewhere on the bed, I heard the sound of him purring, just before I forgot myself. I woke up as soon as a touch of color returned to the sky, I turned on the lamp and prepared myself a cup of coffee, I sat at my desk drinking my cup of coffee as the daylight gradually came in through the window, after the cock cackled for the third time it was time for all the chickens to wake up and begin vibrant conversations, once I had combed my hair and brushed my teeth I went out the back door for my morning walk, I decided that this would be a day for me to enjoy myself, I appreciated the fact that I could still have free time like that here in Riverisle, when I got home after my walk I didn't bother opening the front door, nobody ever knocks on my door anyway, I sat down in front of my rear window jotting down notes reflecting and writing, from time to time I would look out and gaze at the shadows and lights dancing on the mountain ridge and the movement of the plants and trees out in the garden, I walked down the path through the cemetery, the small plum-blossom petals were still longing for the dew, the foxtail bristlegrass seemed thicker and its color was much richer looking more like wolftail than foxtail, gazing out through the wolftail I could see the reservation at the foot of the mountain, it was already existing in a state of "quietude" and there was no other place it needed to return to, I came to a fork in the path and figured that it must lead back to the reservation, but I never thought of passing through that wolftail bristlegrass to get there, near the entrance to the mountain canyon was the Meiyuan reservation, which was originally a subtribe of the Seediq Daya group, at some time in the past one branch of the Daya tribe moved east along the Wukali River and passed over the southern summit of the Qilai Mountains at 3,357 meters above sea level to arrive at the back mountains near Hualian in order to find a new life for themselves, the branch that moved west most likely went over the Western Eye Mountains, which were 2,077 meters above sea level, in order to arrive at the Bukan River, because the area upstream was occupied by the Sekoleq they went downstream through the opening between the peaks, they set up their reservation between two canyons, one of the main reasons that the Remains of Life from the Musha Daya tribe who had survived were exiled to Riverisle had to do with the fact that members of their same tribe were present in Meiyuan, in the late 1930s a new dam was built that flooded the fields of more than 600 people of the Banlan tribe, which was also part of the Musha tribe, they were relocated from Wanda to a place between Meiyuan and Riverisle where they established the Center Plateau reservation, the first time I met Bakan he sighed, "All we have left now are just three reservations," go out to the rear mountains and take a look around at the Daya people who have settled there, since they are far away and the mountains prevent a smooth passage communication is difficult, it was clear that when Bakan talked about there only being three reservations left he was leaving out the Toda Turuku and Wanda subtribes even through they are also Seediq, the primary reason for this change can be naturally attributed to what happened during the "Musha Incident," what repulses me most is that the mountains on both sides of Brow Plateau were taken over by a "state-owned" entity and made into a "privately run state-owned" experimental forestry center, people from Brow Plateau didn't even have the right to enter, whereas the plains people could purchase tickets to go in but even then they would discover that only a small portion of the forestry center was actually open to the public, for the mountains right there in their own backyard to be taken over as "state-owned" really felt like a waste of "nature," it led to a kind of repressed anger that they kept deep inside, this might be the reason I resisted visiting those other two reservations, the expedition I embarked on that day took me from the river through the valley summit and into the "state-owned" realm, during my morning walk I watched the morning sun rise and now I saw it disappearing behind Brow Plateau, I went back the same way I'd come, and from a distance I could see Girl standing in front of the chicken coop as if in a daze, she was wearing a pair of black shorts and a black T-shirt, when she came back to the reservation from Taipei she brought three or four sets of black shorts and T-shirts with her, she often wore a dark red leather jacket, walking on the streets of the "capital" all she needed was her leather jacket and a black T-shirt for her chest to really stand out, which along with her long snow-white legs dazzled everyone around her, I can imagine what kind of nasty thoughts people must have had when they saw her, for the past few nights Girl had been unable to sleep, since there was really no place to go she would just walk out to her six plots of land, "I thought of all kinds of cool plans but none of them worked out," Girl was sure to make it clear that "It's not that there was a problem with my plans, the problem is with this whole reservation," Girl thought about opening a Black Cat Bar, a Warehouse Bar, but none of that worked out, she'll have to wait for her 2020 Bar, when this island nation is reduced to ashes as some people have predicted, those who still want to get "high" will have to squeeze into the Warehouse Black Cat Bar, by that time the architectural style on the reservation will have become the new trend, no wonder there was a period of time whenever I would go for walks on campus I would see the Department of Urban Planning and think to myself that one day they will have to change their name to the Department of Reservation Planning, "It was right after I came back to the reservation and saw a chicken coop that I realized I could raise some chickens," Girl said as she scattered some chicken feed on the ground, "If I turned my six plots of land into a chicken farm it would be at least thirty times bigger than this chicken coop, I would let them be free range so they could live off the land, they could live off those insects in the grass there for a good six months, I would only need to sprinkle some of my homemade chicken feed out there once a day, if I started with thirty chickens I would have three hundred in less than six months, with six plots of land I could probably raise more than 30,000 chickens and there would still be plenty of room for them to eat sleep and roll around, I could set up a distribution deal along Reunion Mountain, and the entertainment resorts near Sun Moon Lake, they would purchase at least 3,000 a day, they wouldn't even have time to lay eggs," "But how many helpers would you need?" "I wouldn't need any, they'd be free range, living on their own, the complicated part would be that I would need to move up there, to prevent people from stealing them, if you don't pay attention someone might run off with all of them in one night," "Naturally," six guys could pull it all off in less than one night, not to mention the fact that those six plots of land are completely naked, "I'd play my chickens Schubert and Mozart when they go to bed each night, even in their dreams they would know that their meat was delicious," "That goes without saying," the chicken's taste is of the utmost importance here on this island nation where competition over food is so fierce, "I'll hang up a huge sign, would you mind thinking of a name for me?" "Remains of Life Poultry Farm," I didn't even have to give it a second thought of course it should be called the Remains of Life Poultry Farm, I waved good-bye cut through the vegetable garden and went in through the back door, Girl called out to me, "I'll drop by after I feed the chickens," I immediately started to brew a cup of pre-chit-chat coffee, it is a necessity to have a cup before any long conversation, I figured that I hadn't had a cup of pre-chit-chat coffee in at least four or five years, it indeed tasted different it was a bit reminiscent of "Mona Coffee," during my Remains of Life I hope to open up a "Mona Coffeehouse" on the bank of the Mhebu River just next to the forest, if I used the sulfur vapor and the mist from the forest to add flavor I'm sure that my "Mona Coffeehouse" would become famous all over this island nation, I guarantee that there would be tons of "super cool" Generation Xers who would drive more than six hours just to taste a cup of "Mona Coffee," it would be so good that it would be worth the Remains of Life of those who drank it, Girl opened the screen door and strolled in, she put the loofah gourd in her hand down on the kitchen counter, the loofah hodgepodge hotpot was fresh and sweet it was just a shame that we didn't have any dried shrimp to put in, Girl sat herself down, and quietly whispered,

"Remains of Life sounds like a great name," it has a soaplike fragrance, Girl looked like she had washed up and done her hair in a neat braid that hung down over her left breast, "Opening a poultry farm is a great idea," I thought of our national treasure Taiwan trout, "Opening up a fish farm wouldn't be a bad idea either," "I'd better wait for my brother to return before I decide, I can't decide anything until he gets back," "Didn't you decide by yourself to come back to Riverisle?" "That's different, I was living on my own away from home and had to take care of myself then, things are different now that I'm home, my mom asked me to help take care of him when he was born, otherwise what would she have done," I thought back to how infrequently Drifter came back home, I wondered if he really cared about his big sister in the same way, "You always appear so calm," Girl was about to say something but I interrupted her, "Not really, you've never seen me when I'm squandering my life away," "There was a period of time when I first came back to the reservation when I felt very much at ease, but now I feel lost, It's hard for me to explain it in words, but people say everything gets all fuzzy and foggy when you drink too much, well that's how I feel deep inside, fuzzy and lost, I've tried to get by without drinking for the past two or three days, but I'm not sure how long I can hold out, when I chew on betel nuts I feel nauseated and want to cry, no one ever sees an Atayal woman cry," Mahong Mona certainly never cried when she was summoned to Puli to identify her father's remains, "I don't shed my tears for any person or thing, I cry for that lost sense of inner quiet that I had when I first came home, even my tears feel lost," complete and utter apathy always brings one the greatest sense of calm, completely devoting oneself to a person object or job can bring someone a great sense of calm, but it is hard to feel calm when one's life is not settled, living a safe life while your heart is restless is a terrible type of calm to endure, it might be easy to write the words how to live peacefully, finding peace and calm between hope and hopelessness, "Perhaps this is just a period of adjustment for you, after all you've had to go through some things lately," I thought carefully about how to phrase what I was going to say, "whether you are seeking peace or not, it's very hard to constantly maintain a peaceful state," Girl swayed her torso and said that she really wanted a cigarette and a strong drink, even a beer would do, "Where the hell did my resolve run off to?" one second she was rubbing the veins popping out around her forehead, the next second she was squeezing her chest, she even bit the neck of her T-shirt, I went into the bedroom and fished out a five-hundred-dollar bill from my pants pocket, which I handed to her, lowering my voice I told her, "There is no need to give up drinking right away, why don't you go down to the general store and see if there is anything you want, there is something I want to discuss with you when you get back," the neck of her T-shirt had lost its shape from her pulling the collar with her teeth, the collar drooped down into her cleavage, in order to get to the general store she had to walk behind Bakan's house, Mrs. Ba was usually out in her backyard talking with other women under the violet trellis, I really wanted to ask Mrs. Ba what she thought of Girl, Girl came back with a bottle of white spirits, two cans of beer, a pack of cigarettes, and a bottle of whiskey, it was a good thing that the winter sun was considerate enough to spare her cleavage from getting too tan, Girl sat down and pulled her arms back covering her cleavage, "I've gotta change my shirt when I go home, I stretched this out when I was biting it," there was nothing I could say, after all to be naked is only natural, civilization on the other hand demands that what is natural must always be covered by this and that, and it has gotten to the point where people now charge astronomical prices for clothing that exposes some cleavage, but is cleavage packaged with astronomically priced clothing somehow more beautiful? I don't think so, the most beautiful set of breasts I ever saw was on a woman who put on a men's dress shirt after sex, "Why don't we start with the white spirits," I suggested when I saw

Girl going for a can of beer, she quickly agreed, "One glass of white spirits," the way Girl smiled showed she was slightly embarrassed, once you get some white spirits down in your stomach it has a way of packaging your true nature and all the plastic artificial stuff can go back to the factory, I've seen Girl's true nature, sometimes I find myself spending a lot of time discussing what is "appropriate" with her true nature, it was still early morning and we each downed a glass of white spirits, "And how about your Quest?" I finally asked, Girl was a bit taken aback for a moment, then another moment, and then another, before she finally exclaimed, "Oh, man!" she jumped to her feet, just missing hitting her head on the ceiling by one or two inches, in the time it took her to plop back down the indentation in the sofa cushion where she was sitting suddenly seemed to appear three-dimensional, "If you decide to go I'll go with you," I was somewhat dumbfounded by what she said, "Hey, *you're* the one who wanted to go, not me, I was just going to tag along," Girl fell silent for a while, "You're right, I am the one who wants to go, I must go, this time I want to ask the Ancestral Spirits how to attain a sense of calm in my life," Girl opened a can of beer, "The only way I'll feel at ease about the trip is if you come with me," "How do we get there?" I asked Girl, she looked at me as if I shouldn't have bothered opening my mouth, "If you just follow the river that runs in front of the reservation won't you eventually just get there?" I laughed, "getting down to the river is easy, but once you're down there are we supposed to go north or south?" "You really think of it as north and south?" Girl looked genuinely surprised, "the Ancestral Spirits never separate it as north and south, they just twist around the bends of the river until they arrive there!" I could tell that we needed to add some whiskey to our white spirits, otherwise the gas might make our livers explode, "The Ancestral Spirits can magically come and go as they please, they can appear at will," I pointed to Girl's dark-tanned legs and feet that were curled up on the sofa she loved to laugh almost as much as she seemed to like losing her temper, "Look at you, you really plan to use those two legs of yours to take you on your Quest, you'll have to rely on them to take you there one step at a time," "I wouldn't know, I haven't researched it," Girl opened up a can of beer for me, "The beer is pretty cold," I took a few sips of the cold beer, I figured that I could drink a bit slower, sometimes if you drink too quickly others have trouble keeping up with you, "Don't you try intimidating my legs, I got them into shape in Valleystream, they wear the same hot pants whether it is summer or winter, just from that you should know that they aren't afraid of anything," those dark and tan legs were gorgeous, take one look from her inner thighs to her curvaceous inner calf and you could see just how firm her muscles were, "I'm the one who's worried about those intellectual legs of yours," Girl squinted as she read the label and expiration date on the beer can, "After a long hike through my Valleystream I'll need to rest for a few days to recover from the soreness in my legs, the Quest won't be easy, but I hope they can keep up with my feet," I squinted at the fair-skinned cleavage between her dark legs and tan collarbone and smiled, at first I wanted to take out my notebook to show Girl the detailed notes I had on the three routes we could take, but I was afraid that my penmanship might hurt her eyes, it has been said that the Ancestral Spirits are the only ones who can understand my handwriting besides me, I had hoped that Girl would take her time listening, so I started with the route that went upstream from Bukan and passed through Reunion Mountain and Qilai, I then went back to explain the second route, which went upstream from the Bukan River before changing course around Eastern Eye Mountain where we would converge with the Mei River, the third route followed the Bukan River downstream to where it met with the Wu River and the Southport River and then went up to Puli where it would follow the Mei River to Muddy River before arriving at the mouth of the Mhebu River, I didn't tell her that in my heart I secretly imagined that the Ancestral Spirits went upstream along

Muddy River and passed over Qilai and Reunion mountains and then went down the Bukan River toward Riverisle where they arrived in Girl's dreams, I hoped that Girl would instinctively choose one of the routes or perhaps the Ancestral Spirits had already given her some hints about which of the three paths would be best for her Quest, but Girl just asked, "Which route is the easiest, and which one is the most difficult?" the first path has the greatest degree of difficulty, just going from Riverisle down to the river and then upstream to Reunion Mountain is a very long journey and it is hard to say just how many days it would take, and that's not to mention all the difficulties we would meet river trekking along the way, only once you are on the road can you really tell just how difficult it will be, it is a good thing that I have already spent quite a bit of time researching the ins and outs of river trekking, rock climbing, and most importantly outdoor survival, so I was ready to trek upstream to the source of life itself and no Bukan River or any other river on this island nation was going to stand in my way, I took a sip of white spirits mixed with beer, but nothing could extinguish my thirst for adventure, I should take a moment to savor my thirst for adventure and enjoy my imagination of what dangers might await me, "The Ancestral Spirits are coming by way of the third path," was Girl talking in her sleep? Or was she talking in her drink? "The Ancestral Spirits aren't stupid, why do you think they spend all their time traveling over the mountains, it is a tough job and not very exciting, following such a long river all the way down Valleystream is lonely enough to make every cell in your soul feel like an empty valley, by the time they finally see the lights of Riverisle, they are all busy providing first aid to each other, it's really horrific, have you seen the movie called *The Valley of Loneliness*? Loneliness can really make someone feel like their heart is a fucking valley, the Ancestral Spirits all take the third path, the road is quite bustling, there are scantily clad girls beside the stream selling them betel nuts,[37] and you can see the small town transforming into a big town overnight, the little neon lights become big neon signs, with all the sounds colors people and voices it doesn't feel the least bit lonely, if it was me, that's certainly the path that I would take—how fucking awesome!" I corrected Girl that one should not use the word "awesome" to describe a matter like this, "the age of Ancestral Spirits was before the age of awesome," Girl blinked in agreement, "The Ancestral Spirits might be able to accept car noise and all the clamor humankind makes, but can they handle the legs of those scantily clad betel-nut girls?" I hid the fact that this path was actually the road to exile taken by the Atayal all those years ago, which wouldn't have been appropriate to bring up, just mentioning it was too depressing, "Wow, you know that Ancestral Spirits love a good party, whenever someone from the reservation builds a new house, the Ancestral Spirits gather around each night staying up until dawn, and did you notice how many rockets were fired on the eve of the Autumn Moon festival this year, they went right up into the sky headed to the moon, half of them were set off by the Ancestral Spirits, in the past the Ancestral Spirits would only come out to watch the show, but this year they actually got in the spirit of things and joined the fun," I was really pissed that Girl's people had all chosen the most difficult path, she was the only one who selected the most easiest path, but it was a shame that I wouldn't get a chance to show off my rock-climbing skills along the Bukan River, it's okay though because later in life I plan to go river trekking through the Ailiao River all the way into the Rukai and Paiwan area, "Maybe I'll even make it to Puli to catch the last screening of *A Bug's Life*, bugs have after all always been my favorite, so let's see just what's so damn scary about their life," I wanted to correct the way Girl pronounced "damn" in Chinese but had to shut myself up, I wanted to tell her that telling someone "You're so damn full of shit" wasn't as good as "You're so fucking amazing," when you tell someone they are amazing it really goes straight to their heart, that is also what it says in that Atayal romanization handbook I read, "I can't say the word 'amazing,'" Girl explained that she couldn't help saying "damn," "but if I say 'amazing' my teeth will fall out," it was a good thing that Girl seemed to have all her teeth in place, damn what the hell does it matter what amazing things she says anyway, "Who else is going with us?" Good Girl for the first time asked a practical question, I sat there all prim and proper thinking about who was "qualified" to go with us, the most qualified candidate would naturally be her little brother Drifter, but Girl would have to summon him home to inform him of our journey, the second most qualified candidate would be Deformo, the Ancestral Spirits would all be delighted to see this little devil who managed to "get his hands on some American tits," we would need to tell Drifter to be sure to inform him if he were to run into any during one of his walks, coming in third would be Mr. Pihu, he was strong and in good shape so he'd be able to carry whatever supplies were necessary, along the way he could also tell us about all the various environmentalist theories and practical actions for protecting the riverbed, I'd be sure to inform him tonight after dinner, "Elder is the fourth most qualified candidate," Girl would check to see if the old man would be interested in visiting his ancestral homeland one last time while he was still of this world, "Priest is fifth," Girl was hoping Priest would bring the Heavenly Father along to bless them with safety during their journey, but I was opposed, the Ancestral Spirits would surely not want to see Priest or the Heavenly Father and in order to avoid them they might even seal the mouth of the Mhebu River to block the passage, Girl stuck out her tongue in surprise, "Okay, I hereby disqualify Priest," Bakan was a busy man and wouldn't be able to get more than a day away from work so he was out, Sapu was too old and he had a bad hip, Girl didn't even know, "When did this young man named Sapu come back to the reservation?" There was no need to even ask Mr. Miyamoto, there was no way he would go but I wondered if his invisible samurai sword could really hold its own in a duel against a primitive hunting knife? "Aha, I forgot all about Old Wolf," without moving I jumped out of my seat hitting my head on the ceiling and then still without moving fell right back down into my chair, Girl looked utterly dumbfounded, "This is what you call being in a state of motionlessness," I explained, "the important thing isn't the fact that I jumped out of my seat, but that I did it without moving a muscle," Girl swallowed a few gulps of saliva before taking another drink of her white spirits-beer mix, "Who is Old Wolf?" I found Old Wolf's phone number jotted down in my notebook, I remember that number being for a phone in the rooftop storeroom, "It is hard to explain who Old Wolf is in just a few words, wait until you meet him, and the two of you can get to know each other!" I immediately called him, the phone rang for a long time, I figured that Old Wolf usually wasn't home, but someone picked up, Old Wolf said that he had been out on the hillside of the rear mountain building a traditional Mhebu tribal house out of moso bamboo, I told him that I was preparing to go with a few other people from Riverisle river trekking up to Mhebu on a "Quest," he told me that he had been waiting for an opportunity to eat and drink with others from his tribe, later he told me that Latino Seediq had wired him some money in Daya Mona's name, with instructions to continue the Mhebu tribal reconstruction project, he was hoping that some other people from the tribe would be willing to stay behind and help out and he was willing to pay them, "So it's decided then," I kept flipping my notebook around as if it was a ball, "There will be at least seven of us going," in a moment of carelessness my notebook accidentally fell onto Girl's breasts and immediately bounced off landing in between my knees, I wasn't quick enough to catch it, "Did you do that on purpose?" I could tell that Girl was upset by the twisted look on her face, "*It* did it on purpose," I didn't have anything to be afraid of, "why would I do that on purpose?" "You're really naughty, I should just take them out and let you play with them like a set of balls," "No need for that, just leave them where they are," Girl reached her hand down her T-shirt, I was afraid that if I didn't play well I might end up shooting those balls all the way up the mountain peak, I was afraid I might even lose them, "Just leave them where they are, they look good there and it's fun to have them around," Girl flashed me a burning drunken smile. Early morning, I am sitting on my front step, looking out at the floating clouds lingering over the mountain range after last night's rain, it is quite poetic when you see floating clouds over the mountain peaks, not nearly as static as usual, when you see static clouds just hanging there over distant mountains without moving it is a price tag hanging on a traditional Chinese landscape painting, but when those floating clouds are drifting over the mountain peaks right before your eyes they appear much more mischievous, someone should hang a price tag on them of three dollars each, I'm sure that these paintings depicting the magical union of "Floating Clouds and Mountains" would magically jump to five dollars each, I hung on to this all morning, the moment I hung a price on it those floating clouds began to move, no wonder people's hearts have many faces and some say true love is like a floating cloud, nature seems to always provide us with these kinds of revelations, the very moment the word "revelation" entered my mind I saw Priest who preaches the Revelations pass by my courtyard wearing a helmet that covered his grayish-white hair and just like always his eyes were fixed on the yellow earth before him, he never dared to look directly into the foliage of the human world, not to mention the whirlwind of ever-changing illusions that one sees in the floating clouds, I used my eyes to draw his attention forcing him to raise his head thirty degrees so he could see me, "Hello, how are you?" that was the kind of standard hello that foreigners often use, I just wasn't sure which one of us was the foreigner, I went over toward him, "Hello, how are you?" Priest said he was on his way to somebody's house to offer a special morning prayer, he also asked how

come he didn't see me at the church on Christmas, I told him that
I had been busy carrying out "ecological research about the reservation," every time I had passed by the church I noticed that the front
gate was always tightly shut, "Oh," Priest said that he was always inside, during Christmas they stay up all night and fast, they don't usually open the doors during that time, the most pressing thing I
wanted to ask Priest was whether he would be able to recommend a
river trekking guide, "A beaver tracking guide?" Priest didn't know
this new term used by outdoorsmen, "No, I'm looking for someone
familiar with the local streams and rivers who can show me around,"
"Oh hallelujah, two doors down and one lane over from where I live
is a guy who knows all the streams and rivers," "Hallelujah indeed!
Thanks so much for your trouble," I passed through the small alleys
of the reservation surrounded by densely built houses of different
heights, I wondered if the house two doors down and one lane over
was the house I was thinking of, during my recent studies of outdoor
survival I learned to be extremely vigilant about one thing, when
hiking in densely forested places like the area around the Mhebu
River one must always use a guide and never enter dangerous areas
without proper authorization, I particularly didn't like this bit about
never entering without authorization, it was obvious that here on this
island nation there were still quite a few mysterious places the people
had no authorization to enter, none of this can be summed up by
what you always hear holiday air travelers saying while on vacation,
"There really are a lot of new things to see here on this island nation,"
but if you have time to ask around you will immediately discover that
international travel agents here on this island nation far outnumber
those specializing in local travel, this seems to attest to that old saying "no matter where you may be born, there is no way to know where
you will die," as I was walking around the church I saw for the very
first time a house on the reservation that didn't have a rusted steel
gate, each night at dusk I would come home from my walk along the

ridges in the fields, and every time I would find myself impressed by how heavy and shiny that impressive steel gate was, although I wasn't quite sure what this system of defense was designed to keep out, "Is anyone home?" I called out through the gate, the shape of that gate was probably designed to imitate the look of prison bars, perhaps they even hired the same designer, "Anyone there?" I raised my voice, "What the fuck?" I took a step back during all the years I had spent on reservations I had never heard anyone pronounce those words with such skill and ease, after what the fuck a person appeared with skin so dark he almost seemed to shine, his hair was all messed up and there was stubble all over his face, for the rest of his appearance I'm a bit embarrassed to even try to describe him on paper, "We'd like to hire a professional guide to take us river trekking," "What the fuck is river trekking?" I never imagined that all this guy knew was what the fuck, but didn't fucking know what river trekking was, but this didn't stop me, there are many levels to spoken language just as there are to written language, I would just have to put it in more simple terms, "A few friends and I would like to go check out the river, we'd like to hire someone who knows their way around the rivers here to show us, we're willing to pay," "What do you mean 'check out the river'?" he approached the steel gate, looking at me through the bars of the gate he was clearly trying to figure out just what the hell I was up to, so I switched to Taiwanese, "I want to find someone who can take us to play around in the stream!" Finally he understood the way I said "play around" or "*ti tok*" in Taiwanese, he kept repeating it and then asked, "What the fuck you wanna play around for?" it was a good thing that I was patient with my words and had a good handle on language, "We're going to play around and look for stuff at the bed of the stream," at last language had helped me complete the first stage of communication, he went inside to grab a rattan chair and sat down, he told me to grab one of the stools lying around outside and have a seat, I sat down on the other side of the steel gate and tried taking our communication to another level through conversation, "I just came back from electro-fishing, I had just fallen asleep for a nap when you woke me up, so just what the fuck is this important business you got going on, I can't tell you how many years it has been since I was woken up like that," oh so he was one of those guys who went "electro-fishing" using electric currents to stun the fish,[38] my oh my, a shame that I didn't have any experience with the nap schedule of electro-fishermen, otherwise I wouldn't have to deal with all this fucking shit, "So you must be quite familiar with all the rivers and streams around here!" "From the Muddy River in the south up to the Three Gorges River in the north, there isn't a river around here that I haven't sent a current through," wow look at what we have here, an electro-fisherman, truly a rare breed on this island nation, he was now being elevated from electro-fisherman to electro-riverman, "I'd like to hire you to be our guide, are you familiar with the Mhebu River near Musha?" "Electro-Riverman ain't no fucking guideman, but I was raised around the Taluowan, Mhebu, and and Wukali rivers, I know that area like the fucking back of my hand," I liked the way that "Electro-Riverman ain't no fucking guideman" kind of rhymed, he pronounced the names of all those rivers so rapidly it was as if he were chanting them off like a Buddhist sutra and just from that I could tell how well he knew the area, "We'll pay you a guide fee if you agree to show us around," from what I'd learned about outdoor survival I knew that he was the one who must be our guide, especially in the heavily forested area around Mhebu, "An Electro-Riverman like me don't need no fucking guide fee, take a look for yourself," he brought a bucket over, it was filled with all kinds of fish that he had zapped, the most impressive were two perch eels, "I never sell my fish, offer me ten million dollars and I still wouldn't sell this big perch eel, just think about how difficult it was for him to grow up into a big perch eel like this, can ten million dollars buy that?" I happily agreed that when it comes to the process of natural evolution, there is no place for money, "And what the hell am I supposed to do there?" he leaned forward and it was only then that I finally got a good look at the green uniform he was wearing, the colors had faded to a youthful green adorned by the colors of the mist, the scent of the canyon and the dense forest had left it windproof, it looked like a uniform redesigned by nature, "We want to hike down to the valley near the Mhebu River to look around," "Humph, so you want to hike around and look around, what, do you think that's the closest river to our reservation, well let me tell you that place is where I come from, I even got lost there twice before, you take one wrong turn in the canyon valley and you enter another canyon, and then another, there are several different ways out, and you end up just going in circles around the different canyons without even knowing it, by the time you finally get out you have no idea where you even are," "That sounds scary, but that's exactly why we need your help," "Let me tell you, I even slept out on that Great Rock in the middle of the river for two nights, I didn't dare set foot in the dense forest, if you lead a group into the dense forest, just like that your entire life will be swished away lost forever in that forest!" wow I had never in the world heard that electro-rivermen were terrified of entering dense forests, after all what could be hiding there, and then there was that spooky darkness in the forest that no child would be able to stand, "You can electro-fish along the way if you want," "What what what the fuck!" wow this idea made him stutter, "As long as I've been electro-rivering I have always done it alone," it looked like we didn't have much hope of getting him as our guide, it looked like I had found myself a lone Electro-Riverman, I expressed my thanks to Electro-Riverman and after thanking him again told him he could go back to his nap, "Beware of the forest," Electro-Riverman rolled his eyes in a weird way, "The bars on your gate are quite pretty, I like the thickness," I patted my hand on the metal bars, "They're new," Electro-Riverman looked out into the distance, "I started working

on it as soon as they removed the official sentry!" "Are there a lot of
fish here in Riverisle?" "I never electro-fish here in Riverisle, I leave
them for the locals to catch, the day I finished my gate a whole bunch
of people drove in toward the rear mountain," "Were they your electro-
fishing comrades?" "Fucking comrades my ass," Electro-Riverman
approached the gate, for a second I wasn't sure what to say, the word
"comrade" couldn't be used carelessly at the beginning of the twentieth century and now at the end of the century it is again a term not to
be thrown around,[39] I turned to see Priest off in the distance about
to step into the church, "Comrade Priest!" I yelled, Priest Comrade
returned my greeting with a tired smile, as he was going in he offered to teach me romanized Atayal, he told me to drop by whenever
I had free time. Spending two autumns and winters here, I gradually went from growing accustomed to life in Riverisle to becoming familiar with it, in terms of the fundamentals there was really
no major difference between things here and on other mountain
reservations on this island nation, most people were looking outside the reservation especially those young people who had long left
everything behind here for a chance to make it in the city, the regular residents were basically the elderly, women, and children, life on
the reservation was quiet, daily chores were the only thing to keep
people busy, occasionally someone from the reservation who hadn't
been home in a while would come back and things would liven up
for a few days and then he would leave again, most of them were
middle-aged men who started to get nostalgic about home, they
could come back and create a bit of a disturbance, that's because
they needed to readjust to life on the reservation, but gradually day
after day all those habits they picked up on the outside would disappear in the mountain air, sooner or later they would figure out a way
to settle down, the quiet life here on this deep mountain reservation
provides many different ways to settle down, in all of Riverisle Girl is
the only one who seems to still be trying to figure out how to adapt,

she keeps going through temporary periods of agitation and then calm, then again perhaps that just happens to be the side of Girl that I saw during my two autumns and winters that I spent here, before that time she had a more stable life, that special place of hers called Valleystream, the bamboo fish trap that she set up in the river, the tall grass under which she hid her barbecue utensils, the river pebbles and pieces of petrified wood she kept in her house, her loofah and Nocturnes, during their day-to-day conversations virtually no one ever mentioned "the Incident," and it was quite rare for anyone to feel like they were somehow living out their Remains of Life in the shadow of "the Incident," but in reality they were living in the Remains of Life of "the Incident," it was "the Incident" that forced them to leave their homeland behind and be banished to Riverisle, they went from developing the land there to reaping its fruits to eventually having a surplus of crops, they went from being strangers here to becoming familiar with this place and ultimately settling down, according to the inscription on the "Memorial to the Remains of Life" erected at the rear of the reservation it has been less than seventy years since "the Incident" took place, on October 27 of each year the government sends a notification to Riverisle reminding them to send representatives to the public memorial ceremony to their ancestor whose effigy still stands in Musha, "the Incident" gave Riverisle not only a kind of officially sanctioned place of honor but also a kind of melancholic yet beautiful sadness, which they had ample supply of, but honor is often quite removed from everyday life, yet if you reach out to truly feel it, that ample supply of melancholic beauty has left Riverisle with a kind of "atmosphere that belongs to history," history has its own depth, and this depth carries with it the beauty of life's trials and misfortunes, "the Musha Incident" has forever left Riverisle with the kind of beauty stained with the blood, tears, and misfortunes of life—I would often feel the presence of these things during my walks, but I could never ask Girl whether or not

she felt any of these things, there are some things that only you yourself can know, I remember the first time I met Girl, she was there in
Valleystream and without even bothering to turn around said, "I am
the granddaughter of Mona Rudao," the manner and tone of voice
in which she spoke made that sentence stand still in the air frozen
in time, after that anything I might ask her seemed superfluous, during dusk as the sun set and the cold air came down from the mountains and in through my window, I too have asked myself many
times whether all my questions about "the Incident" were superfluous, after all history has already decided what its place is to be, the
political has already lauded it with glory and honor, yet I still must
ask, even if it is in a hushed voice, you can say that I need to do my
best to provide some answers to the "questions" I had during my
younger days while I still have some Remains of Life left in me, when
I first began writing this novel I clearly stated what those questions
were, during my Remains of Life I wanted to reevaluate the Musha
Incident, it is actually quite difficult to pose any questions, having
experienced the trials and difficulties of life, I feel there are many
questions that no longer seem worth asking, I read various historical
materials and then came to the actual site of history to live among
the Remains of Life here in Riverisle, I went for daily walks, here is
the place of the Remains of Life, I saw those people who were the
Remains of Life and even personally paid visit to the mouth of the
river where "the Incident" took place, here in this place of the Remains
of Life I meditated on what had happened, "the Remains of Life"
don't need to meditate or reflect, for it is still living right there before
their very eyes, seeing the children laughing and playing each afternoon when they get out of school makes me reflect about how "the
Incident" has already gradually died and ossified like some fossil,
from the scars of history I take those fossils out and place them on
the windowsill in front of my desk where I can examine each one
carefully, clearly even though I am still here in this place of the

Remains of Life reflecting about these things feels impractical, yet "reflection" has its own inherent power, intuition is an ability that we are born with but over time and as you accumulate more experience it can get sharper, reflection is an ability that comes a bit later but over time it too is something that can be honed with additional experience and made sharper, sometimes we might revise our reflections based on external circumstances, but it never ceases, in fact even if the subject of our reflection is completely meaningless and without value it will still not impede our reflective process, "the contemporary" has already as its primary meaning called into question the legitimacy of the dignity of this act of resistance, and later, I fully upheld the historical necessity behind the origin and later development of "headhunting," and now I find myself attempting to explain the various ways the process of upholding this view has been secretly distorted, the contemporary era in which I live has also attempted to use "individual subjectivism" to call the "normalcy of headhunting" into question, I refer to this academic term of "individual subjectivism" simply as "individual autonomy," individual autonomy refers to one serving as his own master as long as he is alive, once acting as an autonomous individual becomes the first condition for existence, then anything that overlooks or threatens to destroy "individual autonomy" reduces existence to a state of empty meaninglessness, and with that all possibilities for one's life are likewise destroyed, the act of "headhunting" in itself refutes individual autonomy, it must have been a primal urge that pushed them to make the jump from hunting animals to hunting "people," or perhaps it was the lure of later benefits that drove them, but I figured there is no reason to jump, just extend things a bit and you can easily slip from hunting animals to hunting "people," after all humans evolved from animals, one of the reasons behind hunting animals is an attempt to satisfy man's primal urge to kill, hunting "people" then can be seen as an even greater enticement for those with that urge, civilization utilized all kinds of ways to subvert this repressed urge, when you directly face the primitive there is no way to resist it, very quickly one crosses that line extending or jumping over that invisible line where one can raise a machete to sever a human head, the prize of the hunt quickly becomes a human head, and in the eyes of the hunter this prized passion rapidly becomes "objectified," just as the hunter becomes objectified as "a great man" and all kinds of practical benefits follow him, the human heads become objectified as "sacred prized objects" that can serve as medicinal remedies, ward off calamities, keep you company when drinking, serve as conversation partners, they are like prized pets that deserve to be kept close to you while others hold your sacredness in reverence you probably only deserve 30 percent of that, my reflections tell me that, the first human head that was taken must have been that of a warrior lost to a primitive machete, but there's no point in waiting for history to confirm that, the second, third, fourth, and fifth heads also may have been warriors or they may have been people who fell into a trap, human heads can be objectified into something both "great" and "sacred," I'm not sure exactly at which point whether or not someone was a warrior stopped being relevant, all that mattered was the fact that it was a human head, it might be an elderly man or woman surveying the fields first thing in the morning or at dusk, it might be a pregnant woman unable to run fast enough to get away, an innocent teenage boy or girl yet to see the evils of the world, or a little boy or girl who had accidentally left the tribal grounds while going out to play, as long as the head was human its age didn't matter, nor did its gender, nor did the method by which it was obtained, any head was enough to attest to the greatness of the hunter, human heads were thus sacrificed for the sacred becoming innocent pets in the process, these individual heads became objectified, and at the same time objectified other individual heads, in the name of "headhunting" one can freely take the life of a stranger, and those victims have absolutely no right to demand that they freely live out their lives without interference, humans gradually became objects to be "headhunted," and so hidden within "the carnival of the headhunt" is the dark sorrowful shadow of what it means to be a man, how truly terrifying that dark shadow is, and so the shadows must be concealed behind the veil of even more carnivalesque façades, "the contemporary" is opposed to the "headhunting ritual interpretation" that Mr. Bakan endorses, if headhunting is a means of preserving the tribe's existing common rituals, then man must use the existence of killing in order to preserve his own existence, this is especially true when it comes to the form of "the headhunt," individuals never achieve autonomy, humans are destined forever to be relegated to existing in a state of killing and being killed, and throughout the long river of history, they have existed in a state of terror, as the threat of death draws near fear itself brings death to their existence, I have a friend from the Pangcah tribe whose grandmother was decapitated one morning while she was out inspecting the fields, that was an "everyday occurrence" sixty or seventy years ago here on this island nation, during her grandfather's later years he would occasionally talk about the heartbreak he felt when he rushed out to the ridge between the fields and found her headless body, it was something that even one's "Remains of Life" is not enough to fully express, throughout the rest of his life none of his friends could understand the reality of this incident, they just found that barbarism hard to accept, people like her grandfather who lived their lives amid "the headhunt" were even in death haunted by the dark shadow of these kinds of killings, "How could people treat one another like this?" I asked myself in sadness, how could people allow for this thing to become "twisted" into an everyday ritual, all the way up until the point that civilization "could no longer stand for this perversion to be looked at as something that was normal" and used its power to prohibit any further "headhunting," that was only sixty or seventy years ago, and let me again stress this fact, as I am so powerfully assaulted by the sadness of existence. Based on what I had learned from studying camping and outdoor survival skills I prepared the supplies needed for two nights and three days, long enough to trek up to the mouth of the Mhebu River, I went out the front door and headed next door to look for Girl, normally when I had my front door closed she knew that I was busy "working" and rarely knocked, Girl left her door half open, there were only a few houses left on the entire reservation without iron bars installed on their front doors, "Anyone home?" I pushed the door open, "Nobody's here, just you," Girl's voice was coming from the bedroom, I could immediately tell that it was a sober voice not tainted by cigarettes and wine, Girl turned to come out, even at home she was still wearing her black shorts and black T-shirt, "I've got something I want to discuss with you," the T-shirt she had on today was in better shape than the other ones she had been wearing, but the look on Girl's face appeared more exhausted than usual as if she had been lying around in bed too long, "Don't you always come over even when you don't have stuff to discuss with me?" "Stop kidding," I tried to stay serious, Girl was about to light up a cigarette, "Please don't smoke," I said, "Don't be so serious, I'll stop smoking when I feel like it," I'm not sure if I was still being serious, but I explained to her what supplies I planned to bring, Girl seemed to be listening, but I'm not sure how much of what I said she was really hearing, "Is there anything else I should add to the list?" I asked Girl, "Anything to *add*?—You need to get rid of all that stuff!" It was a good thing that Girl didn't throw me out on my ass otherwise I would have had to take my ass back down to the plains, I never take advantage of people and certainly never took advantage of Girl she just thought I was a tasty morsel, "What the hell do you need sleeping bags for?" it was only then that I realized that it was already past noon, I could feel the heat on my body coming in from the courtyard, it made it difficult for the young lady in her bedchamber to continue her nap so no wonder she was so upset, "And what—the—fuck is that tent for!?" I decided to let Girl have her cigarette, cigarettes are after all substitutes for other things, they are a means of compensating, and they even serve as a kind of ritual, "I'm giving up smoking, so who is gonna wear this raincoat? and a pair of rain pants?" When I'm particularly happy or particularly depressed or when I'm feeling like life isn't even worth one line of Baudelaire I take some drugs and get a good sleep, so I can understand why Girl gets so bored and impatient with necessary things, there is actually no need to explain any of this, but at this moment I have no choice but to add a detailed explanation, sleeping bags are necessary in order to keep each of us separate and make sure that each of us maintains our manners and decent human form, naturally we need a tent, especially if we are camping in the rain forests of this island nation, they can keep out the rain and mist and keep Black V from sneaking into your pants at night to try to have a good time, Girl listened with a blank look, even though Black V didn't understand her at all she knew that her time with him was like an aborted afterbirth, "You're really a bookworm, ever since you showed up here there has been one more person on the reservation that can read and write, one more worthless nerd that no one knows what the hell he is doing, just another bookworm!" That's not how Girl usually speaks to me, at the least she is usually polite and well-mannered, so I knew without even thinking that her acting out had nothing to do with the time of day, it was all withdrawal symptoms from trying to give up alcohol and cigarettes, "Okay, so I'm a bookworm, but we're still bringing the stuff," "My ass you're bringing it!" "Of course we are, and we'll all be fighting over who gets to follow that ass of yours along the way," Girl smiled but then immediately knitted her brow, she said that she had been feeling uneasy the past few days and it has been hard for her to get any peace and quiet, otherwise she wouldn't have acted like such an ass, I stood up, "Peace and quiet my ass!" I busted out a famous quote, "My ass you want peace and quiet?" after getting knocked on her ass twice in a row by what I said, Girl went back into her bedroom probably to crawl back into bed for a bit longer, I told her I was going into town to pick up some supplies for our trip, "Do you want to come along?" the moment she heard me mention that I was going into town Girl's tired eyes immediately lit up, in a flurry she began to busy herself getting ready and said that she'd be ready to go as soon as she grabbed her jacket, I was actually happy she wanted to go otherwise I would have gotten lost in all the overwhelming delights of the town, even if all I needed was a needle I probably would have been so distracted that I wouldn't have even bought it, Girl threw on her dark red jacket, her pair of once fair-skinned legs were now wrapped in a pair of dark panty-hose, on the way there Girl started behaving like an old nagging granny, she kept explaining why we didn't need to buy a tent, that was because we could stay over at one of her relatives' houses for the first night, the second night we could stay at the tribal chief's house, the third night we could sleep either inside the Great Cave or atop the Great Rock so "there really isn't anyplace to squeeze in a night in a tent," secondly when we stayed over at people's houses we could use their blankets so we wouldn't need any sleeping bags, when we were outside "then let heaven and earth be our mattress!" and you can really see what a bookworm I am by the way I insisted on buying raincoats and rain pants as if I needed to protect my whole body from heaven knows what, who cares if you get a little wet or covered in damp mist or even take a few bites from Black V, it's not like we're gonna die, "Back when I was with him Black V must have shot me up thousands of times and I never died!" true heroes don't bring up the past, I instead focused on avoiding the oncoming traffic, we arrived in town, and after visiting three different stores I was able to buy all the supplies on my list, the only thing I bought that was stipulated by my studies in outdoor survival was a pair of tall rubber boots, the rest was just junk, random items, including snacks for Girl, she also prepared a bottle of sake to give to Old Wolf as a gift upon their meeting, Girl also prepared a bouquet of pure white dahlias and chrysanthemums as an offering to the Ancestral Spirits, after that she started making a fuss about going to see a movie, *New Life of a Licentious Drunkard* was playing, I suggested that we check out the bookstore next door, we could see if they had anything with information that we might have otherwise overlooked, anyway it was getting late and it would be difficult to go home once it got dark, Girl kept pouting, "It's not that I'm into drunk licentious men, I'm just curious what his new life was like," I promised her that I would take her to see the movie some other time, I was also curious what his new life was like, I browsed my way from the front of the bookstore to the back, I discovered a copy of *New Red Crane Tower* that I though was worth picking up, that's because the blurb on the jacket clearly stated, "Racier sex scenes than anything you ever read in the *Old Red Crane Tower*, more flesh exposed and more details revealed," but it would be embarrassing if Girl saw it and asked to borrow it, it would be especially awkward if I brought this *New Red Crane Tower* back to the old reservation where all the buildings' prices had dropped and the price of beds had risen how would I ever be able to settle up everyone on the reservation would go crazy, so I had no choice but to put the book back and approach the register empty-handed, which is where I saw Girl waiting in line with a waxed paper-wrapped magazine in her hand, "Uh, all I could find was this magazine," I took a look, it was a copy of *Playboy* magazine so I immediately bought it for her, from there we went to the supermarket, there we stocked up on the number one necessity, after all "the Ancestral Spirits wouldn't be happy if we didn't buy some alcohol," I had to quote Girl for that, it doesn't take much to figure out that the gate to the Great Cave won't magically open unless it gets a whiff of some good spirits, it was only three or four o'clock when we left town, Girl asked me why I was in such a rush to leave, "I'll only be able to rest easy once I get home and gaze up upon the stars in the night sky," Girl laughed, you can see stars every night, we took a rest halfway home to have a beer with the mountain range over Musha, "Damn!" Girl damned it, "This is my real home!" we passed Yuanheng Temple, Girl asked me to pull over, the gate to Yuanheng Temple was precisely positioned where the mountain road made a sharp 180-degree turn, when I had previously passed by I always assumed that it was a "deserted" temple, when you gazed out from the main temple gate the bamboo forest concealed all of the houses, I pulled over, Girl immediately hopped clear over the short gate, I on the other hand had to half-climb half-pull myself in order to make it over and only then did I ask, "Are you sure it's okay that we go in?" "Too late, we already are in," Girl flashed me a glare, as if she couldn't wait to let me have it, "My crazy great-uncle is the host here," I corrected Girl that she probably meant "abbot" and not "host" after all he wasn't hosting some variety show, the bamboo forest partly concealed the temple on both sides, it was a broad three-courtyard structure, surrounding the building were potted plants of different sizes, but there was no trace of any monks or nuns, maybe they were all out chewing on sacred seeds from the scriptures, the air was filled with the fragrance of the different trees growing out in the rear mountains and the potted four o'clock flowers, and of course the ever-present mountain air didn't forget to soak into the dense forest of sweaty hair covering Girl's armpits, her crazy great-uncle wasn't inside meditating, the entire temple and its grounds were completely deserted, there was a quiet serenity there, "There are people here, but they rarely come out of their rooms," Girl whispered, "If my crazy great-uncle isn't here then he must be out in the bamboo forest," we walked through the broad open courtyard, we could hear a series of snoring sounds mixed with the sound of bamboo leaves rustling, on the ground amid a thick layer of yellow and green fallen leaves was a bamboo chair where the abbot sat snoring, his head was perfectly centered it wasn't drooping or resting back nor was it tilted to the left or right, the wrinkles on his face were so deep that it was really impossible to guess his age, he wasn't completely bald but you could see the scars on his upper forehead from his Buddhist initiation he had a little hair in front and a few locks of long white hair in the back that went down to his shoulders, I stopped in my tracks not wanting to interrupt his snoring, Girl bit the collar of her T-shirt again and it was clear she was up to something sneaky, "Don't even think about tickling me with a bamboo leaf," a voice warned in between the snores, "And don't you dare stick anything in my nose," he snored, Girl covered her mouth in laughter, "Sneezing sometimes triggers strokes," he snored, he didn't sound that old from the way he talked, he sounded like a fat middle-aged ruffian with a beer belly, "And don't bite a hole in your shirt, we don't have any clothes like that for you to change into here," when he smiled the lines on his face resembled the low banks of earth between the fields, and he still had yet to open his eyes, "So who is this you brought along that somehow gave you the courage to barge in here and stay for tea and a meal," "Great-uncle," Girl had a good handle when it came to imitating standard Mandarin, "He's my friend who lives next door, he came here to do some research," the old man opened his eyes to size me up, he stared straight at me with perfect focus and without the slightest hesitation, "Please have some tea," Great-uncle asked Girl to set up a table for tea, he asked me to go over to the room in the left wing to grab two short bamboo chairs, I had been paying close attention to this old abbot and although we had been wavering between action and inaction I stayed close to him the whole time, his Good Great-niece turned out to be quite familiar with all the various odds and ends involved in a tea ceremony from setting up the table and arranging the cups to brewing the tea, and here I was thinking that all she was capable of was mixing white spirits with Whisbih, after staring at me for a while the old man went back to behaving more naturally, he stopped fixing his gaze on the same spot with a lazy indifference, "All we do here is meditate, we practice in the Zen style of Caodong,"[40] after we quietly listened to the sound of the water in the teapot beginning to boil, the old abbot began to speak, he requested that his Good Great-niece just listen and not interrupt with questions, he also told me that all I needed to do was listen carefully, it would actually be more convenient if he could directly cover everything I wanted to ask and everything I wanted to hear without me having to open my mouth, "All one understands is meditation, with all one's heart you focus on meditation, here you can do whatever you want as long as it leads to meditation, our principle lies in the fact that meditation is our sole focus, but beyond that principle we have almost limitless freedom, yet we still focus only on meditation," I have mentioned that I had long learned how to be a good listener, this time I quieted my heart and practiced being a good listener, "I'm a Seediq from the Daya tribe, I was born in Mhebu, in the early 1910s a delegation of Japanese monks visited Musha, they came to spread the teachings of Buddhism and start up a class for indigenous children, my mother was from the Hogo tribe and was enrolled in that class, it was fate that Zen Buddhism came into my mother's life, and she had a deep connection with the monks who taught her, she studied with the monks from the time she was a little girl up until her teenage years, my mother passed her profound attachment to Zen down to me, at the time those monks would travel around all the different reservations to spread their teachings, whenever they passed through Mhebu they would always come to our house to speak with my mother and have some tea, one of the monks would always carry a canvas back-pack that had a tea set inside, there was a teapot and two white por-celain cups, my mother and her teacher would sit under the thatched eaves facing each other and drinking tea, my mother and I shared the same white porcelain cup, often when her teacher came to visit they wouldn't even talk but just sit there smiling and drinking tea, I often wonder what people on the reservation must have thought of that at the time, later I learned that my mother and her teacher didn't care what other people thought, the year I turned thirteen, the monk requested my mother allow me to join the order, since they had so many children my mother was able to convince my father, it helped that I wasn't the eldest son, the monk went with my parents to the police station to take care of the paperwork, the monk brought me down the mountain to a place three kilometers beyond the north district of Puli called Temple of the Slumbering Ox where I stayed, two years later I had my head shaved and took my vows as a child monk at the Temple of the Slumbering Ox, my mother was the only one who attended the ceremony when I joined the order, that was also the last time I saw my mother, the monks' method of passing down their teachings was quite efficient, they would speak in Japanese and use Chinese characters to write down the four words 'focus solely upon meditation,' there was only one rule at the Temple of the Slumbering Ox, monks were not allowed to leave the temple, my teachers hired laymen from outside to take care of the various chores around the temple, the Temple of the Slumbering Ox was no larger than what you see here at Yuanheng Temple, but it was nice that both of them were adjacent to the mountains, when I first arrived there were six monks, they were all different ages, our teacher requested that each of us practice self-discipline and self-cultivation, we were to support one another but never disturb one another, our teacher spent a lot of time on the reservations up in the mountains, but he felt comfortable knowing that Temple of the Slumbering Ox was the most quiet and settled temple, during autumn of the year I turned thirty-three, our teacher called all of us out to the courtyard to announce three things: first, we should focus solely upon meditation as much as we wanted; second, he was going to return to Japan; and third, I would be his successor as temple abbot, I was chosen because I had managed to stay on the longest, of the original six I was the only one left, but there were three others who had come later, teacher didn't say much more than that, and we didn't ask, things continued on for two more years and when I was thirty-five years old one of my younger brothers who had never taken the vows finally found his way to the Temple of the Slumbering Ox, it was from him that I finally learned about 'the Incident' that had occurred seventeen years earlier in my hometown, my parents both died in the detention center, surviving them were two of my younger brothers who had been relocated to Riverisle more than ten years earlier, one of my elder sisters had been married off to the Northern Atayal tribe, my brother tried hard to get me to give up my vows, he said that times had changed and it was a different world now, he urged me to get out there and give it a try in the world, but I told him that I'd already been a monk for twenty-two years, even if I wanted to leave the temple I didn't think my body would listen, that was the only reason, and so I continued on at the Temple of the Slumbering Ox for forty-one years, at the temple we continued to preach the message of those same four words, we still had just one temple rule and it was the same one, one year a middle-aged man from Taipei came down to the temple, he said that his father had been a practicing Buddhist for many years, he had recently bought some land to the west of Puli, he planned to build a small temple where monks could live and his father could spend his old age, I told him that I would be interested if it was a small Buddhist house of prayer, but if he wanted to build a large temple then he had best find someone else, and so we ended up with the single-level courtyard structure you see before you, we planted the bamboo trees later, the old man also chose the name Yuanheng Temple, the reason I came here to Yuanheng Temple was that all of the development around Puli was starting to encroach upon the Temple of the Slumbering Ox, a second reason had to do with the fact that worshippers had started talking about establishing a management committee for the temple, and a third reason was that I was originally told that from Yuanheng Temple you could see all of Riverisle and Valleystream, I would be able to focus exclusively upon meditation and wouldn't have to bother with visitors coming to burn incense, there are three nuns who have their own rooms and they mostly stay inside meditating, the old man's granddaughter also lives here and has been practicing meditation for many years, she was originally forced to come here by her family, I simply told her to focus solely upon meditation as much as she wanted, she could go out to the mountain out back or to Puli as often as she wanted, but I just had one sentence for her: Focus solely upon meditation, not long after that she took her leave telling me that she wanted to leave the temple to lead a normal life, I had just one sentence for her: If you want to come back, feel free to come back, once she left it took her a full six years before she felt free enough to return, she has now been focusing solely upon meditation for almost a decade, the reason I'm telling you all of this is to satisfy your curiosity about this temple, it's not often that anyone passes by that bend in the road and sees our temple and is as fascinated as you, so today I decided to let you know that here deep in the mountains there is still a place where traditional Caodong meditation is practiced, after I turned forty-one I stopped counting my age, I meditated for a few more years then just decided to forget about it, it was only during those six years that the old man's granddaughter left us that I counted each year that went by, the Musha Incident passed before my eyes, but I just focused solely upon meditation, I only was affected by the death of my parents but even that felt like something so distant, I'll throw something out that I'd like you to take to heart: 'the Musha Incident was something that may as well never have happened' one day many years after I had come to Yuanheng Temple, an old scholar brought a young Japanese scholar to see me they first went looking for me at the Temple of the Slumbering Ox and then found me here at Yuanheng, they brought along a book and they wanted to see if I could help identify anyone in one of the photos, in the photo was a man in boots standing in front of a pile of freshly cut human heads, there must have been at least fifty or sixty of them, I immediately recognized that one of them was my father, the scholar asked me what I was feeling, I told him nothing, I just simply pointed out which head was my father's, and then went back to focusing solely upon meditation, 'headhunting' is a misguided practice that follows a wrong path, they don't understand repentance and instead just go on and on cutting off each other's heads in an endless cycle of violence, but this is just something I'm throwing out there, don't take it to heart, once I arrived here at Yuan-heng Temple I never again set foot outside the temple gate, so today I won't be going with you back to Riverisle, from here I can see my tribal brothers there, I'm not sure if it was this spring or last spring, but my older sister who is now a grandmother came up here to visit her little brother with her grandchildren, my little brother is also a grandfather now, he knows that I've always been here, whenever he drives by he always slows down, but he never disturbs me, he just lets me focus on my meditation, the only regular visitors are some members of the old man's family who occasionally come up to visit the old man's daughter who went astray, but Girl here is the only one who is always popping in unannounced," I woke up to discover that all my joints felt they were dislocated, I can't even remember if I heard the chicken's morning cackles, the winter sun decided to stay under the covers, I didn't even drink my morning coffee, not to mention the fact that I didn't even bother washing up, I went out the back door and not long after passing by the "Memorial to the Remains of Life" arrived at Cousin's house, "Do you have a crazy great-uncle who is an abbot up in the mountains?" I called out to Cousin as soon as I saw her in the courtyard sweeping, as soon as she laid eyes on me she was all smiles, "What brings you here first thing in the morning and what's this crazy stuff you're talking about?" "There's an old man who is the abbot up on the mountain temple facing us who says he is your great-uncle," Cousin's eyes turned away she didn't pay attention to her son who wouldn't leave her alone—her older child was at kindergarten—but one look from those eyes was enough to make any man dizzy, "No, we have some family members in the church, but certainly none in the temple," "So was what happened last night just a wasted dream?" Cousin grabbed a round big-belly rattan chair and asked me to have a seat under the mulberry tree, she asked if wanted a glass of water or something stronger, "So last night you had a dream about my crazy great-uncle," the way her hips looked when she hobbled away reminded me of the head of a ghostly spirit, Cousin brought over a glass of cold water, but before she gave it to me she asked me to help her move another big-belly chair over, "We've got ourselves a wholesome reservation here, we don't need college-educated people like you running around talking about your crazy dreams, you'll end up scaring the hell out of everyone here," once I got some cold water into my tummy I felt much more alert, "Your cousin brought me over to see him, we went yesterday afternoon," "Hmph, that pain-in-the ass cousin of mine!" Cousin was all smiles again, just seeing the way she squinted her eyes when she smiled was almost enough to make the winter sun sink into the ground, "Let me tell you about her, first there was a 'godbrother,' then it was a 'godfather,' and then a 'god-this' or a 'god-that,' and now she's got a 'god-great-uncle' who's an abbot at a temple," "I think she was telling the truth, when I met her great-uncle he really had the air of a bona fide celestial being, and your cousin was really well behaved around him," I gave a brief description of the dreamlike visit the day before, "Wow! If he's really that old he must really be a 'god,' because he's certainly not among the living!" Cousin drank some hot water, "From what I can see my cousin has made you lose your wits, but I've heard that you can hold your liquor and know how to take care of business," Cousin came over and grabbed hold of my elbow, she was probably referring to that incident when Girl buried the stone, "Once you finish up your research why don't you settle down here, I'll see what I can do to help you become part of the family," even when Cousin smiled her eyes were still quite large, she was after all a born Atayal, "That's a suggestion I'll have to research," I said with a straight face, "But are you sure you don't have a crazy great-uncle?" "What the hell is there to research, I'll set you up you'll look into each other's eyes and it'll be settled," Cousin was showing off her progressive feminist views, "Don't go thinking that just because you are Chinese all our young girls will be fawning over you, let me share with you a Chinese saying: *Rarities are to be treasured*, these days we Atayal are quite the rare breed, a real treasure, but who cares about you Chinese, you're all over the place!" I held up my empty glass hoping to get a sip of some cold water, Cousin poured half a glass of her still-hot water into it, "Why don't you have a glass of hot water, drinking cold water in winter, it's no wonder that your heart is so cold, you researchers always look distant and cold without even a bit of warmth," I had some hot water, it wasn't too hot, just the right temperature, just like her, if I had known about her earlier I would have come out of my self-imposed sanitarium earlier, by now I would have had a cute well-behaved little Atayal clinging to my leg, "I have some regrets," Cousin interrupted my "decadent ramblings," I could tell that she was still on fire, a product of the "severe decadence" that took root as the fin de siècle approached, "You look healthy and energetic, you don't have any wrinkles on your face, so what is there to feel regretful about? Remember when I told you to home and research your own kind? There's plenty of research to do on the Han Chinese, aren't there tons of you down in the plains all investigating this stuff? Back when I heard that you were here to research THAT, don't you know that there isn't a person on this reservation who hasn't lost someone in their family during THAT, and no matter what actions the dead once carried out with their bare hands, the living can never truly understand those things, instead you researchers come to research those things, I figure a new one of you shows up every three to five years, you are the most recent, it's already been more than four years since the last one came around, everyone was beginning to think that there was no longer any value in researching it anymore, ever since the last one left things haven't been quite the same when the men on the reservation got together to go drinking, a good thing then that you showed up bringing so very much to us," as Cousin came over to take my glass, she gave me a playful bite on the ear, as if she wanted to show me how angry she was that I made them wait so long before finally showing up, in all my years no one had ever told me just how important this kind of research was for the reservation, so many treasures from the past were disappearing, "If I had known, I would have shown up twenty years ago," Cousin came over with two glasses of ice water, she said that my idiot comments were starting to get her worked up, she needed a glass of cold water to calm herself down, "My husband says that you are different from those other people who used to come here to do research, you do other things, but my husband has absolutely no idea what exactly it is that you do, and I don't even want to venture a guess, but I will tell you that if you really have any genuine interest in the Atayal, if you really care about us, if you are passionate about us, then follow the river that runs out in front of the reservation north and the Atayal mountains and rivers that you see there will be enough for you to lose yourself for the rest of your life!" Cousin had to go pick up her son from kindergarten, she apologized for being overly friendly, she had always been overly warm, which is why she decided to balance herself out by choosing to be an elementary school teacher, after she got married and had children she stopped saying what was really on her mind, "I've talked too much today, but remember, you started this!" when I went home I carried with me the "heavy burden of those things we have lost in our lives," when I got to the "Memorial to the Remains of Life" I circled around it a few times, that feeling of loss combined with "those fallen lives that would never be saved" was so heavy that it made me hunch over, I got home and drank two cups of sense-of-loss coffee, I sat down in front of my desk and gazed out at the mountains, the garden, and the west side of the reservation where Cousin lived for a long time, Girl had another older cousin living on the east side, the fact that they were "cousins" didn't mean much and they may have only been very distant "relatives," it is quite possible that Cousin didn't even know that her older cousin had a great-uncle who was the abbot at a temple, there seemed to be a "time-space disparity" between Great-Uncle and Cousin, add to that the fact that the reservation had a church but no temples and the fact that all Great-Uncle did was meditate all day and it made even more sense that no one would have heard of him, and so we come to the conclusion that "Cousin is unable to refute the existence of this person referred to as the Crazy Great-Uncle," so I supposed that when I'd beaten my body up running around all over the place the night before it hadn't been a complete bust, when I returned home at dusk last night, I quickly threw together a hodge-podge hotpot and got ready to jot down a memorandum about the "Crazy Great-Uncle," but I just couldn't seem to get it properly on paper, it wasn't that the words weren't flowing it was that I sensed that there was a big part of his story that had been "left out," not long after that Girl knocked on my door and came in holding that magazine she had bought opened up to a centerfold of a beautiful woman, "Check this out," she pointed to the girl in the picture's long legs, tiny waist, tight stomach, and massive breasts, "This is exactly what I looked like when I was younger, the only difference is that my hair is a different color," she took that image of her younger self and propped it up next to the window on my desk where it could warm my heart during those cold nights, I didn't get up, and Girl gently caressed my head on her way out the door, I stared at that younger version of Girl, her midriff was elliptical like a small lake, and there in the center of the lake was the unfathomably deep abyss of her navel, I struggled to free myself from the abyss and as soon as I pulled my head out I realized that I had "forgotten" something, I turned off the light and got

into bed, and once under the covers I immediately set out for the
Temple of the Slumbering Ox, I needed to urgently inform the son
that his parents were caught amid the fighting that broke out during
"the Incident," the son was only seventeen or eighteen years old at the
time, he was so upset that the tears poured down his face as he cried,
"Please save my mother!" but he didn't move a muscle and instead
focused only on meditation, I immediately left the Temple of the
Slumbering Ox and set out for the Great Cave, amid the crowd of
people inside the cave I recognized his mother sitting there meditating, two small children were napping on her lap, I quietly approached
her and whispered in her ear, "You still need to think about what's
best for your son in the temple," "Since he took his vows I no longer
need to worry too much about him," his mother gently smiled, and
then she asked me to pass some words on to her son, "Life and death
are both unknown, life cannot compare to death, and death cannot
compare to life," I immediately went down to the mouth of the
Mhebu River and rushed back to the Temple of the Slumbering Ox,
it was a shame that her son didn't understand the meaning of his
mother's words, all he could do was say, "Quick, get out of here and
give yourselves up! What the fuck are you doing holed up in this
damn cave!?" I guess all that "meditation" hadn't completely gotten
rid of his fucking temper, I finally thought of a way to save his mother,
"Take that ass of yours that only knows how to sit and meditate
and hop on my shoulders," in a flash we had arrived at the Pass of No
Return and from my shoulders the son could see his parents in the
distance as they fled from the Detention Center, "You can relax now,
don't cry, just sit tight on my shoulders and I'll take you home," but
I never imagined there would be a "Second Incident," I suspect that
his Zen mother also never imagined that she would end up being
hacked to death under the midnight stars as she was practicing
her Zen meditation, however, the one good thing that came out of
running around all night like this was that this Son of the Slumber-

ing Ox somehow was able to reclaim his "Remains of Life," before "the Incident" he didn't know why or for whom he was meditating, but after "the Incident" his Remains of Life were spent meditating for "the Incident"—he meditated for his mother who had died while meditating, strange indeed is the cyclical way history sometimes works, that one little thing I left out ended up making me spend an entire night running around in order to put things back into place, based on my notes and writings up to this point, I think that I have been able to get a handle on the general thrust behind the "Remains of Life," but there are still some random items that I need to tie up, I may as well brew up a cup of "Remains of Life Coffee" for myself, these random items include "idealistic responses," which are at once extremely enticing but also extremely likely to lead one astray, why did that old man think that I was drawn to that temple really every time I passed by, it's not that I'm drawn to every temple I pass by, was it that one of the stars out there somewhere in the universe saw me that day and that night they sent a fax down to the pupils of that old man in the bamboo forest, moreover, I must be careful about how I "define" these Zen terms and Zen practitioners, otherwise my novel runs the risk of losing its way being unable to find its way back and getting wrapped up in an abstract debate about idealistic matters, my first principle is that the only thing this novel attempts to "define" is "the Incident," the issue of "idealistic responses" is another matter entirely and I have no interest in delving into that in this novel, that Zen Buddhist viewed the Musha Incident as simply "something that may as well never have happened," which showed how "the Incident" was seen as "inappropriate" in the eyes of that Zen Buddhist, the only thing he "pointed out was that facts do not offer their impressions," that photograph of his father's decapitated head shows that the raging sea within his mind has long been quelled and is now placid, he was born on the reservation but after being tempered by his experiences in life, he today feels that "headhunting" is a path that is backward and misguided, he seems to be saying that that a primitive tribal life need not follow the path of the "headhunt," there may be other paths other directions that can be taken, his Caodong principle of "focusing only on meditation" doesn't scare my ass one bit and anyway I've long already come up with my own response of "focus only on writing." "Headhunting" has enriched the inner meaning of this island nation, this is a historical fact that cannot be altered, but if "headhunting" was a wrong choice that led us down a blind path, then it perhaps gave rise to an alternative "primal ritual" that also enriched the inner meaning of this island nation in a similar fashion, this is part of a historical imagination that need not be suppressed, thought it may be based on fact, I am not opposed to Danafu's "perspective on the headhunting ritual," nor do I oppose his "views on the culture of headhunting," nor do I oppose things like him opening a "headhunting studio or workshop," during the 1990s I saw my share of "ritual headhunt dances" being performed on various reservations and watched them with great interest, but right now what I'm most concerned about is if I should open up my "Mona Coffee Shop" during my Remains of Life whether or not I should put up a sign for "Headhunting Coffee," that way as people sat sipping their coffee they could imagine what it was really like when someone had their head cut off just the thought would make their hearts shudder causing them to burn their lips on that hot cup of headhunting coffee, by the time "individual headhunts" evolved into "collective headhunting," a complete headhunting ritual had also evolved and taken form, from listening to the call of birds to predict the outcome of the hunt to ambushing their victims from cutting off their heads to the endless carnival of song and dance that followed and from the preparation of the head to placing it on the ceremonial skull rack, once an individual is placed within the structure of the ritual he simultaneously loses his own autonomy, under the violence of the collective the power of the individual is erased, under the will of the collective the will of the individual is completely suppressed, the entire process happens quite quickly and the individual isn't even conscious of what has occurred, but the direction in which the collective moves does not take into consideration the direction of the individual, the eyes of the ritual gaze upon each and every individual, taking everything that is beneficial to the collective into account, when people are still children it injects the new generation with what it means to be a part of the "headhunt," thus those individuals who grow up in this environment have absolutely no critical or reflective self-awareness when it comes to the nature of "headhunting," there are actually many clear examples of the humiliation and destruction that this type of "collectivism" wages upon the individual that we can find throughout the twentieth century in the West, however, throughout my novel I have rarely mentioned people places and things from outside this island nation to reference or compare, I hope that my words flow through the land of this island nation, earlier when I mentioned Georgia O'Keeffe it was only because among the group of books and magazines scattered on the coffee table in my living room, which I would always thumb through, there were two art books among them, one was by Georgia O'Keeffe and the other was by Frida Kahlo, the reason I mentioned O'Keeffe wasn't owing to her portraits of "flowing vaginas" but rather because I sensed that if she were to be sent deep into the mountains to an Atayal reservation she would be an "indigenous person of this good earth" who would have her own individual and independent autonomy, the reason I haven't brought up Kahlo has nothing to do with her paintings it is simply that she as a person has a certain air of an "artist aristocrat," only today does O'Keeffe finally have a semblance of Kahlo's aristocratic flair, but it was necessary for O'Keeffe to escape from a way of life built upon civilization's collective violence in order to become a true "indigenous person of this good earth," I am left feeling sad and angry when I think about all of those individuals who were unable to escape from the violence of the collective during the age of the headhunt—"the contemporary" decries those pages in history in which the collective swallowed up the individual, "the contemporary" clearly opposes "headhunting," "the contemporary" has negated "the legitimacy of the headhunting ritual," "the contemporary" has also refused to accept the Musha Incident as a "large-scale headhunting ritual," instead the Musha Incident is seen as a politically inspired act of resistance, headhunting was simply a tradition that was used as a means for carrying out their political mission, "the contemporary" has placed particular censure upon "the Second Musha Incident," whether it is looked at from the perspective of a grand conspiracy or as a brutal act of retribution, it was a shameful example of a massacre against unarmed nonresisters carried out in the name of "a headhunt." We arranged to meet at 6 a.m. on January 3 at the bridgehead on the reservation, there was a fresh crisp feeling in the air that one often feels just after a holiday, Girl said that Cousin said that Elder said that if he had been twenty years younger he would have called on everyone from the tribe to accompany us on our journey, obviously our invitation had come two decades too late, but Cousin did say that if she weren't so busy with child care she would have loved to have gone to hang out with Girl and "that guy who is researching who the hell knows what," Pihu arrived at the bridgehead at 6:03, he took a photo of us, which was to be sent to the local press and various indigenous culture newsletters in order to promote this "Quest to Mhebu," he apologized for not going but those national treasure fish wouldn't be able to get by without him for three or four days now that he was operating as one of the reservation's independent companies, we tried to console him by telling him that we would call upon the Ancestral Spirits to protect him and his national treasure fish, just before he left Pihu gave each of us a plastic bag and asked us to be careful not to litter while on our journey, we waited until 6:05, which was when Drifter and Mr. Deformo must have run

into each other on the way over, I signaled to Girl with my eyes
and she returned the same look to me, at 6:06 a.m. we went over the
bridge and slid our way down Valleystream and so our "Quest" began, it was a good thing that our supplies were light and wearing our
plastic boots it felt like we could walk through every valley and
stream on this island nation, I even had an extra bamboo sun hat for
Girl I had originally bought one for her not realizing that she had her
heart set on letting her unadorned face take in every bit of nature she
encountered including the cats, the dogs, and the sun, as soon as we
left the reservation we made a few turns and entered the Northport
River, which resembled a massive drainage ditch, you could hear
traffic noise just above one side of the inlaid slope along the river and
on the other side where a wastewater pipe emptied its contents down
into the river, following the bed of the river along the small river we
periodically disappeared behind the wild grass growing alongside,
Girl walked oddly fast perhaps she had long grown accustomed to
hiking through the jagged rocks in the mountains but she was unaccustomed to walking through these kinds of riverbeds down in the
plains, I walked at a different pace and every so often I would fall
twenty meters or so behind Girl, I just assumed that this was part of
Girl's "Searching Steps," along the way she wanted to ponder those
difficult moments in her life and face them, it was also a rare opportunity for me to take a walk through this massive drain that ran
along the riverbed, later I learned that most of the drains like this in
the cities had long been sealed off when I was a kid there was a huge
drainage ditch beside my house surrounded on either side by a row of
willow trees, sometime after the economy took off the entire drain
was sealed with concrete, otherwise just think about how many more
streams we would have today and when going for strolls we wouldn't
have to just stare at equipment and machines after all how could that
artificial stuff ever compare to the beauty of wild reeds and grass, go
from walking on a flat surface to walking on a three-dimensional

space and you can imagine the trend to come, if this island nation isn't a part of it perhaps the universe will be, I went home and designed a multidimensional walking map to give to my younger self that way by the time he got older he wouldn't have to worry about having accomplished nothing in life, according to books on river trekking when you are river trekking you must always be careful of perch eels in the water near your feet, I kept looking out for frogs down by my feet when I got older I developed a taste for the tender flesh of frog legs, but if there are no frogs or eels then I know that Electro-Fisherman must have been here last night I heard that behind his steel gate is a large well where he raises the fish that he has caught Pihu even went to his house and meditated outside his gate as a form of protest but Electro-Fisherman came out and sat down on the other side of his gate and started meditating in protest of the protest, Priest said that during those nights when Electro-Fisherman wasn't home those perch eels would jump out from behind those steel gates some would end up cooling off on the eaves of the church or going into the kitchen to find something to eat and "the whole thing was really quite a hassle," the blade of the large samurai sword that the police department had confiscated from Mr. Miyamoto fifty years ago had grown so rusty that pieces began to flake off, just before the beginning of winter the police sent an official notice informing him that the sword and sheath would be returned to him thus bringing the case of Miyamoto's "contraband weapon" to a close, from time to time I wondered what Sapu's sex life was like during those twenty years when he was living on Dihua Street did he know that if you went to the House of Jiangnan you didn't even need to go upstairs to find some there were plenty of girls right there on the first-floor arcade, from time to time I also wondered about Sapu's sex life during his forty years in Riverisle perhaps after jumping in and out of all those holes over the years he gradually began to implement a kind of "surrogate ritual," the reason that headhunting became a historical necessity was actually owing to "sex" the bloody terror of cutting off a head also has the ability to provide sexual stimulation and head-hunts were always followed later in the night with wild sexual inter-course between the men and women of the tribe but otherwise star-ing out at the serene mountain landscape for too long had turned people's normal sex lives on the reservation into a rather a boring and listless affair, the need to strike a pose and make a show was in com-plete accordance with natural principles they were direct and to the point and there was no need to waste too much time on all the for-malities city people engaged in, just thinking about the elation of breathing the cold mountain air here is enough to add a few years to your life, here on this mountain reservation people know what they see on TV but they don't have a good idea about what life is really like in the cities where people are raised on waste gas and after months and years of that everyone eventually becomes worthless and wasted and when problems arise all anyone knows how to do is kill kill kill, nothing they do is meant to last there is no forever things will be much better the day that pigs start slaughtering people with foot-and-mouth disease here on the reservation instead of having old ladies going out each morning to feed their pigs, the pigs will raise people, looking out as you walked through the drainage ditch river-bed everything looked like a surrealist image that had yet to be cut apart the entire walk was actually surreal, last night Mrs. Bakan secretly gave birth to a little piggy the seed of which was sown by Grandma's hog of a husband he would come by each Monday after-noon to teach her how to read a romanized Atayal version of the Bible and while he was at it he took care of this other matter, it wasn't at all strange to "borrow it for a while," after all in the old days wives of the tribal ancestors would grow lonely when their hunter husbands were out too long on hunting expeditions and they would borrow their son's thing to use for a while, even our own modern Girl knows about "borrowing it for a while and then returning it," no matter where Girl went she never seemed to see the wild grass but all along the wild grass was growing within her wild thoughts, the first choice for Priest's sacred choir on the reservation was Girl's Nocturnes it was pathetic to see him unable to resist Girl's attraction, the gorgeous sight of the mountain mist around dusk being drawn down into Girl's cleavage and "penetrating it" again and again can only be witnessed during the remains of one's life, throughout my life what I have always loved most was looking at dignified women with perfect tits perfect lips a perfect sense of fashion and a perfect diet, but back in my younger days I was far from dignified and far from perfect, it is only because I had those kinds of reservations that I ended up among the Remains of Life seeing the beautiful scenery of the Remains of Life and feeling the wonder of the Remains of Life, but was this some form of rebellion going into self-exile from the city and living a life like a traveling herder going from reservation to reservation investigating researching and writing but this was all just an excuse, if you don't search then there is nothing to hope for just my own personal rebellion against life, after so much bullshit I'm starting to get sick of everything I write and the act of writing has itself become nothing more than a muddle of pure fabrication, actually fabrication is enough since there is no such thing as pure fabrication, it is all about the movement of the soul, the surging power of the mind, the raging force of the blood running through your veins, I started without any real objective perhaps I thought the objective was just the objective or objectives were everywhere, for generations men had grown accustomed to squeezing their women's breasts with the same hands they used to cut off heads and over time this was passed down and made their breasts larger, they became so large that women from other races began to suffer from low self-esteem and by the fin de siècle breast-enhancement surgery had become all the rage in the cities, why don't those brave warriors who rose up think about the fact that simply squeezing breasts enough to make them big was enough for their Remains of Life and once you have that who cares about things like injustice and dignity, after all do beautiful breasts deserve dignity? Can't they appreciate the wonderful sensations of the present moment? Why must they search for adventures that take them to an uncertain future? Just what kind of thought process could lead to hanging one's own children cutting down one's own wife shooting oneself and asking your fellow tribesmen to jump to their death off a cliff what kind of a notion of dignity could lead to these actions, can leaving behind a name in history and a memorial statue that overlooks the falling *sakura* each year even compare with the feeling of embracing another naked body? Is the orgasmic excitement of sex somehow unable to compare with the tense excitement of cutting off someone's head? as the wonder and beauty of sex was lost it must have been gradually replaced with the new climax of decapitation, part of the very definition of what a headhunt entails includes "head-hunting as a primary means of foreplay before sex" but this definition is largely unknown to history and it was only much later that history became aware of this definition, as this was a "sexual incident" there must be a major act of foreplay and in reality there ended up being an overreaction but had history seen too much or seen the wrong thing, the reason that there was nothing remotely endearing about the "Second Incident" had to do with the fact that it took the foreplay too seriously moreover it ended up ruining all the beautiful memories of the first Musha Incident since it came too close on its heels, let the ghosts of those who lost their lives come back one by one to answer the contemporary question "Do you have any regrets?" but all they can do is nod or shake their heads, would you shake your head at the sight of so many beautiful bodies transformed into "tools" bringing their beauty to an end right before your eyes? Is there beauty in death? Writing is unable to extract itself from the conventions of grammar and form but do words have the freedom to rave nonsense? Is raving nonsense a means of speaking the truth or does the truth

bleed into the words transforming language into a cauldron of raving nonsense and chaotic ramblings, without the freedom to express
nonsensical ramblings writing loses its most fundamental freedom
and writing itself also becomes transformed into a mere "tool," if
you do not imbue your writing with true freedom any talk of living
free becomes nothing but glib lip service, both my "writing" and my
"body" have been transformed into mere tools, which is what has led
me at the age of forty-five to arrive at the year of my Remains of Life,
the Remains of Life drag on day after day casting shadows like the
moon and wailing like Mona Rudao until those cries of sadness
transform into smiles, "What are you smiling about?" Girl grinned
back as she squatted on the dirt ridge overlooking the area that led to
the mouth of the Wu River, that is where the drainage ditch emptied
into the riverbed below, Girl said that she had been listening to the
traffic noises coming from the road above them the whole way but
not one of those motorcycles sounded like her brother's, which made
her increasingly upset, and it wasn't until we reached the bed of the
Wu River that she finally began to lighten up, I told her that there
was no reason to worry about her brother Drifter and the whole way
as we walked through the overgrown grass and weeds all kinds of
nonsensical thoughts went through my head until I starting walking
slower and became increasingly depressed and it wasn't until I saw
Girl that I finally began to lighten up, "What the hell do you have
to be depressed about," Girl laughed, so did I, "It's nothing!" I also
squatted down on the dirt ridge, it was already past noon I hadn't
realized how far we had walked, Girl removed some taro from her
backpack, she had steamed it the night before for our lunch, "I've
been sitting here waiting for you for at least two hours you better
believe that I'm upset!" I took a bottle of Riverisle mineral water out
of my backpack, "Are you this slow with everything you do, you're like
a turtle," Girl took a bite of her taro root, I also took a bite she probably didn't know how cute she looked when she curled up like a turtle

going into its shell, "You walk like a turtle too, don't you?" taro tastes
better raw, I'm sure other things must too, "I guess you've always
been like a turtle," Girl smiled with glee, but I didn't utter a word
and just drank my water chewed on my taro and let her have her fun,
after gazing out at the Wu River for a while my turtle eyes wandered
out toward the sea but it was actually just a small oceanic trench,
when I realized that on the other side of that oceanic trench were
more of this island nation's "human" animals I couldn't help but feel
depressed, "Hey Turtle can you carry me; I'm so exhausted that I
can't walk another step," Girl gazed out at a black vulture flying over
an isle in the Wu River and smiled, "Okay but you better not break
my back," All of a sudden as if the world stood still Girl hit me with
her taro root, "Don't you dare start talking shit about my precious
tits again, they never offended you," When I said what I said it was all
true, Girl suddenly leaped off the ridge and slapped the dirt off her
hands and butt, "Let's go, if the others show up they can go there on
their own, if you carry me we probably won't arrive until tomorrow
afternoon, and probably not even then, and I most likely will end up
breaking your back!" We set out on our journey, the strange thing
was that I chewed slower than Girl so I still had half my taro to eat on
the way, as soon as Girl turned her tits around we started walking in
the direction of the Southport River, the riverbed was overgrown
with weeds and wild grass but Girl said that it was still easier to walk
through than the streets of her reservation, I really didn't want to
commit the words "turned her tits around" to paper, but that's exactly as it happened and I need to be loyal to the true face of reality in
my writing, the Southport River flowed past a small village and the
side of a desolate mountain kept obstructing our view, to the east
Girl looked at the scenery while to the west she could see the scenic
highway not far off in the distance, you could almost make out the
rumble of the traffic, but after listening carefully we could tell that it
was actually the sound of the wind scratching against the side of the

mountain leaving its scars, "Why don't you take me to dinner at a
Western restaurant tonight, and I'll treat you to a movie after," looking out toward the scenic highway Girl wanted to go to one of the
Western restaurants there, "Sure, as long as you think you can make
it there," Girl turned around and flashed me a smile as her ass started
picking up the pace, those exiled so many years ago along this road
came via a small trolley operated by the Taiwan Sugar Company, the
survivors of two massacres walked on foot took a trolley and then
continued on foot as they approached a strange new land, I tried my
best to understand the fear and uncertainty they must have felt as
they approached an unknown future, the process in which new soldiers are assigned a unit after basic training is also filled with fear and
uncertainty, the uncertainty of being shuttled around in army trucks
not knowing where your final destination will be, while you simultaneously become conscious of the horrific fact that you are already
part of a system of oppression, moreover as you are transferred around
through different units the people who travel with you are all soldiers you don't know, those other strangers on board with you are
also being controlled by some larger unknown force that is pushing
all of you toward the unknown fate that lies before you, in history
there are many images that are remarkably similar, by the time they
walked on foot from the mandarin orange forest near the mouth
of the Wu River to Riverisle it was already dusk, as they crossed the
small suspension bridge and entered into this place of exile night was
falling, only those living out their Remains of Life who stand in the
corner of a disco facing the wild carnivalesque dance can truly understand that sight and what it must have felt like, there are some
who feel that life isn't worth that price and would rather just hang
themselves, just as there are many new conscripts who would choose
to take their own lives in a variety of different ways in order to avoid
military service among them the strangest cases are those that result
in someone "disappearing forever," after the mass suicides by hang-

ing those who died of disease after they were unable to acclimate to their new environment and those who were later "purged" fewer than 250 people survived, before "the Incident" the population of the six tribes involved in the uprising totaled more than 1,300 people, what happened was a small incident within the scope of human history but a major incident here in this island nation during the 1930s, it was a "major" incident when compared to people down in the plains who only dared to write essays or shout slogans, intellectuals in the cities and countryside had completely given up all forms of armed resistance for a full fifteen years, but the "wild savages" from the mountains seemed to deliver one final blow, just a few years later everyone whether from the mountains or the plains would all collectively march toward "assimilation as loyal subjects of the emperor," and just a few years after that they would welcome yet another group of rulers, which would be followed by an even larger "incident of resistance" where people from the cities and countryside and even up in the mountains would all be suppressed without discrimination followed by a great purge that would last another decade,[41] there are those who cry out and declare 1930 as a year of resistance and revolt against this and that, statues of the rulers were erected on the reservations, later cries for peaceful unification would break out alongside cries for the establishment of an independent state both of which would carry on into the present, history only records "the details surrounding the Incident" but it is unable to get close to the actual sentiments surrounding "the Incident," as rouge politics waves its sword before the collective it simultaneously knocks down "anarchistic" individuals, it is unclear just how long the fear and uncertainty that the individual feels about the fate of this island nation will continue, as the river veered closer to the massive cement support beams supporting the scenic highway above, the flowing river itself seemed to take on an air of fear and uncertainty, "What a humongous—" Girl looked up at the massive overpass above us but her voice was drowned

out by the traffic noise coming from the bridge, once we got past
the overpass, the river seemed to follow alongside the scenic highway occasionally veering left or right along the way, the other side of
the riverbed was backed right up alongside the wall of the cliff, we
walked on sandwiched between the expansiveness of nature and an
expansive engineering project, I wondered if nature in all her expansiveness also occasionally felt that same fear and uncertainty when
facing the never-ending mechanical handiwork of humankind, for
years now whenever the media reports on casualties due to mudslides
the tone of their reports always seems to refer to those deaths as
unfortunate accidents, actually since the 1990s the natural environment of this island nation has already undergone massive changes,
this place called Valleystream deep in the mountains has remained
quiet for ages but now has begun to shift and shake, you need only
take a careful look at the way the gentle flow of water has gradually
etched indentations in the massive boulders here and you can imagine for just how many hundreds or thousands of years things have
been quiet and still, today all it takes is a passing typhoon, as its tail-
winds sweep through Valleystream massive rocks weighing several
tons each fall down the mountains and who knows where they end
up, Valleystream was once beautifully arranged by nature yet now it
looks like some massive excavator descended from space and tore the
place up, virtually overnight mudslides have transformed the middle
section of Valleystream into a flatland and that mountain valley that
people used to come up here to enjoy for their picnic barbecues has
completely disappeared, less than two decades ago when I was still
wearing my army fatigues I would spend my weekends wandering
around the Lu Mountain area, I would get off the bus near that large
suspension bridge just past Musha and let the bus drive off without
me, the other passengers and I would walk over the bridge, at the
time I would look down at Valleystream below and be taken aback by
the stunning depth and beauty, I thought to myself that Lu Moun-

tain indeed deserved its reputation as a beautiful scenic site, for many years my impression of Lu Mountain had been formed by that day looking down from that suspension bridge and seeing the awesome beauty of Valleystream's deep deep canyon, last year while on the way from Riverisle to the mouth of the Mhebu River I passed by that exact same suspension bridge, mudslides had filled in that "deep deep canyon" so that the bottom was now no more than one story below the bridge, here is an example of a kind of "unique and awesome beauty" that has forever disappeared from this island nation, deep down I was so shaken by this that I kept pacing back and forth along the bridge even wondering if I had somehow gotten the place mixed up with a different suspension bridge, nature is of course always in a state of constant change, but unless it is observed over an extended period of time these changes are often invisible to the naked eye such as those indentations made in the boulders from running water, so why have there been so many violent changes to the natural world of this island nation these past few years, I can only offer a superficial answer based on my observations that it is due to the way human-kind has used their machines to systematically destroy the environment one place at a time, the kind of destruction that they have unleashed has caused nature to suffer to the point of collapse, while my heart pains for what nature is going through I am at the same time deeply disappointed in my fellow humans, this disappointment is so extreme that it almost made me completely lose all hope in human-ity, and that is why at the age of forty-five years old as I gazed into nature and then looked back into the soul of human nature I truly felt that I had reached a time when I would see the Remains of my Life begin to unfold, "It's so noisy," Girl was leaning up against one of the bridge's support beams waiting for me, Girl said that she never imagined it would be this noisy here, I told her that this is how it was the entire way along the river and things would only quiet down after we reached the Mhebu River, "It's really a pity for the mountains and rivers here," "It's not too bad, things are still quite peaceful for those rivers running deep in the mountains," "The portion of Valleystream behind our reservation feels quite different from this," "It is different, the air there is also different," "Whenever I leave I always feel like I should never leave again, and when I do I always want to get back home as soon as I can," I wouldn't say I envy her, but I do feel that fate dealt Girl a better hand than it did me, from my bedroom window I can see the verdant green back mountain, standing in the large courtyard surrounded by the mountains you can have a small piece of the heavenly skies all to yourself, it doesn't take much imagination to sense that there are taller and taller mountains that are extending out into the distance, the rivers that run on both sides of the reservation can both be traced back to the Last Canyon deep in the mountains—a small mysterious place that lies beyond the realm of the known, outside the front and back windows of my apartment in the city all I see are steel bars, on windy nights I can even smell the reeking stench of something burning, I can never tell if it is the smell of garbage smoldering in the not-so-distant dump or of someone burning electronic waste again on the banks of that River of Death, the stress that the traffic noise gives me is enough to make me naturally quicken my step so that I can now keep up with Girl, I figured out a long time ago why urbanites walk three times as fast when they go out for a stroll, "It must be a way for them to console themselves," I took out some chocolate for each of us, you can imagine why there are so many convenience stores in the cities so many people there are so overweight that they need to go on diets that's because they need to constantly console themselves, after passing through an area where we were surrounded by large-scale construction projects along the road the river twisted taking us to the Ugyûlan Suspension Bridge before dusk, at that point we didn't really care how much farther we could trek up the Southport River we decided to lie down on the Ugyûlan Bridge, the reason that the Ugyûlan Suspension Bridge is somewhat famous has to do with that "Incident" that occurred during the postwar years for this is where the people fought their sole winning battle against the military, the leader of the People's Army went to Mushu attempting to gain support for the resistance but he clearly was not successful in persuading the Toda, Turuka, and Wanda tribes who had occupied Musha to join them, I suspect that the reason they decided not to participate had something to do with the lesson they'd learned seventeen years earlier during the Musha Incident, at the time the Remains of Life had only been in Riverisle for seventeen years and were going through a very difficult period and they probably couldn't care less about the "large-scale incident" playing out in the outside world, Girl hadn't even been born at the time, if Mona Rudao hadn't taken his own life during the aftermath of the Musha Incident would he have led his tribespeople to join in the "February 28 Incident"? I don't think so, the entire atmosphere on the reservation was already quite different by that time, then again maybe he would have, perhaps he would have seen this as a turning point for the collective fate of the citizens on this island nation, however had Mona Rudao provided limited support for the resistance forces, he would have inevitably been eliminated just like the chief of the Tsou tribe, by the same token Musha also never would have erected any statues or memorial plaques in his honor, when it comes to rogue politics I would like to again stress the word "rogue" to describe politics, the rogue nature of politics and the nature by which history is turned upside down are "truly devoid of the human," this is a small town that Girl has been visiting since she was a child, it is the first stop most tribe members make when they come down from Musha, the long wooden two-story hotel next to the train station that went up twenty years ago was built specifically so people from the reservation would have a place to stay while passing through, "I'm hungry," I could see that Girl's dark face had a trace of red, I also felt that our bodies were long in need of some sustenance, on the main street in town Girl found a Western restaurant called "Life and Death in a Drunken Dream + Old Flames New Sweethearts," it had a haphazardly thrown together classical-style decor, inside they were playing old songs from the 1970s, we ordered steak and salad, Girl told me that this was the first time she felt like having Western food since leaving Taipei, I said that the courtyard seating at the Western restaurant in the city where I lived was so loud and noisy that I hadn't thought about having Western food for years, Girl lowered her head seemingly lost in thought, the draft from the air conditioning carried the stale fragrance of Girl's dense underarm forest over to me, I closed my eyes allowing myself to get lost in the stale fragrance of her dense forest almost nodding off, "Let's go to a movie," at first I thought that someone in my dream wanted to see a movie, but quickly made out Girl's features under the lamplight, "Shouldn't we cut to the chase and get started?" I hesitated, "Start what, who hasn't gotten started? I've been all started up even before I left this morning, no, actually, I've been ready to go since last night, I didn't sleep well last night because I was already started up," Girl didn't have any issues, I was the one with a problem "getting started up," if I waited until tomorrow when we would see Old Wolf there still should be plenty of time, so I agreed to go with Girl to see a new old movie called *Wild at Heart*, Girl had a relative who lived nearby, "Will I ever have the chance to experience those feelings?" Girl turned around to ask me as she led the way to her relative's house, "The feeling of being wild?" I asked, "Wild," Girl lowered her voice and swallowed her wildness down deep inside herself, her relative was an antique dealer and collector who had set up shop in this small outpost town, the door was open and the first floor was filled with all kinds of antiques, we had to carefully walk over all the items on the floor to get through, Girl went over to the door at the foot of the staircase on the second floor and called up toward the bedroom, a woman's voice responded in their native tongue, Girl led me up to the third floor, the third floor bedroom had a hardwood floor and there was a double bed, "Do you want the bed or do you prefer to sleep on the floor, you decide," Girl went into the bathroom, I decided to just settle down on the floor with a thin blanket, Girl returned wrapped in a towel, she said that she had washed her shorts and T-shirt and had hung them up she wondered if they would be dry by tomorrow but wasn't worried since she had a change of clothes in case she needed it, and with that she hopped under the covers towel and all, I went to the bathroom to brush my teeth and wash up and noticed Girl's set of matching black garments hanging near the vent, I lay down on the floor tossing and turning, as we walked through the riverbed earlier that day my thoughts had been too crazy too muddled, my brain wouldn't calm down and now I was also worked up by that "wild" movie, Girl was like a silent animal hiding in the cave of her blanket she didn't make a sound, "Why don't you come and sleep in the bed, the floor is too hard, if you keep tossing and turning like that you'll keep me up too," I said okay, "Come to the bed, but don't even think about taking advantage of me," came a distant and cold voice from her blanket cave, I grabbed my blanket and rolled up into the bed, Girl remained curled away deep inside her cave, "The Ancestral Spirits like it when we come to them in a jolly happy mood, the last thing they want to see are our sad crying faces," I was indeed much jollier and happier when I smelled the fragrance of fresh soap instead of that dense forest coming in through the window, before I turned around to go to sleep I heard her grumble, "What a clueless idiot." We went down to the Mei River, facing the aura of the broad riverbed against the wall of a high mountain, I couldn't help but feel "now this is what a primordial mountain canyon should look like," gazing out to the edge of the canyon one could see a mid-sized boulder, which sat in the center of the fast-running current, to the left was the wall of the mountain and not too far off on the right was the scenic highway, two decades earlier I left this small town on a bus, at

the time I couldn't help but silently exclaim at the strange and magnificent sight of the mountain valley below, as the narrow mountain
road followed the broad riverbed you could see the endless expanse
of the riverbed and mountain valley all laid out before your eyes,
today when you leave that small town there is a series of cheap sheet-
metal shacks densely lined up next to each other along the scenic
highway, we walked alongside the river on the mountain side, all
we could hear were the various car and traffic noises coming from
the other side of those sheet-metal buildings, I'm not sure when all
of this started perhaps it was in the 1980s when the economy started
to take off that they began to broaden country roads like this one
so they could better link up with the cities, that excitement one had
in the 1970s when you could still see open fields and wild nature on the
outskirts of the cities had completely disappeared, one after another
people started opening up stores in those areas just outside the cities,
just like this long line of sheet-metal shacks that were now obscuring
the view from the scenic highway, from that point on the beauty of
gazing out at the magnificent riverbed from alongside the road was
gone, those sheet-metal shacks didn't just serve as homes for the un-
derprivileged they also served as home for greedy opportunists and
both of them coexisted in the days of this island nation's rapid economic rise, "The water is so pure," Girl intentionally walked through
the flowing water at the river's edge, I thought it was strange that
she wasn't wearing the tall plastic boots that are normally required
for river trekking, Girl said that she had taken them off last night
during the movie and left them in the theater, I was so wild at heart
at the time that I hadn't even noticed that she left the theater and
walked through the town barefoot last night and this morning she
just put on the flip-flops that she was now wearing, "The books emphasized not to ever go river trekking without tall plastic boots,"
my knowledge of river trekking was after all far from average, but
Girl just laughed it off, "When I was a kid we always played barefoot

in the river, the only thing my mom warned us about was to be careful of poisonous snakes that might be hiding in the grass alongside
the river, so we walked in the middle where we were surrounded
by water, but I always felt it was a shame that I never saw any water
snakes on my treks," if we caught a small snake we wouldn't even
have to skin it and could just eat it raw, which was the most nutritious thing for little Atayals' growing bodies, I recently heard about
someone who shot a flying squirrel and immediately took two bites
and after chewing it up well swallowed it raw, which really made that
hunter's two balls bigger, after thinking about swallowing those two
I couldn't help but pop open another morning can of Mr. Brown
Coffee which I downed in just a few gulps, "I think you're drinking
too much coffee, you don't sleep well at night, always dozing off with
the lights on," Girl said that she always noticed the way I was sleeping
when she got up in the middle of the night to go pee, Girl had an
outhouse in the back section of her garden that wasn't connected
to her main house, but the fact that the sounds of her footsteps and
her going pee all disappeared in the midnight silence, now that was a
most inhuman feat, but even more terrifying was the fact that while
I was lost in my own midnight meditations someone going pee-pee
was secretly spying on me, no wonder that whenever she went to pee
my inspiration would piss out all over like a tidal flood, from this you
can see the subtle yet mysterious impact that everyday occurrences
can have upon one another, not to mention the strange secrets concealed deep in the mountain valley that was now laid out right before my eyes, "I know I know, but who's the one who dozes off?
whenever you go to pee I see you through the window and when I
have my white spirits they always have a faint pisslike taste to them,"
Girl stopped in her tracks and stood up straight, "Who drinks spirits,
the only thing I drink before going to bed is the moisture from the
dew dripping off my rooftop, ever since I was a little girl my mother
taught me how to collect the dew water in a cup, it's good for your

complexion and helps you retain your youth," her breasts increasingly resembled two large mountains, and the word "magnificent" wasn't enough to properly describe the scenery, she started to get upset, "Aren't you embarrassed to admit listening to the sound of me peeing in the middle of the night, were you just pretending that you couldn't get to sleep so that you could secretly listen to me?" I stood out in the middle of the river and as I let the force of the current push me to the left and to the right, everything "I saw and heard felt good," Girl said she was going to go up ahead to pee, she had to pee so bad that she was ready to burst those precious boots of mine, at least the surface of my boots still had the eternal smell of night dew piss, I loved how lively and fun Girl was the way she talked had a quirky ingenuity that was even more beautiful than when we were back home on the reservation sitting on the sofa drinking white spirits and speaking with her eyes, "The pebbles here are different than the ones back home around Valleystream," after she peed Girl came back with a handful of pebbles from the river that she had picked up, "These pebbles must have been blasted by floodwaters at least three or four times, the marks on them run quite deep, the pebbles in Valleystream are much softer," each pebble indeed was marked with different scars and natural chips, "Perhaps the pebbles in every valley stream are different," I said, "Remind me when the time comes," Girl didn't want to let go of those pebbles, "When we meet the Ancestral Spirits, we need to ask them to collect a few pebbles for me whenever they pass through a different valley stream, I want to play with these pebbles until I'm old!" seeing the way those pebbles looked they were almost good enough to eat, no wonder there are young girls here on this island nation who actually eat sandstone, Girl hit the road this morning on an empty stomach she said that she wasn't going to eat all day because it was only on an empty stomach that she would be able to wholeheartedly embrace her Ancestral Spirits, I told her I was worried that she was too skinny but actually I was more concerned with the fact that river trekking on an empty stomach was another taboo that was warned against in the books, "Don't worry about me, even if I loose some weight it'll only be in the waist area, my mom and grandmother used to always say that Atayal women are just born this way," hearing that I was able to rest at ease, when I first met Girl she was kicking her feet in the rushing water of Valleystream, from time to time she even turned around and tried to pull me in, from that moment I knew that this Atayal girl was no Han Chinese from the plains, later I learned that Girl ate very little living primarily on wild vegetables and taro and the occasional stewed chicken, but she didn't seem to really be losing weight, quite the contrary her subsequent days living with the white spirits actually "enlarged her" to the point that all the mountains both distant and close were shocked by the change, the elders took special care of her they probably felt that no matter what her disposition was like or what she looked like she came closer to what a true Atayal woman should be than anyone else the elders had ever seen, our stroll through the Mei River was especially relaxed and carefree, occasionally the small isles on the river would be blocked by boulders and Girl would climb up and leap around on them, I also got a chance to show off some of my recently acquired rock-climbing skills, the reason we felt so free was that we were standing there in the middle of this magnificent wide-open riverbed facing several layers of mountain peaks that seemed to grow higher as they receded into the distance, "I have an uncle who lives on the Mei River reservation, if we follow the Mei River we'll get there soon," we ended up getting on a bus near the Pass of No Return, we'd have to visit Girl's uncle some other day, upstream on the Mei River there was another stream that seems to disappear somewhere in the Eastern Eye Mountains, we went over the mountain pass and arrived at Musha, all those years ago when her ancestors were exiled they too walked this road with armed soldiers keeping watch on them along the way, they walked down to the

Pass of No Return where a trolley took them along the Mei River
down to the small outpost town below I'm sure they would have been
envious if they had seen a couple like us strolling carefree through
Valleystream on their way, they went upstream along Muddy River
where it meets with the tail end of Emerald Lake, going upstream
from there the mountain valleys start to narrow and water flows
more rapidly, the riverbed is filled with sand and rocks, we passed by
the place where two mountain valleys converge, gazing out to the left
we could see the valley that had been filled in from the mudslides
from the top of the suspension bridge, it looked like a series of massive tumors filled with muddy grout and clay and there were even
more tourists down there climbing around on these tumors of earth,
the Muddy River valley was still pristine quiet and fully intact, all of
those natural places that were inaccessible to people had these "special qualities" of being pristine and quiet, Girl started to quicken her
pace, the degree of incline in the river valley began to noticeably
increase and large pieces of broken rocks littered both sides of the
stream, making our way through a riverbed that lay below a steep
mountain summit meant that we had to wind through the thick
"dark atmosphere" that pervaded, I filled up my empty mineral water
bottle with this "dark atmosphere" and put the cap on tightly so I
could bring it home and put it on my bookshelf to keep me company
for the remaining years of my Remains of Life, Girl was waiting for
me at the meeting spot in the ravine, the broad river flowing through
the wide riverbed on the left was clearly Muddy River, we turned
right and entered to a small mountain valley where the stream narrowed but flowed more vigorously squeezing through the cracks
between the rocks or cascading down over them, Girl's flip-flops
were like the hooves of a mountain goat, allowing her to climb over
large and small rocks with seemingly little effort, I made sure to
remember what I had learned from that rock-climbing book about
getting down on all fours and crawling like a bear when necessary,

Girl kept turning around to check out my rock-climbing form, but I just yelled for her to take care of herself, eventually the canyon opened up and separated into two smaller river valleys, Girl sat atop a large boulder facing those two primordial river valleys, "The opening is so small, how did this big old stupid rock ever make it here," I didn't understand either, after all I hadn't even been born back in the primordial days, so I never got a chance to see the actual phenomenon as it happened, "Like when those little ones of mine were born, they pushed and pushed but only came out when they were supported by the big one, it was a good thing that the big one naturally let the little ones through," I caressed that massive boulder, which really had it rough ending up sitting here after its journey, then I suddenly remembered something I had "recorded" in my mind, "We went the wrong way, this is actually the valley of the Truwan River," I spoke as calmly as possible, "We should have turned right at the second convergence point with the Muddy River," Girl turned around and smiled, she immediately stood up and started walking back, her smile was tinged with a kind of empty exhaustion, I had seen that same smile on the faces of some of the elderly survivors I had met who were living through their Remains of Life years, Girl moved even more quickly than before sweeping past all the large and small rocks in her way, I started to suspect that I might have misinterpreted the meaning behind that smile she flashed me, Girl waited for me where the Truwan River met with Muddy River I was a bit flustered after having to climb up that big boulder again on my way back, I took out two more chocolate bars from my backpack, "You haven't had any, I'm starting to get angry," I shoved one into her hand, Girl nibbled on it one little bite at a time, "Ever since chocolate showed up on the reservation, all the old people started to enjoy watching their grandkids nibble on chocolate," only after I'd gobbled down several pieces and downed a bottle of mineral water could I finally clearly see Girl standing against the mountain scenery, I secretly promised myself that during these years of my Remains of Life I should try to go rock climbing more and I should try to always allow Girl to outdo me, after all you have to constantly climb if you want to ever reach the peak, and when you reach the peak you better not be panting for breath, especially when Girl looks perfectly fine, but there I was panting and heaving trying to catch my breath, I'd probably end up dropping dead at the peak and end up the laughingstock, Girl had a drink of mineral water and was ready to continue on our journey, the bed of rough rocks at the bottom of Muddy River couldn't stop her, I had only seen that kind of energy once before in an elegant and strong female mountain ranger I had met, from far off I could see Girl standing before the Mhebu River lost in deep thought, but as soon as I caught up to her Girl immediately continued on her journey, I took one final glance at Muddy River as it receded into the distance behind the valley of the towering mountains, "See you next time," I silently said good-bye to my upstream trek through Muddy River, Girl was also trekking through the water and rocks in the small gorge up ahead, this time we were really river trekking through the narrow rock crevices of Valleystream, when we got to the most treacherous passes Girl would stop and wait for me and when I caught up she would help pull me up, I didn't say thank you but the smile Girl had in her eyes was that of someone "taking care of a child," a few times I needed to sit down to rest, each time Girl would wait for me and help me up when I was ready to continue, I didn't feel embarrassed and that smile in her eyes actually warmed my heart, during this half-lifetime of mine devoid of struggle I never needed anyone's help and I certainly never needed anyone to warm my heart, I lived a self-satisfied life of lonely isolation, but at this moment when a woman extended her warm helping hand it felt so urgent and real, I sensed a faint melancholy tinged with a touch of joy, just as that hand pulled me up one more time, a white building came into view from the other side of the canyon, shortly after that I could see a multilevel apartment building, I spread out my hands and smiled at Girl, she smiled back, Girl then lunged toward me before suddenly stopping, she tightly grabbed my hands, and then we walked through a large white drainage ditch, we could occasionally see parts of various buildings jutting out over the top of the ditch on both sides, once we emerged from the white ditch we started going upstream through the Mhebu River in a spot where the river was just a few meters wide, off in the distance we could see Old Wolf squatting on the stone steps in front of the Inn of the Elder, "Old—" I tried to call out to him but lost my voice, "Old Wolf!" Girl called out to him for me, Old Wolf turned around surprised and when he saw Girl stood there speechless for what must have been a full thirty seconds, it was only then that he finally noticed me, Old Wolf ran over, "I was waiting for you beside the river all afternoon," I introduced him to Girl, Old Wolf was a Seediq from the Daya subtribe just like her, both of them were born in Riverisle during the late 1960s, they must have seen each other before but they lived different lives and each of them went through their own trials and tribulations in life, but they surprisingly never knew each other, "I spent very little time in Riverisle," Old Wolf said shamelessly, "I lived on the east side of the village, perhaps you lived on the west side," Girl laughed, "When I was a kid none of us from the east side would dare set foot on the west side," Old Wolf invited us into the inn to relax, Girl hesitated, "We still have a while before it gets dark, why don't we walk a bit more and look around," "Okay," I wasn't sure why I felt so energetic, "Let's keep going then," Old Wolf went in to put on his boots, although it wasn't a large river the water was practically overflowing the banks and only one person could pass at a time on the plank on the right side of the river next to the face of the mountain, which was probably the main path a long time ago, the tourists all walked single file on the plank on their way to Hard-Boiled Egg Hot Spring, the three of us waded through the water of the Mhebu River, "The water in the middle is cold, but closer to the bank it is warm," Girl walked back and forth in the water, as I strolled leisurely through the water I felt that comfortable lazy feeling you get when you return home, the vegetation growing on the walls of the mountain beside the river was such that the water seemed to always be hidden away in the dark under a layer of damp shade, this continued all the way up until the river started to broaden as it approached a cliff, the thick smell of sulfur rose into the air with the mist, the river water cascaded down from two sides up high and converged again at the bottom, some of the water formed a waterfall as it came down off the cliff, through the mist we could see at least three thick canyon forests stretching out before our eyes, "I want to go to that canyon," Girl pointed to the riverbed just in front of the thick forest at the bottom of the cliff, Old Wolf led us along that plank path and passing by Hard-Boiled Egg Hot Spring he pushed open a wooden door, behind the sheet-metal building was a misty forest world, there was a small path that had been almost completely hidden by overgrown weeds, the mist in the air was so thick that Girl's ponytail was soaked, drops of water kept dripping down off my bamboo hat, but it didn't feel like rain or even drizzle, instead it was as if the water was contained in the mist, which was so thick that it was easy to get lost in this dense forest, we came to a fork in the road along the path, one way veered up the mountain and the other path went down, Old Wolf said that he wasn't sure where the upward path led, but the path going down would take us to the riverbed, we started to head down but the brush was so thick we practically had to step on wild grass and overgrown branches on the way, through the weeds and grass we could just barely make out the path that was once there, I walked behind everyone and the only thing I could see was Girl's black shorts, which were now completely soaked and looked even darker, the khaki outfit that Old Wolf was wearing seemed to start coming apart because of the heavy mist, only when we finally arrived at the riverbed did we realize that it was actually still quite bright out, before us were a series of four canyons that formed a large depression between the mountains, the only way out of the canyon was up along the route where there had previously been rockslides, the path was littered with rocks and stones of different sizes, water seeped down through the crevices in between the rocks, separating into different trickles and then coming together again, we could see about three or four meters in front of us and beyond that everything in the forest was enshrouded in mist, Girl bounced around through the canyons, as if she was looking for something, "Shouldn't the Great Cave have been just off the ascending portion of that small path we just took?" Old Wolf said, "Maybe," I asked, "Is the mist in late October also this thick?" Old Wolf said that after late autumn it is usually like this every day all the way up until summer when the sunlight is finally able to break through the dense forest during the morning hours, but by two or three in the afternoon the mist starts to move in again, so when Mahong ran away it had to be through this dense forest enshrouded in a blanket of heavy mist, and it was here amid this mist that they slaughtered one other, and the Great Cave is the only sacred hall within this dense forest that is free from the mist, "These days virtually nobody even goes into the cave anymore," Old Wolf's khaki outfit was so soaked that it looked like it was made from a clump of pickled radishes, "The snakes all come out during spring and summer, and then the heavy mist comes in autumn and winter," just before Girl started running around the canyons I yelled out, "This forest feels like it's not even part of the human world!" Old Wolf let out a silent laugh and said, "She seems to be a bit crazy, no?" I suddenly realized that when Electro-Riverman said he never slept in the dense forest he was telling the truth, he was also telling the truth when he said that he could find large river eels between the rocks that couldn't be found down in the plains, if the misty water fumes here in the dense forest could nourish these massive river eels I wondered what other things grew here, I suspected that Electro-Riverman must set out from Riverisle around midnight during the spring and summer months, he would enter Valleystream at dawn and be out before noon, he probably only tried to sleep on a mist-covered rock once or twice, "Why don't you guys walk over that way," Girl's eyes were burning from the water fumes, those bright flames flickering inside were the result of the fire burning within her soul, I understood that Girl had her own personal ritual to carry out just as she had her own vision of Valleystream, I stuck with Old Wolf as he veered left toward the riverbed at the bottom of the precipice, I wasn't sure just how far up the Mhebu River you had to go before you finally reached its end, Old Wolf reached out and drew a large half-circle, "Behind us we are surrounded by mountains three thousand meters high," "Mhebu was once a beautiful place," I lamented the fact that all of the indigenous people on this island nation had originally settled down in those places their forefathers thought were the most beautiful, "If it were happening today," Old Wolf sighed, "the Mhebu tribe would never turn things over to Lu Mountain," "It may not have been easy, but don't give it too much thought, if those capitalist interests were to set their sights on Mhebu, those with money would quickly link up with those in power, it would take quite a struggle not to turn Mhebu into another Lu Mountain resort," "It would take a massacre," "That's right, another form of massacre," Old Wolf and I walked quite far out into the riverbed before we turned around, I hoped that Girl would have enough time to do what she needed to do, the sky was beginning to grow hazy, Girl was standing in the middle of the canyon with her head looking up toward the misty forest, she was standing straight and tall, "Are you guys ready?" Girl smiled and asked us, we smiled back and nodded, there was a peacefulness about her smile, no, it was actually the quietude of the vitality of the forest mist here in this canyon by the river—Old Wolf was the first to strike up a fire, he had prepared a hotpot with vegetables, a roasted free-range chicken, and the preserved meat of a Reeves's muntjac to welcome us, Old Wolf also gave each of us a bottle of white spirits, "Drink as much as you like, no need for any toasts," Old Wolf wanted Girl and me to get comfortable around the fire, he said that Girl must be utterly exhausted, he was taking care of dinner and insisted that he didn't need our help, I handed each of them a piece of chocolate and told Old Wolf to take his time, "The Ancestral Spirits just said that they like watching their granddaughter eat chocolate," Girl moved in closer, "I'll tell you, everything that I've been carrying around inside me, the Ancestral Spirits remember, every night just after dusk they come to Riverisle, they know that I'm the one who always plays the Nocturnes," my heart smiled, "The secret forest is where the Ancestral Spirits dwell, the enchanted mist is just there for their enjoyment, you're right, I also think that no one would ever disturb the Ancestral Spirits' place of dwelling, when we arrive at the home of the Ancestral Spirits, there is no need to open your mouth to say anything, the Ancestral Spirits will know what you want to say, that sense of trust sets people at ease, making them feel so very peaceful," it was at that moment that we smelled the scent of the barbecue meat cooking and the hotpot broth boiling, but the most aromatic scent was the meaty perfume right beside me coming from Girl's thick sweaty forest, it really went well with a bottle of white spirits, we raised our bottles and toasted each other on finally making it here to the original homeland of Mhebu, Girl even raised her bottle in the direction of her Ancestral Spirits' home to pay her respects, Old Wolf started by serving us each a bowl of hotpot broth, after that he brought out a tray of cured pork, by the light of the fire Old Wolf looked a bit thinner and more haggard, Old Wolf said that he wanted to try to complete a row of houses before the rainy season began, "But I haven't been able to hire any workers, it's not that the pay I'm offering is too low, it's just that no one is willing to travel any farther than Chunyang for a job," I thought of all those people in Riverisle just idling away their time, I suggested he see if he could get Boss to contract out some workers for him, but I wondered if Boss's men would be able to take on a simple job like that without messing it up, there was something else that was bothering Old Wolf, the local police would also periodically drop by to check things out, they always ridiculed Old Wolf and told him he was just wasting his energy on this, after all "the final location of the inn still hasn't been determined," Old Wolf went into the small town to send a fax to Daya Mona to tell him what had happened and update him on how the project was coming along, Daya phoned him back and said that Latino Seediq would take care of everything, before long he received a letter from Latino Seediq saying that she was in the process of asking "a rich and powerful individual" to help find a way to turn the inn into a "Mona Rudao Memorial Hall," which would be different from the government's "Musha Incident Memorial Hall," she asked Old Wolf to stay put, hang in there, and continue taking care of the Inn of the Elder, and if it was necessary she would help the elderly Daya Mona make the trip back to this island nation to help put everything in order, "Daya suffers from rheumatoid arthritis," Old Wolf explained as he flipped over the meat on the grill, "He always said his arthritis was caused by all that time he spent in his early years running around trying to speak to people about the Musha Incident," I figured that Old Daya must be at least seventy, I also thought about the moment that Mahong abandoned her baby Daya down in Valleystream, "Life isn't easy!" what would have happened if the Ancestral Spirits hadn't been there to receive him, Girl consoled me with her white spirits, Old Wolf consoled me with his grilled meat, Old Wolf said that he would never leave, because he had already come back to the place that was his true ancestral homeland, "Daya instructed his daughter to open up a bank account in Musha," Old Wolf took a sip of his soup, "No need to worry about money as long as you are careful about how you spend it, and although work is difficult you keep at it every day, but over time people do get lonely, Mhebu is now part of the Lu Mountain district, Lu Mountain is a tourist district, one day people will stop all this tourism business, and only then will Lu Mountain return to Mhebu," Girl urged him to have another drink, Old Wolf obliged by chugging down a third of the bottle, I urged Old Wolf to go easy and take care of himself, he was still young, but had to keep himself in good shape for the day when Old Daya returned so they could carry out their "Return Our Land Movement," as we ate meat and drank wine, Girl sang us a song, Old Wolf joined in, they told me that it was a song that their mothers had taught them called "Song of the Primal Atayal," Old Wolf went into a room with thin plywood walls and came out with a guitar, Girl started to sing one song after another, dancing between the flickering flames, the pulsating liquor running through our veins, and the dense forest of sweltering flesh, that night I lost myself on that nameless reservation, the feeling of not being able to keep from losing oneself, mixed with a touch of confused anxiety and unable to stop myself from falling even deeper into a web of bewilderment, "I'd better go get some rest," I forced myself to get up before I fell even further, Girl helped support my crooked body as she continued to sing, "Old Wolf, be sure to take care of Girl," I held on to the railing as I made my way down the stairs, the first place I went was into the bathhouse to soak in the hot tub, I could feel the aftereffects of the white spirits running through my body, I could also sense that the smell of sulfur was still permeating the cold mountain air, it is difficult when a person is on the verge of death, but it is also difficult when you don't die, either way life is all about suffering, there is no such thing as true happiness, there is no more waiting for visitors to come, but perhaps, precisely because it is so difficult, perhaps you can one day feel a small sliver of joy peeking in from between the cracks of suffering, there is no joy in life that one can truly rely on, the Remains of Life silently pass by amid these small slivers of joy . . .

such a large and pristine hall, surrounded by white *shōji* doors and
tatami-lined rooms, the comforter was such a perfect pure white, I
climbed under the covers crawled out to rearrange the mattress and
then scurried back under the comforter, I was facing the window,
and the window was directly facing the evening mist that descended
on the dense forest of Mhebu, river water trickled by not far from
where I was lying down, I was somewhere between lucidity and a
trancelike state as I laid my head down on this Mhebu pillow, I suddenly realized that the owner of this inn, Mona Rudao, his Remains
of Life were like an absurdist play, his body was discovered three
years after "the Incident" by a Toda hunter, his remains were brought
to the Buk-Tik Palace in that small town and they asked his daughter
Mahong to come up from Riverisle to identify them, Mahong identi-
fied the body and probably put her fingerprint on some official document, the body was then moved to the public hall in town where it
was put on display to all the citizens there, I'm not sure what kind of
truck they later used to transport the remains several hundred miles
away to Taipei Imperial University, there the remains were placed in
a display hall as a model where they remained on exhibit for at least
ten years, later when the new ruler took over the remains were immediately locked up in some archive room, there the remains were
looked at as worthless materials, ignored and eventually forgotten,
twenty-eight years later, his Seediq descendants finally brought his remains back to Musha where they erected a monument in his honor
and finally gave him a proper burial, all together he spent forty years of
his postdeath Remains of Life wandering away from home, it has now
been another twenty-five years since he returned home and has been
able to enjoy the respect honor and tributes that his people have given
him, even after death his Remains of Life played out like a piece of
theater in the modern history of this island nation this kind of post-
mortem performance is unique to Mona Rudao and him alone, when it
comes to inconceivable deaths there is none that can compare to Mona

Rudao's—I could hear the nearby sounds of someone bathing, in my hazy exhausted state I realized that Girl's naked body was now back where it belonged in her ancestral homeland, "Can I...," as I opened my eyes, I saw Girl's body tightly wrapped up in that snow white comforter on that pure white mattress, "Can I sleep a little closer to you?" I had never heard Girl speak so softly and gently, her voice was like the string section from the Nocturnes, "I can't see your eyes," I rubbed my eyes and rolled over to face Girl, in the darkness of the night my gaze entered her eyes, there I saw the sadness of life, the kind of sadness I saw, no it wasn't just sorrow, it was the accumulation of life's trials and tribulations, it was the look of someone who had long been confused about her future, and then there was a look of desperation, a desperation that no action or behavior could provide even temporary consolation for, I figured that the time had come, after that I wanted to go to that place of mountains and rivers where Girl lived, and there I would live a simple life in nature.... I'm not sure exactly when I fell asleep, perhaps it was back when I melted into Girl's eyes, I could clearly feel the sensation of the river water trickling over my body, so soft, and never ending. Each day, I increased the amount of time I spent going for walks on the reservation, I put on a long black jacket, I would stand in different places on the reservation just staring, I wanted to use my soul to freeze those images I saw forever inside myself, I wanted to turn them into fixed images, during this wandering life of mine, there has never been a single place where I could store large amounts of negatives, photographs, or videotapes, I've long grown accustomed to a life of writing where I live out of a single bag, during every stage in life since college I would accumulate all kinds of books, magazines, various items for daily use, and even photocopies of all kinds of research materials that I had "dug up and collected," but each time I moved to a new place I would abandon all of those items, I don't know what the fate of those discarded items was after I left, I suppose they have a fate of their own that I will never know about, just as I face my own unknown future, before I settle down again in a different place I will most likely spend some time wandering through different towns, mountains, and beaches, I very much treasure the two autumns and winters I spent living in Riverisle, when I first arrived I probably already knew that I wouldn't stay long, perhaps I felt a bit helpless when it came to the fixed way of life on the reservation, people on the reservation all looked at me as a quiet visitor who was staying on for a fairly long time so he could conduct some kind of research, I would rather research just how plum blossoms and betel nut were able to simultaneously thrive here in this mountain valley, moreover both of them had a very rich full fragrance when in bloom, I should have studied the Atayal language with Priest while I was here, that way I could have really gotten closer inside of the native language of the Atayal, and not approached this "historical Incident" from the distance of returning to the "historical site" where it occurred, that way I wouldn't have been gazing down from afar in a way that I could see everything but it was all hazy and out of focus, I should have squeezed myself into the tiny cracks between things and carefully examined just one aspect of things, but perhaps my job was to somehow try to combine these two perspectives? I wish that during my walks around this island nation I was able to just deeply observe and didn't have to take any notes, raise any criticisms, or offer any conclusions, but is it even possible to go for a walk like that? Our cultural education doesn't allow for people to "go on never-ending strolls that don't have a clear purpose," not having a clear purpose is actually in order to prepare for having one, or rather having a purpose in purposelessness, but even people who don't know themselves pretend that they don't know, for the past few days I have actually been carrying a heavy burden around with me during my walks, having the leisure to take breaks to stand around and observe the things around me has allowed me to temporarily let go of that burden, that way my shoulders wouldn't get all bruised—but now the time has come, I must offer a conclusion about "the Incident," one day around dusk it was probably sometime in mid January, I got home from my walk and made myself a pot of coffee, but I got a whiff of something burning, I figured that this must be my cup of "conclusion coffee," I faced the nighttime scenery, breathing in the cold air coming from the mountain forest, and one word at a time began the difficult task of committing my conclusion to paper: When the contemporary faces history, the most crucial appraisal that contemporary history makes regarding any given "historical incident," the meaning and value of this appraisal, is one part of "the contemporary's own very existence," moreover through this process of appraisal "historical incidents" are able to reappear within the contemporary, they become living breathing things again in contemporary history, in these years of the Remains of my Life, I came to this place of the Remains of Life in order to reappraise the Musha Incident, historical materials, fieldwork investigation, and deep meditative reflection have been the primary axes of my appraisal, Personally I inherently believe that the contemporary never really affirmed "the legitimacy of the Musha Incident," it used "the primary principle of survival" to refute "the dignity of resistance," and then again used "the autonomy of existence" to refute "the collective will and ritualistic aspects of headhunting," it was only natural for the contemporary to severely critize the "warlike" retributive actions adopted by the rulers, but at the same time, the contemporary adopts the perspective that the "Musha Incident itself was also inappropriate," First off, when the resistance began half of the tribes involved were unwilling to participate, this reveals that the question of whether or not to resist was quite controversial among the tribal leaders at the time, Second, things had not gotten to point where the very existence of the tribes was being threatened, moreover, the contemporary has placed particularly heavy blame upon "the Second Musha Incident"—and so I use this simple conclusion to respond to those "questions" that have been with me since my younger days. I never say never, but it is possible that I might never return to Riverisle, there are still so many places on this island nation that I have never been, and inside me there is a small child who is still enchanted by new places, I want to see those places and go for strolls there, or perhaps I'll stay there longer, sometimes I like to stay long enough for the scenery and culture of these strange new places to seep inside me, it is a nice feeling when you become familiar with a place, it's like being able to continually go back to the primordial womb, once you familiarize yourself with the exterior of a place it is almost as good as getting to know the inner workings of that place, as both of them are equally embracing when it comes to the ways strangers make them feel uncomfortable and upset, Girl brought me to her Valleystream on two separate occasions, she wanted to teach me true outdoor survival skills, I figured that Girl must have had a few other places she could go, but Girl said that she only felt at peace when she was at home on the reservation, "I'm getting ready to leave," we walked shoulder to shoulder on top of the Great Rock as we looked down at Girl's fish swimming in the water below, I suddenly said, "I'm serious, I'm going to be leaving soon," Girl jumped into the water wearing her black shirt and black shorts, she stayed under for quite a while before her head finally came out of the water, "Don't leave, my cousin said that the rivers and streams along the front part of the reservation alone are enough for you to spend the rest of your life exploring!" Girl swam over and grabbed hold of my foot, she gave me a rough pinch from the water, "Don't leave—" I'll be staying until just before the lunar new year, "You won't be coming back," Girl was the only one who saw me off when I left the reservation, walking me to the bridge over the river, the only thing I brought with me when I left was a small backpack, I left all my books and magazines behind in Riverisle so anyone who might be interested could read them, "You won't ever return," I wanted to

respond, but felt like whatever I said would probably sound inappropriate, "You can see that I'm the kind of woman that does what I
want to do, but I could also be a good housewife, I could spend an
entire month in the house without even going out," I smiled, so did
Girl, "I love your smile," we stood there on the bridge as the water
raced by beneath us, I squeezed Girl's right hand with my left hand,
and let go, "You should smile more," Girl squeezed my right hand
with her left hand, and let go, "When you smile think of me." The
day before I left the reservation, I went out around three o'clock,
I first went over to bid farewell to the "Memorial to the Remains of
Life," after that I just wandered around wherever I wanted to go, my
mind was a blank as I felt somewhat lost on the eve of my departure,
as the setting sun was going down behind the distant mountains
I climbed up onto the ridge above the fields before starting to make
my way home, then someone called out to me as I was walking down
one of the alleys on the reservation, he said that there were numerous
times that he had been lying in bed and seen me passing by through
his back window, a shame that we never had the opportunity to talk
face to face, he invited me to have a seat on a long bench against the
wall facing the mountains, on the middle of the bench were two
bottles of white spirits, the ground under the bench was littered with
all kinds of open and unopened liquor and wine bottles, at first I
thought he was just another lonely old man, but then he asked me to
keep my voice down so we wouldn't disturb his wife in bed, "My wife
and I go to bed whenever we feel like it," he smiled as he spoke, ever
since retiring from work, the two of them go into the bedroom
whenever they feel like it whether it is day or night, his shirt was
open and I could see that he was in good shape and was quite muscular for his age, I could even see his calf muscles moving, he poured
me a glass of alcohol, "Drink slowly, and don't forget to take care of
things in the bedroom, and take your time when you do it," he took a
small sip, I downed the glass all at once, the alcohol burned its way

down my throat and made me choke, "Oh my," Old Man patted me on the back, "Drink slowly, do it slowly," through my coughing I managed to ask him: "And what about the Remains of Life?" Old Man understood that "Remains of Life" meant the remaining portion of one's life, he raised his glass, it looked like he was going to finish it off, but instead he just took a tiny sip, "Thanks for not asking me about any of those big complicated things, instead you just asked me about how to live out the Remains of Life, for many years now, from time to time people come here from far far away to research and investigate that big incident that occurred near here, I always tell them I don't know what happened," Old Man poured me another glass and told me to try to follow his lead and drink slowly, and do it slowly, who cares if it's day or night, after all how many days and nights do we really have, "To tell you the truth, when I first came here I hadn't yet turned three, my old lady likes to say I came here when I was thirty, but I clearly remember I was just three, before that there was a period of time when my mom carried me around from place to place not knowing where to go, there were a few times that she thought of just hanging me from a tree, at one point she resolved to jump off a cliff over Valleystream with me but was stopped by the thick trees and brush that prevented her from getting to the cliff, my mother was in such a terrified state that her fevered breathing burned my head, the reason my nose is flat is because my mother held me so tight when she was running away that my face pressed up too hard against her collarbone, I can still remember some things that happened before I was three, my father was a brave warrior, but my mother made me promise never to tell anyone," Old Man raised his glass to me in a toast, and we each took a tiny sip, Old Man kept repeating that you had to let your tongue swish the alcohol around your mouth a few times in order to feel the slow motion of our planet turning, "but I can't remember anything that happened after the age of three, all the various things that happened, like those 'patrols' and those 'damn dogs' who would come to search for things, investigate things, and try to train us to do all kinds of things, one day the patrols would come the night before it would be those damn dogs the next day it would be the police again, I could never make heads or tails of any of that, I never understood the government, they would often allocate us some of that 'modern feed,' and then there were modern tools, I remember my mom and dad one day taking a bunch of those modern tools with them down to the fields, that afternoon they were discovered lying there in the field, they had contracted some kind of modern disease, both of them died on their way to the hospital," Old Man took another sip, he sipped his way from the distant mountains all the way down to the mountains close by, and going from the nearby mountains to the distant mountains was the most legitimate and appropriate time to go to bed, "It's okay if the people on the reservation say they don't understand it doesn't matter, they make up all kinds of rules about this and that, this ruler comes that one goes, but the green mountains and emerald water will always be there, everyone helps out by keeping an eye on them, as long as you are willing to work hard planting rice raising pigs feeding chickens picking betel nuts then that should be enough for you to live on for the rest of your life—when I was thirty years old, that year my wife always mentions, someone from the Toda tribe came to arrange a marriage, everyone was probably still wrapped up in the incident and couldn't bring themselves to face each other directly, those people were all sitting in a silent circle around the incident, this went on for three full days, the man from the Toda tribe who came to propose the marriage couldn't return until the proposal was accepted, the tribal elders forbade Priest from getting involved, the prospective bride from the Toda tribe was the tribal chief's youngest daughter, we Seediq could sense the sincerity coming from this fellow tribe, moreover the age of blood feuds had passed, outside our mountain valleys there was an even more powerful force trying to control us, after three days of song and dance in Riverisle, the peacemaking ceremony was complete, that night the bride was delivered to my dilapidated house, the elders told me that the plains people have a saying that goes "Heaven rewards honest men," I was so honest that heaven had sent her to me and now I had to accept her, I was honest, and very dedicated when it came to work, and I gave up cigarettes and would stare at the stars at night, but she was a girl from an aristocratic family, when I got home from the fields I would still have to cook, clean, and do the laundry, after dinner I still had to wash my daughter from head to toe even her ass, she had a loom she brought with her when we got married that she liked to set up in the courtyard during the day, she never completed a single piece of clothing but in three years she popped out four little runts, my wife normally doesn't smile much, she always feels like she was somehow sacrificed in that "peacemaking" ceremony, she with her aristocratic blood despises simple men like me who don't know a lot, but I work like an animal in bed, I do it so hard and fast that I make her cry, I make her scream, I make her laugh, and my memories from around the time I was three years old all came back, my strength in the bedroom all comes from my father, my father was a hunter among the brave hunter warriors, but talking about it now won't do any good, all I can do is make sure I'm still useful in the bedroom—but you know that without me mentioning it—the brave warriors of the past are still useful today, a few months ago some kind of a scapeland expert, or maybe it was landscape expert, came here from the big city he was cursing up a storm all the time and wanted to flip houses for a profit, he said that those houses we built here in the mountains were like pig sheds and all they did was copy the architectural styles of different eras from the cities, there were iron workers on the reservation, but there was nothing close to a landscape expert, and nobody could answer his questions, I live in a single-level Atayal-style house that imitates Japanese and Taiwanese architectural styles, I've been living here for forty years

and it still has great ventilation and has never leaked, my son and his
wife moved down to Taizhong to live in a new development there,
I heard they have a department store, a supermarket, a Mos Burger
restaurant, and a 7-Eleven in the neighborhood there, my aristocratic
Toda wife insisted that I go with her so she could keep an eye on our
daughter-in-law, while we were there we went to the department
store and Mos Burger, I realized something by the time I got home,
Toda women don't have trouble sleeping like us Daya men, but these
days, Daya men are like that too," the Old Man said that he was
going to finish this last glass and then he was going to bed since he still
had a long night ahead of him, "But thanks again for coming and not
asking me about that big incident that occurred, but now look at all
the crazy things you ended up making me say, I've got quite a few
things to say as far as that 'big incident' goes, but I don't feel like
talking about that now, for now my Toda wife is still around, my
children were all born to a Toda, I'm not sure if you understand all of
this, that's okay if you don't—after I finish this glass I'm going to bed,
I've got a bit of savings and that combined with the money my son
sends from the plains to help out, if I save up it's enough to buy meat
and wine, at the very least I don't interfere with any of those modern
experts' plans, and at least I've had a good couple decades drunkenly
staring at the mountain scenery here, I don't give much thought to
the past destroying the present or the present destroying the future,
that's how I will spend my Remains of Life—in bed with my mind
devoid of all thoughts and contemplation."

Afterword

This novel is about three things:

First, the legitimacy and justification behind Mona Rudao launching the "Musha Incident." In addition to the "Second Musha Incident."

Second, the Quest of Girl, who was my next-door neighbor during my time staying on the reservation.

Third, the Remains of Life that I visited and observed while on the reservation.

The reason I kept repeatedly revisiting these three topics has nothing to do with "time" in the sense of fictional art, but rather has to do with the fact that these three themes are simultaneously contained within the inner meaning of the "Remains of Life."

During the winter of 1997 and the autumn and winter of 1998, I had two extended stays on the Atayal reservation of Qingliu, which was once referred to as Chuanzhongdao, or Riverisle. From time to time I would see an egret flying over the rice fields, and I would go for strolls amid the scent of the plum blossoms.

It is owing to the freedom I have enjoyed in life that I commit these words to paper, and it is because of that freedom that I have lost the one I love.

Notes

INTRODUCTION

1. The "Musha Incident" is derived from the Japanese *Musha Jiken,* in Chinese it is the "Wushe Incident," or *Wushe shijian,* and in the indigenous Tdaya language it is referred to as "Paran Rising," or *mspais Mona.*
2. While a handful of question marks do appear in the original novel, I have taken the liberty of adding several in place of the interrogative final particle *ma,* which functions like a question mark in Chinese.

REMAINS OF LIFE

1. "The White Terror" (*baise kongbu*) refers to a period of political repression carried out under the Nationalist Party in the aftermath of the February 28 Incident of 1947. Martial law was implemented on May 20, 1949, and remained in place until July 15, 1987. During this period thousands of intellectuals, activists, and individuals accused of having communist ties were imprisoned, persecuted, or executed for their political views. Many victims of the White Terror were locked up in the infamous prison on Green Island. Some of the high-profile cases from this period include the persecution of the public intellectuals Li Ao and Bo Yang.
2. Mona Rudao (1882–1930) was a member of the Seediq tribe of Taiwanese aborigines and the village chief of Mhebu. He was an influential figure and even visited Japan in 1911 with other tribal leaders from Taiwan. He led a revolt against the Japanese in Musha (Wushe) on October 27, 1930. Now regarded as a national hero in Taiwan for his role in resisting

the Japanese, he has been commemorated by memorial halls, statues, and his image on the 20 NT coin and has been the subject of documentaries, a popular television miniseries, and a major feature-length film. His name is sometimes romanized as Mouna Rudao, Mona Rudo, or Monaludo.

3. Whisbih is a local Taiwanese alcoholic energy drink marketed as being able to "relieve fatigue, restore energy, enhance appetite, supply nutrition, and nourish the body." Often referred to as Whisky Beer, Whisbih contains 10 percent alcohol.

4. The Seediq (also Sediq or Seejiq) are a Taiwanese indigenous group today based primarily in Nantou and Hualian counties. Throughout *Remains of Life* Wu He alternately refers to them as Seediq or Atayal. The Seediq were historically classified as members of the Atayal tribe; however, in 2008 they were recognized as a separate indigenous group. They are made up of three groups: the Tgdaya, the Truku, and the Toda. The Tgdaya, under the leadership of Mona Rudao, led the Musha Incident in 1930. The other two groups did not participate.

5. The author is referring to the Chinese-language edition of Suzuki Tadashihara's *Investigative Record of the Taiwan Savages: An Investigative Search Into Indigenous People's History* (*Taiwan fanren fengsu zhi: Tanxun yuanzhumin de lishi*), published in 1991 by Wuling Publishing House. As he does throughout the novel, the author omits the word "Taiwan" from the title when mentioning the book.

6. The documentary newsreel footage that the author references here was originally produced by the Japanese news agency Asashi Shimbun during the aftermath of the incident and is featured in the 1996 documentary film *Gaya 1930: The Musha Incident and the Seediq* (*GAYA 1930 nian de wushe shijian yu Saidekezu*).

7. This is a reference to the author's first novel on Taiwan indigenous culture, *Meditations on Ahbang Kadresengane* (*Sisuo Abang Kalusi*), set on Paiwan and Rukai reservations in southern Taiwan.

8. A pun on the familiar Buddhist chant "Amitabha Buddha."

9. This public execution is a reference to the February 28 Incident, during which time numerous executions took place.

10. The image of Sun Yat-sen, the founder of modern China, adorns the 100-yuan bank note in Taiwan. This is a playful reference to the practice of politicians buying off voters in Taiwan.

11. *Qinggong* is a form of Chinese martial arts in which the practitioner harnesses elements of *qigong* to perform gravity-defying feats like gliding on

water, gracefully leaping over buildings, and performing enhanced martial arts techniques.

12. *Otching*, referred to in Mandarin as *zaochi* or *zhechi*, is a traditional custom practiced in ancient tribal societies. It involves striking the central incisors with an instrument to make them protrude or removing them completely, to produce what was considered a desirable aesthetic effect. It was usually performed on adolescent boys and girls and was practiced by several different indigenous groups in Taiwan up until the 1940s.

13. The Slamao Incident (*Salamao shijian*), also referred to as the Qingshan Incident, was a massacre that occurred in 1920 during the Japanese colonial period. In order to suppress anti-Japanese activities initiated by the Atayal Slamao tribe near Taizhong, the government ordered Mona Rudao to lead Seediq forces to quell the uprising. This incident is commonly referred to as an example of Japan's policy of "using the savages to control the savages."

14. "Sayon's Bell" is a famous story about a seventeen-year-old Atayal girl named Sayun Hayun who disappeared (and likely drowned) during a storm in 1938 while carrying luggage for her Japanese teacher. Her sacrifice was later commemorated with a copper bell by the Japanese government. The story became an important propaganda tool during the late 1930s and 1940s, used to exemplify a spirit of subservience and sacrifice. Sayon's story was adapted into songs, paintings, dramatic performances, and even a 1943 film, *Sayon's Bell*. See Leo T.S. Ching, *Becoming "Japanese": Colonial Taiwan and the Politics of Identity Formation* (Berkeley: University of California Press, 2001), 161–67.

15. The Takasago Volunteer Army, or the *Takasago Giyutai*, were volunteer soldiers in the Imperial Japanese Army during the Pacific War, recruited from aboriginal tribes in Taiwan. Recruitment began on April 1, 1942, and during the next two years seven groups of soldiers (each consisting of 100 to 600 men, a total of 4,000) were sent to war. Entire units composed of Takasago Volunteers were dispatched to the Philippines, the Solomon Islands, New Guinea, and other sites in Southeast Asia. More than 3,000 of these indigenous soldiers died in battle.

16. Buk-tik Palace (*Wude dian* in Chinese or *Butokuden* in Japanese) traditionally referred to a series of martial arts training schools for the Japanese samurai class. After 1876 the samurai were replaced by modern police and military and *Budō* became an important component of Japanese education, widely promoted. Buk-tik Palaces were established throughout Japan and its colonies, including Taiwan.

17. This refers to an infamous event that occurred on the eve of the Musha Incident. On October 7, 1930, one of the local Japanese police officers named Yoshimura was invited to observe a wedding on the reservation. In order to welcome him, a tribe member approached him and enthusiastically shook his hand. Offended that the tribe member had sullied his pristine white gloves, he beat the man with a cane. Tado Mona, the son of tribal chief Mona Rudao, witnessed the beating and attempted to apologize and quell Yoshimura's anger with a toast. Instead Yoshimura proceeded to beat Tado Mona. The anger that this incident generated among members of the Seediq tribe in Mhebu toward the Japanese is often cited as a direct precursor to the Musha Incident.

18. Chinese scholar, politician, and public intellectual Hu Shih (1891–1962) and D. T. Suzuki (1870–1966), responsible for popularizing Zen Buddhism in the West, published a high-profile debate on the history and method of Zen (Chan) Buddhism in the April 1953 edition of *Philosophy East and West*. The debate was highly influential and triggered responses from Van Meter Ames, Arthur Waley, and other scholars.

19. River trekking, also referring to as river climbing, river tracing, or river tracking, is a popular outdoor activity in Taiwan, Japan, Hong Kong, and the Philippines. It involves tracing the geography of rivers and valleys utilizing a combination of hiking, rock climbing, wading through rivers, and swimming.

20. The Kōminka Movement (*Huangminhua yundong*), a policy introduced under the 17th Governor-General of Taiwan under the Japanese, Seizō Kobayashi, was an attempt to transform the Taiwanese into loyal subjects of the emperor. The three main components included a "national language movement," which implemented Japanese as the official language in Taiwan, a "name-changing program" under which Chinese names were replaced with Japanese ones, and a "volunteer system" under which Taiwanese were encouraged to serve in the Imperial Japanese Army and sacrifice themselves in the name of the emperor.

21. Obin Tadao (a.k.a. Obin Tado, 1914–1996) was the widow of Hanaoka Jirō, one of the central figures in the history of the Musha Incident. Hanaoka Jirō was a Seediq from Mhebu who was educated under the Japanese and served as a police officer in Musha. His role in the uprising is somewhat ambiguous and has been the subject of numerous novels and films. He took his own life in the immediate aftermath of the Musha Incident. Obin Tadao is better known by her Japanese name, Hanaoka

Hatsune, and later in life she changed her name again to the Chinese name Gao Caiyun. Obin was one of the few survivors of both the Musha Incident and the Second Musha Incident. She is the subject of the book *Dana Sakura: The Truth Behind the Musha Incident and the Story of Hanaoka Hatsune (Fengzhong feiying: Wusheshijian zhenxiang ji Huagang chuzi de gushi)* by Deng Xiangyang, which was later adapted into a television miniseries.

22. Miyamoto Musashi (1584–1645) was a Japanese rōnin renowned for his expert swordsmanship and for being undefeated in traditional duels. He founded his own school of swordsmanship and authored a philosophical treatise on strategy entitled *The Book of Five Rings*. Miyamoto Musashi was later the subject of numerous comic books and films, including the *Samurai Trilogy* (1954, 1955, 1956) directed by Hiroshi Ingaki.

23. Here Mr. Miyamoto is employing a corrupted version of the Japanese term *baka yarō*, a curse word that means "idiot bastard."

24. Georgia O'Keeffe (1887–1986) was an important American artist known for her innovative paintings of flowers, skyscrapers, landscapes, and bones. The author's reference to her being "Mexican American" is a playful comment on the fact that she spent many years living in New Mexico. Many of her paintings of flowers bear a striking resemblance to female genitalia.

25. This is a reference to Kingstone Books (Jinshitang), one of Taiwan's largest retail bookstore chains.

26. Mr. Brown Coffee (Bolang kafei) is a local Taiwan canned coffee product produced by King Car Group.

27. A local Taiwanese folk belief calls for dead cats to be hung from trees for 49 days in order to purge evil spirits from their body and allow them to continue on their voyage to reincarnation.

28. *The Analects (Lunyu)* and the *Mencius (Mengzi)* are two of the cornerstone works of Confucian philosophy. *The Annals of the Eastern Zhou Dynasty (Dong Zhou lieguo zhi)* was a popular historical epic novel written during the Qing dynasty. *The Biography of Saigō Takamori* chronicles the life of Japanese rebel and statesman Saigō Takamori (1827–1877), the military leader during the Meiji Restoration. *The Biography of Tokugawa Leyasu* traces the life of Tokugawa Leyasu (1543–1616), the founder of the last shogunate in Japan. *D. T. Suzuki and Zen* is most likely a reference to *Zen and Japanese Culture, Studies in Zen*, or *The Essentials of Zen Buddhism* by the noted scholar of Japanese religion D. T. Suzuki (1870–1966). *Bungeishunjū* is a leading Japanese literary

journal that was founded in 1923 and awards the prestigious Kikuchi Kan Prize.

29. Mr. Rukai Auvinnie Kadresengane is a reference to the subject of the author's first novel on Taiwan indigenous culture, *Meditations on Ahbang Kadresengane* (*Sisuo Abang Kalusi*).

30. Formed in 1928 in mainland China and relocated to Taiwan in 1949, Academia Sinica (Zhongyang yanjiuyuan) is Taiwan's leading research institution.

31. *Shigu*, the rite of excavating the remains of a loved one and reburying them, was the subject of an earlier short story by the author entitled "Digging for Bones" ("Shigu"), inspired by his own experiences.

32. The Little Theater Movement (Taiwan xiaojuchang yundong) was a small-scale experimental theater movement that began in the 1980s and was centered around the Lan-Ling Theater Workshop.

33. The author's period of seclusion in Danshui is also the subject of another semiautobiographical novel, *Dancing Crane in Danshui* (*Wu He Danshui*).

34. Decapitating chickens in public is part of a folk tradition that can be traced back to Fujian province (from where more than 70 percent of Taiwanese immigrated). The chicken serves as a stand-in for the individual decapitating it, and the act of beheading is meant to display the innocence or honesty of the individual. During elections, many politicians perform chicken beheadings at local temples as a means of illustrating their resolve and proving their integrity.

35. A reference to the end of Japanese colonial rule in Taiwan in 1945.

36. Black Beauty Restaurant (Hei meiren da jiujia) was an important meeting place for businessmen during the 1930s. It was founded as a coffee shop and later became an entertainment house. Black Beauty is also important for its close proximity to the site of the outbreak of the February 28 Incident. It is now preserved as a historical site.

37. The phenomenon of the "betel-nut beauty" (Binglang Xi Shi) refers to roadside stands or stores where scantily clad young women sell betel nuts and cigarettes to passing drivers and pedestrians. The stands are typically made of glass and adorned with flashing neon lights. The majority of the betel-nut beauty stands closed down in the early to mid-2000s.

38. Electro-fishing involves using two electrodes to deliver current into the water to stun fish, which then can be caught in a net.

39. The Chinese term for "comrade" (*tongzhi*), strongly associated with communism throughout most of the twentieth century, took on a new

meaning in the 1990s when it was appropriated by homosexual and LGBT groups to refer to members of the queer community.

40. The Caodong school is a Chinese Chan Buddhist sect founded in the ninth century by Dongshan Liangjie (807–869). It is regarded as one of the Five Houses of Chan Buddhism.

41. A reference to the February 28 Incident of 1947.